T0161272

TEETH
UNDER THE
SUN

TEETH
UNDER THE
SUN

IGNÁCIO DE LOYOLA BRANDÃO

TRANSLATION BY CRISTINA FERREIRA-PINTO BAILEY

Dalkey Archive Press
Champaign · London

Originally published in Portuguese as *Dentes ao Sol* by Brasília/Rio, Rio de Janeiro, Brazil, 1976.

Library of Congress Cataloging-in-Publication Data

Brandão, Ignácio de Loyola, 1936-
    [Dentes ao sol. English]
    Teeth under the sun / Ignácio de Loyola Brandão ; translation by Cristina Ferreira-Pinto Bailey.
       p. cm.
    ISBN-13: 978-1-56478-438-4 (alk. paper)
    ISBN-10: 1-56478-438-X (alk. paper)
    I. Pinto, Cristina Ferreira, 1960- II. Title.
    PQ9698.12.R293D3813 2006
    869.3'42--dc22

                                        2006016858

Partially funded by the Illinois Arts Council, a state agency, and
the University of Illinois, Urbana-Champaign.

www.dalkeyarchive.com

Printed on permanent/durable acid-free paper, bound in the United States of
America, and distributed throughout North America and Europe.

Translator's Note

Ignácio de Loyola Brandão's *Teeth Under the Sun* presents some stylistic challenges for the English-language translator, in part because the novel's style reflects the protagonist-narrator's state of mind. According to the author, the protagonist is based on a friend of his, a man "of great talent, who was afraid of fighting for his dream . . . [and] went crazy in real life." Dialogue is not predominant in the novel; instead, the reader is granted intimate insights into the narrator's thoughts, which become more chaotic as the novel progresses. The narrator expresses himself foremost by the use of very short sentences or by phrases that do not have a conjugated verb. A non-linear syntax is common, with adjective or adverbial clauses displaced to the middle or to the end of the sentence. In addition, the narrator does not employ conjunctions or other syntactical connectors, but rather makes a pause between phrases that would normally constitute a complete and longer sentence, if commas and connectors had been used. Another characteristic of the text is the enumeration of nouns, adjectives, and verbal phrases, often arranged in long paragraphs. The result is a fast-paced narrative that is often ambiguous and at times confusing, even for the Portuguese-language reader.

The protagonist-narrator makes reference to various historical names, political parties, places and publications of importance during different moments of Brazil's political and cultural history, most notably the so-called Vargas Era (1920-1945), and the military dictatorship that lasted from 1964 through 1985 (the novel was first published in 1976). Some of them are noted below:

Arena, or "Aliança Renovadora Nacional" (Alliance for National Renewal), was one of two parties instituted in 1966 by the military government; it was the ruling party, while the other party represented the opposition.

Catete Palace, or Palácio do Catete, was the headquarters of Brazil's federal government and the official presidential residence between 1897 and 1960.

Getúlio (Getúlio Dornelles Vargas, 1882-1954) was leader of the provisional government that took over the presidency in Brazil between 1930 and 1934. He was elected president in 1934, and in 1937 installed the "Estado Novo" (New State), a populist dictatorship, giving himself all legislative and judiciary power. The "Estado Novo" lasted through 1945, and after a short period away from politics, Vargas was elected President of the Republic in 1950. He committed suicide in 1954.

Integralistas were the members or supporters of the "Ação Integralista Brasileira" (Brazilian Integralist Movement), a political movement of fascist ideology founded in 1932.

Jackson de Figueiredo (Jackson de Figueiredo Martin, 1891-1928) was a politician, journalist, writer, and leader of the right wing lay Catholic movement that in the 1920s fought against Communism and liberalism in Brazil.

Pasquim, first published in July 1969, was the first and most influential oppositional newspaper during the Brazilian military dictatorship. It also addressed social issues still considered taboo at the time, such as sexual relations, divorce, and drugs, and was characterized by its humor, and irreverent and satirical language.

Pereira Lima (Antonio Tavares Pereira Lima, 1918-77) was an

engineer for Araraquara Railroad, a soccer enthusiast, and a visionary spirit. In 1946 he established a new soccer team, the America Futebol Clube, and was elected its president. Initially the team was created with the idea of defeating other local teams, but it joined the state of São Paulo's league, then the national league, and played against first-division teams.

Some Brazilian Portuguese terms used in the translation should also be explained here.

Caboclo, according to the fourth edition of the *American Heritage Dictionary of the English Language* (2002), is a person of mixed Brazilian Indian and European or African ancestry. For Brazilians the term also implies that person is from the countryside.

Cachaça is a strong, white rum made from sugar cane; the word appears in the fourth edition of the *American Heritage*. Pinga, also used in the translation, is a synonym for cachaça.

Escola de samba is the term used for the samba schools that parade on the streets all over the country during Carnival.

Guaraná is the carbonated soft drink made from the guaraná berry native to the Amazon region.

Jaboticaba, a term also found in the *American Heritage*, is a purplish-black berry commonly used to make jams, desserts, and liqueur.

Marcha and *baião* are two forms of popular music in Brazil. The *baião* is typical of the Northeast region, while the *marcha*, characteristic of the urban Southeast, is a popular form of music played at Carnival balls.

CRISTINA FERREIRA-PINTO BAILEY

Teeth under the sun
And the dark moment
Of the sunflower on the wall
Going insane

(Hilda Hilst,
Joy, Memory, Novitiate of Passion, 1974)

To:
Raphael Luiz Junqueira Thomaz,
Laís Vendramini, Joaquim Pinto Machado
Jurandir G. Ferreira, Gilda Parisi,
Maria Aparecida Valério, José Luís Brandão.
And to Rodolfo Telarolli, who loved Araraquara
and knew its history like nobody else.
To the "Rum Club" (Araraquara, 1953).
And to André, who was born on the same day
I felt I had found this book's definitive structure.

They gathered the citizens on Largo da Câmara and held a public referendum. Since the town is far from the sea and there are no oyster shells here on which to write my name, they used ballots from old elections, which the barbers always keep in stock. The barbers use the ballots to clean the soap off their razors. The results were unanimously against me: ostracism.

Only the town's name is real.
As are the names of streets, squares, and places.
All the rest (present and past characters and situations) is fictitious.
Any similarity to real people, dead or alive, is pure chance, mere coincidence.

The tired projectionist turns endless reels, positions them, removes, repositions, removes again, turns the cranks, closes the films in round, hermetic cans.

My window-turret faces the projection room— there, where the adventures are born.

A window in the mountains, and impenetrable drawbridge doors, and the smell of dust from the room-grotto sterilized according to Rottingen's method.

The town buried by sand, white sand that the wind blows on Wednesdays and hides my buried teeth.

In the theater lobby, the wavering, fearful, false, eternal hope.

Around the white clock.

Time reversed. I walk around the clock, toward the beginning.

And the corpse of Ceres Fhade, the liberator, floating down the theater aisles, the old man's corpse on the pharmacy floor, eyes empty, and the Northeasterners' mutilated bodies, ripped apart at night by the hired mob, the priest's vengeful curse over the town, buildings rising up, white boxes, cement tombs, the end of open spaces, ah, Eduardo, how unstable the future seemed on those nights at Pedro's; and how secure I was at that job with the Railroad.

And I, who got to know, am now condemned; isolated for wanting to know.

The town's memory.

I, inside and outside my town, not belonging to what has never belonged.

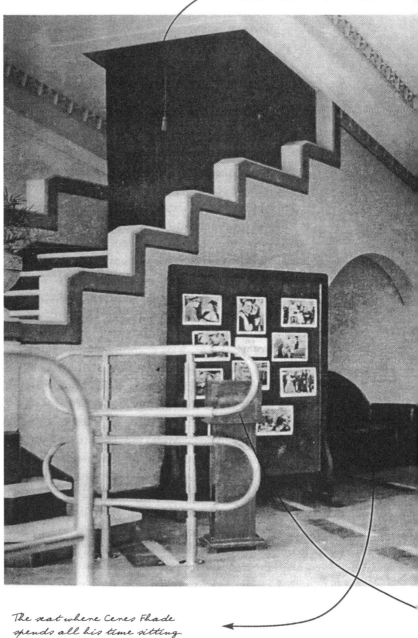

Stairs to the balcony; closed to the public. They use the stairs on the other side.

The seat where Ceres Fhade spends all his time sitting.

Access to the
projection room.

The box where the
ticket stubs are kept.

On summer nights, or every night, after dinner, the father leaves the table. Still holding
his coffee cup, he walks toward the square box.
The goddess of the bluish beams awaits his
touch, for then she can emit sound and light,
images and movement. Everybody gets settled.
The father gets the best seat. Nobody talks.
There's nothing to say. The father brings nothing home from the streets, from his day-to-day
life, from the office. The children don't ask,
they aren't allowed to interrupt. The woman
plunges into the soap opera, or the movie.
Everybody knows no one will come to visit. If
someone was coming, they'd come before the soap
opera. Sparse conversation during the commer-
cials. The feeling is that being together is
enough. Nothing else. Quiet, the family con-
templates the bluish box. Their eyes excited,
their minds inflamed. Receiving, receiving.
As long as their bodies can stand it, they'll
stay there. Later, they'll press the button
and the goddess will rest. Then they'll all go
to bed—lie down and dream. About the things
they've seen. Always seen through the box.
Never felt or experienced. They are vaccinated
against life itself.

THE TOWN
Memoirs of Exile

They return. On the day of some important game, holidays, the town's anniversary, Carnival, Christmas, New Year's. Danilo came by train. I was stunned. The only one I didn't expect. He disappeared fifteen years ago. I watch him from my post behind the door of São Bento Hotel, where I always position myself when people are arriving. Danilo has changed. A lot. He's flabby, not fat, swollen, sickly, disheveled. I'd been told he was doing well. Police chief in Goiânia. The Danilo I see coming down the stairs is almost as old as his father, the watchman at the store. He carries his cardboard suitcase with difficulty, sweating. He stops twice on the stairs. He's walking, even though the parking lot is full of taxis. I never heard anything after he disappeared from São Paulo. It took him twelve years to finish law school. Luís Carlos visited him once at his home, a studio apartment on São João Avenue. He didn't see any furniture, only a china cabinet with the glass panes broken, holding a half-dozen bottles of cognac. Danilo never drank *pinga*, only cognac. Any brand, from *São João da Barra* to *Palhinha*, even the cheaper ones. His face is wrinkled, his hands heavy. His fingers wrap themselves around the suitcase handle with difficulty. Why did he come? He always hated our town—even when his mother died, he didn't come back. When we sat at Pedro's bar, he used to tell me:

"You need to leave. You can't stay here. You've got no chance here—none. Do you want to get married, get fat, hang out at bars and cafés chatting? This town will kill you. It's like quicksand. You have to leave, if you want to write. Go to São Paulo, go work at a newspaper, go get fucked, get drunk. It's better to fail there than here. Here, we're born failures."

He talked slowly, all night long, railing against the town; against the people, the gossip. It wasn't just small talk; it was real hatred. Danilo felt ill when he was here, anguished. There were times when everything he exuded even made me feel bad. So much so that I rebelled: I started to like our town, to find it flawless. You could have a good life here. São Paulo was no paradise either.

But at least Danilo was sincere. He disappeared for good. Who knows—maybe that's why I feel affection for this odd figure walking down the street. He was consistent. He disappeared and cut all ties. He wrote me for three years, insisting that I leave. When I sent him an invitation to my wedding, he fell silent. He stopped writing, though I kept sending letters to his old address. I sent them without a return address, so they couldn't get returned. When I wanted to say things, get it all off my chest, I wrote, even though I knew Danilo wouldn't get the letter. It would end up in the trash, or be read by someone who I'd never meet. I wonder what all those unknown people thought, all these years, reading me pouring out my heart, my doubts, the questions nobody could answer, what depressed me and excited me? I don't care. I stopped writing; now I don't produce even one line, whether it's a letter, story, novel, or diary. Danilo isn't going to like it when he finds out.

2

I belong to the generation that witnessed the birth of *The Safe Guide to Leaving Home*, the Manual of the liberator, Ceres Fhade. I'm hopeful that one day it will be understood and accepted, and widely used. Not everyone from my generation respects the Manual. Most think it's a dull, heavy book about meaningless problems. What's generally accepted shouldn't be discussed, they say. It's like someone saying the Earth doesn't orbit the Sun. The Manual was a joke, one of those absurd theories that try to contradict established and proven principles. Some people don't think like that, though; they know the Manual's value. What's the point in wanting to change anything on this Earth? What happened to Ceres Fhade? He had to abandon his research, his kids were expelled from school, they scattered salt on the soil around his house. His effigy was strung up at every gas station. When this kind of thing happens in our town, it means the guy is considered dead. We can't talk to him, hire him, sell him anything. His credit gets canceled, his bank account closed, they shut off his electricity, water, and gas, and he and his descendants to the third generation are denied membership at the Club. He can stay in town, but nobody's going to talk to him. Exile is recommended; it's the best thing to do. The guy moves to São Carlos, a friendly place that welcomes everybody and gives people jobs in the Red Street Car Company. I'm not afraid of doors because I've read the Manual. It was a great revelation, a true initiation, to plunge into its recommendations, to discover the grandiose simplicity of leaving your home, and going outside. After studying the Manual, which took me a whole year of readings and comparisons, it dawned on me: my fear was gone. For me, doors had lost the frightening connotations they have for everyone else. I felt they were normal objects. They were a natural thing in nearby towns, why not in Araraquara? We grew up used to being afraid. Doors were something dreadful in our lives, like good and evil, reward and punishment. We lived with them without touching them. In the same way we lived with danger at every moment. For some of these dangers, we had found a solution. Falling down in the bathroom, for example. Since the '50s, bathrooms had been equipped with hooks and chains for hanging on to when we shower, eliminating the risk of falling, hitting our head on a corner, passing out, and smashing our face on the floor. After reading the Manual I was called crazy: fearless, I defied doors. I touched them, pushed them, slammed them. On rainy days I leaned against them. I peeked through their keyholes, scribbled stuff down, things about the people inside. Osbcenities, invectives, insults, slander. And through the cracks in their windows, or through the peepholes every door was required to have, they were watching me. I knew it. Over the phone, anonymously, they denounced me. So I called people at random and screamed, "DOOR." They hung up every time. I made flyers (copied from the *Encyclopedia Britannica*) on the history of the door, their function and why they're necessary. Late at night I would leave the flyers at people's houses. I tried to interest a publisher in Ceres Fhades's Manual. No luck.

3

The usher scrupulously checks the ticket, looks at my student ID, and compares it to my face. He returns the ID and suspiciously tears the ticket into four absolutely identical pieces. He's right; a forty-year-old man is no student. But this usher is behind the times; there are a lot of people my age studying at the new liberal arts college. People like me who never moved to São Paulo, because they couldn't, didn't want to, were afraid, or never had the right opportunity. In fact, my ID is fake. I found it in the restroom at the main square; it was easy to remove the photo and glue another one on. Working slowly and precisely, I retraced the official school stamp using a ballpoint pen and a wet rag, like a spy forging documents. It was something fascinating that kept me occupied every night for two full weeks. I didn't go out and realized I didn't feel the need to. My home is as stimulating as the streets. What a reactionary thought for someone who fights with people to leave their inviolable dens. It was exciting to perform the experiment with the usher. I started with this theater, so rundown that not even the popcorn seller stops here. It's the town's old theater, poorly maintained. 1930s Hollywood style, baroque, in tones of fading blue, with greasy brown curtains at the entrance, and over the screen heavy drapes that were golden forty years ago, when I was born. In the foyer there are golden railings that are polished daily: the only clean thing in the place. An old-fashioned window display shows goods made here in town: a can of Dianda Lopes oil, a pair of dusty socks, coffeepots and darkened aluminum pans. Everything has an air of things long forgotten.

I tested my ID here because it's across the street from where I live, and the usher is strict, he doesn't let anything get by. When I was a kid, the big initiation we had to go through in order to join the gang was to sneak into the Paratodos matinée. No one ever made it. The doorman, with his eagle eyes, watched the entrance and the stairs that led to the balcony; the same stairs Ziza Femmina now climbs, disguised by a mustache. He goes up there to see if there are any men around. At the other theater there are so many people going in that the ticket-lady doesn't even look twice, unless someone has a really strange face. It's always the same people who go there, especially nowadays, when everybody stays home, glued to the TV set. I don't feel like seeing today's movie; it's just a test. The room is empty, and the movie starts in five minutes. I walk up to the usher. He might as well cancel the show, as far as I'm concerned. I'll come back another day.

"Okay, but what about the ticket? I already tore it. And there are people in the balcony."

"Lots of people? Give me another ticket."

"The ticket counter can't issue you another ticket. There's someone up there."

"Talk to him. It's only Ziza, he won't mind. You can give me a voucher."

"We don't have vouchers."

The usher's face looks vaguely familiar. The way he talks, dragging his *r*'s.

"You can make one. Write: 'Valid for one admission' and sign it."

"I have no authority. It's not legal."

"It doesn't have to be legal. It's just a voucher between the two of us, so that I don't lose my money."

"I'll call the management and ask what to do."

"Why bother the management? It's a voucher between you and me."

"What if there's another guy here the day you come back?"

"What other guy? I've been watching you take the tickets since I was a kid."

"It could happen."

"Then it's my problem. Go on, make the voucher."

"I can't, it's not right."

His face intrigues me. It looks familiar. I've seen his picture some-where. Where?

"Okay, I'll watch the movie. Then I'm going to denounce you to the management. Do you know how much this is going to cost in electricity?"

"It's none of my business. I'm doing my job. Nobody can say any-thing."

Where had I seen him before? It was a very small picture. It had to be him. This man is not this man. It's that other one.

4

Whenever the nights are warm and the smell of honeysuckle suf-focates me, I remember Nancy at the window, looking at the sta-tion courtyard where three women sat. Quietly sitting, looking at Nancy. Their faces a chestnut color, their dry skins taut. Sweating, they never moved except to cool themselves with taped-together cardboard fans. From the office door I spent hours observing the three women, until they left, though Nancy stayed, her gaze lost in the dark. I felt she was watching me because there was noth-ing else to look at. There was only the platform with half its lights off (the last train, a passenger-freight combo, hadn't passed by yet), and everything else—brushwood. I let her eyes follow me while I walked around counting the rocks and listening to the crickets. In the dark I could bear Nancy's gaze. Its weight diluted, filtered by the shadows, it reached me softened, and I imagined it was the same look as when we flirted. Whenever I turned around in our English night class, there she was, at the other side of the room, looking at me. We didn't talk to each other for months; we just comforted each other with our satisfying, calming contemplation. I had enrolled in the free extra classes because I wanted to understand the movies in their original language, read books and magazines, and later—much later—live in San Francisco, or Los Angeles, or Hollywood, writing movie scripts.

5

We were intoxicated by American movies: discussed the long sequences in *A Place in the Sun*, and Montgomery Clift's performance; suffered because *Citizen Kane* was never shown; and hallucinated with *The Bad and the Beautiful*, because Hollywood was breaking away from its own formulas. We wanted to visit the Vera Cruz studios, and saw *The Bandit* hundreds of times. Bobby Driscoll in *The Window* left everyone in anguish. Mitzi Gaynor's legs drove us crazy, and so did Maureen O'Hara and Jane Powell. Then, one day, everything changed. They began to show French movies on Monday nights, and we would go to the balcony to pay Françoise Arnoul our solitary homage. Her breasts were the first ones we saw in the movies because the American movies, the only ones they showed, never went beyond legs and cleavage. But Françoise Arnoul exploded in the dark, while we exploded almost at the same time. The movie was *L'Épave*, and I don't remember anything about it, except for Henri Vidal walking in on a half-naked Françoise, her face hidden by her hair. Now I wonder: was it really Françoise? Later we saw other breasts, Edwige Feuillère's in *Lucrèce Borgia*, and Martine Carol's. And the French movies, in shattering the American movie rules, also ruptured something inside us. They unleashed the mystery of sex—something simple, millenary, atavistic. The discovery of this new cinema, which affected us so, took place in the darkness of that balcony.

6

I'm watching the enchanted wall of Miguel the Barber, a seventy-year-old man in incredibly good shape. He looks fifty. Five years ago (around the time I was leaving the railroad), Miguel began to draw and to sculpt clay forms on the wall around his house. Soon it was entirely covered, and his neighbor let him continue on his wall. Nobody had imagined Miguel had a talent for that. The forms were colorful, the sculptures perfect, cheerful, almost as if they were alive. Kids came to see, and Miguel asked them to paint the shapes whatever color they wanted. Kids from other neighborhoods came too, and the old man taught them to draw and sculpt. Grown-ups came, ready to make fun of the madman. But they stayed quiet. Teachers came, ready to criticize. But they said nothing. Journalists came and did news stories. The authorities came and warned him not to get too full of himself with all this attention, but Miguel ignored them. Every day, he kept painting and sculpting. Now he was using all the walls on the whole block, and was starting to turn the corner. People from other neighborhoods came and offered him walls. A rich guy from the Fonte Luminosa district offered him millions if Miguel wanted to use his huge wall, sixteen feet tall and over three hundred feet long, a whole block. Miguel preferred to stay with the children; making up, reproducing, and telling stories through the paintings and sculptures on the walls. There were all kinds of things: dragons and space rockets; red-eyed birds, airplanes, and dogs; men with ten-foot-long arms, winged women, gigantic eggs, angels, saints,

Madonnas, and movie stars; trees that had automobiles in their limbs, pools that swallowed people, dinosaurs, and groves made of wire; trains, red engines, plants that devoured humans, and insects of all sizes. The stories, characters, and times intertwined because Miguel and the children were creative. They weren't the least bit worried about mixing everything up. They assure you of something to this day: everything that exists in isolation can exist together, it's only a matter of eliminating the difference in hours, minutes, and seconds, and consequently, in days, months, years, and centuries. And if there's anything capable of producing this effect, it's our minds, within which there are no obstacles—we move at astounding speeds. Legends, stories, facts, truths, and lies sprout from Miguel's mind; and from the children's minds scenes from comics, TV, and the movies are reborn, as are events that take place behind the walls or that their parents tell them (when the parents do talk to their children), in those rare breaks from work, television, and the other usual, if mysterious, occupations of adults.

7

That morning I was thinking of Miguel's walls. Imagining how I could draw a woman getting out of the water, the sun reflecting on its surface, when I realized: people are walking by in a hurry. The kids were excited. I figured they were probably looking for the Formula One Champion. He was playing tennis at the Country Club. He'd come to inaugurate the Automobile Club and choose the site for the race track. We're going to have races. I followed. There were so many people that I had to climb on the big wall behind the tennis court in order to see him. The people were very curious. The

Champion was a strong man with buckteeth who smiled pleasantly. He looked at the people and smiled. Looked at his wife, a pregnant blonde sitting by the pool, and smiled. I've never seen such a beautiful woman. Maybe there are women like her around here, but I've just gotten used to them. The Champion played well, and won all the sets. He hit the ball violently, and I imagine he got his arm strength from exercise and training. It can't be easy to control those cars. I admit I was probably more excited than anyone to see a famous person, someone who runs all around the world: Paris, Monte Carlo, Barcelona, Nurburgring (I don't even know how to pronounce it). Because I can understand. What a champion is. The hard work, the effort he makes. The traveling, the cities he gets to know. He's only twenty-five years old, and he is completely at ease in all these places, even in South Africa. It must be nice to be someone like that, someone who doesn't feel like a stranger anywhere. In my curiosity, I let the book fall. It stayed there, in the tennis court. I was at the Independence Gardens with *Scenes from a Marriage* when I heard about the Champion from a group of kids who went by. I was reading some dialogue between Marianne and Johan:

MARIANNE: I must have been wrong all along.
JOHAN: Tell everything to go to hell. It's a very comfortable solution, to always take the blame. It makes you feel strong, noble, generous and humble. You didn't make any mistakes, no, and I didn't make any either. It's no use displaying your guilty feelings and your bad conscience in such a way that even chokes me. It's all chance, a cruel accident. Why should you and I be spared from humiliations and catastrophes?

I went after the kids and noticed that the avenue was crowded, the buses full. How could there be so many idle people on a Tuesday? There was no doorman at the Club; he'd given up trying to control the crowd. Around the tennis court it was thick with people. And the Champion smiled and played, accustomed to audiences. In his place, I would have been paralyzed, afraid of making a wrong move. He, however, hit balls against the net, balls out, and smiled, waving at the people. He looked like a sly fox, and I believe that's how it really should be. His gestures and gait, the way a champion moves, are different. Decisive strides, like someone who knows what he wants. Energy, quick thinking; you can see if someone is quick-thinking by the way he moves his feet. Even if I didn't know this man from photographs, television, and the movies, I would be able to tell that he's different. Especially when compared with the locals. We're weak, indecisive, doubtful. We take forever with words and gestures. We have all the time in the world, and time is nothing. Eternity is this: inutility. My book fell. It's there, a red cover on the brown tennis court.

That evening, the cars in town roared furiously, their exhaust pipes spewing, in races of two or three cars, or just by themselves. Down the street, up the street, modest VW's transformed into potent MacLarens, Lotuses, and Ferrari Formula One's.

8

"What were you doing in town all these years?"

"I don't live in town, I live in São Carlos."

"São Carlos? Don't you live in the duplex across the street from the Veneza Theater?"

"No, I live in front of the Paratodos."

"What Paratodos? They renovated that place fifteen years ago. Even if it was the Paratodos, then it means you live in Araraquara."

(Danilo wants to confuse me, like the Araraquarans do every day—whenever they manage to find me. Disrupting my thoughts, filling my head with doubts. Why, if he's my friend? Who knows? Maybe he isn't. He too is one of them. I have to keep repeating it: I live in São Carlos, the town that welcomed me.)

"I think you're mistaken. I live near São José Theater, that one on the streetcar line."

"I don't know any São José Theater. And there was never any streetcar here."

"Remember when we were kids? That's how we knew we were different from São Carlos: they had streetcars over there."

"Let's get together. Give me a call."

"How long are you staying?"

(He's not going to be in when I call, and I'm not going to call either. He won't find out what's been going on.)

9

It's really embarrassing to confess, but I've never seen an airplane in my life. I mean close up, on the ground, in front of me.

10

I failed in everything I've tried. Failure is an atavism of Araraquarans. I'm starting to believe it. I have an excuse. There wasn't enough time. The data collected was scarce. My town's history doesn't come to much. There are no historical facts. Only a set of small, sometimes insignificant everyday events that determine everything, but are hardly detectable. Who can be sure that this prevailing temperament didn't originate in the years following that night in 1897? A fact I established: the old politician who was assassinated was a man of influence, well known in town; the head of a family that dominated and silenced everything. It seems obvious, simple, but even the old man's existence has been denied. In the years that followed there were disappearances. People vanished and were said to be traveling, or to have been transferred to other towns. The jail filled up with people who said things about that night, with people who said they'd seen people holding knives in their hands.

11

"What about Jackson?"

His name was given to him by his father, an old member of the *Integralista* party, in honor of Jackson de Figueiredo.

"He embezzled from the bank and disappeared. He was last seen in Goiânia, quite fat and wearing very thick glasses because he was nearsighted."

"Fat? He was the skinniest guy in school. And in the shooting competition, no one scored more points than he did in the 200-meter-target."

"And Clélia?"

"She got married, has three kids."

"Norma."

"Got married, has two kids."

"Verinha."

"Two kids."

"Lúcia."

"She got married old, just recently."

"Olga."

"Got married, separated, four kids."

"Marilene."

"Three kids."

"Regina."

"She hooked that millionaire farmer. She's unbelievably rich. Five kids. The famrer is a *machista*. She disappeared, never leaves the farm. Doesn't go to the Club, only to the movies on Mondays."

"'Wasn't it Regina who said she was going to travel around the world?"

"She only got as far as São Paulo."

"And Ondina?"

"Crazy crazy Ondie? She was the Spring Games Queen twice. Then she married the Games organizer. Each spring she has a child."

"Chiquinha."

"She's in Rio, working in TV. You didn't know? Haven't you seen her? She's in soap operas."

"And Andrea, the sophisticated one, Maria Gertrudes, the Arruda girls, the wonderful Pamplonas, the Godóis, Magda, Roberta, Maria Paula?"

12

All the facts checked out. But if anyone looks at a map, the town isn't there. Or no longer is. It's the elders who did it. Not out of revenge, but as a decision of the council. Prejudices against outsiders are longstanding; they date from the great old days of the School of Odontology. Young men came to study, dated the girls, and promised to marry them. Then they brought their real girlfriends and fiancées to graduation. The town girls got upset, and locked themselves up at home. They grieved to the end of their lives, withering in silence. That was a long time ago; the girls today don't even look at the Odontology or the Pharmacy students. When they date an outsider they call the guy's hometown, write letters, and have people investigate him. Nevertheless, certain prejudices remain. It may seem like a silly way to justify their attitudes, but it's the only explanation I know. With my binoculars, I keep an eye on the paved road. No one arrives or leaves. I think they may have had another road built, behind the mountains. If the Sancarlans would let me leave, I could investigate. But no exile is allowed beyond the 187 square meters we're allotted in the frozen mountains. Besides that, I'm only allowed to take the red streetcar, No. 13, and go to the movies. I go down all the way to the rotary in front of a park with swings, a merry-go-round, shooting stands, animals in cages. The streetcar is open to the air, and since I don't pay, I travel standing in the back after showing my pass. The streetcar moves slowly and I enjoy looking at this town that preserves so many things no other one has. I don't know if it's because of the way they welcomed me, but I love this place. Each day I discover new things on the streetcar's route.

THE DISCOVERY OF WRITING

He tried to write and they showed up, confiscated everything, and left. No explanations, but no recriminations either. They didn't say anything; they just looked around and took away what was on the table.

He tried moving to another place, to no avail. They showed up the instant the pen touched the paper. As if that touch could send out a signal, perceptible only to them, like a high-pitched sound to a dog. They took all his papers. And when he tried to buy more, the stores wouldn't sell any kind of paper, nothing, without an official request form. Even notebooks: each child was kept to a strict ration. Misappropriation of notebooks was punished with exile for life. He checked out some bakeries and found out they wrapped their bread in thin, transparent plastic sheets. And when he tried to buy a newspaper, he saw the margins weren't blank. They were covered in a black band, to keep people from writing in them. Once, late at night, he wrote on the walls. And in the morning he found out they had come and painted over everything. He wrote again. They painted again. The third time, they knocked down the walls. He tried to take boxes apart, to use the cardboard on the inside. They'd already thought of it: the insides were full of drawings, or had been manufactured in such dark colors it was impossible to write anything on them. He tried white cloth, flaxen cotton, or lightly colored fabrics in yellow or baby blue. They'd thought of that too. The ink stained the clothes, blotted; the letters got all muddled.

They didn't prohibit, jail, or censor. Patiently, they watched. Controlled. Day after day—minutes, seconds. They kept him from writing, without saying anything, just taking things away: pencils, pens, stumps of charcoal, brushes . . . whatever he came up with.

Two, five, twelve years went by. He tried to make paper clandestinely, in basements and shacks hidden in the countryside. They found out, broke all the machines, and destroyed his supplies.

He experimented with everything: glass, wood, rubber, metal. In time he realized the men who came weren't always the same. They changed, taking turns. Loyal, tireless, silent.

He let time go by, pretended he'd given up. He just kept thinking, writing everything in his own head. He waited two years, five, twelve. When he thought they'd forgotten, he put some materials in a car.

He went north, toward less-inhabited regions. He crossed swamps, woods, deserts, mountains. Heat, cold, humidity. He reached an immense plain; only rocks, as far as the eye could see. He stopped there. With a hammer and a chisel, he began to write. Engraving the signs deep into the rocks. There he could work, non-stop.

And the chisel slowly gave shape to As, Bs, Cs, Ds, Ps. Lines. Words. Drawings.

THE BODY

Memoirs

The manager turned off the light and pulled down the gates at the movie theater. He picked up the box with Tuesday's receipts, and put it under his arm. He walks two blocks down to the office, comes back to eat a grilled ham-and-cheese, and goes home. I go after him. If I killed him, or robbed him, I would have money to buy a round for everyone at Pedro's. Ten till eleven. At the hotel bar there's only Carvalhinho, the realtor's son, drinking his *pernod*, alone, as he does every day. Fat, rich, young, and alone. They talk about him. Pedro comes to the door, huge, gray hair, the only decent waiter the town ever had. The only bar we went to, every night, was the hotel's. It became Pedro's Bar.

"Nobody came today?"

"No, nobody."

What's happening is that they must be meeting at someone's home. When they come back to the town, they meet and hide. Why don't they show up at the regular places? Maybe Nelson, from the newsstand, has seen one of them. At the corner, a group of people talks about soccer. A driver sleeps at the wheel. A red car zooms by like a bullet. I thought of Caldeira, a millionaire, who owned an Italian sports car. But I haven't seen Caldeira in two years—he may be dead; he drank like a madman, did drugs, hosted big orgies at his farm. He used to drive around the deserted town at night. Always drunk, unshaven, his pants filthy with cow shit, wearing dark glasses. I'm sweating; it's midnight and the gravel is still hot from the sun. I walk across the garden. The night watchman climbs into a plant bed and looks at a tree. On the trunk, a cicada slowly strips off its shell. It seems like it will take years. No hurry. It has all the time in the world. Like me.

15

Someone called the police saying the house had been closed for over a week, and that Nancy's grandparents had disappeared. They were a shriveled-up old couple from Ceará, and sold vegetables door to door before the supermarkets opened and started offering bright and appealing displays of produce. But the old couple's vegetables, grown in their backyard, were tastier, fresher, stronger, and had an earthy smell. They sold them for no reason, just for the love of their work, and to keep busy. In the end, all their children were well off, all college graduates. The police knocked down the door; the old couple was dead and there was a huge inexplicable hole in the roof. The house was in complete disarray. "A robbery, and one of the most violent I've seen—such a mess, it's like they broke everything down with a pickaxe," declared the police chief.

16

Jacques arrived in a silver Galaxie, the latest model. He drives only the latest models. I was walking down Fifth Street, wandering around. He honked.

"When did you arrive?"

"Just now, a little while ago."

"You came earlier this year."

"I'm on vacation. Who's already here?"

"Danilo, Luís Carlos, Faruk."

"Danilo? He's still alive?"

"Alive, but looks bad. Super-fat, swollen."

"He's going to explode, and when he does, better not light a match nearby. Where are you heading?"

"Nowhere. I'm free."

"Get in, let's go for a ride. Let's see if the town has made any progress."

"There are three new buildings."

"Condominiums?"

"Two are condominiums, one's an office building."

Soft seats, rolled-up windows, air conditioner. The sun hits the car roof and burns my eyes. They're starting to hang ropes up on the lamp poles, in two days they'll start to decorate the streets for Carnival: the King of Carnival, made of Styrofoam, Colombines, Pierrots, whales, fish—all kinds of things, enormous.

"What have you been up to?"

"Freelancing, I got fed up with bosses."

"You left the Railroad?"

"Some time ago. Can't get ahead working as a public servant."

"I thought that was a shitty job for you, but I never wanted to say."

"I thought so too, so I left."

"What kind of freelancing are you doing?"

"I help in the radio station archive, do some typing."

I'm not going to tell him about my pension from the Railroad, otherwise I'll have to tell the whole story, and it's already disrupted my life. It's enough to have Nancy, who keeps repeating non-stop, "It was your fault, you were an idiot, a pawn."

"Does that pay anything?"

"Enough to live here, sure."

"Do you have a car?"

"No."

"You haven't gotten a car yet?"

"I have a bicycle. I like it better. It's good exercise."

"You need a car, man."

17

The bus moves. When it goes by the old station, it slows down. I watch the kids standing next to a small cedar tree hedge, right across from the station. From the other side of the hedge, the noise of balls being thrown. Once in a while a ball crosses over the hedge. The kids fly over, grab it, and run, far away from the cedar trees. They don't return the balls. They're there to steal them.

18

The anonymous calls began on a stormy Wednesday. At first, it was thought that they were from someone who had nothing better to do. The rain had started at six in the morning, so heavy that by seven-thirty most of the streets were flooded. The underground run-off canals couldn't take all the water. People who didn't have a car stayed home, people without a phone couldn't call in to work.

At four in the afternoon (we found out later), the husband of Miss Maria do Carmo, the town's most illustrious lady, got a phone call. The husband hung up at the third sentence, upset with what he referred to as "the riffraff." He, an elegant man, had come to the town twenty years before to open a hospital and build a big mansion. People called him crazy when he planted oranges, because the exhausted and decadent land wasn't worth anything. In three years the orange trees began to produce, but the town didn't see a single orange: the trucks went straight to the juice-processing factories. Miss Maria do Carmo's husband got many phone calls that afternoon, and as much as he repeated, "riffraff," he ended up getting in the car and going home. His wife wasn't there. When she got back later she said, "I was stuck in a store because of all the rain." "And why didn't you call me?" "I did, but your phone was always busy." At least that was true, he thought. Or was everything true? How come I know all this stuff?

19

I intended to stay until I found out everything. It's stuff you don't find out easily. I worked for ten years on the lynching. I should have managed to find a way to get my material out. Documents, testimonies, newspapers—I had everything there. The guy in the drugstore next to the church, the old man going in, the argument, the smacking with the cane, the shot, the arrest, the lynching in the wee hours of the night, over there, yes, next to the church that for so many years displayed the families' stained-glass windows. Suddenly, nobody remembered the drugstore; the old church had become a modern, concrete box, and the stained-glass windows were buried in the basement of the old Physical Education Department. Even the old man with the cane had never left home. He was very sick, but nobody had died. I tried to establish whether the year 1897 had existed, or whether it had been skipped. Because, according to what people say, the old man's influence was such that a whole year had been skipped in the town's calendar. In other words, the town moved ahead, but by doing so, it fell behind, because it got stuck in the same old rhythm. And the following year it did the same things as the year before. It seems that the first resolution forbidding people from leaving the city limits began at that moment, because there was so much confusion. The orders placed by businesses arrived a year late. Invoices were issued with the wrong dates. Bookkeeping was confusing, and the government issued fines. Some went bankrupt. And the windows were shut tight. There were select groups that began meeting behind the walls. Huge walls, twenty-five to thirty feet tall: white, brown, yellow, faded red walls, made of ivy-covered stones, of brick or concrete. The elite met behind the *Carrara* marble-finished wall that extended all the way down Father Duarte Street. The most beautiful and traditional walls were located in Largo da Câmara. Sometimes somebody got kicked out of a group, and seeking revenge would tell some story about something that had taken place behind the walls. Real or not, no one will ever know, just as little is known about the lynching that night in 1897, that, according to what everybody says, cursed the town. I didn't believe in curses, and they knew it. They knew my work, the research I was doing on the lynching. When they took away my notes, I had nobody to appeal to. Not one lawyer embraced my case. The notes didn't exist, they said, just like no crime had ever taken place in the town. I tried to reconstitute my work, but entering the Court was forbidden, unless there was a trial scheduled. In the library, they closed off certain rooms. And when I wanted to go to Piracicaba,

Sorocaba, Tietê or other places with connections to the town's history, they blocked the roads—to everyone. You could leave town, but not get back in.

I know there was a man who defied everybody, sneaking by the guards. He managed to leave and return with impunity. Leave, get away. This man fascinated me. But they hunted him down. It wasn't easy to catch him. He knew the town and the area well. Inch by inch, alley by alley, street by street. One day he was caught. His captors were scared to death. They used mousetraps, fox traps, ant poison, nets, lassoes, and whips.

20

The men came for the third time, long before the show was supposed to start. When I arrived, they were in the foyer talking. The manager had turned on all the lights—more than necessary. As if the happy Sunday shows were back. In the last several years the order had been to not change the burned-out lightbulbs, and to turn on only every other one along the sides. The men climbed up to the balcony. The woman working the ticket counter hadn't arrived yet; in October she showed up only after the blessing of the rosary at the Cathedral. The men had measuring tape and notepads. They measured the foyer and the stairs. The projectionist went up, put on Judy Garland's song "For Me and My Gal." The recording was very old and had been around since the time the movie was shown. The projectionist: in his forties, thin, single, works during the day at the Notary Public notarizing signatures. He's proud of knowing the signature of everyone in town. The men unfolded a blue paper on the floor and started taking notes on it. I wonder if they're thinking of renovating the theater. It won't do any good; nobody will come, unless they change the schedule. If they do, as I've suggested to the manager, people could have supper, watch their soap operas, and *then* come see the movie. The woman working the ticket counter has arrived, turned on the light in her cubicle, and arranged the tickets side by side. She knows she won't be selling any, but she does it anyway. She's been arranging the tickets this way for thirty years, since the movie theater opened after a renovation, the only one it's had. She says that night they showed *Kismet* with Ronald Colman, and they had floodlights on the street. There was a line of cars, and people dressed formally. That night they weren't selling tickets. She took the invitations and led the VIP's to their seats. The seats were well-positioned; your view was unobstructed even if there was a tall person or someone wearing a hat sitting in front of you. Now we can watch the movie comfortably too: we can choose a seat and change as many times as we want, since there are no more than twenty people in the audience each night. Ziza Femmina goes up to the balcony; old Roque arrives dragging his leg.

THE FAMILY
Memoirs

Click-click-click-click. Where was Bernardo the night of the rally?
I don't remember having seen him. But he must have been somewhere. Fighting somewhere. Click-click-click-click. November. It
could have been December, or July. I'd have been here, getting away
from my job. I try to get away from it whenever I can. Can anyone
be ashamed of having a job? I am. Of having a job, and precisely
the one I have: miserable bookkeeping in a decrepit hardware store.
I leave the job—when I manage to—all covered in dust. Metal dust.
Click-click-click-click. Even in the shade I sweat, not even all these
shade trees are able to alleviate the dull heat. It smells like straw
cigarettes and pigtail tobacco: it's two gardeners. I stretch my feet,
rest my elbows on the back of the bench. I notice my pants are worn
out around the hem. And I dressed like this to go to the Tennis
Club, to check out the people at the pool. I found out there's a door
in the wall. It's for employees. It's always open. I can go around
the loofah vines and calmly watch the pool. Click-click. A tanned
body emerges from the pool, climbs out, drops of water sparkling in
the sun. My worn-out pants don't matter; nowadays kids wear their
jeans cut up with scissors, threads coming off. His open umbrella
tilting to one side, the Italian man walks by slowly, looking for some
shade. Dark glasses, waxen skin. When he was ninety years old, he
shot a man to death here in the garden. Nobody ever found out why.
He didn't say anything, didn't defend himself, didn't want a lawyer.

He spent two years in jail, and then had a heart attack. They let him go. Click-click-click-click. The afternoon trickles away; nobody wants to talk. Danilo is in town, but I'm not going to look for him. I wouldn't know how to face him, tell him why I stayed. From time to time somebody crosses the garden. Some circle the oval flowerbed on the right, others on the left. It's the same distance. Young women walk down the side where fewer men are sitting. The hunched pharmacist, thirty years older than his wife, approaches, leaning on his crutch. He lost his leg to gangrene when he was in jail for being an accomplice in an embezzlement scheme at his company. He never went out with his wife again. I think this is the first time. People say they have money in Argentina, money that their daughter took with her on her honeymoon. Celinha walks by, dark glasses on. She doesn't have that same daring, ironic little face she had in her school days. She was always glued to Clarice, the party girl—in school, at the movies, at tennis. Nobody else had a chance. She greets me like a lady, with dignity, nodding slightly. Miss Maria Célia. Click-click. The retarded girl holds onto the arm of her mother, a fat old woman carrying a parasol. She waves lethargically: "Ciao, handsome. Have a good trip, sir. Hi, good-looking, ciao." When they pass beneath the trees, everyone lowers their parasols, as if to preserve them or to feel the breeze. A bunch of kids run to the ice-cream parlor and come back eating colorful popsicles. Click-click-click-click. I used to come study chemistry and math here, listening to the cicadas, watching the people, waiting for the day to pass. Waiting for the girls to come back from school. They're women now. Click-click. "Do you want a shine?" I don't, and the little German boy keeps walking, stopping at each bench to ask his question to the idle men and the retirees who spend the afternoon enjoying the fresh air. He stops on Fourth Street, in front of Marilia's house. She's disappeared. Bernardo has told me he sees her sometimes at theater openings in São Paulo. I liked her. Everybody did. I look at the house and remember the serenades on cold nights. Now I do nothing at night, I go to bed early. Click-click-click. The woman in the bench across from mine pulls down her skirt so her legs don't show. The gardeners are talking, while the one smoking the straw cigarette prunes the cedar topiary and trims the edges of the star in the middle. Click-click-click. The sound of the scissors, rhythmic. The only noise in the garden. I've known the star in the topiary since I was a child. I've heard they're going to renovate the garden, change the wooden benches, and put in mercury lampposts and illuminated urns, maybe a fountain. They think there are too many trees, which attract too many insects. Click-click. Slow pregnant girls. People walk slowly in this town. The sun has moved, it's hitting me on the back. I change places. In front of me, one of the new granite benches: "In São Paulo, stay at Além Mar Hotel, your home away from home. Telegr. Addrs.: Almar." Click-click. A man with a basket of eggs, a worker from the tax collector's office with his briefcase, a store clerk with his girlfriend, couples with kids. Clothes of faded twill cotton, worn-out shirts, white or navy pantsuits, Sunday morning family dances, television. I can hear the town's every noise. A silent town at four in the afternoon. I don't know what to do with so much silence and tranquility. Suddenly, the world is gone, nobody stayed. Nobody wanted to stay anyway. The usher of the movie theater walks by carrying a shopping bag. He knows me, greets me. I go to his grubby theater every night. Ziza sits down, flustered as always.

"What are you doing here?"

"Protecting myself from the sun."

"Why don't you go to the pool?"

"I'm not a member."

"Not even of the Railroad Club?"

"Not any more."

"How come? In a town with the sun this strong!"

"I don't care. My son goes to the Railroad."

"What about the dentures? Do they feel okay?"

"Still hurt a little."

"They just need an adjustment. My brother's a good dentist, isn't he?"

"I don't know how I'll be able to pay."

"Pay in a hundred years. My brother's nice."

A funeral procession goes down Fifteenth Avenue. A child. Four girls carry the white coffin. Behind them, a chaotic line of eight- and ten-year-old kids in school uniforms. At the end of the line, some old women. Nobody sad, no red eyes. They walk on, carrying wilted flowers that must have been in buckets since morning. Ziza jumps.

"Funerals are bad luck. And if we stay here in this garden we'll end up seeing funerals all day long."

"There aren't that many people dying, anyway."

"Sure, dead people can't die twice."

22

The other day I saw a really thick book in the library, the *Who's Who*, listing the addresses and professions of people from all over

Brazil. I know this sort of book exists for every country in the world. So I had the idea to start writing to all these people —to as many as I can, or to all of them if possible. I don't know what to say yet, except to write, to see if they reply, what they tell me. Then, try to get other *Who's Whos* from countries around the world.

23

Probably what the townspeople fear most about me is that I might break the Premonition Oath. It's the great secret. The town's great secret, which keeps everybody united. Something that only Araraquarans are allowed to know. The ceremony is held at the moment when one becomes aware of the world and is ready to face it, which traditionally in our town is at the age of sixteen. It happens every year, and kids look forward to it, because there are celebrations for three days, with homemade bread, sweet wine, and dairy products, like shortbread cookies, butter, and different types of cheese.

Premonition Day. Only sixteen-year-olds can get in, because they understand the meaning of the responsibility they'll be taking on, no matter how heavy or how terrible their fathers' revelation to them on this day.

The day before, the boy is taken to his grandparents' home, takes a bath at five in the afternoon, and begins to receive those of his friends who haven't yet turned sixteen. They talk, and each brings him a gift and a letter.

In this letter they write everything they think of the boy who'll be confronting his Day. Good or bad, the truth must be written.

These letters will be read after a month and will help the boy reflect upon his relationships with the world and with other people.

He'll know if there has been malice or hypocrisy, and he should be ready to face them.

The letters have one objective: to instill distrust in the boy after he turns sixteen. From then on, unless he's exceptional, the boy won't trust anyone. That's a virtue in our hometown, so that he will grow up, succeed in life, and find peace of mind.

The sixteen-year-old boy therefore distances himself from others. He won't talk to them anymore. Sometimes ex-friends will see each other, start to say hello, even raise their hands, but draw back. With time they forget each other. It's necessary to forget, always; to learn how to isolate oneself; to obey the community's rules.

On the second day at the grandparents' home the boy is left alone.

On the third day he drinks wine and eats cheese with his new friends, until the moment when his father tells him the truth about the Premonitory Children.

It began many years ago, maybe eighty years, for no particular reason. At first the families involved hid it. Suddenly, a family said something, and then another. The cases spread, multiplied. Each family had one—so, it wasn't any kind of prodigy, nothing to be proud of. In this way the parents of the first Premonitory Children lost their status a little. It was a terrible blow, quite a trauma: parents in shock, in sanatoriums, crazy.

To this day most of them haven't re-adapted, because they don't believe in psychiatrists and psychologists. "They're all charlatans."

When the children learned to speak, one of the first things they told their parents was how they would die. As soon as they gave their prophesies, they forgot them. At first, the parents thought it was just a children's game, imagination. As time went by, some of the deaths happened exactly the way they'd been foretold.

Two coincidences? Three? Sure. But fifty? A hundred? No—they became scientific, proven facts.

Many tried to protect their children from the premonitions. It was no use. At the right time, they were fulfilled.

Is this one of the reasons why people don't leave their homes?

That's the secret the fathers tell their sons at the age of sixteen. How they're going to die. So that they accept death, live with it, like a bullfighter on a Sunday afternoon. Only an Araraquaran can understand certain things that happen in this town: certain attitudes, morals, traditions. Everything can be justified, since they know how they're going to die. They just don't know the date. They try to figure it out using the most absurd methods. There was a time when a con artist sold an infallible method for predicting the cause of death. He did very well. Sometimes someone faces something incomprehensible. An enigma. He tries to decipher it, like a riddle. I have a friend whose premonition stated: "You're going to die by *mints julep*."

This word was not in the dictionary, neither the old nor the newer editions. It was gibberish. It wasn't a scientific device, a vehicle, nothing. The two words were completely unknown. I don't know if they still are. Mine will be simple, elementary. My premonition says: "You will die by a revealed secret."

THE TIGER

He got home for dinner and his wife noticed he had deep cuts across his chest. She questioned him. He answered: it was the tiger. His wife wanted to know more. He told her he was walking down the street when the tiger came out of a store and walked toward him. It stroked his chest with its paw, hurting him. His wife got frightened. It could get infected. She applied an antiseptic and put on a bandage. Days later the husband came home. He had come across it again. The tiger. It acted friendly and was quite concerned about his wounds. It was relieved to hear they weren't serious. After having a spumoni ice-cream together, they said goodbye. But the man was hurt a second time. His wife tended to him and was afraid. This was persecution. She called the police and they replied that they didn't go after tigers, only men. Well, she thought, men and tigers. They all have ears. Apprehensive, she saw her husband come home covered in blood again. She didn't know what to do. They had to win the beast's friendship. At noon the man had seen the tiger. "Why do you persecute and hurt me?" The animal didn't answer because it couldn't talk. It hit the guy with its paw.

THE CAP

He couldn't talk; he had a beer-bottle cap on his mouth. He didn't know how it got there; it'd been quite a long time now. In town he was known as "the cap-mouth man." He suffered, because whenever he wanted to kiss a woman, she asked: "Do you think I'm a beer bottle?" He went to the doctor, and ran out: the doctor had a cap on his mouth too. He went to a psychoanalyst to find out why men have beer-bottle caps on their mouths. The psychoanalyst choked. He hypnotized his patient but wasn't able to find out. The cap-mouth man was getting neurotic. He wandered alone, and dreamed of thousands of bottles surrounding him. Dark bottles, all without caps. They had terrible faces, as if they were accusing him of hoarding all the beer-bottle caps. He woke up covered in sweat. One night, walking down a street, he saw a sign: "Caps, Caps & Sons Inc." There might be a solution there. At seven in the morning, a man arrived.

"Are you with the company?" he asked.

"Yes," the man answered.

He pointed to the cap, and the other understood. He brought a bottle opener and took it off.

THE SIMPLE LIFE

Memoirs

Whenever the night is warm and the honeysuckle smothers the acid, oily, unpleasant smell from the juice factory, I remember Nancy, at the window, looking at the patio. I strolled around, thinking of the English classes where we silently looked at each other, and how we continue to look at each other silently. I should be in the United States by now, writing scripts. I would come back to Araraquara once a year. Not on the seven o'clock train; not on the bus either, but in an airplane. I would arrive at the airport, like the politicians and the generals. I didn't write. I knew I could do better than the others, but didn't. I sat down in the movie theater seat, watching the movies three or four times. There weren't any more shows than that, two at the Odeon, two at the Paratodos, and then another show-ing, with two feature films, a serial, cartoons, previews, and other filler: the discount night. I memorized the dialogue, the cuts, how the scenes were set up, the movies structured. I knew everything about scripts. I could write one with my eyes closed. I just lacked the stories. I didn't have a single original idea, and resigned myself to being an adaptor. After all, an adaptor is a creator, because there are two languages: that of the book and that of the cinema. One is different from the other, and it's foolish to talk about faithfulness to the original. One thing is the written word: expressions, phrases, dialogue. The other is images, spoken dialogue. I studied English to read screenplays and books that were unavailable in Portuguese.

That's why I worked so hard in those classes, and even more so after I met Nancy.

I forgot everything, except her eyes in the darkness of the patio (of all sixteen lamps on the platform, only six could be lit, according to regulations, except during very busy times or at festivities or inspection days). Because I didn't know if she was crying, blaming me, or if she felt indifferent. If she felt indifferent she wouldn't have taken the train back on a Sunday night.

"I can't stand it any longer, not one minute more. I'm going crazy, completely crazy."

"Crazy?"

"I am! I can't stand it anymore. This station, the trains that never stop, the quiet, your silence. You've become mute since we got here."

"We always got along well. I've always been quiet."

"Quiet, not mute. I don't know what you think, what you want, if you hate me, if you like me. I can't get through to you, there's a wall in front of your face. The Railroad isn't punishing you—it's me they have in solitary confinement. I don't have anything to do with it, except the fact that I'm your wife and I promised to support you in everything. But not in that stupid strike."

25

Nancy was right, she had no reason to stay with me at the station. She didn't even love me that much anymore. Or—who knows? Maybe she did. However she was quiet too, and we didn't exchange any words, about anything. Except about non-trivial things that happened in our lives. And nothing happened except the trivial. I sweated on the platform, looking at the dark, without the courage to cross it and reach her. I liked Nancy, even though she hadn't encouraged me. I got into it on my own, without even knowing if I believed in what I was doing, thinking it was an attitude. I didn't sweat from the heat; there was some organic imbalance that caused me to get soaked, my clothes drenched, stinking. I was ashamed to walk into the house smelling like that. So I waited until Nancy left the window. Then waited a little longer, after the station was already closed and the lights out. There weren't any trains between midnight and five-thirty. I waited until I could take my clothes off right there, between the rails, and ran to take a cold shower in the backyard. I walked into the house refreshed, free from that smell, and put on lots of deodorant after making sure the doors and windows were properly locked. I lay down next to Nancy. I wanted to touch her. I could see, in the lampshade light, her sweaty neck, her teeth half-closed. I wanted to, but didn't touch her. I've always denied myself.

26

I know it must be somewhere, I know it is. I have to find it, I haven't thought of anything else for two days. If I could only remember what it is, it wouldn't be a problem. The solution is to start with the bundles of tied yellowed newspapers and magazines. These storage rooms hold all sorts of things. I'm never going to use anything here, but I feel bad throwing any of it out. Each newspaper has some bit of news, a photo, or an ad that impressed me. I keep everything, as an archive. What for? Everybody is a packrat in his own way. I have a cousin who worked for years at the same job. One day he opened his drawer and saw the mess. He dumped everything in the trash. He hadn't ever needed anything in it. Thus he concluded his job was unnecessary too. How can I find a small newspaper photo in this maze? Piles cover the windows; the room is always dark. I like the darkness; it's a relief after the sun outside.

On to untying bundles, looking at newspaper after newspaper, magazine after magazine. I don't remember why I kept most of it. The newspaper on the table: I look through the whole thing, leave nothing out, and I don't find it. The solution is to throw all the junk out.

The doorman's face. Was it something to do with the police? It wasn't the "Wanted" section. It was a report—but about what? What?

I've already gone through five bundles. It's evening; I go to my observation post. The girls from Lupo are gone, the two old men who meet for coffee at seven-thirty have just arrived; the one with glasses orders the coffee. Three young guys at the corner. They look at my window intently. Are they watching me? Or maybe they're planning a break-in? They're suspicious. I thought I'd better not to go out today, especially to the movies. Lee Harvey Oswald was killed in one, and Dillinger was killed as he left another one the night they showed *Manhattan Melodrama*. No, that's not right; Oswald was just arrested in the movies. He got killed later.

In a little while the *Brazil Hour* will start. They don't play "The Guarani" anymore. They changed the opening. A disk jockey announces that there's a woman who calls him late every night saying the world disappears after midnight. She says several times that she looked out the window and didn't see anything. He can look as much as he wants, the town disappeared a long time ago; he just doesn't know it. The news: an interview with the police chief. He soothes the population, announcing that the man who stuck his kids inside a washbasin to burn in the sun has been arrested. In jail, he hasn't said a word. I'd like to talk to this man. I think about him, about the miserable small town where he lived, dry and whipped by the sun. They won't let me. They think I ask too many questions.

Ziza Femmina goes by in a hurry. The doorman at the movie theater is there in his spot. Nobody will come, but he stands there until the show starts. Ziza stops, turns around, looks at a movie poster, looks left and right, tears off a photo, and sticks it in his shirt. He has tons of photos. Not all of them stolen. Ziza writes to distributors, to producers, to newspapers and magazines, and to American studios too. He has pictures of actors from India, people we'd never seen before. The owner knows Ziza steals the photos from the theater. He doesn't say anything. Ziza goes to the movies every night; always sits in the same seat. Unless he stays in the balcony, hunting. He runs from one place to another until he meets someone. If he doesn't meet anyone, he runs out. He's always running. He's been running since high school, when we used to follow behind him to touch his butt, nice and round, and his white thighs.

Faruk. How come? Maybe he just got here today. I had all the information, how could I have missed this? Faruk never misses Carnival.

27

I can't believe the town has gone crazy over the man who lives in the telephone lines. The whole town talked about it so much that the

Telephone Company had to publish a statement in the newspapers, and had it read on the two radio stations too. Inconceivable. The TC said it was a terrible mistake: there wasn't any voice, just electronic noises that sounded like a human voice. They explained something about inference, radiation, transistors, wires. Of course there was some agitation. I took the statement to an electronics professor and he assured me that, from a technical viewpoint, the TC's argument had no basis. I tried to publish the results of my investigation. The editor-in-chief asked me if I would support the newspaper if the TC accused it of slander and had it closed. The radio stations asked me to leave my report, they'd look into it. I looked for the mayor at his tailor shop, but found him having a scotch with the TC director. They invited me over, offered me a drink, and we had a nice friendly conversation. I tried to change the subject to see if I could find out anything, but all the TC's director and the mayor talked about were the women at the Golf Club. They asked me if I knew a certain woman who really gets around. I do.

28

Behind the movie theater there's a new condo; Luis Carlos designed it. Little white balls fall from a tiny window (it must be a bathroom) on the tenth floor. There's no pattern: sometimes a whole day goes by without a single one. Other times, they keep falling, one after another. After Ziza was gone, I went down, jumped over the side gate at the movie theater, and turned the trashcans inside out. The projectionist always cuts strips off the movies and I collect them. Then I jumped over the wall in the back onto the patio of the condo. The little paper balls were there, five white balls. I bent down and poked them, with a small stick. I thought, what if Faruk went by and saw me squatting, poking at some little paper balls? Good thing he's still at the corner waiting for the new traffic light to change. He might be singing a bolero. "Anguish" was the one he sang best, but "Siboney" made me long for I-don't-know-what, especially during the serenades. One night, all the lights in town went out. It was very cold. We started walking; Danilo couldn't play his guitar, he said he couldn't see the strings. All of a sudden, in the middle of our walk, the lights at Dianda Lopes came on, and we stopped, blinded by the cooking oil factory's lights (it probably had a generator). Faruk got excited and sang "Siboney," and to this day it touches me to think of the empty street, and the factory all lit up.

I open the little ball with the stick, it's tissue paper and there's nothing inside. It hasn't been used. Tissue paper of good quality, two-ply, silky. I hate paper that's so thin it comes apart in your hands. I sit on the edge of the wall waiting for more balls. Certainly the light has changed and Faruk is gone. He has a white Chevette, and what fascinates me is not the car, but the license plate. From São Paulo. It's a stamp, a mark. It defines the individual, classifies, explains him.

I'm going to write to Cid, ask him for a job at the TV station. I don't know what I'll do, maybe scripts. Cid can help me, I'll ask him for advice, some guidance. I can't go on seeing people and saying, "I'm still working part-time in the office at the hardware store." They come back in new cars, fancy clothes. I even noticed Faruk smokes a bright yellow cigarette, very expensive, just like the hero in the seven o'clock soap opera. You can't find that brand here; it's imported. I read about them in the "Life" section of the newspaper.

It's nine o'clock (according to the clock at the Lupo Sock Factory) and I make up my mind. I go talk to the custodian. They haven't thrown any more balls, but this can't go on. I don't have time to watch this foolishness.

I show him the little ball.

"Have you seen this?"

He takes the ball in his hand, and examines it.

"No."

"Did you know somebody has been throwing these little balls from the tenth floor?"

"Really?"

"Yes, somebody has. Can you do something about it?"

"Why? They don't bother anybody."

"They're irritating."

"No, they're not. I'm not irritated."

"I am."

"Do you live in this condominium?"

"No."

"So . . . Wait a second, I know you."

"You do?"

"Aren't you the one who went from apartment to apartment asking questions? Why had they moved to the condo? Why wouldn't they rather live in a house, etc.? Aren't you?"

"Yes."

"They talked about you at a homeowners meeting. They're worried. They want to know why all these questions."

"Research."

"What for?"

"For myself."

"What are you going to do with the research?"

"A study."

"This is very strange. They're going to talk to you. Watch out. Don't waste my time with this talk about little paper balls!"

29

The day those strangers got killed, the crowd filled up the station. They wanted to see blood, bones, flesh, guts. They looked for fingers, clothes, shards of glass—as souvenirs. The machine guns must have ripped the men apart because the crowd found lots to look at, to keep and to talk about. There wasn't even time to clean the station or cordon it off. A crowd came running as soon as they heard about it. The police tried to hold them back, but to no avail. The stationmaster was desperate. Fifty years without a single accident. Not even a derailment, and now this mess, a big one. I spent the afternoon sitting on a bench on the platform, watching the developments. Everybody was there. The police soon had to resort to violence so that the forensics team could do their job.

Who were the two men the inspector denounced? Nobody got to see their faces. They were disfigured. What if one of them was Derly? I haven't seen Derly for a long time. We weren't friends anymore, we don't think alike. He left Araraquara fifteen years ago, but always came back. Almost all of them come back, on important holidays, the town's anniversary, Christmas or Carnival. He didn't talk to me either; just waved and asked out of courtesy, "How are you doing?" So courteous, so polite. It's easy to be polite and courteous when you're doing well, away from this town, doing what you want, working on what you like, dying for something worthwhile. Like Derly. If he didn't die today, he's on his way. Tomorrow, the day after, it's inevitable. I saw the billboard, it had names with *X*'s over them: eliminated. Once in a while, the town gets agitated, like today. Then it's a party. Groups of people on the corners, the cafés full, not one table free in the bars, all the garden benches taken. With one difference: they are the only ones missing. I like this, the streets alive, all lit up. And when everyone goes home, there are papers and ice-cream cones everywhere. The human heat remains, the excitement from the conversations, the buzzing of the voices, the young women's perfume—an aura of people who left their homes, talked, touched one another. I feel alive, not isolated. In the last twenty-five years there were only a few days like this: the night the Communists' theater at the Largo da Câmara was destroyed; when Cleia Honaim, elected the Coffee Queen, returned from Colombia; when Pereira Lima won the election; and when the Railroad soccer team went back up to the first division. I've kept newspaper clippings. Today I felt like investigating again. Go around asking questions, finding out what happened. We won't know anything; tomorrow the news will talk about nothing, hiding the truth. I open the window wide, there's nobody out. It's late at night; I'm not sleepy, the sky's bright. A goddamn sky, that irritates me, troubles me, just as it did twenty years ago. Like during the serenade nights. And the smell of plants; the honeysuckle has begun to bloom; in one month they'll be overpowering, strong, suffocating. The ice-cream shop is closed; they're washing the sidewalk. I imagine there's noise coming from the movie theater. They're probably showing some x-rated movie; the doorman told me they show some good ones. Just for the bigwigs. Jerks. Imbeciles. I stay at the window, I'll catch them all, and one day they'll invite me. They won't. There's not a single noise, except for the generator at the oil refinery. Crickets, I don't know where. I keep watch, I need to watch; it's my mission. I feel calm today, no shadows from the past rising up to intimidate me. In a short while I'll go for a walk, to finish my stories. A fresh breeze blows, bringing a little bit of sand; very little.

30

These are proven facts. But if someone looks at a map, the town isn't there. True, maps don't prove anything. At night, I see the glow of lights from the mountain and know people are home. They don't go out, don't go for a stroll, don't visit each other, don't get together. There's no restaurant (not anymore), bar, café, hotel foyer, club veranda, or pool hall where people can meet and talk. Any stranger who arrives—and it's incredible how they find a way of sneaking in (and why would they want to?)—is detected. Strangers can't relate, can't find anybody to talk to. It's this silence that obsessed me. I wonder: is this the reason for my exile? They couldn't accept seeing me on the streets, fearless, day and night, going back and forth. I could feel them looking at me from behind their closed blinds. The town was famous for the eyes behind its blinds. And for the peepholes, through which people kept watch on the streets, looking for strangers. And at night, the holes were used from outside by the voyeurs, a group (practically a cult) that walked around looking into the houses, watching with pleasure what couples did inside their rooms. I realized, as each day went by, that the tension was mounting behind the windows. But the shutters didn't open. Not even a catastrophe like the one in 1947 was enough to make people show their faces. I heard that in 1939, during the fire in the Dianda Lopes oil refinery, there was some excitement. Some people are born, live, and die in hiding. Only their families are aware of their existence. Gophers. I've always been curious about these houses, wanted to walk inside, see what they're like, their architecture, how the space is set up (some say there are beautiful inner patios with fountains). There are thousands of unknown faces in this town. Once I was caught trying to force a gate open. They started to target me even more. Voices whispered angrily, asked questions; I could barely hear them. A voiceless monologue: "go away, go," "you're just hurting us," "you bother us," "go away, we don't like you." I didn't see anybody, so I tapped on their windows, rang their bells, threw pebbles, and the whispers stopped. But when I walked away, I could hear them again. Me, alone, in the middle of the street, in the Araraquara sun—and the sun can melt rocks—with people whispering. Nothing else but the whispering, like a summer creek. Me, alone, at night, catching frightened peeping toms by surprise.

31

I don't know how, but they found out about my research on the apartment buildings. Suddenly, people were advised not to answer my questions. I received judicial notices, ordering me to destroy the questionnaires that had already been answered, and informing me that nobody would confirm their answers now. I was intimidated, summoned to hand over all my material my conclusions, or all my notes that led toward conclusions. I said I wouldn't do it, that the principals at the Progresso School, where I had studied, kept everything. They were old friends of my mother, from the remote times when people visited each other. Since the school was a free territory, autonomous, untouchable like a foreign embassy (I don't know why), I was exempted from the summons. (Nobody can touch the school because our fathers and mothers had studied there, though nowadays only girls do, since it stopped being coed in order to avoid promiscuity.) The school educated generations and generations of Araraquarans. My room was searched, but only blank copies of my questionnaire were found. Two hundred questions, with which I was trying to determine why people—in a town like ours—would move from houses into condos. There used to be large open spaces around town, near familiar houses and gardens. The town was joyful, full of flowers, full of trees, shady. There were many orchards and lots of fruit: mangoes, guavas, oranges, plums, coconuts, peaches, grapes, tamarinds. Then they began to build. São Paulo had skyscrapers, so did other towns in the interior. So buildings started to go up, white boxes covered with windows, made by architects with no imagination. Cold blocks. The families sold their houses and began to pile up inside the new buildings. That was one of the first causes for the silence. People didn't see each other, didn't visit, and didn't talk—except over the telephone. The most interesting thing is that if the people who confiscated the blank questionnaires had seen the completed ones, they would have been surprised. There were practically no answers. There were large blanks that corresponded to the surprise of the interviewees at my question: why did you move to an apartment? There were the ones who stopped me halfway through and kicked me out, even if we were acquainted, or if I'd been recommended by my family, my father. After all, my grandfather had been somebody: the first stoker on the Railroad. Until the day when he got tired of burning wood and became a cabinet-maker, making beautiful things with wood instead of throwing it on the fire.

I lost friends and was left alone. I had few friends to begin with, because of my manias. What are you going to do with your life? What do you want? I didn't know what to say. There was nothing I aspired to, except for vague, airy stuff, like writing, and who knows what else. Nothing certain and solid enough for them, such as: engineer, attorney, accountant, industrialist, loan shark, priest.

32

Reports come from the non-existent and inaccessible Araraquara, not located in the interior of Brazil, and are handed to the exiled man who lives in the mountains of São Carlos. He plans to survive only on the perfume from the honeysuckle, which between September and December form a mushroom shaped cloud over the town. Eating crickets, locusts and honey, drinking mineral water, the exile—opposed to the decision of the non-inhabitants of Araraquara—tries to reconstitute his own history.

The major difficulty about Araraquara and its strange, straight streets is how to pronounce its name. At the Mário de Andrade Municipal Library, there are 229 studies that attempt to determine the correct spelling and exact pronunciation of "Araraquara." It's no wonder, then, given the complete impossibility of pronouncing its name, that people don't talk about Araraquara. For a long time, it was believed that the town didn't even exist. There were symposia, seminars, congresses: the town was as lost as Atlantis, Lemuria, or Mu. There are Araraquarans all over the world. They have names, bodies, regular jobs, they read, write, drive. They just don't talk to each other. The Araraquaran is considered the most perfect example of modern man, with his anxieties, longings, little problems, and mystical quests. The town sits there, in the center of the state, with its banks, schools, saunas, supermarkets, drive-ins—its businesses empty (there's a serious financial crisis sweeping the country)—its racetracks, golf courses, its club with dances on Sundays, another club with a lake and boats, its hotels, colleges, two soccer fields, and all the amenities that constitute a town made for human life. But it's a town without access. The maps don't show it. There are no signs on the roads. The trains never stop there. The telephones are just for decoration. Weeds have taken over the airport. They say the town is 160 years old, give or take. It doesn't matter. Nobody knows the town's history. The elders, eyewitnesses, live in twenty-three nursing homes, and the nursing homes are in the mountains, inaccessible, like the monasteries in Meteora, Greece (see *Encyclopedia Britannica*).

These reports were taken from inside Araraquara. Nobody knows how. Written papers don't leave the town, nor do tape recordings. People's memories blur. There is a big mystery surrounding these narratives, which constitute a real cosmogony. An enigma as impenetrable as that of the Bible's authorship, or the true meaning of the Egyptian pyramids. I state this with confidence, from my observatory in the mountains of São Carlos, where I am able to see the nocturnal glow of the town that has exiled me: Araraquara. I was born there, in 1936. I don't have any proof, or any documents; you'll just have to take my word for it. The reason for my exile: I spoke the word "Araraquara," and believed in its existence.

33

It's nice to watch the movement from behind this window, in the tranquility of this room. See the people, without being seen. They have surprising gestures and attitudes. They stick their fingers in their noses, suck their teeth, cough, spit on their own clothes, touch their penises, roll their heads, fart, and burp. I can hear the noises when the movie at the Paratodos is quiet. The best people go by this window, many at the same time everyday. After six, the girls from the sock factory go down in groups. I've known some of them for years. They're getting old. Others disappear; sometimes I see them on the streets, with their husbands or children. Every night, an old relative of mine goes down at seven o'clock, buys the *Gazeta*, folds it, places it under his arm, and goes back up. A bachelor, he's crazy about the movies, didn't miss a show. Now he doesn't go anymore; he watches soap operas. I don't know why he buys the *Gazeta*. He never reads it. He gets home, has supper, and leaves the newspaper on the hat rack; he's only read the headlines on the first page. I can't understand how he doesn't despair, seeing how different the town is nowadays. The movie theaters have been renovated, the pavement downtown has been changed, trees have been torn down, there are no more graduation balls, the girls don't parade back and forth between the movies and the Club anymore, the Club is moving, the Roses Esplanade has changed, the promenades are over, they shut down the *Araraquara Reporter*, the hotel bar is now a travel agency—I've heard it's going to be made into a fast food cafeteria. How come he doesn't notice? I don't know where to focus. People have disappeared. And the guys from our gang? We were united, we could have stayed together; we should have made an oath, cut our arms, mixing blood with blood so we would never part ways. We abandoned each other, forgot we exist. They forgot I exist. I walk down the street and it's as if I were invisible, as if I had taken a magic potion and become transparent. I could have died and it wouldn't have made any difference. That's what I'm going to do one of these days. The other day, a nanny saw me and moved to the other side of the street. They didn't have to be afraid of me, but rather of the things that hide behind walls, of the people who disappear in swimming pools and reappear God knows where. They should be afraid of the people who keep me from writing, break my door down and take my things away. They should be afraid of the people who place barbed wire around their yards, of the wind that every Wednesday shakes the town and brings sand. Afraid of strangers who leave rocks for us to deliver. Why don't they look down on Miss Maria do Carmo and her poorly explained adventures? No, they're afraid of me, who, secretly, doing dangerous, patient spying, gathering the testimonies of the dissatisfied, was able to reconstitute everything, putting together the most remarkable story of this town ever written. I'm going to send it to a publisher in São Paulo. Later, I'll be able to see my friends again—with something to show. And I'll return with them, on the seven o'clock deluxe train; or on the bus; maybe in my car. Leaving on the 6:10 train, on Ash Wednesdays.

34

I worried. I wondered if the Rt. Hon. Paul Meerne Caedwalla Hasluck, P.C., M.A., M.P., Australian historian, politician, and diplomat (born April 1, 1905), had received my letter. It had been five months since I wrote him. Mustapha bin Datu Harun Datu,

O.B.E., from Borneo, hadn't answered either. I went to the post office to complain. I took a pink piece of paper that read "Brazilian Communications Company." I went from window to window, and nobody could explain anything. One of the old guys thought it'd be better for me to write another letter asking what had happened. And if this second letter didn't get a reply, I should send another one. Five, ten, twenty letters if necessary. And if two hundred letters didn't help, the best thing would be to go to Borneo or Australia in person. I thought the old guy wanted to increase the BCC's revenue, but I took his advice about a second letter. Only one; exactly like the first. I just added: "In the belief that you have not received my initial letter, and hoping that you are in good health." I waited for two months, while I wrote to other people, like the Soviet surgeon Liev Konstantínovitch Buguch (born 1905), from the Central Institute of Tuberculosis, Yauza Railway Station, Moscow. Dr. Liev had won the Red Star Lenin Prize in 1961 and could be found on page 161 of the *International Who's Who*, where I'd gotten all the names, biographies, and addresses. I poured over the *Who's Who* day after day, choosing the names. I wrote the letters in English. My night classes had been helpful. Worried that I was writing in American English, I enrolled at the British Cultural Institute. In five weeks I was writing in proper English. The letters were short, five lines. Straightforward. They contained my request, nothing more. A simple request many people from the *Who's Who* complied with. I kept the replies, from all over the world, in my closet. In another closet I kept stacks of forms from the post office.

I wrote whenever I got home from my job. Clerk in a hardware store on Nove de Julho Street, the old business district in Araraquara.

I spent the day in a wooden cubicle, among tables covered in metal dust, lit by yellow lamps, deciding who I would write to that night. I ate and rushed home. I sat at my table, leafing through the new *Who's Who*s from India, England, Jamaica, Chile, and Afghanistan. I wrote in a round hand; in a calligraphy I learned at the Di Franco night school, from seven to nine (and I missed dinner at my boardinghouse, so I would eat a pear, bread with butter, some sugarcane juice). I attended the school for two years, and was awarded an honors diploma. The principal hugged me and cried, "You are the last calligrapher to graduate from this school. What you learned is useless. Nobody writes by hand any longer. You should have learned to type!"

But I hated typewriters, those round keys where you pressed your finger and a letter appeared ready-made, without your having to work carefully to form it, create the letter artistically, design it, like an architect designing a house. I simply couldn't understand the typists in the office, typing all day long without even knowing why they were typing, without understanding what they were copying. Twenty-two young women sitting all day, from eight to eleven and from one to six, typing, their little hands always in the same positions, their fingers running and pressing the small round keys mechanically, eight hours a day, forty hours a week, two hundred hours a month, two-thousand-four-hundred hours a year, twenty-four thousand hours in ten years. And the day they retired, their fingers, dull from pressing the small, black, round keys so much, would have typed for seventy-two thousand hours. And none of them would have ever improved a letter, worked on a word, created anything in a sentence, put anything into alignment, because everything was ready, easy, quick.

THE MEMBERS
Memoirs

I looked at the town, whipped by the sun, the tall buildings down-town, the scarce trees.

"Dad, tell me that story about the fish that ate Grandpa's fish."

"Again? I was just telling it on the bus."

"I didn't pay attention on the bus. I was looking out the window. Tell me!"

"It'd been sixty days and your Grandfather hadn't caught any fish, and was feeling discouraged."

"Sixty? You said fifty on the bus."

"Yeah? You weren't paying attention? I've calculated it right; it was sixty. It'd been two months since your grandmother had died."

"What did she die from?"

"From old age. She died quietly, one night your Grandfather arrived bringing a bag of *içás* to fry."

"Why haven't we ever gone to catch *içás*, Dad? You talk so much about it. I want to go someday."

"We have to go at the right time."

"And when is that?"

"I'm not sure if it's in July or December. We have to wait for a rainy day followed by sun. Then the *içás* start flying, fill the fields, cover the ground, flap their wings, trying to burrow into the ground. We get a bag, and just start picking them up."

"Do they bite?"

"I never got bitten. I would go out with your grandfather in the evening and the fields were black with them. Your grandmother would cut off the lower bodies, cook them in hot oil, and serve a big plateful to each person."

"Tasty?"

"Yes! Very tasty. I'll tell you, I haven't eaten *içá* in thirty years. Haven't eaten? I haven't seen one! Who knows, maybe they don't exist anymore."

"What's it look like?"

"It's a big black ant with wings."

"A big ant with wings? I've never seen an ant with wings, not even on TV. Is it time for them now?"

"I don't think so. It's more toward the end of the year."

"What about the fish? Did you forget?"

"It was huge. So big it didn't fit in the boat."

"You were saying he hadn't caught anything in sixty days."

"After Grandma died, he got upset, very sad. They had been married for fifty-four years. Maybe his sadness kept the fish away."

"Do they know when we're sad?"

"Yes."

"And plants too?"

"Who said so?"

"You, on Christmas day. When I asked you why you didn't use the little pine tree for a Christmas tree, you said we shouldn't cut down trees or pull their leaves out, because they felt it."

"And it's true."

"But Grandpa was sad and tried to fish, and couldn't get anything. Then he got even sadder."

"He didn't even mind; he would sit staring at the water and thinking of your grandmother. I think that's why he didn't catch anything. He didn't pay attention to the line; the fish would eat the bait and go away."

"Why did he fish?"

"To eat. And to sell."

"Did he sell the fish?"

"He sold them in the market."

"Wasn't Grandpa a cabinet-maker?"

"That too. He did a little of everything."

"How long ago did he die?"

"Fifteen years."

"I don't have a grandfather, right, Dad?"

"No."

"The other boys do. Why?"

"Because they haven't died yet. But they will too someday. And then the boys won't have one."

"Grandfathers are very weak, aren't they, Dad? Why?"

"Most of them are old."

"Why aren't there young grandfathers? Child grandfathers? That way they'd last a long time."

"Because it takes time to become a grandfather. It's not easy."

"What are grandfathers good for?"

"What do you mean, *good for*?"

"Fathers are good to sleep with us, play, tell stories, get upset, make us do homework. And grandfathers?"

"They're good for . . ."

"I know, for grandfathering."

"Right, for grandfathering."

"And what does that mean?"

"It means playing grandfather."

"You don't know what it means, do you, Dad?"

"No, I don't."

"Then find out, so you can tell me."

"I'll look it up. Next time we go out, I'll tell you."

"You take too long, Dad. You say you're coming for me one day, and don't show up. Then, you show up, and my mom doesn't let me go out."

"I'll pick you up every week . . ."

"Do fish eat *içá*?"

"Yes."

"But does the *içá* go in the water? Can it swim?"

"No. And when it falls in the water, the fish swallow it."

"Without frying it?"

"Without frying."

"Doesn't it taste bad?"

"Fish are different from people."

"What about the fish Grandpa caught? Did the other fish eat it whole? Do fish eat fish?"

"Big fish eat little fish."

"Do big men eat little men?"

"Sometimes."

"How come, sometimes?"

"It's very difficult to explain to you . . ."

"But Grandpa caught a fish that was bigger than the boat. How did the other fish eat it?"

"An even bigger fish came and your grandfather couldn't do anything."

"Did Grandpa hit the super big fish?"

"As much as he could. He spent many days fighting it."

"How many?"

"Four. He was old and tired, but he decided he needed to face the creature. He did, and won."

"But you said the super big fish ate the other. So, did Grandpa lose?"

"No. Grandpa fought to catch the first one, huge, strong. Then he tied it to the boat because he couldn't put it inside. Then the other one came and ate the fish Grandpa had caught."

"Does it mean it was all for nothing?"

"Yes."

"Did Grandpa get sad?"

"Grandpa knew that's the way things are. He knew he had to fight for his fish. And he did. He tried to fight with the bigger fish that came to eat the fish he had fought for. But he didn't have anymore strength. He was exhausted."

"Was anything left from Grandpa's fish?"

"The skeleton."

"What did he do?"

"He left it on the beach so everyone could see it. But I was the only one to see it, because the tide came and the waves carried it away."

"Wasn't it in the river, Dad?"

"In the sea."

"You told me it was in the river."

"I think I was mistaken."

"Is this story true, Dad?"

"The truth, pure and simple. I wouldn't lie to you."

"But you lie sometimes. Don't you?"

"No. Really."

"Do you like me, Dad?"

"Very much."

"Why don't you come to see me everyday?"

"I can't, I work a lot."

"You should come see me. I'm alone. Mom goes to work. Why don't you live with us, Dad? Like the other dads?"

"How many times do I need to explain? I think you're old enough to understand it."

"I didn't mean it. I thought, maybe if I mention it, you'll come back. Don't you miss me?"

"So much."

"Mom misses you."

"She does? Has she talked about it?"

"Yes. The other day she said, 'A home without a man is hell.'"

"I can't go back."

"You're stubborn like Grandpa. If he weren't stubborn, he wouldn't have caught the fish. Isn't that right?"

"Could be. Your Grandpa never left anything half-finished."

"I've never seen any photo of Grandpa."

"There aren't any."

"None? Not one? Nothing? The other boys have photos of their grandfathers, grandmothers, everyone."

"Your grandfather didn't like pictures. He said if someone took his picture, he would get very, very weak. The picture would eat up his energy."

"I'm tired, Dad. Enough climbing. Can we rest a little?"

"Under that shade over there."

"I want a *guaraná* soda and a sandwich."

"Now?"

Sitting under a tree. Far away, the town was immersed in a blur of shadows. But the fields and hills around it were sunny, shiny, covered with orange trees. A car went up a dusty road.

"Let's go to our tree today?"

"Don't we always?"

"You like that tree, huh Dad?"

"Don't you?"

"I do, but you like it more."

"When I was a kid, I used to come here with Grandpa. When I was young and it was a holiday, I would come up and sit under it reading. There were no buses; I walked up all the way from the church."

"I could walk it too. You want to bet? And I'd get here first."

THE EYES

He sold his eyes in ads for eye drops. He was the most famous Araraquaran. His eyes could be seen all over the country on big billboards. Thousands of women were in love with him. Mothers bought eye drops so their sons would grow up to have eyes like his—a pure and limpid, light blue color. Girlfriends broke up with their boyfriends, brides with their fiancés. Couples split when the men didn't have clear blue eyes. Even he contemplated his eyes on the billboards, and tears streamed down his face. He looked at the mirror and cried out of happiness. They were sky-blue, sea-blue, blue-blue. Then, he stuck his pocketknife in his left eye and removed the globe. Then, the right one.

THE TEETH

He hit his teeth with a rock and broke them, all of them.
He had thirty-two white and perfect teeth and he had been
the object of study at the School of Odontology. He broke
them because his girlfriend said, "Your smile seems like
something out of a toothpaste ad." He broke them because
he was ashamed of opening his mouth and showing all that
whiteness, sparkling every time the sun shone on them. He
was ashamed because he didn't go to the dentist twice a year,
he didn't know what a cavity or toothache meant. He never
felt the caress of the drill or the little jet of water. Nor had
he had a root canal or nerve extraction. It was humiliating:
he didn't even have bad breath. He woke up in the morning
with a taste of nectar in his mouth, and the women he'd
slept with cried out of happiness—his breath smelled like
blossoming orange flowers when he woke up. How many
times had he woken up with women sticking their noses in
his mouth, inhaling his breath like ether? He hit them with
the rock and went home: toothless and happy.

THE LEGS

He had a car but didn't know anything about engines. He got stuck twice on the side of the road because he'd run out of gas. He couldn't understand why cars wouldn't run without gasoline. He'd filled the tank with water and it didn't do any good. Thus, he preferred to walk: he didn't have to shift gears, step on the brake, accelerate, control his speed, watch the gas, the oil, or the lights that came on to indicate problems. But, walking, he found out he could get the flu, colds, backaches, headaches, muscle pains, lumbago, eczema, hemorrhoids, gonorrhea, neck pain, ingrown nails, tuberculosis, cancer, ulcers, nephritis, hepatitis, paraplegia, blackheads, dandruff, lice, hives, swelling, diabetes, mononucleosis, leukemia, strep throat. So he neither drove his car nor walked. He stopped and stayed still; his arms hanging, his head drooping, his eyes closed.

THE BRAIN
Memoirs

I know that for many, many years there was a man who was officially designated by law to be the guardian of the trial records. This was the title passed down from father to son: guardian of the trial records. It was a secret title, not even relatives knew about it. It was a source of pride only to its holder, not a glorious coat of arms to be displayed. At a certain age, the father passed on to his middle son the secret about the title, his honorary duty. Actually, the guardian of trial records was kept in complete ignorance of what the records contained. He was vaguely informed that something important was locked up in those unopened shelves, which were never accessible to any person. The bookshelves' doors were equipped with elaborate locks, and the keys didn't exist any longer. Nobody knows if they had been thrown out, lost on purpose, or locked up in the safe of one of the twenty-one most powerful families in town. People talked about "twenty-one families"—who were they? One could add and add, and end up with many more, or much fewer. Listing the largest fortunes, they added up to more. In the list of tradition and prestige, they were quite fewer. Where, then, did the number twenty-one come from? Or is it a secret society, or a political organization? What I know is that everyone tries to forget or to hide his participation in the horrible crime. In the trial records are the names of those who participated, and their families are still alive today, some decadent, others stronger than ever. They try to bury the crime under an avalanche of contradictory and paradoxical information, and harm the investigation with leads that point to other, minor crimes that took place at different times, and have nothing to do with that night in 1897, the night of agony and fear.

37

I look at the doorman from afar, walk closer, pretend I am looking at posters. My God, whose face is this? Certainly it's not that of a doorman's. I'm sure I saw the doorman's picture last week in an old magazine, when I was going through the papers in the storage room. It was a photo, about 2 x 3". If that room wasn't such a mess, or if I were more organized, it would be easy. I don't like to go through it; it's full of black dust and sand. The yellow sand keeps on falling without people realizing it: the sand that will doom them.

38

I walk by in front of the dead vegetable growers' house. I am fascinated by it, by what may have happened inside. Over a year has gone by and the mystery continues. Nobody cared anymore anyway. The windows closed, the dust accumulating in the garden paths and in the verandah, the weeds choking the plants. It used to be a beautiful and neat garden. They say they both took a gardening course in Europe. They say. This is a town where the most commonly used words are "They say." Life here has existed, was witnessed, contemplated and even lived by an invisible group of people who say things. They tell and re-tell, and we never know who has seen, heard, met, and lived with these "people."

They say they exist.

39

It's not raining; it's not cold. There isn't any special movie showing at theaters. There isn't any party anywhere; there isn't any game. It's an ordinary Tuesday. Before, the evening students used to come down after classes. They're gone. I'm curious: what do they do? Not all of them go out with girlfriends, or are married and need to go home. They came in noisy groups, spread out, and moved on. Soon, other groups came. For a good half-hour downtown was alive, and then we would go home with the comforting feeling of having seen people, having heard shouts, voices, and laughs. Things a man needs, that make him feel protected. This is it: the sensation of being in a vacuum. I often think I am going to plunge into the dark and will have nothing to grab on to. I seem to stagger as if drunk, and the idea that people see me in that state terrifies me. But I'm not drunk; I haven't had a single beer in a week, and now I feel like going to a bar, grabbing the frosty glass with my hands, and feeling its sweat. Nothing else. It's not a desire to drink; it's the contact with the cold glass that will make me feel good. The glass seems to me human, it conveys this impression. It's frosty. It communicates with me through this sensation. The frost touches me, penetrates me, and remains for a few moments. I feel alive, because the frost disturbs me, upsets me. This glass makes me alive. I still have reactions. Many times I even doubt myself. I walk, eat, look; like a robot. Mechanically. Two weeks ago, I stepped on a nail, and didn't realize it. It bothered my heel; it was a quarter-inch deep into my foot.

40

The certainty I have is enormous: sand will eventually cover the town if the wind stays violent and keeps bringing as many grains as it does now. I wipe the window every hour, and come up with a handful. I've already collected a bucket of it in my room since yesterday. I'm vigilant; if I feel the desert is dangerously advancing, I'll call the mayor and all the authorities about the state of emergency. It's easy to call them: they are a block away from here, playing cards at the Club. They play every night. This is why nobody works at the Town Hall in the morning.

41

I was writing. Rather, I was trying to write the script, without being able to create even one scene. Nothing to worry about; just an old routine. I'm used to it. I even stopped having headaches and tightness in my neck. All I did was sit down in front of the window everyday at three in the afternoon. I sat down after cleaning the fine yellow sand accumulating on the window, table, and books. Why doesn't the town heed the danger? I scribbled on wrapping paper: lines, circles, arrows, spirals spinning incessantly. I have kept all the papers. I don't throw any away. None. Sometimes, an occasional phrase comes up in the middle of it, representing whatever situation I see from the window: on the sidewalk, in the café, in front of the movie theater. At first, as a way to warm up, I copied phrases from their posters: "RAVISHING. VIOLENT DRAMA OF EMOTION AND TENDERNESS." Later I realized the phrases were tirelessly repetitive. One day I went out at the moment the painter was writing something, and found out he copied phrases from a small greasy notebook, its pages dirty and torn. The painter was fond of certain phrases and adjectives. All the movies at the

Paratodos became RAVISHING. But I had given up copying such phrases, and began to describe people's faces. It was good practice for depicting a character physically. Besides, the people going by at the same time were always the same: the girls from Lupo went up in the morning and came back in the evening; Old Lopes with his *Gazeta*; Big Mendonça and his belly; Miss Maria do Carmo's husband having coffee with the bank managers; those three old men at seven o'clock; and so on. I gave up. Who would find these people interesting? Danilo or Bernardo would laugh at me if I talked about these monotonous, repetitive characters. As if I, or my life, weren't the same. However, my life is not being reproduced nor is it the subject of a biography. Danilo told me, "Leave. Break free and jump out." But if we don't break free by the time we're twenty-five, it becomes more difficult. Only someone who has lived in a small town knows that. I too am trying to find what has kept me in the cage, what ties me down. A prison without bars.

I finished the lines, circles, arrows and spirals. In a while I'll begin to contemplate the blank paper, imagining what to write. I have a list of ideas and topics; I just have to develop them. I could open an agency for ideas, and sell them to other writers. I should say: sell them to writers. I am not one, definitely not. What use is there in lying? I write my diaries, an adolescent thing, the diaries of a young man going through puberty, full of matters of love, insecurity, timidity, loneliness, and plans for the future. Ridiculous. If anybody knew!

Meanwhile, the ideas:

1 – The man who changes into grass is eaten by a donkey, becomes shit, is defecated and used as manure for lettuce; becomes part of the lettuce. He's eaten in a salad, goes to the stomach, part of

him is absorbed into the organism, becomes again part of man.

2 –

3 –

4 –

5 –

6 –

I'll fill them in later (I had so many ideas, where are they?). Now I'm going out, to have a coffee, see if the afternoon newspapers have arrived, find out why everybody is running toward Vila Xavier.

42

Nancy ran among the people. The café was empty. Nobody came to wait on me. On the street, everybody was running, as if a herd of buffalos were after them. At intervals the street got empty: a throng would pass, and then everything got quiet again. I don't know why, but a vision, a memory, something like that hounds me: an old house, a hallway on the side, and an open gate. It's a Sunday afternoon or a holiday, and the street is deserted. I look at the ground surrounding the house and see weeds growing among the rocks, a sign of abandonment. Later, it's Sunday night, I'm on the sidewalk, and all I hear are my Aunt Quita's silver bangles when she moves her arms; there's a bunch of young women—cousins and friends—and they are going down for a stroll.

Why I remember this, I don't know. The café, empty. I stand leaning against the counter. A kid comes in, I ask:

"Why is everybody running?"

"Someone said the dam burst and the water is rushing down. There's nobody left up there."

"Is that right?"

"How am I supposed to know?"

"But if the dam bursts, the water is not coming here."

"How am I supposed to know?"

I stay there. Hearing the wind. No sign of water. I think people have been watching too many movies. The wind brings sand and it suffocates me a little. I cough. The counter is full of sand, the cups, the floor. I can feel the grains of sand dissolving under my shoes as I walk. It gets in through the hole in my shoe. Is that why everybody was running and not because of the dam? The desert is coming at last. I shall wait for it. Maybe it's dangerous, the sand may cover me. One day, this town will have disappeared, and I want to walk on the dunes, trying to locate where the square used to be, the movie theater, the house where Nancy hides with Eduardo. The wind is awful, the grains of sand cut my skin; I can't open my eyes or move one step ahead. I can't do anything; only wait for the storm to be over, so I can go look for my son. Find out if he is safe. Eduardo, don't despair, I'm coming, I can't walk; coming, Eduardo, where did your mother hide you? The tears bind the sand onto my motionless face. A furrow of sand goes down from my eyes to my chin: a painful line.

43

"Do you watch TV all day long?"

"Yes."

"Don't you have anything else to do?"

"No."

"Don't you want to talk?"

"No."

"Nancy, what do you want?"

"To watch TV."

"All day long?"

"All day."

"How can you stand it?"

"I just do."

"That's not possible, you can't be normal."

"Maybe I'm not."

"And you admit it?"

"What's wrong with it?"

"You act like you're a fool."

"Maybe I am."

"Nancy, I'll come back unexpectedly, and if you're watching TV like everybody else, I'll kill you."

44

At two in the afternoon, on Sunday, the town is empty. It's the best time to go out. Testing doors, studying keyholes and examining the locks people often use to guarantee their isolation. One can hear the snores of the sleeping, stuffed with spaghetti and beer. Burps come from stomachs full of risotto and chicken-fried steak. The snore of gluttons gorged with empanadas, pork loin, cocktails; children's screams, TV music. The town is hypnotized by talk shows for eight, ten hours straight. This is fortunate for me because I can work in peace, with my magnifying glass, notebooks, rulers, compasses, keys, pliers, and wires, because some of the locks are strange and I'm not able to catalog them. I think of some of the unusual models, full of tricks and devices. At this point, it's unlikely I'll find a lock I'm not familiar with. Or one I can't find in catalogs. My pantry is full of filed, well-organized catalogs. They are an essential part of my work. The large majority of them were sent by my correspondents in Sweden, Finland, Australia, Panama, Tierra del Fuego, Chile. For twelve years I have been collecting catalogs, brochures, ads, newspaper clippings: everything concerning keys, keyholes, locks and doors. This was in part responsible for my isolation from Nancy. A minimal part, but in a sense it contributed to it. Because I spent money on paper and stamps, and sometimes I had to pay for a catalog. Only certain specialty shops get them for free. I had the great idea of having a notepad printed, making up a fictitious business. It paid off: the companies sent everything. From time to time they sent supplements, outlining the changes that were made in the models.

Hundreds of houses have very complicated doors. Some took weeks for me to understand. I need to examine the locks at the old man's house; I've heard they are special. The most important part of this work is that, with time, we learn to define the individuals, physically and psychologically. We get to understand the homeowner. He expresses himself through the door, its thickness, the style, lock, keys. Everything faithfully portrays the owner: height, weight, character, manias, teeth, illnesses. I discovered something curious, just by chance: people who suffer from hemorrhoids use very small keyholes. The smallest I've seen. In one of my studies, I noted three completely identical keyholes. I know the owners; they suffer from hemorrhoids. I thought it was a coincidence, but took note. When I found sixteen more, I did some research among acquaintances, friends, family doctors, and relatives. All had the same disease. I was puzzled. As much as I try, I can't find the reason. True, I'm lacking the necessary medical background. I already have an appointment with a specialist, but in Ribeirão Preto. I don't trust the doctors here, nor do they trust me.

45

Pedro's bar is being demolished. Old wood partitions are piled up on the sidewalk. They were part of the private rooms that in the '30s sheltered couples having tea; or women who, in the afternoon, got together for chocolate and pastries. The wood was engraved and the doors' glass panes had drawings: palm trees and swans, mermaids, flowerpots, small roses. And the sun—which is everywhere. In some of the drawings one can see what people say is sand in the background. (The desert that used to exist in town?) Long ago women stopped attending the bar because of the salesmen. Later came the fags, who kept making out, forcing the management to remove the door locks so that the private rooms would always stay open. So many fags showed up in this town. They came out, paraded around, impudent. In 1950 they got beaten, a lot. On Sunday nights, whoever had a car dropped his girlfriend off at home and then went out. Driving along the meeting points—the airport road, the tuberculosis hospital—beating the homosexual couples they found. They beat everybody: the passive and the active ones. On Monday, those who showed up at school all beat up, we knew: a fag. He got labelled.

46

"Let's talk first, and then I'll examine you."

"It will be just a conversation, Doctor."

"So tell me what you feel."

"I don't feel anything. I just need some information for a project I'm working on."

"What kind of project? What information?"

"I'm a door and keyhole researcher. I'm an expert in keys, locks, everything."

"And what is the connection between a keyhole specialist and a hemorrhoids specialist?"

"I'll get there. I have studied all types of locks for several years. And they have taught me something fundamental: the keyhole reflects the homeowner, his life, character, fears, tensions. Most importantly, however, is that keyholes also reveal the homeowner's diseases."

"Give me the details. It seems to me a strange but curious topic. And since you are paying for the visit, you can continue."

He scribbles on his notepad while I talk. Maybe he's recording. I'm not sure it was a good idea to come to Ribeirão Preto. I've been told you can't trust the doctors in Ribeirão; they write long dossiers against the people of Araraquara. But no doctor in Araraquara would see me. They don't take me seriously. Now I'm already here, I've spent money on the bus ticket, the visit, very expensive.

THE ILLUSTRIOUS LADY

1 – Miss Maria do Carmo, forty-five years old (and more), society's distinguished lady, was sitting in the patio of her house at 9:30 on a Tuesday morning. Miss Maria do Carmo's patio was on high ground and had a glass wall, as if it were a greenhouse. Miss Maria deserved a greenhouse; she was a rare individual in town. Her father had been a doctor, land-owner, mayor; and very rich. Her grandfather had been rich, just like her great-grandfather, and the great-grandfather's father, and the great-grandfather's grandfather. Two hundred years ago, Miss Maria do Carmo's grandfather's great-grand-father had founded the town. Miss Maria do Carmo was a good-looking brunette, dark hair, slight Indian features, full figure. Elegant, well dressed, perfumed, tanned by the sun at her house's pool, whoever saw her wouldn't say she was more than thirty years old. On Tuesday, Miss Maria was watching (a little bored) people walk by her house when she saw: the man ringing, the maid saying the man needed to talk to her. She walked down to the gate, greeted him, heard the man say:

"Honey, let's make a little love?"

Miss Maria do Carmo opened the door, the man walked in. She took him to her bedroom, took off her clothes, he did the same. They went to bed.

2 – Miss Maria do Carmo, forty-five years old, sitting in the glass-enclosed patio, on a Tuesday in December, one of the first days in December without rain. She thought she should enjoy the sun and go to the pool (in the back of the house), but stayed in the patio, lazily, watching people walk by. She didn't like the town's people, even though her husband was very important, and her family had lived there for two-hundred years. She didn't like them, but belonged to the Rotary, the Lions, the Brazilian Legion of Assistance, the SOS, and to all the institutions of charity and social aid, and to charity hospitals, and contributed to private emergency clinics. She organized tea parties, bazaars, festivals, balls. Miss Maria saw when the man rang; rang again. Nobody answered; the maids were probably in the back wing of the house situated on the other side of the block. Then, Miss Maria do Carmo walked down. She spoke to the man. The two walked in, went to her bedroom. The man pulled out a sharp sickle. He struck Miss Maria on her head, her neck (severing her veins), her breasts, her thighs, cut her toenails, sprayed blood all over the bedroom, over the expensive dresses Miss Maria bought in Paris: Cardin, Courrèges, Chanel, Rabanne.

3 – Miss Maria do Carmo, society's *"distinguished lady"* (as a local society columnist, who liked to use foreign words in his column, called her), elected the most elegant, was sitting

on the patio. The rain had stopped a little; outside the sun was burning, but the patio was air-conditioned, cool. Miss Maria do Carmo, with nothing to do, while her six maids cleaned the house and fixed lunch, washed and thought of Christmas. She looked at the street, bored, watching people go by. Everyone turned and greeted her. Everyone looked at Miss Maria do Carmo. She was respected, a monument. Loved by the poor, whom she helped; by the priests (she had helped build five churches, which had been under construction for the past twelve years); and by the employees at her husband's factories (for whom she organized the Christmas party, the Mother's Day party, and the Father's Day party). Miss Maria saw the man stop, ring the bell. She didn't hear the bell, because it rang in the small backroom, where the maid, the attendant, was. She saw when the man talked to the maid and the maid walked up. Then, Miss Maria went down and returned with the man. They walked in the house, went to her bedroom. Miss Maria do Carmo took the iron letter opener that her husband used to open book pages, and stuck it in the man's chest. One single stroke, in his heart. Bloodless.

4 – Miss Maria do Carmo, a good-looking brunette, eyes like those of an Indian (they say she was born from a *mestizo* mother, for her grandfather had kept a harem of Indian women at the back of the farm), was sittingon that December morning in her glass-enclosed patio, on high ground, from

where she could see all her yard, and beyond the yard, the street. Her house was in a central location, but was quiet, because there were acres of land surrounding it, with gardens, small woods, a lake and three swimming pools. She tanned there, with her friends who arrived from the capital. Miss Maria do Carmo hated the town's women, those country bumpkins, ill-dressed and with such bad manners. She spent the mornings watching from afar the people who walked by, as if they were curious little creatures. She had the walls built low, so that people walking by could see: her gardens, her yards, the marble busts brought from Florence, Lebanon, Greece, Asia, all the places she had visited. And so that they saw the fountains, lakes, lights, arbors, benches, centenary trees. Her house was a small Versailles (as her friends used to say). Miss Maria saw, on that morning, the man stop at the gate, ring, the maid answer, shake her head "no," point at her, shake "no" and "no" and "no." And the man nodded and walked away slowly. Miss Maria hurried, got in her white sports car (she didn't have anything black, not even maids), and drove off on the sunny street. She followed the man. She was far from her house, outside the town, when she ran him over. She ran over him again and again, until he became pulp.

5 – Miss Maria do Carmo was sitting in her patio. Looking at the street and at the people who, on that day, seemed to be out, en masse, for a stroll. The first day of warm sun in

December. It was a holiday. On holidays, people came to the square in front of her house to see the statues of her great-grandfather (who had been a hero in the Paraguay War); of her grandfather (who had fought in the north with Antonio Conselheiro); of her father (a pioneer of manufacturing industries: socks, preserves, metallurgy, dark beer). Miss Maria saw the man enter her garden. The maids, in the back, in the service wing of *Petit Versailles*, as her house was called. She walked down; it was hot outside the (air-conditioned) patio, Miss Maria do Carmo wore a light, see-through dress (by Biba of London). The man looked at her, at her suntanned (Capri, Marbella) body, her legs and breasts. At her neck where there was a stream of sweat, at her eyes (some say they were Indian eyes, others that they were Japanese; her father had overseen a tomato plantation and the workers were Japanese, there were beautiful *nisseis*). He looked at her nail-polished fingers. He was a filthy man, grime on his neck, yellow teeth. His mouth stank. Miss Maria do Carmo smelled the stench when he breathed. His hands were thick, his nails, black; his clothes, clean, nevertheless. Clean as if they had come out of the laundry room. Miss Maria do Carmo approached the man.

THE WORK
Memoirs

I am horrified to think people may consider me to be the judge of my hometown. I'm not; I'm averse to judgments. What I do is relate events, hoping to reach positive conclusions for everyone. A man needs to understand his people and his hometown to live happily. He needs to know himself and see himself within the environment where he lives. Otherwise, he will be unhappy. I don't even know if these are the issues that should be raised. I must say, and this is true, that I feel uncomfortable in the world, as if I can't find my place in it. But nobody makes it easy for me either. There are little things, disguised here and there, that in the end become gigantic: a phrase, a denial, an ironic smile, an obstacle, an endless postponement, a veiled persecution. All this proves: repairs are necessary, small maintenance jobs, so that the world can be made into the right size, as if it were a shoe, or clothes. When we're talking about the world, it's more complicated, because each individual tries to make it fit in his own way. Length, width, and details are not the same for everybody. And what happens is that when it fits some, it doesn't others. What I can assure anybody, cross my heart, is that so far it has not fit my dimensions. I always feel left out. I tried to explain this to Nancy. However, she could only exclaim, "It can't be this way, it won't work out." I just wanted Nancy to understand certain issues of mine; then it'd be easier for me to understand hers. Maybe I really shut myself off, without being aware of it. I didn't know what to do to live in peace with someone else. And I wanted to; more than that, I *needed* to know how to live together. So I wouldn't feel the loneliness I feel now. I also needed someone to encourage me to fight. Obviously, the others are to blame; I needed them like crutches, to support me.

Today I was reading my notes about the men who were killed at the station again. I drafted some scenes for a movie about violence and death. Both fascinate me because they were never part of my life. I don't know either. I'm referring to physical violence and death, not the type of violence that is just the consequence of situations, a pain inside. It may turn out that the men at the station were not bandits or terrorists. Nothing. It may happen they were not even fugitives. The inspector's and the policemen's panic may have caused a big misunderstanding and so they destroyed the guys. It must be a strange situation, to die like that, without anyone knowing who you are. In any case, death nullifies one's identity. This is another thing I wish I could express but can't. An individual dying like that twice becomes a zero. Because his life and the name that distinguished it, making him its affirmation, have been taken away from him. An average town shaken by a tragedy. A mediocre man, on the verge of losing his job, tries the lucky strike that will make him secure when facing his employer—the State. This will be the character. If I turn his life inside out, it will be made up of two scenes: the daily sweeping of the train platform, and the moment he dialed the phone to call the police. At the instant he dials the last number, his fate will have been sealed and his life transformed. These are the moments that fascinate me. The moments when we determine changes, through a gesture, a word or thought, without realizing it.

I can't go beyond the first scenes, I am stuck on them. I don't know how to continue. Was everything over then, in the morning and afternoon? The movie has to unfold in a single day. In this one day I can develop everything.

What good is it to dream of a movie here, away from everything? Who will be able to help me? I'm already tired, I have nine scripts in my mind.

48

It's like I've forgotten how to be a human being. I haven't had normal attitudes in a long time. I don't laugh or feel sad, but I feel shaken, emotional. As if I were a swamp and whatever falls in, dies. Quick sand, apparently motionless, and destructive. Everything alive that penetrates me dies. It's not a pleasant realization. I had depressive moments but was generally cheerful, ironic. My friends liked me because I was able to come up with the right, funny words at the right time. Not that I was the clown in the group. I had enough of a skeptical mind to face every situation with a healthy irony, the only way of confronting the world without going crazy. Now, my lips are tight and my muscles don't move, because I have no desire. It's dangerous when desire starts to fade away. I needed to find friends, but people avoided me, as they avoid Drunk Rio. It's possible I smell too much like the past, or that the strike has left its mark upon me. I'm not old, I'm only forty, and that's nothing and at the same time everything. It's everything if we worry and take our daily inventories. It's nothing if we behave as if we were starting out. In fact, I'm always starting out, and that's what keeps me young. The time is coming when I won't know *what* to start. A time when I'll look in from outside. The other day I filled out an application for a job at a car insurance company. A big company that's opening a new branch.

"Forty years old?"

"Yes, forty years old."

"Go ahead, if you want. But it won't do you any good at that age."

"What about my age? The ad didn't say anything."

"Nothing. You're just not going to be selected. In fact, I shouldn't even let you continue to fill it out."

He took the form and kept looking at me, expressionless, this kid I didn't know. An outsider. The little shit.

"I am forty years old and as able as any twenty-five year old," I said, not even believing myself, knowing it wasn't going to help anything. Besides, the sentence was completely silly and meaningless, a cliché. Nevertheless, I was willing to fill it out. I wasn't going to get the job; I could waste my time and the company's. My time was worth nothing and theirs was precious, as my interviewer would say.

"Can I at least try?"

"It's no use."

"If you'd let an application slip by . . ."

"Not yours! I don't even know you."

"I want to finish my application."

"They're not going to select you."

"I have the right to try."

"And I am under orders to not let you."

"Let's talk about who gave you the orders. It's unconstitutional."

"I don't know if it is or not."

"Call the manager, I want to talk to him."

"There aren't any managers. They're in São Paulo. I came ahead of them to choose the candidates."

"Then, call them. I'll wait. One of them will come."

"Call São Paulo and wait for one of them to get here?"

"I'm not getting out of this chair until I talk to a manager."

"You're going to have to excuse me. I have a lot of people to interview."

"Only after you talk to me."

"I've already talked."

"Not yet. I'll wait."

"It's over. If you don't leave, I will."

"So, go."

He left. I stayed sitting in the chair. Until 5:30, when a man I'd never seen in town came to close the door.

The next day I was the first in line. There were ten people behind me. I went in right away and sat down, the little shit hadn't arrived. I started to read the newspaper. When I put down the paper, there he was. Looking upset.

"We don't have anything else to say."

"I want to be interviewed, to have my application filed, to compete for the job."

"Get out, this property belongs to the company. I have the right to throw you out."

"I'm the one who's calling the police. So, your company doesn't hire old people. I am going to the newspapers, I am going to cause a scandal, to force some kind of intervention."

"What proof do you have to say that? None. So, we'll sue you for slander. You simply didn't get the job because you're insolent. We'll show you didn't fulfill the job requirements. Get out."

"You get out of my town."

"You have one more chance. You're getting on my nerves."

"I'm getting on *your* nerves? You refuse to hire me because I'm forty years old; coming from outside to shortchange people here. To harm the townspeople, that's what it is. Well, for your information, we've had enough. There are too many people in this town coming in through the backdoor. You're one of them."

"What are you talking about?"

"Outsiders are unwelcome here!"

"Even those who are bringing jobs, like us?"

"Jobs! What jobs? You've just rejected me."

"Not me, the company."

"It's the same thing."

"No, it's not. Listen here. There was nothing in this town before we came. Do you know how many jobs we'll bring? Twelve hundred. How many other companies will come behind us? Hundreds. The region is important. There will be lots of jobs. And you all complain. I've never seen anything like it! From now on, people won't have to leave to make a living outside the town."

"How nice. Your company has come and solved the region's un-employment problem. What do you think?"

"What's your problem?"

"I've come to defend."

"Defend?"

"Defend, defend, defend."

I'm down and out now, but once I had a pretty good job. I couldn't stand it. It was right after the Railroad, in the big corporation. I simply couldn't put up with it. Every day, wearing a brown suit, being called by a number, sitting in a cubicle. We were all confined. I tried to write my stuff there. They prohibited it. They took away my papers, my typewriter, my pencils, everything. One day, they removed my green tie, demanded my brown suit back, and asked me to return the tags with the numbers that identified me and made me an individual inside the building. I was kicked out. Without the number, I regained my name. What was it?

49

It's him. It can't be anybody else. Ceres Fhade, full professor, who'd had his constitutional rights revoked, author of *The Safe Guide to Leaving Home*. It took me a long time to realize it. The same angular face, the hooked nose. The professor seems to have lost his intelligent, lively air. It must be self-defense. I'm going to talk to him right away. How could he hide something like that from me? Me, his biggest fan, the only man in modern times who knows his Manual by heart.

50

Happy, at the bar table. Faruk, the singer-dentist, and Jacques, the crystal palace architect, called me. They saw me in the foyer of the movie theater, and invited me for a beer. *They* were the ones who called *me*. I wasn't the one who approached them under some pretense. Faruk has wrinkles under his eyes and looks tired. Jacques has kept his well-parted, gelled blond hair. He hasn't got into the long hair thing. His shirt has double cuffs, with gold cufflinks and his initials. The beer saves me from the awkwardness of the situation; the lack of things to talk about. Once we've had the first sips, we'll have to talk. Jacques was never much of a talker, although he could easily answer the math questions of the entire class. Faruk was more open. I hope he'll start talking soon. I'll have a beer in one gulp, to warm up the engine, and will order another one, very cold. They'll pay. Just like in the old times at Pedro's, when they used to treat me. Faruk sent me a telegram when Eduardo was born. He was the only one to acknowledge my announcement. It wouldn't have been too hard to send a letter, or a note, it wouldn't have cost anything. After all, I spent money I didn't have, having the announcements printed. I wanted to show them I was doing well in life. To this day I owe the Railroad printers, although they've given up trying to collect from me.

"I saw you on TV, singing on the Sílvio Santos's show."

"I was the special guest. If it weren't for that, I wouldn't have gone. That show is depressing."

"You sang well. Very well. I've always thought you sang well."

"I'm trying to bring back the boleros. Nostalgia is in."

"Funny, you say '*nostalgia*.' Not '*nostalgeeah*.'"

"It's an American word; we have to pronounce it correctly."

"I've always liked the show. It reminded me of the time you sang at the August 22 Club."

"But now with much more experience, huh? Everything I learned during that whole time. Did you know I'm recording an album? When I went to São Paulo to sing, all I did was become a dentist. It was the bolero period; I sang boleros, and nothing happened. Now that I'm old, my career is here. Who's heard of someone starting at the age of thirty-nine? Now I'll close the office, sell everything, and get a divorce."

"Divorce?"

"New life, new home, new wife."

"Don't you get along with your wife?

"It's a joke. Don't you get a joke?"

(The way they talk is not the same. Nobody understood the group better than me. Their dreams and aspirations. Nobody kept up with what they did better than me. I was sure Faruk had given up on singing. He didn't even sing that well.)

"Sure, I was joking too. Don't you remember? I took everything seriously, but made fun of you guys."

"You and Celso were a pain."

Three more cold beers. And an order of Gorgonzola cheese.

"Celso was a pain. And on top of everything, a jerk."

"What happened to Celso?"

"He's dead."

"Dead. Shit. How old was he? About thirty-five?"

"He died from alcohol."

"That's right. He was a jerk, and got drunk with us. That's right. He died okay."

"They found him dead in a hotel in Avaré, a cheap hotel, at a bus station. His heart exploded."

"Heart? At that age?"

"He had just left rehabilitation."

"Dr. Moura didn't have any luck, not at all. One daughter, a whore; another with two husbands; Celso, a drunk; his wife sleeping with the whole town. And he, president of the local Medical Association. He tried to cover it up, obviously."

"A strange man. He wasn't like everyone else. He's been drinking now. The father takes after the children."

(Faruk: "The obituaries. He knows everything about who's died, who's sick, dying, or sentenced. He knows everything about accidents, murders, missing people. Listening to him, I get the strange feeling I'm disconnected, I have no frame of reference. I don't belong to this town any longer; I had nothing to do with these people.")

"So many of our generation have died, huh?"

"Carlão and Maneca from leukemia. Maneca had always known he had leukemia, that's what's hard. That's why he was always lonely, didn't date anyone; it was much worse. Rubinho died from heart problems; Edith from complications in childbirth. Do you remember her? Skinny, but beautiful, beautiful. Have you heard about Rosemary? She was a bit mysterious; people said she smoked pot. Her husband killed her in Jabuticabal. He committed suicide later on. Her third husband."

("As if I were reading the obituaries section in the newspaper: the list, the report he gives me every year.")

"And Dr. Marcovan? He was shaving in the bathroom, felt a pain in his chest, told his wife, 'Call the doctor, I'm having a heart attack.' When the doctor arrived, he was dead. The town was shocked; he was the best doctor of our generation."

Faruk listens to me with a mocking look. I don't get it. He gets me started, wanting to know who's died, who's sleeping with whom, the scandals. I think of all my friends' deaths. They offer me some perspective. Is it my permanence? The possibility of thinking over my life and what I've done with it? What shitty philosophy after five beers. Their deaths don't touch me. They hurry me, in some obscure way, and at the same time tell me not to worry. It will all come at the right time. For everything there's a season, says the bolero. Or maybe it isn't a bolero? It's a samba song by Tito Madi. Everything's mixed up; I want to put some order into my mind.

"Derly is worse; have you seen that? The police are chasing him."

"They haven't arrested him yet? I saw his picture in the papers about two years ago."

"They're not going to arrest him. When they find him, they'll shoot. He's considered dangerous."

"Derly? Dangerous? A guy who used to drink a few beers with us? He just wanted to be a pharmacist."

"Who knows what happened."

"That's what I'd like to know: what guides, what shapes an individual; what changes him, what sets him astray. Peaceful Derly who drank beer and ate Gorgonzola; and Derly, the dangerous terrorist who robs banks. I can't reconcile the two in my mind."

"Well, I can in mine. He's into something else, into his own world. He knows why he did it. Just like me: a dentist, I became a singer. It was something that had always been in me. You know, our world is something that's over, for us and for him. It was over the moment I stepped on the train and left for São Paulo. So, I understand him."

"Do you? Why?"

"Look at yourself. What did you gain from the Railroad strike? Forced retirement and great difficulty finding a job."

"But I got into something illegal. They didn't even want to know if I was guilty or not. I got taken, you know."

"Look, I have no idea if you got into it by being a fool or not. That's over. I thought it was good you got into it; you got rid of that shitty public servant job."

"But I had stability."

"And that's what you fought for. See the result?"

"Something went wrong."

"Wrong is the system we live in. Wrong is defending things one doesn't believe in. You, defending workers' salaries, better working conditions. That wasn't you. Nice, loyal, but it wasn't you. It wasn't heartfelt. You weren't engaged in it, you didn't really believe in it. You were pushed into it, something was putting pressure on you, and it wasn't exactly idealism. True or not? In fact, the whole story of that strike was very confusing; it was a damn game of self-interest, you were used. A public servants' strike—no way!"

"We've talked about the dead. Do you want to know about the women who've been fooling around?"

"That's good."

"I just know what I've heard."

"Tell me, damn it!"

"Do you know the wife of that new lawyer from Rio? The one nicknamed Castelinho?"

51

Behind the windows, they observe me. They know when I walk by. I realize they're very close when I try in vain to force open the door locks. The doors don't open. The Araraquarans don't leave their homes. They stay locked up, out of fear or pride. And they find it strange that I walk around, free, unencumbered. I, the only one who isn't afraid of facing what they fear: the streets. The thick doors, the locks, the alarms, the peepholes—everything is intended to make the streets inaccessible, from inside to outside: I don't get it. I examine the street closely: two sides, poles, wires, sidewalks, and trees. Nothing else. God, they're exactly like all streets in Brazil, identical in all the cities I've visited. What kind of spell or evil could exist in them? I looked it up in books, even though all the books in the public library aren't sufficient to enlighten me. It's something that belongs to the past. It could also be something from the present, because it's out there, pulsing, circulating. It weighs down on them so much they refuse to talk. Not only to me. Bernardo used to say there's a spell on this town, acting upon all of us; and that it was necessary to break the barrier created by the spell. Did he say it? Or would it have been Ceres Fhade, the ex-college professor who had his constitutional rights revoked and was chased away? Ceres doesn't know I've uncovered his true persona: political refugee; the exiled man who has requested asylum and is in hiding. I'm not telling anyone; even if I did, nothing would happen. Ceres is not wanted, and people from Araraquara never go to São Carlos. They cannot leave: the locked doors don't let them.

52

"*Malagueña, qué bonita, quiero besarte*," and while the snuffling, squeaking record plays, I hand over the ticket. The doorman checks the photo on the ID card.

"What are you waiting for?"

"I need to talk to you, sir."

"Not now, I'm busy. When the show is over."

"Only then?"

"Move out of the way, please."

"Out of the way? There's no one trying to get in."

"Please, don't disrupt my work."

He stayed there, ready to take tickets. Standing still, next to the box where the stubs were kept. When he heard the bell he moved away, pulled the curtains, and returned to the same position. Inside, the usual music from the newsreels. Old newsreels, from six months before, shown just to follow the rules.

"Can we talk now?"

"When the movie starts."

He continued standing and took one more ticket, from Ziza Femmina.

"I'm going to the balcony," said Ziza.

"There's nobody in the room downstairs."

"I like it up there."

"Ok, but don't throw candy wrappers and don't spit on the floor."

Ziza went up.

"I don't know why this gentleman goes to the balcony every night. He watches the same movie four, five times. Some nights he goes up, comes back right away and leaves. He likes to spend money."

I went in; when the movie started I went back to the foyer. They were showing *We Were Strangers* with John Garfield.

"And now?"

"What do you want to talk to me about? We barely know each other."

"You see me here every night."

"Yes."

"What I'm going to say is important. You can remain calm, sir. You can trust me. I know everything, but I'm on your side."

"You are?"

"Absolutely. You were right to do what you did. You are a courageous man."

"I am?"

"Very courageous, my friend. You may count on me, always. We'll confront the town together, if it's necessary."

"If what is necessary?"

"To grab the bull by its horns."

"Bull?"

"I found out your real name, by accident."

"My name is José Carlos."

"Right. José Carlos for *them*."

"Them, who?"

"You know who I'm talking about."

"I do?"

"You don't need to pretend. You can open up to me, you can relax."

"I can?"

"Of course. I don't like them either."

"Them, who?"

"The people who make your life hell."

"Ah, have you noticed it too? I've got to have a lot of patience."

"Count on me."

"Will you help me?"

"Of course, two are better than one. Tomorrow we'll be three.

Little by little, an army."

"I don't know what to do anymore. If this goes on, I'll end up losing my job."

"Shake here, Ceres."

"Ceres?"

"Yes, I know your name. I know it very well."

"I'm José Carlos."

"For me you continue to be the great Ceres Fhade."

"Who is Ceres Fhade?"

"The Manual's glorious author."

"The Manual?"

"The Manual, the brave book. The man who defeated the town with his brain."

"Ah, it's a book you want me to read? I don't like books. I've never read any; they are our ruin. Neither books nor magazines."

"Well, well, Ceres, you don't need to pretend."

"We just met today."

"Ah, so that's it? You don't trust me?"

"I don't trust or distrust you."

"All right, let's do something. I'll come every night and we'll talk, until I convince you."

"Come if you want, but I don't like to talk."

"Would you rather watch a movie?"

"A movie? No, no; I've never watched a movie in my whole life. I'm a Jehovah's Witness."

"You've never seen a movie? Have you never been inside the theater?"

"Not after the movie has begun, no!"

"Don't you know what cinema is?"

"Yes, from hearing about it. I can't watch it."

"Have you never been curious?"

"Not about forbidden things."

"You didn't use to be this way, Ceres. I read your biography. You were a talented man: lucid, progressive, inquisitive. Don't deny what you are. You even made documentaries for the University."

"What are documentaries? What did I do?"

"Documentary movies: a kind of report captured on film."

"I don't get it."

"Ceres, don't provoke me, don't do it to me! You don't have to test me."

"I'm not testing you at all. If it's a movie, I didn't do it. Movies are forbidden."

"When you taught at the University, you started a sociology lab, the best one in the whole state. People even came from the University of São Paulo to copy it. And they made movies on social evolution in a mid-size town like ours."

"Look, I don't understand a thing you're saying. It must be a mistake."

"Ceres . . ."

"José Carlos . . ."

"It doesn't work with me. You are Ceres."

"You're crazy, I'm sorry to say it."

"Are you afraid?"

"Afraid of what?"

"Of me; of them."

"They? You? Why afraid? Why should I be afraid? I trust the

Lord. I work honestly. I don't do anything wrong."

"I'm not one of them, I swear."

"Are you making fun of me? You belong to that gang too. A man your age associating with those punks."

"I don't associate with anyone. I'm alone."

"Is that right?"

"I swear."

"That's better. Men were born to be alone. This business of associating with gangs never worked."

"I wanted to tell you, sir, that I admire you a lot. You and your work."

"You don't have to call me sir."

"Not to mention the Manual, your documentaries are fantastic. That one about an empty town is incredible. Dramatic. Definitive. The small goddess Television, as a student says in his testimony, being worshiped every night. Her cult is faithful; nobody abandons the home-temple. The goddess of the brilliant images, of a thousand possibilities, hypnotic, mesmerizing, omnipresent. She ties people down in their homes, and the streets are empty. People don't visit and don't communicate with each other anymore. The goddess of silence has killed conversations and mutual understanding. One single goddess, but she lives within us all, within each one of us. She deserves an award."

"You'll have to explain everything, please. I don't watch TV."

"Of course not, on principle."

"I'm a Jehovah's Witness. It's the oldest religion on Earth that follows the true Christ."

"I've never heard of these witnesses."

"Would you like to meet them?"

"Yes."

Slippery, smooth, like an eel. Typical of Ceres. Perfect for a man who suffered what he did: being persecuted, having his constitutional rights taken away. To deny, to deny everything may be a method he learned in prison. It won't be today; I need to have patience, to slowly penetrate his shell.

"We have a small community in Vila Xavier."

"Do you have a church, and services?"

"No church; nature is our temple."

"Do you meet outside?"

"Under the open skies. This way our prayers vibrate freely and don't suffer any interference."

"Is there something like that in Araraquara?"

"A wonderful group."

"Sir, you . . ."

"Don't call me sir.

"Are you studying this group?"

"I belong to it."

"Have you converted?"

"I was born into this religion."

"You've converted. You were an active man of the left, Ceres. You confronted quite a few battles for your department before losing your rights."

"What left?"

"The left, which is not the right."

"Right, left, I'm confused."

"You're right to deny it, to want to hide."

"Deny what? Oh, Lord, tonight's my night. Give me strength. I'm sorry, let's stop this conversation. I don't understand one bit of it, absolutely nothing."

"It's okay to pretend. I understand it very well. I would be afraid, very afraid. It can't have been easy to adopt a new persona. I would deny it too until I was sure of who I was talking to."

Someone clapped and whistled from inside. They stopped, then started again. A mulatto man came out.

"So, are you going to continue the movie or not?"

"Did it stop?"

"Right after it started. What's wrong with this shitty theater?"

"I'll check right now, stay calm."

"Calm, no. I want my money back."

The doorman, or Ceres, pressed a button hidden behind the curtain. He pressed it several times before the projectionist showed his face on the stairs to the balcony.

"Stop bugging me. The projector stopped working and you keep ringing that bell!"

The mulatto shouted, "I want my money!"

"I'll call the management."

"I want it now."

"You'll have to wait."

"It's a pain in the ass, go ahead. Fuck. They should have closed this theater a long time ago."

THE MAN WHO HASN'T COME
SITS AT THE SQUARE EVERY AFTERNOON

"Give me a word beginning with X."

"Malaria."

"Malaria begins with M."

"It's X."

"Then give me a word beginning with M."

"Package."

"It begins with P."

"With M."

"And how much is ten times ten?"

"It's 165."

"And 76 take away 18?"

"986."

That is how it went, every day. He sat at the Largo da Câmara. The kids around him asked questions. He answered. That was the entertainment, in that place where there was no theater, TV, radio, or train. The man arrived one afternoon. He settled down, and stayed. Thin, malnourished, with dry and taut skin like the people from the North, a sparse beard, yellow eyes. He knew things nobody did. He spoke a new Portuguese, with new words, as yet un-invented expressions, letters that would only appear later. He knew the new numbers. He could add by dividing, multiply by subtracting, subtract by adding. He could live dead, cry laughing, listen with his nose, smell with his eyes, eat with his ears, listen with his fingers, run standing still. He didn't say where he came from, how old he was, if he had been married, if he had served in the Army, what job he had had, any birth marks he had, who his parents were. He kept quiet. And the kids remained curious. Until the math teacher went to talk to him. They talked about lengthwise numbers, numbers opposite to curves that were the shortest distance through three points, divergent parallel lines, and triangles without vertexes. And then, when the conversation was over, looking at the man's eyes, which reflected the children's, the math teacher understood.

THE ENCOUNTER
Memoirs

Sounds of shots and horses' hooves. The projectionist turns the cranks, changes the films from one reel to another, rewinding them. He stops, grabs some scissors, cuts a filmstrip, puts it in his pocket, and glues the film together. The Sunday afternoon turns endlessly like those reels: sunny, quiet. The people are at the stadium, or at the clubs, or at the pools. The craze of private pools has caught on. Three companies have already opened, specializing in filters, vacuum cleaners, chemical products, construction and maintenance. One of these companies belongs to Eugenio, who had studied with me. He was the school janitor's son, but we only found out about that after he left. And when he left, he promised he would only come back when he was married to a rich woman. I don't know if he got married; he came back two years ago, has two grown-up daughters, a VW, an average house, and it isn't even in the Luminosa district. He doesn't recognize me anymore, or pretends not to.

Ceres Fhade, his arms crossed, is at the door of the movie theater. I wonder what a college professor, stuck in a job like this, may be feeling. I go down; someone scores a goal on the radio in the café, the announcer is excited. At four-thirty in the afternoon there is someone playing soccer on every field in this country.

"Very busy?"

"The matinee here is always busy. It's very cheap."

"A boring afternoon, isn't it?"

"Very calm, nice."

"Too calm, I can't stand it."

"I like tranquility."

"That's because your life was active, Ceres. Maybe now you want some peace and quiet, to think about what you're going to do in the future."

"I was active when I was young and this was the only theater in town. It filled up every night, there were lines. It was hard to control them."

"No, I'm not talking about that. I mean your life at the University."

"I never attended college. We didn't have it during my time. I finished elementary school and went to work."

"You're just hiding behind this facade of being a doorman. You must have suffered a lot in their hands."

"Not really. The theater owners have always been nice to me."

"I'm not talking about the theater owners, but about the commission that convicted you."

"What commission? Convicted me of what? I don't understand you."

"I'm almost like you: an exile.

"Asylum."

"Asylum, where? Exile."

"Can you explain, please?"

"When they confiscated your book and convicted you, you ran away. You changed your identity, you had a wife and children to protect."

"I *had*? No, I have."

"Then that's it. Afraid, you're afraid. But nevertheless, you were the only man to oppose the town."

"Oppose what?"

"Oppose the town."

"Did I oppose the town?"

"Sure, with your Manual."

"My manual?"

"Of course, Ceres. The great Manual. It's something that will live forever. There's no point in censoring a book, you know? You may burn it, tear it up, kill the author. But once an idea has been written and read, it remains."

"Has anyone burned one of your books?"

"No, your Manual."

"I don't have any manual. I don't like to read, not even newspapers. I only have books from my church, but they're different."

"Don't worry, Ceres. I'm on your side. Okay? There are two of us now. Maybe tomorrow we'll start a group. And a group can begin to resist. We'll fight, we'll win the cause."

"Are you a lawyer? Do you defend causes?"

54

The tree sat on top of the hill, at the highest point around town. You could reach it by walking along an old fieldstone wall that followed the hillcrest. Nobody ever knew who built it, it looks like those ruins you see in movies set in Ireland or Scotland. The impression you had is that the tree had been planted at the end of the wall on purpose.

"Dad, why are you hugging the tree?"

"Because it feels good. It *does* me good."

"Is it good to hug trees, Dad?"

"For me it is. Every time I'm nervous, weak, upset, I find a way to hug a tree. I stay like this for about ten minutes. And I feel much better."

"Really? Why?"

"I send whatever is bad to its roots and try to suck in the tree's vital energy. I make a transfusion and the tree responds, it understands. My depression, my troubles go away. It sends positive energy."

"Very complicated, Dad."

"The bad stuff goes away and I receive the good."

"And the tree keeps the bad?"

"No, it sends it away too. Just like with the lightning that strikes it."

"You're really strange, Dad. People say so at school."

"People say it? And what do you say?"

"Nothing. What can I say? Either I get in a fight or stay quiet and listen. It doesn't bother me anymore, I know you're cool."

"Do you think I'm strange?"

"Sometimes. At first, now I like you. I like to go out with you, to see the things you do. That's a good one, hugging a tree!"

"You can try it too when you're upset."

"Do I just hug?"

"Hug it tight. Stick your whole body to the tree. Make it feel you like it, that you need it. I'll tell you something else: I come here all the time, alone, and talk to it."

"And does it answer?"

"It just waves its leaves, when the wind blows."

The two of us stand there hugging the tree, our backs to the town.

THE WRINKLES

"I'm twenty years old and my problem is the small wrinkles on my fingers. Look at your fingers and observe the small wrinkles. I bet you had never noticed. I first noticed them when I was fifteen. I had a boyfriend and one day he stroked the wrinkles with his finger, and I felt a horrible sensation. I began to squeeze my fingers with my hands. Since that day 'they' make me feel nervous and depressed. Do you know I can't put my hands inside a drawer? Nor inside a small container? I feel an itch, begin to tremble and to blink, and my mouth puffs up. When I chop eggs, tomatoes, onions, I feel like cutting my fingers too. It's such a horrible sensation that if I didn't love life so much I would've killed myself. Not too long ago I tried to sandpaper the wrinkles, but they bled, and the skin and the wrinkles grew back. I tried to file them too, but the same thing happened. My father thought I should find a job, and I started to learn to type. But at school they placed a piece of cardboard over the keyboard to hide the letters. And my fingers rubbed against the cardboard and I could feel the wrinkles shrinking. Then I struck the keys hard and pulled the cardboard off, but the instructor didn't understand it was because of the small wrinkles, and he had me expelled. I didn't have money to pay the doctor, and even though my father pays for health insurance the insurance company said it wouldn't pay. Now, my ears are worse than the wrinkles. I have the same sensations around my ears that I have on my fingers. I'm always grabbing onto them, trying to pull them off. Nobody can touch them, except me. I feel like breaking everything I see, killing whoever shows up. I feel like cutting my ears off and killing myself. When I help my mother grind beef in the grinder, I keep imagining myself grinding my ears and fingers. I feel more desperate with every movement I make. I can't be next to a closet with its door open; it feels like my ears are going to fall off, I can't explain what happens to them. I can't walk by a short wall either, when it's about as high as my ears. And I don't like to see people wearing those headbands that cover half their ears, nor do I like to see people holding their ears. A doctor I saw said it was nothing; it was something sexual."

HOPE
Memoirs

Nobody knows exactly how the coffin got there, right in the middle of the wedding. The fact is it was delivered, and when the bride came back from the photographer's with her family she found the coffin in the middle of the room, on top of two chairs, a bunch of people standing around it. They didn't know if they should keep watch or go have a whiskey in the garden. Eight Ball, the cook-waiter, said the hearse stopped suddenly in front of the door.

"Is this where Mário Cerqueiro lives?"

"That's right."

The men from the funeral home looked embarrassed in front of the guests, who were spread around the garden holding glasses of wine or beer, with appetizers in their hands. They hesitated a moment, but finally opened the back of the van. There were only two of them, so they waited for one of the guests to step up and hold one of the handles. The guests, however, stood astonished, drinks in their hands and canapés in their mouths, chewing and not tasting anything.

"Hey, sir, help us over here!"

The man in question stretched his hand to lift the handle. He was holding his glass of scotch in his other hand and looked around for help.

No one grabbed his glass, so he placed it on top of the coffin. And they started to walk in like that, just the three of them, until an elderly man, looking on disapprovingly, grabbed the fourth handle. The procession entered the room. The women looked startled and got scared. Some screamed. An old lady dressed in red lamé and a hat ran off.

"What is this? What does this mean?"

Since she didn't know what was going on, she wondered if someone in the family had really died and they were expecting the body. She found mixing a funeral and a wedding to be in bad taste. She considered, however, that these things are not decided down here. Weddings, yes, but not death, as she said.

"Is this the home of Mário Cerqueiro?"

"Yes, this is it."

"Then, delivery made. Who can sign here?"

The room was empty and the coffin lay on top of two chairs arranged by an attentive neighbor. A gentleman in a gray suit and silver tie approached, probably the best man. Self-possessed.

"Can you please tell me what this is?"

"It must be someone in the family. We were just told to deliver it. Here's his name."

"Didn't anyone come along?"

"No, not in the van. A VW was following us. We lost them on the road, I don't know how. We kept asking people along the way. Luckily Mário Cerqueiro is well known here."

"He has to be. He was the mayor. Who died?"

"A young man. Thirty-four years old."

"Died from what?"

"They found the body in an apartment. I don't know anything else. The men in the VW have the documents."

"Cerqueiro didn't have a son this age. Or did he? Would you two mind waiting a minute? It must be a mistake."

"We're running late. We have another body to deliver in Bauru. We're doubled up. There's a crisis in the transportation industry. Lot's of people dying, you know what I mean!"

"Would you like some coffee?"

"I prefer a whiskey if you don't mind. Do you want me to open the coffin?"

"No. Leave it the way it is. I'll get Mário, he's at the photographer's with his daughter."

The room had filled up with people who weren't holding any drinks. They were beginning to put on grave expressions, as was expected in the presence of a coffin. They started to gather, apprehensive. A maid brought a pack of candles without being told to. She didn't know where to put them. The funeral home workers drank their whiskey and left. The garden was full now. Other guests kept arriving, the neighbors standing at the doors and windows. The news spread. One of the female guests had someone fetch a rosary and began the prayers, saying it didn't matter who had died. A relative or not, it was a soul. And souls require miles of rosaries in order to get out of purgatory. I walked into the room, I wanted to see this conflation of funeral and wedding, and I was there when the bride and groom (newly married) arrived, alarmed by the crowd at the door. They all ran: the groom, the bride, the in-laws, the best man and maid of honor, and tardy guests. Pushing people with their arms, elbows, hitting and kicking, forcing their way in with their shoulders, until they managed to get in, curious and panting. They came face to face with the coffin. The bride began to cry. Without knowing why, without the slightest idea of who was inside it. Crying because the party was hopelessly ruined, and because the coffin would bring bad luck to her. She held on tightly to her husband, crossing her fingers to nullify the effect of the unexpected, and uninvited, guest.

The bride's father, indignant, asked, "What's going on here? Who brought this coffin here? Who's in it?"

Everyone knew as little as he did.

"Candinho has to be behind this, he wants to demoralize me because of the elections. The *Arena* party uses all the weapons it can. But this is too much, ruining my daughter's wedding. I bet there's nothing inside."

"Let's open it and take a look."

The bride's mother cried, "No!" She was sure it wasn't anybody in the family. The relatives, all from Araraquara, were there at the party. The sons who lived in São Paulo had come too. She wasn't going to allow the coffin to be opened with a dead, and probably stinking, body inside.

"So, what are we going to do?"

"Where are the delivery receipts?"

They couldn't find them. The men had handed them to somebody. How to find them in that confusion? The bride's mother told the servants not to serve anything. There wasn't enough. Most of the people were there out of curiosity. The coffin still sat in a corner. On top of it were whiskey glasses, canapés, empty plates, napkins. The bride's father decided it was better to put the body in the garage and form a commission to study the matter. A banker and member of the city council, he always thought in legislative terms. The garage, however, was full of tables holding pastries, appetizers and beer kegs.

They decided to put it in the maid's room. The maid shouted, "No! I'm not going to sleep in a room where a dead body has been."

"There's no other place."

"Put it next to the laundry sink. Or in the bathroom in the back of the house."

"The guests are going to use that bathroom."

"So what?"

"Who's going to pee looking at a dead body?"

"So what?"

"It's disrespectful to the dead."

"Disrespectful? Nobody knows who it is."

"It doesn't matter!"

"Okay, but don't leave it here."

"It's going to stay here," said the bride's father.

"Then you pay me. I'm quitting."

The gates were locked. They threw out as many party-crashers as possible and tried to resume the party. Nevertheless, there was embarrassment and uneasiness. A beer keg was opened, and I stood next to it, chatting and handing out cups. I wanted to see how everything was going to turn out. I even suggested that the host turn on the radio. Someone was probably looking for the body. A few people headed toward the police station. If there had been any complaint, the police would know. They considered the possibility of leaving the body at the station. The police chief could try to find out to whom it belonged. If nobody claimed it, it would be placed for a certain period of time in the Lost and Found room, and then buried. A drunk thought they should take the coffin to the front gate of the cemetery and leave it there with a sign: "To Whom It

May Concern." Someone else wanted to form a search party. They wandered through the streets to locate a wake without a body. I don't know if it was due to the situation, or to the heat, but in a little while everybody was drinking way too much. Mixing bottled beer with scotch, *pinga* with draft beer, cognac with rum, and lacing soft drinks with vodka. Men, women, young people, kids, were suddenly overcome by an endless thirst. It *was* hot, but to guzzle a Cuba Libre in one gulp, as if participating in a chugging contest, was not normal. An old lady was served coffee and screamed: it was liquor, the strongest kind. To tell the truth, this kind of thing wasn't unique to this party. There was nothing exceptional, except that during the day people seem to notice it more. All the parties in town are like this. People feel the need to have fun, as if it were the last time they were going to be together and have a drink in their hands and could dance. And when they dance they grab on to their partners, and hold tight, suffocating each other.

Bottles appeared fast, disappeared swiftly. I looked for a bathroom, but they were all locked. I went upstairs. A small group whispered next to the phone, and looked at me. They stopped talking briefly. I went into the toilet.

". . . All reading porn books. See if she remembers it, how she liked to kiss the other girls on the mouth."

I was listening through the door. The voice was muffled. Whoever was talking didn't want to be heard. There were brief moments of silence, then the people on this side of the conversation resumed talking. They had passed on the receiver.

"Here's Olguinha. Rosa knows me, from the Municipal dressing room. Now the theater has been torn down because of some deal, you don't know how sinister it was. We got in through the downstairs, went to a dressing room and stayed there, smoking pot and holding the guys' penises. Later on, Rosa had sex with everyone in front of everyone. She loved it and the bigger the penis the more she screamed."

There was silence again. I had finished but wanted to listen. Who were they talking to? The same girl began again:

"We did a performance late at night. The theater was full. Men left their beds in the middle of the night and went to it. They paid big money to see. A damn good show. What a damn show. It had everything: obscenity contests among the girls, fucking, strip-tease, peeing, defecation, sucking . . ."

Whoever was on the other end of the phone was either having fun or was infuriated. He didn't seem to reply. Maybe there wasn't anyone on the line. They could be saying all these things for no reason.

"So, pal, are you going to get out or not?"

Someone knocked and knocked. I opened, looking upset. They didn't care. The short guy pushed past me, and went into the bathroom. The others stood around the phone. I went downstairs, leaving them there, to drink some more, like everybody else. And so, with the night falling, the stereo on, the room crowded, people danced in the verandah, in the garden's narrow paths. Some had begun to fall in the corners, sliding down along the walls, passing out, or staring wide-eyed, motionless.

In the bedrooms, the bride's mother, the mother-in-law, and the bride took tranquilizers, assisted by the doctor.

Nobody was able to stop the women from gossiping. They came, desperate, wanting to show solidarity in sorrow and in mourning.

They walked in crying, hugging everybody, exploding in tears. Most hadn't come for the wedding, but left in a hurry when they heard about the coffin. They cried a little and went downstairs, to the maid's room, hoping to see the corpse. Disappointed, they stayed around, talking, praying, and crying a little if some relative of the bride showed up looking upset. Little by little, a wake formed in the back of the house, while the people in the front were getting more excited at the party, forgetting about the dead body. They even forgot to look for the coffin's real owner and, whenever someone brought it up, it was between jokes and references to the corpse-less funeral that was likely taking place somewhere in town.

Drunk. Annoying, having fun, or both at the same time. The bride herself forgot about everything, thinking of better things for the next few hours. She had been assured the body had been moved and the matter solved. The best thing she could do was eat, drink, and dance a little with the young men. Because now, a married woman, she would have to dedicate herself entirely to her husband. It would be a kind of farewell to the single woman's life. She found the idea exciting because she was a married woman, but not yet a woman, and she'd be in the arms of young men.

It was night already. The neighbors had left the street. Only a few remained in their chairs, pretending to talk and watching the party. And then, at least for a day, for a few hours, the old habits were resurrected. Others were already in their homes, dining on a thick bean soup with small macaroni noodles, the old Wednesday tradition, whether it was hot or cold outside. After dinner, satiated, watching the seven o'clock soap opera, settled in their faux leather easy chairs, people got on the phone. They kept calling the party non-stop. Maybe they recalled those days when automatic dialing was first introduced and all hell broke loose. For the first time one could talk anonymously, with no operator to interfere, to listen in, always aware of who was talking to whom.

"Has the corpse left for the honeymoon? And the bride, is she buried?"

Or, "This is the corpse's owner. Please return it, or you're all going to join him."

"This is long distance. It's the dead speaking. I'm in the wrong tomb. Could you please move me?"

"Does the body stink?"

"I've heard the party is so good, it's to die for!"

"Is the party so good that even the dead are having fun?"

The phone was left off the hook. The party, ruined. There was no point in trying to keep it going. The groom was disheartened. He turned off the stereo and the lights.

"What is this? He has no manners."

"It's not a question of manners. He's a newlywed husband, and can't wait to go to bed with his wife. Go to bed, but don't put an end to the party!"

"Me, with this family—never again."

Instead of leaving, they sat around on the sidewalk, holding their drinks. A deep silence descended. Except in the street where the guests (only men had stayed) let some time pass and jumped over the garden railing to steal a beer keg. With the gate locked, the only solution was to pass the keg over the wall, or leave it in the garden and have someone pass the cups. The problem was that a lot of maneuvering would be necessary to pass the cups over the wall.

They looked for a stepladder, but didn't find one. They forced the garage door open, and went into the maid's room.

And they found the coffin. Instead of getting scared, being fearful, or showing respect, they started to think.

"There are about twenty of us. We could buy some candles and have a funeral in the middle of the night. We'll go down the street singing, people will appear at the windows, we'll invite them for the funeral."

"Stop it, we're so drunk we can't even carry a drink."

"Then come up with a better idea."

"We can open the coffin and leave the body at somebody's door. Then wait for the morning to see their face when they open the door."

"It has to be something better."

"We'll tie a rope around the neck and hang it from a lamp pole in the garden."

"Let's take it to the red-light district."

"Leave it in a seat in the theater."

"Bury it behind the Ferroviária's goal. It'll put an end to the team's bad luck."

"Shit. Such an opportunity and we can't come up with a single good idea. We'll end up burying the guy on our own."

We now had two problems. How to pass the keg over the wall, and how to use the body for a joke.

"Wouldn't it be more fun to get the body out of the coffin?"

I jumped over the wall, and went back to the street. There was something unpleasant about that whole thing. I didn't take any pleasure in being drunk, singing, swearing, or in trying to think of something to do with the dead body. I was always an outsider in these situations, observing with a critical eye. That keeps a person from participating, from enjoying himself. Somebody like that is bothersome; for himself and for others. It's like a closed circuit, constantly on, transmitting. He doesn't let the others feel comfortable, or close to him. I wondered what was wrong, why I didn't react. It could have been a funny situation if I wanted to use my imagination. What we were doing was a kind of challenge to death. A lack of respect, a disregard for death, for the fear we have of it, a way of confronting it, calmly and humorously.

There was some construction going on and lots of lumber two houses over, and I had an idea. I started to pull out some boards, and placed them in front of the house where the men were gathered. I leaned one end of a board against the garden wall, making a ramp. We did the same thing from the wall to the garden. All we had to do was push the keg up the ramp and let it roll down to the other side. If we wanted to take the coffin, it'd be the same operation. I didn't know the name of any of those young men. They were all in their twenties, or younger, like our gang at that time. They thought my idea was sensational. Belonging to a group again should have made me happy, and yet I didn't feel anything. I didn't feel like belonging to this gang. Kids today are different. In our time we could talk, discuss, argue over a book, over a movie, we knew so much and tried to keep informed. We didn't learn more only because there were so few magazines and newspapers. Practically nothing came from abroad. I couldn't belong to this gang because I had nothing to do with it. In the same way, and for the same reason, I can't belong to this town. And since I don't have any place outside of here, I float. This is the exile's condition: to float, to levitate, not to belong anywhere, knowing however that there *is* a place for him. His own true place is forbidden. This may be the worst position to be in, to have the ground pulled out from under one's feet. There are two ways of doing it: by hanging or exiling him.

The coffin was in the street. The guys were sitting on it, looking desolately at the beer keg. After all the effort to roll it up over the wall, there were only about thirty cups left.

"I know what to do," said one of the guys, the one who seemed the least drunk. "Grab the handles."

"What for?"

"Surprise. A damn good idea."

They took the coffin and began to walk up Fifth Street, on the sidewalk. A couple that had been leaning against a tree ran away.

"Come on, tell us. I'm not going to be carrying the coffin during the night. It's bad luck."

"Nonsense!"

"How far is it?"

"Not too far."

They stopped, and rested the coffin on the ground.

"Okay. Okay. We're going to take it to Miss Maria do Carmo's house. Her husband is a doctor. The worst doctor in town, even though he's the richest. We'll leave the coffin in front of the house and hang a sign on it: 'THIS IS HOW HIS PATIENTS END UP.' Later we'll call the newspaper, so they can take pictures."

"We can do that, but there's no way the newspaper will take pictures. It has connections with everybody in town. And Miss Maria do Carmo's husband is a member of the Rotary, the Lyons, the Business Bureau, and a director of Charity Hospital, every scam imaginable."

The doctor's house was situated at the end of the street, in a huge lot, almost a small farm. It was a tall mansion, with a glass-enclosed verandah in the front. The hedges and walls weren't high enough as to keep Miss Maria Do Carmo from seeing what happened in the street. A beautiful and haughty woman, she kept her distance from everybody in town, and almost never attended any events. She was never seen at the movies on Sundays. Not even when she was young. She went on Mondays, and waited for her chauffeur to buy her ticket. When she heard Tchaikovsky's *Nutcracker Suite*, the last musical piece played before the movie began, she walked in and sat in the third row in the back, in the fourth seat counting from the main aisle. She never sat anywhere else. Skinny Vanderlei, the usher, made sure the seat was always available and that there weren't many people around her.

People say Miss Maria Do Carmo has a lover in Paris, who sleeps in a separate room and does cocaine. I've been hearing about what goes on inside the Children's Park mansion for twenty years. Two or three times a year the whole mansion is lit up, the gardens are filled with tables, and an orchestra from another city is brought in. The cars that come up the street don't have Araraquara license plates. Four or five private jets bring guests. They rival Candinho's parties, but with one difference: Candinho invites everybody. He wants to be mayor, senator, then governor. He brings people from Brasília, but also invites janitors and trash collectors. Miss Maria do Carmo's parties exclude the town's people, I don't know why. They talk about revenge or hatred, but I've seen Miss Maria do Carmo's husband in person several times. He's a very tall man with huge, heavy hands. He looks more like a boxer than a surgeon. Once in a while, in the middle of the afternoon, he walks down to have coffee at Municipal, standing at the counter, talking to everyone. People approach him like a politician approaching the big boss, obsequious, submissive. They have coffee together, his big hands engulfing the cup. Then the doctor walks back, waving at people inside stores and banks. The bank managers, in particular, rush out when they see him walking toward the café. They grab their jackets and run. They walk in absentmindedly, five or six bankers at the same time, and express surprise at "such a coincidence." They compete to see who buys the coffee first, only to be outdone by the quick doctor, who's already ordered ten cups and is smiling, because he must realize it's all for show. For five years it's been the same scene, and it may continue to the end of time. They exchange trivialities. (You should come more often, sir; you only come to make a deposit, never a withdrawal.) The surgeon's bank accounts are fat, but inactive, like everybody else's. People refuse to make allocations, investments, take out loans. There are those who say Miss Maria do Carmo and her husband loan money at very high interest rates, and that's why their money multiplies in an amazing way. I don't know anyone who has borrowed money from them, nor do I know anybody who knows anyone who has paid them interest. These are rumors that come out of nowhere, and go around in circles without anyone knowing their source. Like the story about the singer who committed suicide in our town, jumping from a building in front of everyone. They say he came to solve a problem involving a large sum of money, and the couple refused to compromise. They demanded payment, or they would take measures. I don't know what kind of measures a couple of loan sharks could take. Unless they had bank bills, promissory notes, legal paperwork. Something from which the singer could not walk away, to which he was irrevocably bound. Just like I'm bound to this town. Bound because I signed too many promissory notes, I made too many commitments. In fact I didn't make any. I worried about false debts, fictitious bills, and let time pass me by.

The guys stopped at a door. Black banners indicated a funeral was taking place. Inside they could hear the monotonous voice of an old woman praying the rosary.

"Let's go in. If there's no dead body, we've found what we're looking for. If there is, we'll split the prayers between the two of them."

There *was* a dead body, that of a young woman. She was dressed in white and her coffin was white. Ten sleepy people were keeping watch. Surprised when we showed up, two young girls ran inside. An old man got up as he saw our coffin, the others, astonished, remained silent. Exactly like the wedding guests when the body was first brought in. From the back of the house came a short man with gray hair.

"What is this?"

The drunkest in our group replied, "Our corpse doesn't have a funeral. It needs one. We saw yours, we thought we could share the prayers."

"What are you thinking? A bunch of drunks playing a hoax? I'll call the police right now! What do you want? To ruin my daughter's funeral?"

And looking at the white coffin, "May God keep her, poor girl!"

"No, we're serious, we respect our corpse. It needs prayers."

"Who died?"

"We don't know."

"So what are you doing with this coffin? This is a students' prank. I'm calling the police. You're going to jail. Jerks!"

"It's not a joke at all. We're serious. The body was delivered to us, we don't know who it is, we're taking care of it the best we can. We can't keep walking around carrying it all night. It's not fair. Who knows, maybe the corpse wouldn't even like this. The dead should be kept quiet, peaceful, with people, flowers and candles around them. Poor thing, our corpse doesn't have one single flower. Can you imagine?"

Whatever the reason, the man was touched. Maybe his daughter's death and his loneliness led him to allow the coffin to stay while he considered the situation. It was the first time something like that happened, and he had no experience with that kind of thing. He just wanted to have everything in order and reflect a little.

"Let's have a nice hot coffee. It's getting cold outside."

"Don't you have a bit of *cachaça*?" one in our group dared to ask. I didn't know his name. I didn't know any of their names. Hearing the question, the owner of the house—and of the funeral—looked upset, but this time for no reason, because a shot of *cachaça* would be really nice. If they gave me coffee I would have thrown up everything right there. And not only did they serve coffee, they also served fritters filled with banana, small cheese rolls, and ham sandwiches with the bread a little stale. A good snack for three in the afternoon, but not in the middle of the night with a stomach full of beer.

The host dragged the kitchen table to the living room. We placed our coffin on top of it and lit candles, improvising candleholders in bottles. One of the women wrapped the bottles in colorful tissue paper, disguising the starkness of the scene.

"I swear I don't know what I'm doing, nor why I'm doing this. I do it because I'm a good Catholic and I can't leave a corpse in the hands of vandals. However, I don't understand, God forgive me, I don't understand anything. But let's move on, my poor daughter, let's move on.

He sat down holding his head, sobbing, who knows if it was for his daughter or the situation. The old women seemed to be praying the rosary more quickly, happy with the sudden increase of clients in need of prayers.

"In the morning you can get the coffin and leave. I'm just letting you stay during the night because I'm compassionate, humane. It's not right to have a dead body wandering in the damp and cold weather. Who knows what he died from? Do you understand? In the morning you're leaving."

In fact we were planning to sneak out, leaving our corpse there, for it'd be well taken care of. But nobody left. I don't know if it was because of the lady's fritters or the bottle of cognac someone found in the kitchen pantry. We stayed. Two of us even helped the old woman lead the rosary with solemn voices full of energy. After all, they had just arrived at the funeral, their blood still fresh and vigorous. A woman remarked that the young generation wasn't lost, her faith in young people had been restored. She hadn't seen a young person in a funeral for more than fifteen years.

This was indeed funny. In the old times we had never been able to do anything like this. But I don't want to compare, or I'll end up feeling disappointed with my old friends. But I have to recognize that the night's adventure was much more exciting than any of the intellectual conversations we had at Pedro's Bar. We only talked about books, politics, movies, the town's provincialism, getting out of there fast. The funeral beat everything—even the day we walked around the block completely naked. Or the day we defecated on the steps of the Town Hall; or broke into a mailbox, read the mail, and switched around the letters and envelopes; or built a wall in front of a door using material from a construction site nearby; or broke all the lamps in São Bento Street; or set the alarm off in a bank and the police came running over, the street filled with people at four o'clock in the morning; or we got a train engineer drunk and detoured the train. I need to think. I don't know if we had as much fun as I was having now. Nothing was as daring as this. It's like we were playing with death, laughing at it, destroying the solemn, spectral tone, the fear.

Nobody knew how this big farce was going to end, but they believed us. Were we going to keep it going or were we going to give in? It depended on our imagination. As absurd as it may seem, the farce was simple and touching, and no one doubted us for a moment. I'd like to belong to this gang, go out with them, suggest ideas. Maybe they've never thought of defecating on the steps of the Town Hall, or of buying panties and leaving them on the seats in the theater and waiting to see people's reactions at the intermission.

I think of Caldeira, the playboy. He knew how to do things. The other day I was imagining what I'd do if I were rich and untouchable like him. One thing I'd like to do is let a tiger loose in the middle of town. A real, live ferocious tiger that would begin attacking the people. How would they explain it when they got home?

What would they say after showing up wounded? A tiger attacked me downtown. How come? A tiger in the middle of Araraquara? "How can it be?" the women would ask. And they wouldn't believe it. And, along with the tiger, I would let loose doubt.

At dawn I woke up suddenly. I had dozed off, a large cup of steaming coffee was in front of me. Inviting. I drank the coffee and realized the room was full of relatives and friends of the dead girl. None of the guys who had come with me were there, nor was the coffin. I got up quickly and felt dizzy, had to sit down. I'd been suffering from fainting spells. After they pass, there's a sensation that I'm stumbling, that something inside is out of balance, and it lasts for almost an hour. I walked outside onto the sidewalk holding the cup. The sun was coming up. The young woman's father: "You're still here?"

"Where's everybody else?"

"They left more than an hour ago."

"They didn't wake me up."

"I was going to, but they told me to let you sleep. They said that you weren't part of their gang, they didn't even know you well. I said you were probably a relative of the corpse, but they insisted you weren't. 'Some old man who came along uninvited,' that's what they told me."

"Which way did they go?"

"Toward the Largo da Câmara."

"So long, sir. And my condolences once again."

I ran up the street. All the way to the Largo da Câmara. Got there very tired. Really tired. Mad, rather than tired. Uninvited old man. The little shits. They'll see who's the uninvited old man, motherfuckers. I didn't want to miss out on how the adventure was going to turn out. I was really upset. After all, I was the one who had the idea of placing the board over the garden wall to get the beer keg and the body to the other side. The Largo, empty. I went up and down Seventh Street: nothing. The misplaced body had disappeared along with the young men. I'll find out tomorrow or the day after. This story will spread all over town, it'll be as famous as the Railroad's Games. I knew one of the guys. He's always sitting in front of the Club. He was a thug, smoked pot. Smoking pot with them could actually be fun. I sat down on the abandoned fountain facing the Largo. Overwhelmed, incredibly tired and with a pain in my neck. The best thing that could happen to me would be to contract meningitis and then everything would be over with. I thought about falling asleep. From the top of this fountain, in 1953, Múcio and members of the *Integralista* party headed the attack on the Communist Elisa Branco's political rally. That's what they said: the Communist. I remember the Brazilian flag being carried among the crowd and the screams. Later, the fear. I thought: somebody spearheaded that. Múcio had no idea of what communism could be. For me it was a big adventure, an endless night. Décio stood right here, where I sat, screaming. What was he shouting? What was it? I was exhausted; I can't survive all-nighters anymore. Before it was easy: I'd go on all night non-stop like this, and still go to class, play indoor soccer, and watch the Progresso School students getting out of classes. I went to sleep right there. Those guys can go fuck themselves, the town can go fuck itself. What was Décio shouting?

THE BIRTH

He stopped, astonished. Looked at the ground. The round iron lid had moved. He was sure. Around it life went on, everybody hurrying, back and forth. The filthy lid was making an effort to stand up. Someone was forcing it up in an attempt to get out. The lid moved at regular intervals, making squeaking noises that sounded like laments. The passersby were insensitive. The lid opened. The observer, surprised, stood looking at the man who slowly emerged. Dirty with oil, he looked tired, and the afternoon sun hurt his eyes, which he kept half-closed. He got out, and with his hand pulled on a thick black cord. The observer didn't hesitate. He armed himself with scissors and ran. He cut the cord with difficulty. Then he found a telephone and dialed an emergency room.

"Everything's fine. I provided the initial medical care. I cut the umbilical cord. The street has just given birth to a man."

THE FALL

The lamp was tired of being boring. All day long the sunlight hit it, and when night fell and it got ready to go to sleep, the brightness came on inside. It never understood why it glowed so, and never knew what it held inside itself. That thing burned, blazed, and it spent nights awake, feeling desperate. It looked down and was able to see a long foot, round and black, next to which stopped ardent lovers, drunks, and irreverent dogs. For this reason it began to believe these lovers, drunks, and dogs had something in common. It found out it could escape. If it tried hard, unscrewing itself from left to right, it would free itself from its cradle. And it left unhurriedly. It was surprised to see the light inside went out, and an inner peace arose. It started to fall and tried to support itself on its black foot, but wasn't able to. The foot was flat. It was falling, falling. It felt terror, and then it crashed to the ground, dark and with a great void inside.

THE SEARCH
Memoirs

I argued a lot with Danilo. He always said "nothing happens by chance, there's a reason for everything." He was clear, objective and practical. He didn't believe in curses, atavism, or fate. "The reasons are inside the individual. That's where we have to search, in the individual and in society. Everything else is bullshit, justifications." What has conditioned this town? What has shaped people's temperaments, led them to hide? What do the facts behind the walls really mean? I said that a generalized madness had settled in, like a collective neurosis. Danilo disagreed, and said that it wasn't neurosis or something imaginary, it had really happened. "Why not calmly face the facts straight on? Certain things happen. So, let's establish the causes. They can even be political." Besides thinking a lot about Danilo and what has happened to him, with all that wire, I've told myself the cause may be the sun, but may also be the cold rocks in the Melhado district. It may be the lack of fluoride in the water. It may be the seven-o'clock wind, which doesn't let anybody go out, and forces everybody to have the shingles on their roofs cemented. It may be the desert surrounding us, dry, without a single oasis, even though most people here deny the desert's existence. They seem afraid of it. It may be. Years ago it was far away. Then it began to expand. If it continues, it'll swallow the town. In reality the desert and the town are very much alike, considering people here are flexible and change like the dunes, sterile like sand. They're quiet and arid. Ask any Araraquaran where the desert is and he'll look at you like you're crazy. If it's somebody from here, like myself, he'll whisper, "You? Don't you know, if we all believe the desert doesn't exist, it'll disappear?" They believe in the power of the mind, and every night they think with all their might—they've all agreed on it in advance—in order to conjure up a tornado that will whirl violently and blow the sand away. They say the desert doesn't exist.

But if you manage to drive into town—which is impossible—look for an avenue called November Fifteenth. Drive up and try to locate the old house where Maria Helena Belda had lived. From that house go 1.27 miles and you'll be stepping in the desert, with its fine sand. From these mountains I can see its yellow shape.

57

Railroad vs. Santos game:

In the stadium, Railroad is winning. The first half ends.

"I'm still researching the lynching. There isn't much information. Some sources are missing. They're scattered everywhere. I don't have money to be traveling back and forth. If I could get a grant . . . But only the University offers them. And I have no chance, you know."

"Two things," said Bernardo. "It's good to bring up the issue. It was taboo in town for many years. Not any longer. There's always some prejudice left, but very little, just on the surface, so nobody will say people have forgotten. The old timers, and that's it. The younger generations don't even know. Your mistake is to try to explain the behavior of a whole town, of generations after generations, through a single act."

"But that's my approach. Think, Bernardo, about the extension of this single act as you say. It's funny, a guy like you, a writer, lucid, denying the influence of a historical fact, an event that traumatized a village and determined its future. Remember, it was a collective act."

"No, it wasn't. It would've been collective if the whole town had participated. But it was a small group, most of them following orders. Remember that some reacted against it. Some of the residents had a black band painted on their houses as a sign of mourning. You should read the study by Ana Maria Correia about that. Very good, well substantiated. Fundamental to contextualizing the case."

"I'd like to talk to you about it calmly, not in the middle of a game. And the second thing?"

"You could apply to the Liberal Arts College, do some good coursework. You have a good background; we went to a good high school. You just need to bring yourself a bit up to date, take some refresher courses. At least you'll get a teaching job later."

"At my age?"

"You're obsessed with your age. Don't get into that. Forget it."

"*You* can forget. You feel fulfilled, have a career. It's easy to offer advice in your situation. You're a good journalist, you have prestige, three books published, easy access anywhere. You were lucky. I wasn't. I struggle every day here, like a wild animal."

"I was lucky?"

"Weren't you?"

"I worked damn hard. Damn hard indeed. I left the town without a penny. If I hadn't got a job in the first week I would've gone hungry. Luck? Here?!"

"Okay. In any case, you're well off now. I'm not. I don't even know if I'm going to eat tomorrow."

58

Railroad vs. Santos game (end of second half): RSA 2 vs. Santos 1.

"Are you going to the Club?"

"No."

"You're not going to the Club? What are you going to do then?"

"Sit in a bar, have a beer, take the bus, go home."

"Good."

"Come with me. I don't have anything to do. I just came to watch the game and go back."

"I'd like to have this kind of flexibility. I'd be happy."

"You got boring. How can you put up with yourself? Happy or unhappy, going around moaning is getting old. When I moved to São Paulo, in '57 or '58, it was fashionable. It was Sartrean. Everybody was anguished. One day I read a book by Camus, you know? That was when I was starting to write. He impressed me. There was a sentence: 'I'm happy or unhappy. The matter is of little importance. I live with such enthusiasm.'"

"It's just a sentence for him, for you. Not for me."

"The problem is enthusiasm. You never had it. That's why you didn't leave Araraquara. You stayed here passively."

"What if I'm passive? If that's the way I am?"

"Where are you going with this? You want an excuse, a justification."

"I stayed for something important. The book. You know that. A great book about the lynching."

153

"Where's the book? I left eighteen years ago and you were already talking about this book then."

"It's going. It may take thirty, fifty years. One day I'll finish it."

"I've told you. It's good you're bringing up all this stuff. Who knows, maybe you'll have to get out of here because of this book. You may be kicked out, get pressured. It's an explosive subject. You're going to have to explain yourself, discuss it, prove, demonstrate, get into debates. A book isn't a game, a joke. It's you, above everything else. It's what's left of you; what you transmit, pass on. It's not simply having your name on the cover. Do you know exactly what you intend to do with it and what it's going to be?"

"I don't know what it's going to be, I don't have a crystal ball. I know what I intend to do: to study fear. The fear that took hold of this town after that night in 1897. It fascinates me. People's silence, the town's hostility toward foreigners, the aggressive behavior, the indifference toward everything, the false superiority. Everything came from that act. It left marks, solidified traditions, crystallized beliefs, oppressed the town."

"All suppositions. I agree, it's fascinating. I just don't see how you can base a thesis on suppositions. You need concrete facts, and for that you'll have to go through eighty years of history."

"I'll confess something, Bernardo. This book scares me."

"Fear. Fear is imagination. We create it. We slowly generate and expand it. It impregnates our brains. Before something happens, we make up situations and suffer in anticipation because of them. We create the possibility that these situations may exist. So, therefore our fear increases. The town assumed it couldn't speak up. It believed in the curse the priest supposedly had cast, and feared retaliation from the powers-that-be. The simple fear that the past could possibly interfere in the future resulted in the past actually interfering in the future."

"Look, I don't think I'll be having a beer. I'd like to go to the Club again, just once."

"I'm not a member. I never was. I was there twice in my life, with Hugo Fortes. And I'm worse off because of that. I don't miss it, and never did. Can you tell me why it's so vital for you to go to the Club?"

"I'll get off at this stop."

He pressed the bell in the trolley.

59

Whenever the night is warm and the perfume of the honeysuckle suffocates me, I remember Nancy at the window, looking out. And then I recall again the nights spent in the English class, and old Pimenta trying to explain *Did the flea flee?* and coming up with wordplays that were still incomprehensible for us. I always left class in a hurry to catch the second show at the movies, where I closed my eyes and tried to follow the English dialogue. Nancy sometimes went with me, but we weren't dating yet. We were just friends, and in those times friends couldn't hold hands or kiss. We had to keep a distance. And it wasn't so very long ago: twenty-three years.

I've forgotten everything, except her gaze in the dark of the railroad station courtyard. She had warned me: she was pregnant, and wouldn't support me if I joined the strike.

"How come you're not going to support me, knowing it's important to me?"

"I'd support you if I knew you'd been in this from the beginning, that you're in it because you're a fighter, because it's your cause. But no, dear. You joined without knowing what was going on, and you don't know where it's heading. Can you be so blind? You know public servants can't go on a strike, only the workers can. You have a different work contract. Besides, why this sudden interest of yours?"

"I found out my co-workers need me."

"These are just words, empty words. I've known you for ten years. You've never shown leadership abilities, or any feelings of class solidarity. On top of that, I don't think you're convinced of your decision. What's going on?"

"There's nothing going on."

"Of course there is. They're getting you involved in something and you don't see it. Let's talk."

"I've made up my mind, Nancy."

"But you're not the only one making decisions in this house. There are two of us. And they're going to use you. Don't you realize that? They're using you."

"No, they're not. I've agreed to it. I thought I should participate."

"Oh, yeah? And how many are participating? The entire Railroad? Is everybody together in it? Will it be a general strike, from the chief accountant to the inspectors and the porters?"

"No, for now it's just a few people. But the movement will spread. We just have to do some work."

"Do some work? The strike is set for the day after tomorrow and you're still trying to convince the guys? Are you crazy? You just don't see it. You've gone totally crazy. You want to be arrested or lose your job."

"Nobody in the Railroad has faith in me, Nancy. If I'm able to win this one, to fight for them, they'll accept me. They'll respect me."

"Dear, this is not the way you're going to get their respect. It's going to make it worse. They can see the role you're playing, dear. You're playing the fool."

"It's the only thing I can do, Nancy. I need to do it."

"Do you know what your problem is, dear? You don't believe in this strike or in the Railroad. Your mind went blank a long time ago. I noticed and have been hoping you'd talk to me. But you don't. You keep ruminating, but can't say it out loud."

"No, I like the Railroad, I like my colleagues."

"Yes. You love all this."

"Not that much."

"Not at all. Admit it."

"Yes, a little."

"No, you don't. Say you don't."

"I can't say it."

"But SAY IT."

SAY IT. SAY IT. Speak, shout, let go of everything. But admit that's not it. That it's all a big mistake.

No, it wasn't a mistake. I also knew it was probably all wrong. Nevertheless I needed to play this hand, any hand. I knew I'd be punished, fired. Deep down inside, that's what I wanted. I hated the Railroad, its offices, the bovine workers who spent their lives at their desks, waiting for promotions and retirement. I didn't have enough courage to leave it on my own. I'd been dominated by an idiotic sense of responsibility. It wasn't only me. There was Nancy too. And she was pregnant, and I was scared, confused. And at the same time I wanted it, I kept imagining going for walks with my kid, I had so many things to show him. We could sit down in the Independence Garden and talk.

"TALK."

I didn't talk. I felt like hitting her. I didn't. How could Nancy put up with me? Soon I found out.

She wasn't putting up with me any longer.

60

"Who are you? From the police? The Railroad? Some newspaper? Come on, explain yourself, or it'll get worse. I've already told an investigator you've been coming around with lots of questions about the men who were killed here. They're watching you. And leave the inspector alone. The man is crazy, he thinks it's his fault that those two died. What is this about writing a book? I bet you can't even write. That's a good one. A guy shows up all raggedy, I bet he can't even read, saying he's writing a book. Write your name here, I want to see it. Ah! It's not a book; it's a movie! And you're going to be in it, I'm sure. As an actor. You're going to play the role of the starved dog at the station, always waiting for the train that brings the dining car."

61

"Dad, when I grow up, will you let me participate in the Railroad Games?"

"No."

"Why not?"

"How can I explain it to you, son, the horror and violence of these Games that no one dares to ban?"

I change the subject on purpose, or else he'll ask me why the Games exist, if they're this way or that, what they are like. And I won't be able to answer. Eduardo will get to know this town's meaningless people, and their meaningless behavior. He'll find it strange: pools where friends disappear, streets opening up to give birth to men, men who break their own teeth or pull out their own eyes, lampposts that are able to get off their bases on their own, young girls who go crazy after noticing the wrinkles on their fingers.

62

At seven, between two soap operas, Cid's commercial comes on. He's bald and fat, but has success as a little crazy guy who goes around the stores on a shopping spree, screaming the whole time. It's the funniest commercial I've seen, everybody talks about it. Cid is on top of the world. The news today said madness is the illness of the '80s. At seven, the battle has been lost to the juice factory.

Everyday there's a war in the air and it turns my stomach. It's a fight between the acrid smell from the orange juice factory, the smooth aroma from roasted coffee, and the indecipherable dry odor of the hot air (does it come from the desert?). One can smell the roasting coffee from the coffee processing plant from any place in town: sweet, penetrating, pleasant. It's the only thing to mitigate the unpleasant smell from burned orange juice, as if someone were continually throwing orange peels in a huge bonfire.

Having coffee with Ceres Fhade, I noticed that, as I drank it, the amount of coffee in the cup decreased. I didn't say anything so as not to alarm him. I repeated the experiment and got the same results. Scientific repetition, for months and months. I tried with different variables: drinking it fast or slow; with more or less coffee, or drinking so slowly the coffee turned cold. The results were always the same, so that it wasn't a casual, random fact. I began to pay more attention. Water, soft drinks, ice-cream, food—everything decreased, not only the coffee. Therefore, something was happening and I couldn't tell anyone. Not even Ceres Fhade, who is my friend but is too conservative and gets scared easily. Maybe Eduardo will understand and will be able to help me. Children have a very keen sensitivity; they grasp everything quickly. It's possible he'll under-stand, and achieve what I'm not able to anymore because I've lost my mental dexterity. When this kind of thing happens, it's necessary to determine if it's happening by chance or by design. Since I haven't found the fortuity, someone must be behind it. I don't know with what purpose. Maybe to drive me crazy or ridicule me. I notice I'm not taken seriously. Last time my friends were here, they looked at me in a strange way and got upset if I approached them. Luís Carlos uttered sounds like a cat's meows. That's why I stayed behind the tree in front of the bar, just watching them. They were drinking whiskey. They've abandoned the beer with gin.

So, I return to my room. I face the struggle against myself until I, exhausted, win. Always. At what price! I turn myself off, just like the lamp that gets loose and explodes on the ground with a great void inside.

63

"I envy the job you have."

"It's like any other."

"No, it's not. It's richer. You see different people."

"People are the same. I don't look at their faces. I just look at the tickets, so that I don't get cheated. These people are sly. There are those who pay half-price and try to get in unnoticed."

"Can I take a peek at the movie?"

"Sorry, you can't."

"What difference does it make?"

"It's not right."

"No one will lose anything. The movie is showing anyway, for nobody."

"I'm sorry."

Ceres irritates me. He's stupid, stubborn. Or he hates me because I know his identity. He should try to keep me happy, so that I won't tell anybody. He probably remembers how I lashed out when they found the Turks, the denouncers. Those three were accusing everybody of being communist to the police. They denounced people they didn't like, and destroyed many lives, especially professors at the university. When the head of the Political Order made the Turks' identities public, because they were getting dangerous even for them, we almost killed them. They had to move. I suspect they'll come back. I saw one of them in a car recently. Or maybe they haven't left, they're still around, working quietly for the police. Now, Ceres could very well let me sneak in the movies, he could. He knows I can't pay, especially on Mondays. All my money goes to Eduardo's Sunday matinees, candy, hot dog and *guaraná*, ice-cream and a toy.

I'll end up having to sell a bundle of newspapers from my archives. The solution is to photocopy what is of interest. Then I can get rid of the old papers; then they won't keep collecting dust.

64

Ziza passes me a printed flier. He has a bunch in his hand. They're all colors, green, pink, yellow.

"What is this?"

"I had these printed out of my own pocket. They're things I've been observing for a long time. Things people have stopped doing."

"And what good will it do to distribute them?"

"It's the beginning of a movement. I'll hand them out to every house, read it on the radio, publish it in the newspapers. I'm going to the TV station in São Paulo. Will you help me?"

"Let me see what it is."

"Things people have stopped doing:

Giving their seats up for women and the elderly in public places and public transportation.

Saying 'thank you.'

Saying 'please.'

Greeting each other.

Being tolerant.

Not harboring resentment.

Listening patiently.

Leaving the inside of the sidewalks for the elderly and women.

Looking up.

Walking slowly.

Keeping up a good conversation.

Using handkerchiefs.

Drinking fresh mint, peppermint, and chamomile tea.

Keeping a running tab at the grocer's.

Cultivating the friendship of cousins."

"This is the first list. I've been taking note of everything. I'll make several lists. Do you think Bernardo will publish it if you send it to him?"

"If I ask him, I think so."

"I'm not so sure. He's so full of himself he's going to find this very provincial. Bernardo is a revolutionary, the hard-core type. He's not going to pay attention to these things."

65

I walk up and down the aisles and between the seats. The movie theater is completely full. There's not one single seat empty. Everybody's here, the Sunday musicals attract people. Tchaikovsky's *Nutcracker Suite* is almost over. The bell will ring soon. They're all in their usual seats, talking, getting agitated, and the air fills with the murmur of their voices and laughter, now dead in time, mingling with diluted perfumes. But all has been found again.

66

People have been careless lately. They don't read the inserts that come with their medications. It's very dangerous. It's such a fatal indifference that I'm going to write a letter to Flávio Andrade suggesting that he should submit a bill in the Senate. I don't know what kind of bill. Flávio can decide that, he's the expert. It would have to be some kind of decree, ordering schools to teach children how to read the inserts, which is not at all easy. They're written in a special language, a kind of code. There are scientific names, quantities, dosages, uses, warnings, and side-effects. If we got in the habit of reading the inserts as children, so much harm could be avoided. It's something that amuses me, a job I'd like to have: writing medication inserts. They're the only texts we can be sure are written to produce sound health. They produce improvements and changes. It's a rewarding feeling to write something knowing it's for the common good. Ziza will like my idea. *Rewarding.* This word has been stuck in my head for a week. I was dying to use it. I found the right place for it.

THE FIGHT

He tried to climb up the smooth wall. He held his head between his hands, jumped, and was in his room.

The fight between him and himself would take place there, where he, exhausted, would defeat himself. The difference was the rats. Every night, the same mathematical problem, full of square fractions left and right. He rationalized the numbers so they'd behave. That night, besides the battle against himself, he had the following equation: "If two blue rats have yellow tendencies, what is the proportion of fear to be provided in the satisfaction of the tendencies?" It seemed easy, but tendencies are complicated, irresolvable and unsatisfied. Everybody has tendencies. Men like to have them with stupor. Everybody has legs too. He simply equated everything, leaving them unsatisfied. He remembered the rats climbed up the wall squeaking, and gargled with pleasure, while devouring them.

THE HUMAN BODY SPLIT IN TWO

The hunt lasted almost a year. It wasn't easy to catch him. He knew every inch of the town, alley by alley, street by street. He knew doors, windows, recesses, garrets, roofs, basements, attics, yards, sheds, bridges, overpasses, walls. He had a photographic memory. He could remember every detail. He could escape, fool, cheat, disguise, deceive, lie. Whenever someone thought he had been caught, he ran away. Until, one day, between mousetraps, fox traps, ant poison, nets, lassoes and whips: he was caught. He was a normal man, average height, dark hair, brown eyes, dressed and speaking normally. He wasn't scared or fearful. He faced his captors calmly, indifferent to the beating the weak men in the group gave him, indifferent to the guns, knives, rifles, spears, daggers, machetes, bats, and everything else his frightened captors pointed at him. They made him kneel down next to a tree, and beheaded him. But his body got up while the head rolled away. The head looked at the headless body. They were now two distinct things living separately. The body didn't have anything else that could think, and the head didn't have anything to command. Both felt something was missing. The head spoke, and the men ran away scared. The body couldn't speak, and waited, forlorn and useless, blind, apprehensive. But one of the captors, an anatomy professor, came back. The head was sleeping. The professor waited, lying on the ground next to the head, looking at it. And when the head opened its eyes, the professor was afraid, and understood.

THE COMMUNICATIONS
Memoirs

Flags from the countries he visited are tied to a pole in his bicycle's basket. He rides around the garden and people throw money in the shoebox at the bottom of the fat coconut tree. He has quite a bit of money. People are dying to help with these things. I look closely at the flags, none seems to be from Europe. Only from Latin America. He rode around here, up and down hills, climbing the Andes. I want to see him ride his bike to Europe, and in Paris. How ridiculous: circling the Arc de Triomphe, leaving the box to collect money by the symbolic fire. Sure the French would give him a cent! This guy bugs me. Pedaling, pedaling, I have to walk by him every time I go home. He looks like a Bolivian Indian, dark-skinned, greasy. Worse than a Brazilian *mestizo*. He's going to be pedaling for two hundred hours, non-stop. On the first days people came to see him. Now he's pedaling alone, out of breath. He slows down, approaches me. The bicycle almost stops, balancing precariously.

"*Me hace un favor, Ud.?*"

I think that's what he said. I observe his pockmarked face.

"*Me llena la botella de agua?*"

"*La botella*" is a banged-up aluminum bottle disgusting to touch. He makes an effort to smile, pedals. I stand still. He circles back, extends his hand.

"Not now, wait a little. I'm going."

He circles again. I shake my head. The Bolivian Indian smiles with difficulty, and keeps going.

He's going to crash. It's obvious he can't go on anymore. For two days he's been living on the raw eggs and orange juice Dr. Juan Do Jabá, the doctor here at the square, brings for him. On the way to the public restroom where there's a faucet, I see Ziza Femmina.

"Hi. How are you doing?"

"I'm fine. And you?"

With his white, chubby thighs, Ziza Femmina sat next to Diojão, the guy who kept showing him his penis in the middle of class. Ziza didn't want to look, turned away, then looked. He realized the whole class was watching him and he started to cry.

"I've been wanting to talk to you for some time. Can it be now?"

"Sure."

Now, tomorrow, what difference does it make, Ziza Femmina, the class babe? How hard we tried to catch you behind the bathroom during recess. Years and years, and not one moment of rest, running away from the boys. Always running away. When you left during class to drink water, two or three boys would leave too to give you a squeeze, and you couldn't drink water. You couldn't pee, were afraid of medical examinations, asked to be excused from P.E. classes because the teacher hated you, he made you jump sixteen feet down to a canvas mat. The teacher would make you run for hours until you'd fall exhausted. He made you play soccer and shouted, screamed, and asked the others to kick you, so you would become a man, or give up.

"I admire you a little."

Admires me? Someone admires me! And it had to be him, the

one who ran away like a frightened virgin. Was running away a game you played? You excited everybody a whole lot, during the four years of high school. That's why you had to jump from that window.

"Why do you admire me? What have I done?"

"You're a guy who likes our town."

"I do?"

"Yes, really. Remember? Your whole gang left, and you've stayed. You belonged to the coolest gang to ever come from here. A terrific group, really cool people. There isn't one of them who hasn't made it in life. Did you know I follow the lives of everyone who moves away? I follow everything. Do you want to stop by my house?"

"To do what?"

"So I can show you my scrapbooks."

"I do, but some other time. I promise."

"Okay, I'm not going to force you. You come whenever you want. Not to do anything, really. Just to look at some newspaper clippings about your friends."

"I said I'll go, I'll go."

"I always thought you hated me."

"Why would I hate you?"

"I don't know. I watched you at school, always keeping to yourself. You didn't talk to anyone. You only got excited over soccer. You played well. I used to think you were arrogant. Can I tell you something else? My mother told me to watch out, not get close, not be too friendly."

"Was it the same with all the boys back then?"

"I can't say. The boys bothered me a lot. I hate them. I know every one's name. I've memorized every one's face, especially those who tormented me. I wished one day they'd need me."

"They're not going to need you. You can forget that."

"You had an advantage: you were famous for being brave, tough, courageous, of being up for anything. Some of my girlfriends admired you, but wouldn't get close. You were always hanging out with Nancy. Pretty, wow, how pretty she was."

"I don't want to hear it, don't talk about that woman to me."

"I won't."

"Enough talking. I have to take some water to the cyclist. He's dying of thirst."

"I'm sorry if I've offended you. What was it? Nancy?"

"Nothing, you faggot. Nothing."

"I'm not a faggot, never was. I swear. Why did you all do that?"

"Nobody did anything. This is not the time to walk down memory lane. I don't have time. If I don't take him water, he's going to die."

"Go ahead. Take it. He needs to leave with a good impression of our town."

"Do you want to take it?"

68

"Dad, why don't you want me to participate in the Railroad Games?"

"Because they don't make anybody proud, son. I don't want to lose you. And I know that if you go, you'll never come back."

"Not even if I practice, Dad?"

"Not even."

69

It doesn't make any sense to walk around with a string connecting your left ear to the big toe of your right foot. It's ridiculous to join the left and the right, because the string crosses in front of your leg and unbalances your walking. But the townspeople don't seem to be thinking and insist on using the crossed string, which causes all kinds of tumbles and falls, in the middle of the street. An old woman who could barely walk ended up under a bus because, eager (eager, eager, what a funny word) to tie the string properly, she tied both feet to both ears, thinking that this way she'd eliminate any chance of making a mistake. From my window I saw her coming over, hopping, without anyone realizing her mistake and warning her. We even laughed when she fell: she looked like an old crumbling pot, plop, out of kilter, because her bones were no good for sustaining anything anymore. What nobody had anticipated was that the 5:10 bus to São Paulo was absolutely on time, with asbolute precision. And that's where the old woman got screwed, because if it were one second late or ahead of schedule, circumstances would have liberated her from that ridiculously theatrical form of death. These killer buses, how I hate them. One of the first things the police investigators tried to establish was the exact schedule of the bus. I was looking when they exonerated the driver. He was exact, millimetrically exact. I am very careful when I go out, making sure the ends of my string are correctly tied, and examining its length, so that it doesn't restrict my movements. I usually use a fine string that breaks easily, so that if I stumble the string breaks and I won't fall. It's a simple trick. I don't know why more people don't use it. Maybe out of fear, because it's forbidden. The requirement says to use thick string, almost a cord. Or maybe out of ignorance. I take other precautions: I check bus schedules, and choose times when I'm sure no bus will be going by. However, the schedule alone doesn't help. The best, the simplest thing is to look around. To stop, look and listen.

70

Ziza Femmina lives in a small townhouse surrounded by rose bushes. "They're the symbol of our town, don't you think?" The living room is narrow, the hallway and the bedrooms decorated with old and new photos of Araraquara. Second Street at the beginning of the century; the Independence Garden; the square with the gazebo on Spain Avenue; the tree-lined streets, before they pulled out the trees; the big, noble mansions, the Vaz's, the Carvalho's; Progresso School; the old public high school; the Largo da Câmara. And also: posters of festivals, exhibitions, shows, openings; paintings by Araraquaran artists; a landscape painted by Ernesto Lia; framed invitations from Bernardo's first autograph event in São Paulo; telegrams from Araraquaran personalities and politicians; postcards from town people who had traveled. Photos showing projects by Araraquaran architects built in Rio, in Belo Horizonte, in Recife.

"This is like the town's museum."

"Isn't it true? I add to my collection every day. Do you know what I've been promised? Pedro José Neto's knife."

"Did Pedro José Neto use a knife?"

"He must have. I've been promised it."

"What if it's not authentic?"

"What can I do? At least it's something related to the founder."

"Did you know he was a bandit?"

"He was no bandit."

"He was running away when he got here."

"For other reasons."

"What other reasons?"

"I don't know yet. I've been doing some reading, talking to Alberto Lemos, to Ana Correia."

"What for?"

"They've written the town's history. Haven't you read it?"

"No."

"Why don't you act like an Araraquaran? Why don't you care for what people from your hometown are doing? There are many people doing good and important things."

"I know. But they're out there, and we're here."

"You could have left and done something. The history teacher liked to read your exams, remember? Your ability to sum things up?"

"That was high school stuff. Nothing to do with literature."

"Yes, but Bernardo, far less smart than you, took off."

"What about you, why didn't you take off?"

"I didn't have anything do to out there. I can be a good pharmacist here or anywhere. I like my hometown. Besides, if I leave I'm making room for somebody else, and it may turn out to be an outsider. And there are already enough people coming in through the town's backdoor."

Ziza opens a closet and takes two folders out. The closet is filled with them, numbered and catalogued.

"This one is about Múcio. His whole career, since he began in amateur theater. Look at the opening of his first play in Santos, in that festival. Do you want to see something precious?"

He pulls out a labeled envelope, and from the envelope, a certificate.

"Múcio was awarded this certificate in the Santos Festival for directing the best play."

"How did you get it?"

"He gave it to me. It was a great demonstration of his friendship."

Friendship! Múcio never cared about these things. He never kept a review, or any piece of paper. He had a mania for not getting attached to anything. "To any kind of shit." What mattered was the show. No clippings or photos could ever offer an idea of what the play had been like, alive on the stage. He felt a little frustrated about it. Nothing is permanent in theater. The play, the acting, the direction—everything dies the moment the season is over. Once in a while, when he came to town, he admitted his frustration, before he left Brazil for Portugal and disappeared. He was seen in Angola or Mozambique. Many times I asked him to write. He never did. He hated letters, notes. He threw away even the notes he took about his plays, as if he wanted to erase himself completely, to not leave anything about himself or about his work behind.

Ziza opens more folders, and shows me some photos and clippings I don't really see, I can't pay any attention. A large archive about important and unimportant people, poetry published in the local newspaper, xeroxed short stories, office newsletters, birthday dates, reproductions of paintings by Sunday painters, flyers, programs. I don't see anything, I don't want to see, I'm not interested, I don't know what I'm doing here. Just because I didn't have anywhere to go this afternoon, and the cleaning lady was at my house and I couldn't stay there. It's raining, and everything is boring—boring in town, boring in the world. I don't feel relaxed today, I feel discomfort. If I were in São Paulo, I'd go see a movie, the shows begin in the afternoon. Once the movie theaters here showed a weekday matinee during a film festival. One time in twenty-five years.

"Ziza, have you ever taken it in the ass?"

"Huh?"

"Haven't you ever?"

"Never."

"You're lying. You always looked like you did."

"I didn't."

"Of course you did. Not here, and you were right. Otherwise they'd ruin your life."

"They ruined my life without me ever doing it."

"Then you should start now."

"I'm old, I'm not good-looking like I used to be."

"But at least you admit the possibility of doing it. There's still time. You're soft, your skin's smooth."

"Don't touch my butt. I hate people who touch my butt."

"Start now and fool around with everybody."

"I wouldn't dare."

"You just have to get started."

"It's a sin."

"A sin?"

"A sin. A sin, understand? Who do you think I am? I'm Catholic, very Catholic."

"Maybe you are. So what? Catholics get laid too."

"But done right. Not a man with another man."

"It's the same thing."

"No. A man with another man is a horrible thing."

"Not at all. At least not any longer. Have you seen the kids today?"

"Do you want to know something? Do you? Well, I'll tell you. I did it, just once."

"And?"

"It burned me. It still burns, to this day."

"Did it hurt?"

"No, it didn't. It really burned!"

"Why don't you let me fuck you?"

"Me, with you?"

"Of course. We're alike, the two of us."

"Alike? Do you want to get fucked in the ass too?"

"No. We're just similar. You never got laid, and I never got out of here. And we don't know why. For no fucking reason. Because they didn't let us. They didn't and still don't let people like us. They won't, do you understand? It's going to be a long time before people like us are able to do anything."

71

Luís Carlos walks down the stairs holding his briefcase. He closes his jacket to protect himself from the damp air. He's walking home. He likes to walk. He was always suggesting long walks. "Those who walk never die from heart attacks." Once, walking along the railroad tracks, we went all the way to the next station, and spent the afternoon in the train yard reading a book by Lombroso. He crosses the street toward the hotel. He can't have seen me, I'm behind the door looking through a crack. A crowd of people are waiting for the taxis to return under the glass marquee at the station. Not as many people arrive by train as they once did. Almost everybody has a car or takes a bus. In a little while I'll go down to the bus station. I'm going to wait for the seven o'clock Cometa bus. Later I'll go see the arrival of the 8:30 Cruz Express. Only Luís Carlos; he arrived in the Deluxe train. I'll wait. The taxis have picked up all the passengers. The inspector—the informant—sweeps the stairs looking disheartened. A bell rings on the platform.

Soon people will start to eat supper. The people who have arrived will join the people who had been waiting. They'll open beer cans. They've prepared steaks and chicken, hot soup for a cold and damp day. I push the pedals with difficulty on the hill up São Paulo Avenue. It's lack of exercise. Even the bicycle has been forgotten. I only ride it once in a while. It's always dusty, its tire flat. I don't know how it happened. I follow Luís Carlos. He has the same hurried, steady stride, holding his head high. They return. Tomorrow, Tuesday, they should be meeting at the Hanai Bar, across from the Club. They should. Because the Hanai Bar has been closed. They're building an apartment complex, and the Club moved. It's behind the stadium now. People don't sit in their rattan chairs anymore, like little kings on their thrones, watching people go by. So, they'll be at the Club. I won't go in, I'm not a member. Or they'll be in one of their homes. I need to follow them to find out. Later I'll wait, leaning against a wall, or under a tree if it's drizzling like today.

Bernardo was your hero. Still is? The most politicized and rebellious guy in our group. But do you know where he was the night of the rally? Do you? Do you have any idea?

The daily, repetitive scene: there must be about fifteen people doing their *footing* between the two movie theaters. *Footing*: to promenade, stroll, walk. Nobody walks: *nothing*. I should propose a change. Many people go by in cars. They appear and disappear. I can't reach any conclusion regarding these people's disappearances. Why did they hide in their homes? Is it just the TV? This may have been their justification, their final argument. The revelation. When I visit my relatives, I'm in awe of the ritual that is religiously celebrated in the main room. The square goddess emitting her blue radiance, and people sitting silently in front of her, observing. No other goddess has dominated men as much as this one. Men have abandoned everything. They have surrendered themselves for her sake. Nevertheless, sometimes I ask: did she attract them, or was it the men who have run away, from the streets, from the sidewalks, from the open sky, from the aroma of honeysuckle? I remember my street on summer nights in the old days. There was a huge congregation of chairs on the sidewalk. The chairs gathered in front of the doors and reached toward the middle of the street. One could assess someone's popularity by the size of the group gathered around him after supper. The chairs were taken away little by little, and only some isolated, lonely recalcitrant, who doesn't have anybody to talk to, remains. One of these nights he'll get run over by a car. I abhor the idea that people think I'm the high priest of a nostalgic cult. What I want to say is that there were more humane situations in the world. Human contact, meetings, the exchange of ideas, conversations, mutual enlightenment, happiness in coexistence. Have people isolated themselves voluntarily or unconsciously? Suddenly streets have become scary. Or was it the bluish goddess's power of seduction that changed everything?

74

"Dad, look at the ants I've drawn, the way you taught me. The kids on the street are all jealous because of all the things I know. Now, Dad, let's make a deal. We'll get together everyday on the corner near my house. Mom doesn't have to know. You come and bring one of those big books, full of words."

"The dictionary?"

"Remember when you looked up the words and taught me? Each one more difficult than the other?"

"And why do you want the dictionary?"

"I'm selling words to the kids on the street."

"How?"

"I say a hard word. If nobody figures out what it means, I get a marble, or a trading card."

"And do I have to choose the hard words?"

"Sure. You're the one who knows everything. You're the one who writes."

75

Trying to work on the book. In the confusion during the move from here to the station, and from the station to here, I've lost all the chapters. I only have the thirteenth. Once in a while I tinker with it. As much as I look through this pile of papers, I can't even find my notes. The solution is to start over. There were two titles: *The Man in Bas-Relief* and *The Exhausted Dream*. Or: *The Exhausted Man*. I was going to decide at the end, once the book was finished.

I don't have a title. Chapter thirteen was difficult. I didn't remember the details, the newspaper published a small note. I interviewed people, wrote letters. All my friends participated, against the *Integralistas*, obviously. There was a lot that I had to change in the text. Múcio, for example, can't be called by his own name. I need to work on the sentences, polish them. Each time I delve into this chapter I feel anxiety. At that time, 1953, we were seventeen years old. So I get stuck, unable to reproduce my thoughts from around that time. If I write this book (about me) about my friends, about the town, I'll be free. I'll destroy everything and leave.

I speed up so the rain doesn't quite catch me, and walk into the theater. Ceres is sitting down deep into his seat, curled up, cold. I know he doesn't have any wool clothes, only this beige linen suit, ragged at the sleeves, that he wears every night. A college professor debased to this condition. He has two jobs, but he can barely support his three children. The other day I saw the youngest son, a blond, skinny kid. Malnourishment has made the boy's hair a watery color, between corn, straw, and sand. Having his university chair taken away must have been very traumatic for Ceres, because he denies that he was ever a professor with a Master's degree in physics. Maybe it's a secret he wants to keep, so he won't be persecuted anymore. There's a cold wind in the streets. Ceres could very well stay inside the theater today. Nobody goes out to the movies on a Tuesday like this. Much less to see a movie that has already been showing for two days at the other theater. And if someone wants to get in without paying, so what? The show hasn't started. There are only five people in the theater, one of them is old Roque. He has a lifetime pass and uses it. Every day. Roque is eighty-one years old and has seen all the movies that have shown in town. The lot where the movie theater sits once belonged to his family. They sold it on the condition that they would be granted free admission to the theater, in perpetuity. It's been a tradition for thirty years. People here worry a lot about perpetuity. In the cemetery, for example, there are only perpetual mausoleums. There isn't one inch of land available. The mayor is going to have another cemetery opened for the newly dead, outside the town limits.

THE SWALLOWING SWIMMING POOL

Every late afternoon they got together at their friend's house. There was a lawn and a swimming pool with blue water. White benches, round tables, mats, chairs with flowery throw pillows, a portable bar filled with scotch, gin, Campari, bitters, vermouth, Angostura liqueur, vodka, beer cans. They talked, drank, laughed, sang, ate, argued. Most of the men were in love with the thin young woman with green eyes. These passions were kept hidden from their own wives, and also from the husband of the thin young woman with green eyes. She had a child-like demeanor, a natural smile, was always willing to listen to the problems of others and was able to figure them out better than an analyst, putting things in perspective, this is this, that is that. None of the men knew the others were in love with her. She was the only one who knew who liked her. She didn't seem to care or else enjoyed clandestine games. She walked with small steps, and the women didn't like her green eyes, but they kept their dislike secret, because it seemed like she was loved and admired.

Every weekend they got together. Sometimes they stayed Saturday and Sunday, drinking, eating, sleeping around on the couches, even on the lawn if they were really drunk.

They were always in a group, never alone. The only thing each one did alone was to like the young woman with green eyes. When one of the friends traveled, they held a farewell party and they all went to the airport. The postcards that came were addressed to everyone, and were always humorous cards, repeating jokes they'd told previously, using phrases and expressions known only to the group and that only they could understand. When the traveler returned, they all went to the airport and sat in the bar, at tables they pulled together, and drank and waited, and later kept drinking to celebrate the arrival, and from there went to the blue swimming pool and the green lawn, to listen to the stories, because all who traveled followed the same itineraries, and looked up the same people, friends in Europe or friends who had also traveled and had agreed to meet there.

One Sunday morning, they were all drinking and talking, the men looking surreptitiously at the young woman with green eyes. And she, who had been standing next to her husband, dove into the pool. Those who were furtively looking at her turned to look at their own wives' eyes, or at their drinks, or at something else. No one saw that the young woman with green eyes didn't come back. An hour went by before they realized that she hadn't returned. They looked at the pool. There wasn't anybody in it. One of the friends, dark-skinned, short, with a black mustache, put on goggles, grabbed an oxygen tank and dove in. He disappeared.

They were all sitting now. Sad, they were thinking about how cute the young woman with green eyes was, how intelligent, elegant, well spoken. And each of the men secretly remembered how she had solved so many of their problems and how much he had liked her. What would it be like, without her to look at and to love, without her saying things and traveling and telling stories and smiling spontaneously? The sun was getting strong and one of the friends jumped into the pool. He disappeared. Soon, others followed: the friend who owned the pool, the disappeared man's wife, the husband of the young woman with green eyes. Nobody found anything. They got worried and sat down to drink a scotch and watch the water, which was getting murky, brown, a light coffee color. They talked about what was happening to them, and then the smiling dark-complexioned guy with small spots on his chin, who did aerobics and spinning, dove in to see why the water was clouding over. He disappeared. And when he did, the water appeared darker and thicker, of a density like that of chocolate mousse. And that's what one of the women said, "Let's get some spoons and eat the mousse from the pool."

They all laughed and complimented the host, because on that Saturday many spectacular things were happening and they were having a great time. They drank, while the host contemplated the paste that had taken the place of the water in his pool. Some pipe must have broken and brought in mud—all the pools in the area must have been like that. The weekend was ruined. Then the woman who had suggested the spoons dove in the mousse paste, laughing and saying: "What a great Saturday! There'll never be another one like this." She didn't come back. After that they all began to shout excitedly. And they kept diving, looking for the woman with green eyes, for the smiling dark-complexioned man, for the woman who had mentioned the spoons. All disappeared, one by one, dissolved in the gelatin-like mousse-paste water. Soon, among the white benches, the flowery pillows and the Broom shrubs blooming with yellow flowers, only the host remained, looking at the empty chairs, the empty mats, the glasses filled with drinks, the stereo playing Joe Cocker. He contemplated the pool as the sun began to set. A servant came and saw him, his body extended, his arms stretching in front of him, as if he was about to dive. And then he relaxed his arms, and kept staring at a spot in the bottom of the pool. As he did every night, the servant turned on the lights, four mercury floodlights.

LEISURE

Memoirs

I've bought a book with James Agee's scripts. I want to study his technique, dialogues, how he structured his scenes. Agee was a little older than me when he died in glory. I started to read the book with some difficulty, stumbling on the colloquialisms, especially when Bogart speaks in *The African Queen*. As I kept reading, going from the book to the *Michaelis* dictionary and to a glossary of slang and idiomatic expressions, I realized I was light-years behind these men, who did what I'd aspired to do. And I didn't move one step ahead. It wasn't Nancy that kept me from accepting the Cultural Union scholarship for the specialization course in America. The first-place student for four years, and today I can barely read English. I lack the vocabulary. And the moment they placed those papers in front of me for me to sign, I felt lost. I'd be in a strange country, without any support, and having to prove I was what I had been with ease before: the best student. That contract, or document, or whatever it was, placed right in front of me, represented the first step in my ascension. It was the scissors that would cut my ties to Araraquara. Two years in the United States would be more than enough for me to change. Two years studying the language. I don't know how many more before I could write correctly in English, and as many again before the doors to the publishers or a movie studio would open to me. How many years would it take? And that was really what I wanted to do with my life. I only hesitated once—when I was faced with those papers. Instead of signing them and changing my mind later (what consequences could there have been?), I decided not to sign. I gave up my place to the next person in line. I spent the night throwing up.

I've always been one for extremes. For me, that momentary, normal doubt was sufficient to wash everything down the drain. I thought: if I hesitated, I wasn't sure, forgetting that we only achieve certainty by adding all the doubts we've had. Once we give in—and this is a cliché—we always give in, either to justify that first time or to reinforce it. Signing those papers would have meant courage, detachment. I thought I wasn't tied to the town, because I hated it for its narrowness and the limits it imposed on me. Now I know: we were both narrow-minded and limited. What good is there in knowing? I can try again. So many years were wasted, and nothing is ahead of me. I have nothing to lose. I'm not risking anything—safety, comfort, an income, family. I am completely available, as if I had just been born. There's nothing to influence me. An exile can try everything. He doesn't even risk losing his country, since he's already lost it.

77

"We didn't move to São Paulo because of you."

"We didn't because you never wanted to. Every year we were going, every year you postponed it. You said you hadn't finished some research."

"See? 'Some research.' The most important thing in my life and you don't even know what it is."

"How can I know? Have you ever said?"

"Have you ever asked?"

I have the feeling my head is a tape player, playing the same events, situations, dialogues over and over again.

"You made a face every time I got close to your notebook. I bet that notebook is blank. There's nothing written in it."

"There isn't? I'll show you if there is or isn't."

"Show me, I want to see it."

"One of these days I'll get fed up and show you. All the enormous work of these last six years."

"Show me now."

"Not yet. Wait and I'll prove you wrong. And you'll see how unfair you've been."

"Do you know something? Now that everything is over anyway, I want to tell you something. What have you been running after? Why do you live so restlessly and full of anguish? I swear: I'd love for you to open up and tell me. What's happening? You grab onto this mysterious research as an excuse for what? For not having gone to São Paulo? You didn't want to go. You kept postponing it and making excuses. What were you afraid of? When your old friends show up, you go after them like a puppy dog. And they don't even care. Do you know why? They don't want anything to do with you. They're good-for-nothing. They snub you, humiliate you, and you keep running after them. Have you realized you don't even have anything to say to them? When you get back home I ask what you've talked about. Nothing. Gossip. Live your life. Forget about them."

"Don't talk to me like that about my friends. Don't say anything else. They're my only friends, we were in middle school and high school together. They're the people who've made it in life, they're good role models for me."

"Role models, what role models? You're better than any of them. That Bernardo, full of air, the so-called writer who's always giving you writing lessons. Tell him to switch places with you! I'd like to see if he could get one book published."

I search for a vision that's constantly coming to me: a shiny body emerging and the sun reflecting off of it. It's an obsession, a dream, a vision, I don't know.

"He's made it in life. It wasn't easy for him either. He was poor . . ."

"Poor? Come on. How has he made it? He's graduated, yes, like all the others. Ambulance chasers, abortion doctors, sloppy engineers. Look, dear. What have they done? Everybody knows. What do Valente and Clécio do? Abortions for the socialites. And what about the other two who show up in a golden Cadillac? The lawyers. They sell habeas corpora to thieves and killers. You've read about them, the newspapers talked about the law suits that resulted in nothing, except for fame and money for them. I feel disgusted when I see you with those two, drinking beer and gossiping about women. And that architect you said went out at night peeping in and listening at windows. He came from a good family, didn't he? Rich. And what happened? Why doesn't he show up anymore? Because of that corporate fraud. They built twelve condominiums, made lots of money, and handed over twelve shacks instead of luxury apartments. And people selling their houses so they could buy apartments, and have a bird's-eye view."

"Bernardo is nice."

"Has he ever sent you his books? You had to buy all of them. Has he ever helped you get your stories published? Do you remember when he read one and laughed, said you were out of touch, stuck in the past?"

"And I was. His criticism was right. And who are you to be saying all these things? You're not even my wife anymore."

Before I know it, I'm thinking of that body again. In the same way, my last argument with Nancy in our living room on a hot night replays in my mind.

"See how funny? We had to split up so I could say all these things that you refuse to see. I did everything so our marriage would work out. I liked you. I wanted you to do the things you dreamed of. I even sewed for others when the State laid off all the substitute teachers and the unemployment crisis started. I didn't mind sewing dresses for a half dozen imbeciles who took the labels off from old dresses bought in São Paulo. I don't mean to rub it in. What I did doesn't matter. What matters is what you *didn't do*, either because you couldn't or because you had nothing *to* do."

"What do you mean, I had nothing to do?"

"Maybe, dear, you were chasing a pointless dream. You wanted to be something that wasn't you. And you never accepted what you are. You mirror yourself in others, but it's not *your* image you see in the glass, it's someone else's."

"It makes me despair, to be this way and be unable to change."

"You despair because you're a romantic. You're fighting a battle with the wrong weapons. You wanted to be like your friends. They were all restless, couldn't stand the town, felt suffocated by it. Not you. You like it here, you love this life, and you want to connect with the people. You looked so happy on those relaxing Sundays when we barbecued in the backyard. It was the most peaceful, the calmest thing. I hated that Sunday peace, I looked forward to the end of the day and hoped another one would never come. You spent each second of those afternoons drinking, dozing off in the sun, in shorts, your belly sticking out, growing bigger with each beer. At the end of the day you were distraught, thinking that you had wasted another day, blaming me. You blamed my mother who was visiting in the evening, blamed the town where nothing ever happened. You never blamed yourself, you who didn't know what you wanted."

On that street there was a jasmine bush, and its aroma was suffocating. However, on that night, in the end, I suffocated from hatred for her.

"I always said what I wanted: to be somebody."

"But you needed to have an objective, and you never had one."

"I had many. I had, no, I *have*."

"Many means none."

"I still have the same ambitions."

"Hoping that things will fall into your lap. You never lifted a finger."

"Enough talking, Nancy. You didn't come here to talk. You came to ask for money. Today is when I should get paid."

"You're so cruel. You always have been. You never realized I loved you. I could see you wanted to be somebody and didn't know how. I tried to help you, but felt so rejected that I began to hate you."

"You were too insistent. That wasn't encouragement. It was pressure, nagging."

"Because you lied, and I wanted to find out the truth."

Soon after I wrote down our dialogue, because by writing I seemed to escape it, I freed myself from its burden and control. Today I read it and it sounds to me like an excerpt from an absurd play, a meaningless situation. Or else very meaningful.

78

TV news. They focus on a magazine cover: *Le Nouvel Observateur.* A yellow title, "Les héritiers de la débâcle," on a brown cover, about the end of the Vietnam War. The end? The photo shows a boy with thin hair and huge eyes. The boy's perplexed stare pierces the pages, penetrates my room, and shatters my stare, which is now more perplexed than his. The boy's gaze breaks through his country's borders—fixed on the photographic film—to reproduce itself in me, perplexed and quizzical. The boy's perplexed and quizzical look breaks through my room's borders, bringing in the disquiet of someone who doesn't understand. He doesn't understand the world, and I, him. Both of us are perplexed. The photo shows the boy sitting alone on a brown tile floor, as brown as the burlap robe he's wearing. An abysmal light reflects on his face, coming from the eternity of a time that is both finite and infinite: a flash of light, announcing not the future but catastrophe. A calm, yellow, apocalyptic light caresses his face. Our difference lies in that light. The one that reaches me is permanent, repetitive, ordinary. His light is frightening in its calm. Light not from the sun, but from a bonfire—the flashes of exploding bombs engraved on his perplexed face. The sunset light that touches me is frighteningly destructive, piercing like a laser, burning like acid, corrosive in its violence. Falsely peaceful. We're the heirs of a tragedy, the two of us, this boy whose roots were cut and who was left loose and isolated in the world. And I, who have deepened my roots, am also loose and isolated in the world. Exiled. We're alike in that, where we're most different. This is the mystery that perplexes and confounds me the most. It stunts my thinking. I walk to the mirror and look at myself, trying to find out if my eyes reproduce his perplexed and quizzical gaze. Almost facing the mirror, I step back. I'm not brave enough. It won't do me any good even if I find out. On the contrary, I'd return to my observation post, to the streets, certain that, outlined against the window frame, I'll be seen by those walking by down below, in the same way I see this boy from Vietnam on his magazine cover: what are my eyes searching for? My brain works fast, thinking in high speed. My and the boy's stares: bewildered, frightened, believing. Even so, a belief: the photo of a boy, a Vietnam refugee, alone on a brown tile floor, without parents, brothers, relatives. No pain, plea, or supplication—there's nothing in his eyes. Only an abyss, a question: I.

79

Auctioning the furnishings from the old RSA: clocks, rings, train lamps, benches, ticket window bars, two-way radios, telegraph machines, staffs, wicker chairs, tables, inkwells, desks, baskets, stools, bells, carbide lanterns, scales, signal flags, typewriters, ticket-stamping machines, shelves, hutches for the tickets, cabinets.

The old chief, his kepi a little crooked, is followed by a policeman,.

"That's the guy who's been asking. He's been coming here for the past month."

"He must belong to the gang. He'll be squealing. Give me those papers."

I did.

"Nothing's written on them. He's certainly come to draw a plan of the station."

"The station doesn't exist anymore. Why would I want a plan of it?"

"I don't know. I don't understand you people. Nor do I want to."

The policeman, "Your situation isn't good at all. I had your file checked. You were forced to leave the Railroad. You joined a strike. Now you're investigating those men's deaths. Why?"

"In order to write a TV special."

"What's a TV special?"

"Every two weeks the TV airs an hour-long show, a whole episode. I thought the men's deaths or the end of the Railroad Games could lead to something."

"You're making this up. What Railroad Games are you talking about?"

"Are you from here?"

"I've been living here for fifteen years."

"The Games stopped twenty years ago."

"I've never heard of them. You're the first one. And I talk to everybody: to the judge, lawyers, teachers, the mayor. Everybody. I never heard anyone mention anything about that."

They left me incommunicado. That was unnecessary. I have no one to come visit me.

I do.

"Ceres Fhade, what are you doing here?"

"Ceres? Even in jail? I found out yesterday. What happened?"

"Who told you?"

"The woman who works at the ticket counter lives around here. She saw it. What happened?"

"A mistake. They got me mixed up with someone else."

"What are you going to do? How can I help you?"

"I know nothing. I'll stay, they're not treating me badly."

"You can't stay here."

"I don't have anything to do outside."

"If I weren't so afraid of the police, I'd talk to the police chief. Do you want me to contact anybody in your family?"

"No."

"A lawyer?"

"Do I have money to pay for one?"

"I'll go to the Social Services."

"That's just for medical needs."

"To the Court."

"Forget it, Ceres. Sooner or later I'll be out of here."

"Doesn't it bother you to be in jail?"

"To be or not to be, we're always in jail."

"What?"

"Think about it. You, every night in the foyer of the movie theater, you're not allowed to leave your place. Aren't you locked up? An individual, everyday in the office, thirty-five years before retiring. Isn't that a sentence? We're all condemned to thirty-five years of continuous and boring work."

"I don't understand this stuff you're telling me, that you're always telling me."

"Never mind."

"Any friends of yours? Someone from your group?"

"They all live out of town."

"But we have to do something."

"You can bring me magazines, newspapers, candy, cigarettes."

Wow, Ceres is nice, worrying about me. Here I am, locked up, super-relaxed, and there *he* is, worrying, feeling scared. The good thing is that here I can think. I can spend the whole time thinking.

She wore her black, straight hair, very straight and black, parted in the middle. Her face was thin and her nose aquiline, and only later I found out she looked like an English actress who worked in Italy: Barbara Steele. I saw her in *8 1/2*. It may have been my neurosis, transference, or an escape from reality, but I liked the coincidence. The first time I went out with Nancy, clumsy in the shoes my brother let me borrow, we went to the movies. To the Paratodos, on one of those Sundays when the theater is completely full, people walk up and down the aisles, and the candy sellers see their candy sell out. I associated Sunday nights with the smell of mints and Chita candy. Nancy sucked on candy the whole movie, non-stop. She admitted to me she dreaded having bad breath. She brushed her teeth compulsively. There was nothing better than watching the movie and holding Nancy's hand, her sweaty palms, her nervous fingers. And during breaks, when the movie wasn't so interesting, we kissed. Maybe she lost her interest because we kissed. That's what we most liked to do in the movies, indifferent to the people around us. And the Paratodos audience was full of curious, gossipy, cheeky people. Every time we kissed, the kids started:

"1 – 0."

"2 – 0."

"3 0."

"What a score!"

And if we stopped, "Encore, encore, encore."

Nancy laughed and turned her face, offering me her whole mouth, her small, white teeth protruding slightly. She was good-humored and happy. There was no reason for her not to be. She was seventeen and had lived her whole life in Araraquara, in a house with a verandah and a garden full of roses, like all the gardens in town. She led a carefree life, from home to school, from school to the Club, her girlfriends' houses, church on Sundays. She moved around within a restricted, small and perfectly safe circle. She believed she was protected and invulnerable. And that's what allowed her to show up everyday looking fresh and rosy, smelling like Phebo soap, her face glowing. I think she expected everything from the future, and I was the future. I couldn't disappoint her. I didn't want to. I just hoped that Nancy's world would never disappear, not simply so that she wouldn't suffer, but so that I could be a part of it and feel protected too. I didn't see that everything surrounding her was fragile, and that she was even more fragile than her circle.

Ah, that fragility: a lie I told myself. Later I found out how strong Nancy was, and it was thanks to her that, once the whole affair was over, I was able to endure the Railroad massacre. During the whole week when they were discussing what to do with the strikers she didn't say one word, didn't make any accusations. Even though she had warned me she was against me, that what I had done was insane. The day they didn't fire me, only transferred me to the station, to that three-month long purgatory of trains, desert, whistles and the torturing and endless clicking of the telegraph, she said, "Let's go, but this is the last time I'll support you. There won't be a second time." She was right. She was one or two months pregnant, I don't remember well. How did I come up with this idea of Nancy's fragility? What for? The world that surrounded her was about to disappear, I thought naively and romantically.

80

I go back to the same topic many times, like an ox chewing its cud. The ox takes something new from the food that's gone to its stomach and back. So do I. I hadn't been able to interview a single eighty- or ninety-year-old individual who would tell me the truth. There weren't many left. They had been picking up the elderly and sending troops of them to the nursing homes in the Matão Mountains. There were always different versions of the same story and not one single point where they coincided. Either their memories had deteriorated with the years, or they learned to lie since that night in 1897, when the meek hid and the bold were in the Largo da Matriz watching, not participating. Watching only to keep quiet later. "We don't discuss our problems with strangers," they said. I'm not a stranger, I was born here, I've lived here for forty years. I belong to you. It's *our* history I want to know about. History, they said, is the present and the future, not the past. You want to bring up the same slander that the surrounding towns did for years. The whole State talked about us, against us, and hated us, and we couldn't defend ourselves. Where are you going to write it? In a book? In the newspapers? In magazines? On TV? Write a soap opera on a lynching that didn't happen. Make up your characters. Write the truth, write about real things, son. This truly happened, Mr. Teófilo. We all know it. We were born and grew up hearing about these things. They forbid us to say anything, and the grown-ups stopped talking when children walked into the room. There was no curse, Mr. Teófilo, only guilt. People locked themselves in their homes out of guilt. Guilt made everybody aggressive. Here people always attack first. Nothing is allowed. You ask me for proof. There is the cemetery, where the brothers are buried. "That's no proof of anything. An abandoned cemetery taken over by weeds, the tombs in ruins. What is it proof of?"

81

"Hold my hand." Nancy's small hand. "I want to touch your face."

Nancy's small hand on my face. "You never let me touch you like this."

Her small hand on my hair. "Why don't you let me? Your hair is so soft." Her small hand, sliding down my neck.

I see the sparkling body emerging, and the sun. The intense light dissolves everything. Only a blank space remains, and there is Nancy, with her small hands. The desperate recollection of a gesture that never reaches completion, because I sketch it in my mind wishing for it to be repeated, and for Nancy to be at my side.

She's lost forever. For I've lost her. I lose everything that I love and that I need. Right now I wanted Nancy's small hand on my skin. The nights we spent sitting on a garden bench hugging, holding on to each other. Even if it was a cold June night everybody went to the garden with their dates, there wasn't one single empty bench. We had to arrive early. Nowadays nobody goes there, it's a sad place, people just walk by it. In the afternoon, between four and six, old retirees chat, then go have dinner and watch TV. Once in a while I stop by, and stand contemplating the bench where we sat, expecting Nancy's hand to touch me again.

The police chief has declared that without flagrante delicto, proven guilt, or preventive custody he can't keep me in jail longer than twenty-four hours. The station chief should have pressed charges but didn't. Nor was an incident report filed, so he will let me go early tomorrow morning. He warned me not to get in trouble again. What trouble? I spent the whole time in this stinking cell thinking about how to write the paradoxes, one for each street in town. They'd be the epigraphs for the chapters, each one about a person or fact related to that given street. Like the fantastic story of Miss Maria do Carmo, about whom nobody says a word since her husband, risking ridicule, sued three people for having spoken disparagingly of her. Each one had a different version.

First Street Paradox

There was a free prisoner, because, having been set free he was still locked up, since every prisoner lives a special situation of full liberty and use of his senses, whereas the free man lives under extreme pressure from freedom itself, which imprisons him as much as any prison.

Second Street Paradox

He saw without seeing anything, because, having his eyes uncovered he found himself blind, since every blind man lives a special situation of full vision and use of his capacity of observation, whereas the man with a vision suffers the unbearable pressure from everything he sees and must face and confront, this being the extreme pressure of those who possess vision.

Third Street Paradox

Paraplegic, he moved about, because all those who are immobile are in movement, since all mobility is a special condition, extrinsic to mobility, opposite and parallel to it. The immobile man suffers pressure from his own mobility, such mobility being the result of the inversion of being immobile.

I get mortally depressed about not being able to express myself, being unable to let out everything I hold inside. I don't know if the world is interested. I'm afraid I'll produce one of these insipid books written on Saturdays and Sundays about gray existences, without a single event to shake the boredom from years and years of life in a provincial town. Someone who has something to say can't have such misgivings.

I never had a girlfriend in town. On Thursdays and Saturdays I wandered around the streets. I watched couples standing in verandahs, near walls and trees, walking down toward the garden, walking into the theater, hand in hand. The eight o'clock show on Sundays was full of couples, side by side, holding hands, hugging, kissing. The great Sunday show: an experience I missed out on. It was denied me, and why? There was nothing I could do except try, and when I did try it resulted in nothing, except for humiliation.

"But later you got married, had a son. That means your attempt resulted in something," you may say.

My marriage, Nancy, everything means nothing. Have you met Nancy? No guy was willing to go out with her. She was ugly, talked in a high-pitched voice. The advantage was that her father had money. People said he won the Christmas lottery, a lot of money. That's why they respected that man who walked around in a blue suit, yellow tie and white socks, carrying an umbrella with a wooden handle they said he'd brought from England. Nancy never mentioned this trip or talked about her father's money. I never saw any money.

82

The man at the Notary's office was a relative of mine. Still, he never let me consult his files to look up the death certificates.

"Those who have died have died. You'd better not disturb the dead."

So that's what it was about, it disturbed the dead. I worried about them, wanted to decipher indecipherable things, to elucidate enigmas that weren't enigmas, but clear situations.

"A demon trying to whip us," the mayor had told me. And the mayor had been my schoolmate. He had even dated a girl that I liked.

He sat down with me in his father's tailor shop. We sat there in awkward silence. After all, we weren't exactly friends, we had just met at school. And around election time I received envelopes from him with his *curriculum vitae* and flyers showing which office he was running for. His *curriculum vitae* included classes in Odontology, specialization courses on prosthesis, conferences attended, trips to São Paulo, two or three articles on new filling materials; the positions he had held in the business association, the tailors' association, the Tennis Club, the Nautical Club; the good things he had done for the town: mercury floodlights, illuminated fountains, sidewalk cleanings, donation of seeds for the campaign "a vegetable garden in each yard for the people's economy." And I voted for him. I confess.

"People say you snoop too much. You want to know everything. You're always sticking your nose around, talking. What are you going to do with this stuff? What everyone wants to know is simply this: what are you going to do with all this material, or whatever you call it. Nobody holds anything against you, but it's best to make things clear, the situation is very unpleasant. I've been asked to intervene. You know, things move fast here, they spread like glass beads on a slope. Tell me so I can calm the townspeople down." As if I were a monster, scaring a hundred thousand people. Because a hundred thousand people live in this town. Will it do any good if I tell the mayor I just wanted to find out why the suicide rate is so high? And particularly in the 18-25 age group? They hid the details, but we pick up the rumors in the air. It wasn't only rumors. There were my friends too. One jumped from a building, another one ingested ant poison. The third one died on the job. I saw that one and it was awful: his mouth foaming, blood running down his nose, his eyes wide open. He was twenty-three years old and had a two-year-old son, who was standing next to him, watching. He was a normal guy, with an average job, had just paid off his car. There was a time when he wanted to leave town—he said it suffocated him. Then he calmed down, really, he was fine. He wasn't a rebel, nor was he frustrated like me, or a failure, as people are saying. I had the feeling he had chosen this life. He also chose death. He was a fragile person, everything looked fragile when I saw his contracted body, his foaming mouth, his son watching.

Therefore: they hide the deaths, these suicides following one after the other. "One suicide generates another," my relative at the Notary's told me. Very simple, no need for more explanations. One action leads to another, same thing. It's like a principle of physics. I ended up telling the mayor I'd vote for his re-election. He thanked me. He'd rather have my vote for the Senate.

HELLO

He was rich, well-traveled. Every time he came back, his suitcases were full of phone books. His friends brought him phone books. His offices had instructions to get him phone books from every city in the world.

Large storage rooms kept phone books from El Eglab, Mecca, São Paulo, Herat, Jodpur, Norislk, Radan, Alabama, Montevideo, Ouagadougou, Caracas, Apia, Santos, Wellington, Utrecht, Kuwait, Byblos, Lautoka, Sneeuberg, Salisbury, Léopoldville, Khartum, Jerusalem, Phnom Penh, Prek Veng, Yaoundé, Matara City, Fort-Lamy, Beijing, Fushum, Zibo, Budapest, Eger, Hong Kong, Reykjavik, Tokyo, Kyoto, Corfu, Kofu, Athens, Tirana, Ulore, Elbasan, Sarapuí, São Carlos, Tanger, Sétif, Luanda, Pago Pago, Lobito, Avellaneda, Sydney, Graz, Nassau, Manama, Bridgetown, Hamilton, Antwerpe, Tashi Chho, La Paz, Chi-Chi-Shima, Cayo, Brunei, Sofia, Yangon, Bujumbura, New York, Paris, London, Roma, Vienna, Moscow, Stockholm, Amsterdam, and thousands of other capitals, cities, towns and villages.

So one day he had every phone number in the entire world. He hired technicians and computers and started. He entered the numbers on cards and fed the computers. Eventually, a computer spit out a card with a number that was the synthesis of all the telephones in the world. And he dialed, and all the telephones in the world rang simultaneously.

"Hello," people said, in Bulgarian, English, Spanish, Portuguese, Swahili, Persian, Scandinavian, Spanish, Turkish, Greek, Swedish, Norwegian, Polish, Danish, Scottish, Burmese, Ladino, Mongolian, Rumanian, Check, Serbo-Croatian, Tibetan, Korean, Hungarian, Hindu, Malay, Melanesian, Papuan, Samoan, Vietnamese, Togolese, Nepalese, Thai, Swazi, Tamil, Somali, Tagalog, Diveli.

He could barely hear.

"Hello, hello," he shouted.

"Hello," the others shouted in the world's languages.

He hung up: the world was out of order.

WHO'S TALKING?

He made the decision, irrevocable. He looked at the black phone on the table, the wire stretching out on the floor toward the wall. He made up his mind and climbed into the phone. He sat there hiding, waiting. He heard it ring, one, two, seven times. His wife answered. A man was calling, the grocer, he wanted to know where to make the delivery. They hung up. The day went by. His children talked on the phone many times, arranged games, appointments, dates for the movies. Ordinary people, nothing extraordinary, just everyday life. He waited another day, and another, and another. He saw when his wife, worried, called the police, called friends. Their voices were screeching and hellish, interposed with tearing sounds. To stay inside the phone was pure torture, but he adapted. He had adapted to situations his whole life, this was just one more thing. One month. At first the calls followed one another with hallucinating constancy. Then they began to decrease. He then left through the wire and got into all sorts of telephones. He heard business deals being made, dates being set, lovers talking, conversations in foreign languages, women gossiping non-stop, escort girls talking to clients, wives betraying their husbands, husbands betraying their wives, and numbers, and long-distance and international calls. The first phase was over. He began to interfere in conversations. Mr. So-and-so was talking and suddenly through the wire came a small, strange, extraterrestrial voice. They cursed, hung up, called again, and there he was, not budging. He spent weeks interfering in the same telephone. Then he moved on to another, and another, without ever getting tired, without stopping: a small extraterrestrial voice in the middle of the conversations, cursing and shouting. All of sudden, everyone in town had heard that voice. Everyone talked about it: crossed lines, but very strange crossed lines. They complained to the phone company. The company sent out technicians, moved heaven and earth. And when the technicians talked from one phone to another, they heard the same smiling voice, the voice that laughed and mocked and cursed. The technicians couldn't find him. So the company brought technicians from the United States, from Germany, from Switzerland, from everywhere. And the small voice from hell continued. Hellish. In all of the telephones, until the whole town went crazy: completely, irrevocably crazy.

RELATIONSHIPS

Memoirs

The buildings downtown formed a compact block. There were also occasional towers spread out in the distance, between the rows of houses and the long tree-lined streets. We're under a tree, protected from the sun. Drops of sweat form on Eduardo's forehead.

"You're okay today, aren't you, Dad?"

"Yes. I'm very well. How do you know?"

"You haven't hugged the tree."

"I'm very calm."

"The last few times you didn't let go of the trunk. I didn't even feel like going out with you."

"I'm fine now."

"You didn't come get me for a long time. What happened? Mom didn't want to tell me, or she didn't know. She just said you were gone."

"I traveled. I went very far away."

"Will you take me on a trip?"

"I will next time."

"By train."

"Sure."

"Tell me the story of Grandpa's fish."

"No, not again. Let's think of another one."

"I like that one. You've never told me the whole story, only pieces. It's hard for you to let everything out, eh, Dad?"

"You're the one who interrupts me all the time. You're like your mother."

"So, Grandpa had been in the boat for a hundred days and the fish came . . ."

"No, it had been sixty days that he hadn't caught any fish and he got in the boat. His only friend, a boy, came, and told him not to go out on the boat, the sea was rough, he wouldn't find any fish."

"Can you find an old man for me?"

"What for?"

"To be my friend."

"Don't you have friends?"

"Only in school, but in the afternoon I'm alone at home. I can't go out before Mom gets home from work. It would be nice if I had an old man."

"What about the stereo I gave you?"

"You gave me the stereo and only two albums, I can't stand them anymore. You promised to give me an album each month. I'm still waiting."

"I'll get one for you tomorrow. What album?"

"What album? Any one. I only have two."

A bell rang far away, with regular strokes. Sometimes the sound disappeared, then it would come back.

"Dad, why don't you write Grandpa's story? Aren't you a writer?"

"I will. I've been working."

"Does it take long? When I was small you used to sit at the kitchen table writing."

"It may take a lifetime. It's very hard."

"I don't want to be a writer, Dad."

"What do you want to be?"

"I don't know. A soccer player."

"A soccer player? Don't you want to be like your Dad?"

"Dad, I don't know what you do! Besides, I'm playing really well in the youth division. The tournament is about to start. You have to watch all the games. All of them, okay?"

"Okay ('I don't have anything to do anyway, I'm fed up with that hardware store. They're going to end up firing me— I do shitty accounting.')."

I stand there hugging Eduardo for the longest time, my hand over his chest feeling his heart beat fast. How much apprehension because of this kid. And nevertheless he's growing up safe, peaceful. Nancy told me his teachers like him, that he's intelligent, bright, calm, not at all affected by the separation.

"Dad, look at those tractors. What do you think it is?"

"I don't know. Let's go over there, and see what it is."

Tractors, trucks and steam shovels had parked at the bottom of the hill, next to a bright blue wood house.

"What are they going to build here?"

"A lime-processing plant."

"Are they going to tear down the hill?"

"Only part of it on this side for the facilities. On the other side it's all calcareous. They're going to get the limestone there."

Eduardo was fascinated by the big yellow engines. We sat down while he ate his sandwich and *guaraná*. I only brought one for him, I didn't have much money. I think I'll sell those old newspapers and magazines, by weight.

"Dad, are they going to cut down the tree?"

"I think so."

"Then let's take a branch from it."

"Let's not. Why keep things that will only tie us down? You'll be tied down by the memory of this tree, son. What for?"

"That's good, Dad."

"No, it isn't. I know very well it isn't. It would be good if we forgot everything. Our memory is like a prison, a chain."

THE SAD MEN

The men walked, and next to them, the women. They walked slowly, rhythmically, as if they were marching. One could practically hear drums keeping pace with the march. The men were dressed in brown with green ties, and had sideburns, long hair. The women wore really cute dresses. They seemed to replicate each other, to be copies of one another, to look the same. He looked on, and started to shiver.

"Why?" She asked.

"Who knows? Happiness. I'm not that way any longer."

"But you're nothing else either."

"It'd rather be this way. I haven't got used to it yet, but it's better like this. Now I know the feeling a donkey has when it's freed from the cart, and its harness and blinders are removed."

"And what good does it do?"

"At first, nothing. We're free and don't feel it. Then we begin to realize we can scream, wake up at any time we want, sit down at the typewriter and write whatever we want."

The men in brown walk slowly, the sun hitting them. The clock on the white tower shows six o'clock. It's December 31.

"There was a party today," he said.

"Party? And everybody so sad?"

"It's the end-of-year party, the only one management allows. They prohibit protests, birthday parties, newsletters, bulletin boards, jokes, not wearing a suit and tie, wearing the same shirt more than once, not polishing your shoes, not brushing your teeth, laughing, humming, writing anything that is not for the Railroad, going to the bathroom at unscheduled times (Ah, did you know their bodies have adapted perfectly well?)."

"But the party, no one leaves a party like that. Look at their faces!"

"They're happy. That's the way they are. Did you know? Upstairs, on the floors, noise is not allowed. Everyone has a phone, an invisible miniature earphone. Through the earphones they receive the boss's orders, phone calls, communiqués. At the end-of-year party they dance to the music they hear through the little apparatus. It's strange to watch the December 31 party: everybody dancing and not one sound. Everything is carpeted and covered in special acoustic pressed-wood plates."

"And you put up with it for ten years?"

"They paid well, really well."

"And did you like it there?"

"I was going crazy. I worked all year long, Saturdays, Sundays, holidays."

"Every day?"

"Yes."

"No days off?"

"No. Do you know something? I realized I liked it. Just like they do. Can you believe they like it?"

"And how can they stand it?"

"They are the ones who ask for it. They want to work everyday. They say it's better."

There were twelve floors. The building—horrible, ugly, visible from any point in town, the very symbol of the town itself, and its largest industry—had its facade covered in stainless steel plates that reflected the sun. The metal mass was so bright you could barely look at it. There weren't any windows. There was one entrance, and a parking lot full of late-model cars. Men in uniform strolled back and forth. They were near the river, close to an entrance, looking through the fence. "Warning: Electric Fence." The men in brown kept walking slowly. They didn't look at anything, not even at the women.

"How funny these people are."

"Did you know they make the highest salaries in this country?"

"Really?"

"And that's their life: that building. They leave it to go home, from home they come back here. They don't talk to anybody, don't go out with anybody."

The men walked in their rhythmic strides, slowly, as if they were marching. They got in their cars.

"They look sad, very sad."

"They are sad, very sad indeed. They reached such a degree of sadness that it was hurting their performance at work. So their boss talked to the boss of the boss's boss. And a close-circuit TV system was installed. They spend the day watching cartoons and comedies. The sound on the TV sets is off. They hear everything through earphones. And do you know something?

"What?"

"They don't laugh. They can't anymore. I had a cousin, the one who got me a job here, who went crazy. Don't be surprised. Almost everyday somebody goes crazy in there. Look carefully. Do you see that square building in the back? That's where the ambulance is, always waiting. It's normal. The first day you hear the ambulance siren, it's scary. On the second day you get used to it. On the third, some imbecile is gone. In the end, somebody got liberated."

"You're kidding."

"Not at all, really. Do you want to see something? Come on."

They circled the building. Araraquara's typical, deep silence dominated the afternoon. The back part of the building was gray: one single wall of concrete.

"Can you see over there? Those lines? Look carefully. See? That's the door for suicides. Not one month goes by that someone doesn't kill himself. When it happens, they remove the body through this door. But everybody's gotten used to it. I don't know if they don't care or just pretend not to care. Inside, nobody knows what the others think."

"And no laughter?"

"You mean, why don't they laugh? That's something they chose when they agreed to work here. They choose and don't choose. Practically everybody there had talent, great talent. People who believed they could live off creating things. They started out here believing it. Then they became prisoners. The building owns the people, completely. It asks for everything, demands everything. I know a bunch of people who had the potential to do things: write, direct movies, plays, paint. But they're not allowed. Nobody can do anything outside the building. Nothing. They can't write books, can't paint, can't direct movies—nothing. Do you know what this means? They can't waste a single line, a sketch, an idea. There's a tradition here: the ideas you come up with are immediately put on a pink file card. The card is placed in a little box. At the end of the afternoon an employee gathers all the boxes in the building and takes them to a room. The Ideas Team reads, lists, studies, develops and applies all the useful ideas. Whatever is left over is sold outside. Ideas are very much in demand everywhere. Those who produce the best ones receive enormous bonuses. It's said they get very happy. They squeeze their minds even more, ideas pop up, they make more and more money."

"Why don't they laugh?"

"The doctor who examined my cousin noticed something strange: my cousin couldn't laugh. The muscles that controlled laughter were dead, hardened. You know how it goes, you stop using something and it loses its function. It deteriorates. Look at their faces. Nothing moves. Nothing."

"Who knows, maybe they're laughing inside."

"If someone laughs, he laughs on the outside. The problem is that they don't find anything funny. And it's hereditary. The ones who have children will have laugh-less kids."

"Those who have?"

"Yes. My cousin was infertile. Many of the others are like him. Once someone starts out in there, the whole thing absorbs him—he gets passionate about it. They don't think about anything else, only work. Some have forgotten they were married. Others find their wives can't stand them. The women were slowly left alone. Each man in there is the loneliest man in the world, closed in his acoustic pressed-wood cubicle with his TV. But they have their work. They work as many hours as they can handle. So, maybe they forget."

Almost all the men were in their cars, but weren't moving.

"How can they stand it?"

"They have the highest salaries in the country."

"So what? What do they do with the money?"

"They buy brown clothes, houses with pools, country

homes, host parties for each other, have houses on the beach, travel to Europe."

"Can they travel?"

"Yes. The boss knows they're constantly thinking about the building. They adore the building. When they're traveling, everyday, at six o'clock, they turn in the direction of the sun. See, the building faces the sun. They turn and think about the building, about their work, and make a commitment to returning. They think they're being watched. They're not, but think they are. As soon as they begin working in the company, they spend months in a special recruiting department that implants the code of regulations in their heads. Once they have it in their heads, they can never liberate themselves from it. That's why my friend went crazy."

They stood very close to the gate. They heard a whistle. The men in their cars started their engines. Another whistle: the cars pulled out in reverse, turned. A third whistle: they moved in line, and began moving through the gate. A man in uniform took note:

"License plate?"

"1 – 167."

"Parking slot?"

"145."

"Section?"

"PAX 35."

GUTS

Memoirs

My endless script. I admit: the only one I wrote. I mean, I wrote part of it. It's not finished. All the stories I said I'd written, I hadn't. Not one. I lacked ideas. I sat at the table in that room, and kept watching the sand that the breeze brought in. When I walked, my steps sounded rough. I swept and piled the sand up in a corner. That fine, yellow sand obsessed me. It came in everywhere, it was on the bookcase, between the books, in the drawers, boxes, clothes. The sand distracted me whenever I wanted to finish the story. I gave up, there was no point anyway. Write for whom? These are the facts, exactly as they happened on that day. I changed the time: the men died in the morning. I set the action in the afternoon. Why? Poetic license.

THE RAILROAD MEN

"An empty platform. Ticket booths closed.

Shot of the clock: 1:10 in the afternoon. The semaphores show green lights: the trains can pass. Deserted benches, closed bar. The sign at the bar reads: TAVERN.

A porter in a frayed uniform walks along the platform.

The camera (porter's perspective) focuses on the brown tiles that cover the walls; focuses on the sign: LADIES' WAITING ROOM.

The room looks like a middle-class home, furnished in an old style with wicker chairs and sofas. In the center is an oval table.

Two men talk, sitting next to each other on the sofa.

The porter keeps walking to the end of the platform.

Shots of the rails, a curve, tangled wires. It's drizzling.

An electric locomotive's trolley pole hits the overhead line and the line gives off sparks. Noise (buzzing) from a locomotive's engine. Through the window's damp glass the machinist gets ready.

The porter returns, observes the waiting room. The two men continue in the same position, talking very closely. One of them has a beard.

Shot of the clock: 1:18. Afternoon.

Shots of the old station's iron arcade.

The camera goes through the glass doors. Beyond, leaning against wood tables, clerks work, bending over papers. The lights are on, as at the end of the day.

A hand dipping a pen in the inkwell.

Blotting-paper being used on the books.

An old piece of rail (narrow gauge) serving as a paperweight.

Close-ups of old armoires. Tables with turned legs.

The camera proceeds. It stops suddenly, turns back quickly. It slows down as it approaches the waiting room.

The two men look over papers. There's a bag open on the floor, by the sofa. The camera has stopped at the door. The two men sense the porter's presence. They look at him quickly, surprised. They resume their conversation after realizing it's only an old man.

The porter continues his work. It's very windy now. The switching locomotive is on the patio, moving in reverse.

Close-ups of the cars (preferably, wooden) being hit by the rain; windows closed.

The clock shows 1:48.

A bell rings, sharp, long. The sound continues to reverberate even after it stops ringing. The porter enters the waiting room without looking at the men. The men break off their conversation. The porter realizes one of them has put away a piece of paper. The porter goes into the bathroom.

He stands leaning against the lavatory door. The lavatory is old and filthy. Flies, a bad odor. The man walks to the door, puts his ear against it.

A noise at the door. The porter moves away quickly, hides in one of the lavatories. One of the men, the one without a beard, walks in. He looks carefully around the bathroom, at the closed door.

A quick shot of the porter's apprehensive face. It lasts one second.

The man without a beard leaves.

The porter waits after hearing the door slam. A lightning strike followed by thunder.

The porter crosses the room. The men are sitting apart from each other. The bag is now closed and sits on the table. He glances at it.

The porter walks out onto the platform. A freight train goes by, loudly.

The light between the passing cars casts strange shapes on the platform, at the porter's feet.

The clock is showing 2:05. The camera must always be in such a position as not to focus ostensibly on the clock. Since the clock is in the middle of the platform, any angle that frames it will do.

The porter knocks on the bar door.

Someone opens. He walks in.

A granite counter. Cups of coffee turned upside down on saucers. The bar owner turns a cup up, turns a faucet on the coffee machine. The bar sits in semidarkness.

PORTER: There are two strangers in the waiting room.

BAR OWNER: They must be waiting for the train.

PORTER: Train? The earliest one isn't until 6:30.

BAR OWNER: Maybe they arrived too early. They must be travelers.

PORTER: Do travelers have beards?

BAR OWNER: Why not?

PORTER: I'm not so sure. They were talking, but stopped when I walked in.

BAR OWNER: Stop imagining stuff, Alvaro. You must be tired, you begin your shift very early, and spend the day hammering away at the trains' wheels. Don't go looking for trouble.

PORTER: I don't like the look of those guys. Honest people don't come to the waiting room to chat.

BAR OWNER: Have a cognac. You must be feeling cold. Leave the men alone.

The bar owner walks to the corner, turns off the only light that's on. The two walk out to the platform.

PORTER: Let's walk by the waiting room. Just take a look.

The two walk slowly. The locomotive goes by quickly, and disappears at the end of the patio. Far away, beyond the rails, there is a woman with an umbrella.

The honking of horns coming from the street. The ringing of a bell. Silence.

The porter and the bar owner walk by the waiting room. The two men have pulled some chairs close to the table and are talking in front of a map or something similar.

The porter and the bar owner look at each other. The bar owner shrugs. He now seems apprehensive too, but doesn't want to admit it. The two continue to walk on the platform to a passenger car that's parked. They walk back, but don't look at the room.

At the exit, the bar owner says goodbye. The porter gestures for him to wait, but he leaves.

The porter continues, stops in front of a door: STATION CHIEF. He goes in.

The chief is reading the newspapers. On the table, a coffee pot, some leftover bread, a pack of cigarettes.

CHIEF: What is it, Alvaro?

PORTER: Have you seen the men in the waiting room, sir?

CHIEF: No. I don't watch the platform. What are they doing?

PORTER: Talking.

CHIEF: Since when is talking prohibited?

PORTER: They're very strange.

CHIEF: You're strange. Don't bother me.

The porter leaves. A window in the ticket booth is open. The ticket seller looks out. He sees only the wet, empty lobby, the clock showing 2:18.

The ticket seller opens the ticket-stamping machine. He puts a pile of tickets in the machine, and closes the lid with a thud.

There's no music. The everyday noises in a station, and silence. Voices coming from somewhere. The buzzing from the locomotives' generators.Wheel trucks thumping when the cars touch each other.

The porter crosses over the rails toward the watchman's sentry box. He walks up the steps. He's rather wet.

The watchman is sitting on a stool, smoking. He's middle-aged, and has an air of boredom, apathy.

PORTER: You have to help me.

WATCHMAN: If it's money, I don't have any.

PORTER: It's something serious. It'll require the police.

WATCHMAN: Did you kill somebody? Rob the ticket booth?

PORTER: That's not it. There are two very strange guys in the waiting room. I was suspicious of them and went there. They're planning a robbery, at a bank here in town.

WATCHMAN: Come on, come on, stop acting like a fool. So two crooks come sit down in the waiting room to plan a robbery?

PORTER: They have a bag full of guns.

WATCHMAN: So call the police.

PORTER: Can't you call for me? I'll watch them while you do it.

WATCHMAN: Don't you know I can't leave?

PORTER: The next train isn't coming until 6:30.

WATCHMAN: I've never abandoned the sentry box in twenty-six years. I'm not going to start at my age, just because of your crazy ideas.

The watchman looks at the patio through the foggy windows. He sees the red light turn green. He gets up, pulls on a lever.

Through the window the switching locomotive can be seen moving back and forth.

PORTER: None of you ever cared about me. I've always been ignored. All my life I've walked the line and never got a promotion.

WATCHMAN: Don't start this now. Damn it. On a rainy day like this I want peace. Go take care of your bank robbers.

The watchman looks at the locomotive. He seems fed up.

PORTER: So does that mean you're not helping me?

WATCHMAN: Help you how? Grab a gun, walk over there, and shoot them? Stop pestering me.

PORTER: I'll do everything myself. You'll see.

He climbs down the sentry box steps.

Close-ups of the train yard: car wheels, couplers, a faucet dripping at the edge of the line.

The porter on the phone seen through the bars of the telegram window.

He looks excited. It's necessary to define *excited*. In other words, as excited as a forty-eight-year-old man, worn out, frustrated, single, who lives in one room, eats at the station, is poorly paid, and sees in the situation his opportunity—he doesn't even know of what.

He hangs up, looking unsure.

226

A loud ring at the platform. The clock shows 2:57. The porter walks by the waiting room. The men are still there, each holding a notebook. They seem more agitated. The porter stops in front of the door. The men look up, ignore him, and continue to 'exchange information.'

A cobble-stone street that ends right in front of the station entrance. The street slopes down, then up. The station sits right on top of a hill. A car goes down, turns in front of the station, disappears.

The street is deserted. Two men walk by a corner. A horse-drawn carriage approaches slowly.

The porter, standing in front of the station under an old marquee, looks at the street. Another car comes.

Close-up on the porter's eyes as he waits.

A ring at the platform, loud.

The police paddy wagon comes down the street at high speed. It turns left, drives onto a ramp, stops in front of the station. Four policemen get out. The porter approaches them.

PORTER: I was the one who called.

SERGEANT: What's going on? Where are the men?

PORTER: They're in the waiting room, making plans.

The sergeant pulls his gun.

SERGEANT: Are you sure you heard them talking about a robbery? It wasn't a bomb, was it?

PORTER: They were talking about robbing—I don't know what.

The sergeant walks in to the lobby where the ticket booths are located, followed by the three policemen. The man in charge of telegrams looks through the window. The ticket booth opens.

As the sergeant and the three policemen walk out onto the platform, the station chief leaves his room hurriedly, but very collected, in his frayed suit.

The clock shows 3:26.

CHIEF: What's going on, Sergeant?

SERGEANT: We got a tip about two dangerous men. They're here.

The chief looks at the porter: surprise and reproach.

The sergeant, the chief, the policemen and the porter walk toward the waiting room. The porter, proud, walks a few steps ahead of the others.

The porter appears at the door, a sneer on his face. He can't contain himself.

PORTER: The police are here, pals. It's over.

The two men jump, surprised for an instant. They throw all the papers in the bag and run toward the platform. They pass through the door, grabbing the porter's arm. They are face to face with the sergeant and the policemen. Shoving. The policemen pull their guns.

One of them gets ready to shoot with a heavy pistol.

Right as he shoots, one of the men turns around, positioning himself behind the porter. The shot explodes near the porter's face.

The man lets go of the porter and runs toward the gate. The sergeant and the policemen shoot at the same time. Shards of glass from the bulletin boards, the clock, broken tiles. The station chief shouts, 'Watch out!'

The second man is running in the opposite direction across the railroad yard. At a turn he sees the switching locomotive coming slowly. He jumps on the footboard, tries the door. It opens.

The locomotive approaches. The platform is empty. When the locomotive goes by the lobby, the sergeant and the policemen can be seen getting into the paddy wagon.

The chief returns to the platform where the porter is lying on the floor: pale, trembling. Other employees start to arrive.

The machinist is frightened. The man takes advantage of it, takes over the command of the locomotive, pulls on the lever.

The locomotive takes off. The station remains behind. It crosses the end of the patio, goes under some overpasses, takes the trunk line. Up ahead at a railroad crossing are the paddy wagon, the policemen and the sergeant on the tracks, shooting their machine guns in all their killing power.

All the information says the men were killed on the station platform. But what is reality if not what we most want it to be?"

PLEASURE

Memoirs

The days: fragmented. The nights: organized. The alarm clock set for 2:30 in the morning. Punctual, the beginning of the vigil. Two and a half hours spent contemplating and watching the sleeping town. The feeling that no one else is awake. To think about the town and the people, write the facts behind the walls, compare, take notes. Two and a half hours during which I analyze myself, in order not to despair. Few people know what it means to be exiled in one's own hometown. To speak the same language and not be understood, to try to communicate with others and be looked at as though you're invisible. It's the same as sitting at a table in front of the window trying to understand things. But it's not possible to understand only by looking at the buildings, the church steeples far away, the lights of the streets and squares, first yellowish, now silvery: mercury floodlights. To extract from the walls and stones—still warm from the sun—what they have to say. To relate the houses and streets to the individuals and find the correct equations and formulas. There is a powerful radio or stereo somewhere playing a classical music concert: a violin ensemble, or a solo, flutes and oboes. Like Danilo I was starting to enjoy classical music. We listened to the albums, he commented on the different pieces, showed me the composition's structure, told me the stories he had found in the magazines and books that were piled in his house and tied together with string. There was a shack at the rear of the backyard, sitting between two mango trees, that was Danilo's refuge. He could play his music as loud as he wanted and not bother anybody. Marcelo would also come by, between one and four in the morning. He wouldn't say a word, but would sit down, his head in his hands, looking at a spot on the floor. Motionless, as if he had suffered a cataleptic attack.

Ziza waves at me.

"Have you heard about the prize Múcio was awarded in Italy?"

"I haven't read the paper yet today."

"It was on TV, on the hour-long show."

"My TV isn't working."

(It's a lie. I never bought one. Nancy kept the old TV, I never had money for another one.)

"He said Bernardo is going to write a play especially for him. Isn't it an honor for our town?"

Bernardo is becoming a renowned writer, slowly taking on the respectability of having an established, reputable name. He never risked anything, carefully working his way up. The opposite of Múcio, whose unconventional work is explosive and dazzling. Múcio gambled a lot without any guarantees. He fell very low, and pulled himself back up many times. That's not Bernardo's game. He, a strange guy who in the old times didn't have a penny to pay the bills at Pedro's. Bernardo and Múcio both made it, each one in his own way. I don't know which one I prefer. Múcio's dazzle fascinates me more than Bernardo's patient and calm hustling. Which one has the real talent? Would they still be able to have a conversation today, as when they both lived here? I don't believe Bernardo is writing a play for Múcio. He's a good writer, but conventional, exact, nothing Múcio would want to set on stage. Or would he? What good does it do to be thinking of it here, so far away from them? I've lost contact with them, and see Bernardo only occasionally. There was a deep connection between us: ambition and the desire to leave town.

Bernardo. Why does he return so rarely, unlike the others? What's hidden behind his quiet face and thick eyebrows? It's hard to relate to him, not knowing what he's thinking. There's violence in the sarcastic smile he's always wearing. His twisted, ironic mouth, ready to lash out. I always expect him to attack, but he never explodes. He always seems calm, expressionless. I had a woman friend who hated Bernardo's demeanor, "He's incapable of screaming, and I don't trust anyone who doesn't scream." You get the feeling that Bernardo lives two distinct lives. One doesn't know the other. There's a rebellious, restless Bernardo who represses himself. Why? It took a lot of courage to leave town so indifferently. He didn't even say goodbye to us. He left one afternoon on the 2:45 train. When we went looking for him, his mother said he had moved. Before leaving, he took down everything in his room, the famous refuge that had four Marilyn Monroe movie posters, foreign pennants, collages, magazine clippings, photos. A nice room, where our friends got together and talked. There were some afternoons when Bernardo didn't go to the Municipal Library, but rather stayed home writing his stories or letters. He corresponded with foreigners, had joined an international pen-pal club. At first he met only young girls who wanted to exchange pennants, but later found some intelligent people who were willing to discuss ideas. Bernardo was poor, and the money he got went for books, especially books about the movies. It was sad to see the walls of the room full of tack holes, glue stains, the bed without sheets, the bedding folded in half (why do people fold the bedding

232

in empty rooms?). Bernardo was gone, and it was like he had never existed. Never. How could he have left like that? He rarely came back. Didn't he want to? Or wasn't he able to? Legends surrounded Bernardo, just like the strangest stories circulate about Múcio.

"Is it true you went to Israel in 1966?"

"Me, in Israel?"

"You went to write an article, stayed during the war."

"What did I have to do with that Jewish war?"

"People say you stayed out of idealism, for the thrill."

"Since when am I a thrill-seeker? Where did you hear such things? I shit my pants if I hear a shot."

"You, a coward? You're the most courageous guy I know."

"You know! You know, how?"

"To leave town required courage. To not come back required even more courage. If that's not enough, I'll tell you more. Remember that night when the guys from the cultural center, those little shitty *Integralistas*, turned over the truck where the Communists were holding a rally? Remember how you confronted those guys who came charging with knives and bats in their hands?"

"That was crazy. I was eighteen years old. Today I wouldn't get into another situation like that. That was an adventure, because nothing ever happened in town and at that moment something was happening. It was either then or never! How many times did we talk about that night? Years and years."

"But leaving was brave."

"I left because I had to. Sooner or later things become unbearable. Araraquara had become impossible, as far as I was concerned. I left. And now São Paulo is also reaching that limit."

"And are you going to Europe?"

"I'm coming back to Araraquara."

"And Paris, did you always dream of Paris?"

"I did. It wasn't real. It wasn't true."

"Paris is Paris."

"And a common place is a common place. I visited Paris often enough to realize I have nothing to do there."

"What does this realism get you? This pretentiousness?"

"Who wants to get anything?"

"I don't understand it, but I think you're playing a role, posing. You're pretending."

(Me, saying all this stuff to Bernardo. But he bothers me a little, so sure of himself, with all his integrity. I know it's not real. He wants to humiliate me, acting like, "I've known the whole world and nothing interests me anymore.")

"This is me. You may think what you want."

"I don't believe it. I can't."

"That's your problem."

"It's all very proper, everything in its place, correct. There's something that's not working."

"Do you want to know the truth? I've never been to Israel."

"But I read your article."

"Excellent articles can be written from Paris. What do you think guys from the Brazilian press did? Did they go there to be in the middle of all the shooting? With so many French agencies and magazines investigating everything?"

A conversation as meaningless as one from twenty years ago, with all our friends together at Pedro's. Except at that time they talked about everything and knew nothing, they wanted to rebel and save the world. Today we don't want to save the world. We make excuses for ourselves, because we've lost our capacity to be iconoclasts. It hasn't been renewed, stimulated, it's been compressed under our alleged experiences and clear vision. This is more depressing than anything, more than me not having left: to have lost our aggressive outlook and capacity for irreverence and disrespect—the only way of changing things—because it means not accepting the world as it is or as it has been elaborated, positioned. What saddens me is to have become part of a cheap philosophy and recognize I'm not capable of anything better, to feel impotent to define situations and where I stand. It's as if I were wandering in the desert, walking in circles. I was under the impression Bernardo knew where he stood, but he doesn't. He may know less than the others, because he's in a comfortable position, as if the journalist and the writer owned the world, were its judges and critics. Or maybe I hate Bernardo for having done things I wanted to do and didn't. Shit, how confusing! It must be this beer with gin.

86

Ziza climbs down from the balcony in a hurry. He seems scared, quickly goes up the street, walks into the café. I want to know what's going on. Maybe he picked up somebody and the guy tried to cross the line. Ziza's gone. It's always the same.

"Maria Aparecida and Candinho are going to Europe," he tells me. "They're having a party now. Do you want to go?"

"They don't even know me."

"Everybody's going. One more or one less . . ."

"Those parties are boring."

"They're fun. They have the best parties in town."

"No, I'm going to write."

"Let's go to the party. Don't drink that coffee, no, it's going to leave a bad taste for the whiskey!"

"I don't have the right clothes."

"Nobody pays attention to clothes."

"To walk into that party arm in arm with Ziza, hang out in the garden holding hands. Tomorrow people will talk, not about the party but about the date, which would infuriate Maria Aparecida. Every person in this town who goes to Europe puts on a big public hype. First, dinners for their friends. Then, dinners at their friends'. Finally, the big party on the eve of the trip.

"Have you noticed that more and more people are traveling to Europe? Do you know we've beaten São Carlos? They're ahead in trips to the United States. But you know, it's business trips. It's not like our people, who travel for leisure, and enjoy their money. Wow, how much money there is here! It's that no one shows off. My aunt alone has made more than thirty dresses for this party. There'll be quite a competition. Anyone who doesn't look elegant tonight will be finished for the season. Do you know what I was thinking? Have you imagined Paris full of Araraquarans? Full of them!"

"You should be the Tourism Secretary, Ziza."

His habit of saying, "Do you know . . ." or "Wow" is irritating. If he were a real faggot, it'd be better: flamboyant, letting loose around town. He's a character, but he represses himself, trying to act manly.

Nine o'clock, in front of the flowery arabesques of the iron gates. The doorman gestures for us to wait.

236

"Invitations, please."

He checks a list.

"His name is not here," he says pointing at me.

"You know, we're the nephews of the seamstress. We've come to represent her. Check her name: Olinda Martins."

"It's here."

"It's her invitation. Let us go in."

"Go ahead, go ahead. I'm not going to bother to keep everybody out."

He looks at us with the peculiar disdain of someone charged with a noble mission.

"Fix your *foulard*," Ziza says.

"I've never worn one before."

"Relax your head."

"If I move it comes off."

"You should've put on the silver bracelet."

"It would've been too much, wouldn't it?"

"It's the latest fashion."

The sound of an orchestra playing a rumba was coming from hidden speakers. Floodlights everywhere, fake colonial lampposts.

"What a garden!"

"You haven't seen anything yet."

"For someone who started as a clerk, this is very nice. We can always have hope."

"He loans money to banks now."

"Of course, the bankers lose everything on his gambling tables."

"Don't go around saying that. Candinho isn't a bookie anymore."

"Does his wife still stand at the stove, cooking for the gamblers?"

"Maria Aparecida is among the most elegant of all."

Initially, the mystery was this: how Candinho, a clerk at an accounting office, found a way to pay the monthly dues at the Country Club, the most exclusive in town. People said he gave up eating sometimes so they wouldn't get behind on the payments. On Sundays, Candinho and Maria Aparecida followed the ritual: the elegant eight o'clock movie show, sitting in the right wing. They practically had reserved seats, in the middle, where everybody knew each other. Next they went to the Country Club, to dance all night long, as if desperate to make use of their hard-earned money.

"The sauna, Ziza, I want to see the sauna."

"It's in the back."

"I know everybody, but I don't have any friends here."

"Stop messing around with your *foulard*."

"The scotch, where's the scotch?"

"Look, the waiters. Wait a little. Let's say hello to the hosts."

"What for? I crashed the party anyway."

"To make your crashing official."

Candinho, in black tie, welcomed the guests in front of the bar, shaking everyone's hand.

"Should I kneel down, Ziza?"

"Stop making jokes."

"Do I kiss his hand?"

"Hers. It's very chic."

It was like I was kissing my mother's hand, or my godmother's, for she handed me an envelope. She sensed my surprise:

"It's your number, for the raffle of a piece of jewelry."

"Ah!"

"It'll be tomorrow at breakfast. At eight."

"Yes, yes."

"Make an effort to hang in there."

"It'll be easy at a party like this."

"And write your name on the envelope. We'll send you a postcard from Europe."

"God bless."

I felt like walking away backwards, faced with such royalty.

"Scotch, Ziza. I didn't come here to be kissing hands. I want to get drunk!"

"How rude you are!"

"More than these hicks?" Look at the flags: they have photos of themselves, God. In Paris, Rome, Amsterdam, Athens."

"My aunt said that each lamppost represents a city around the world they're going to visit. Look, the names are painted on."

Outside the house there were flags from the places they were going to visit. Every other year they made the trip, flooding the town with postcards. People got two, three every week. The newspapers received photos: Candinho riding a camel in the Sahara, Maria Aparecida shopping on Via Condotti, the couple dining in a restaurant on the Emerald Coast. The radio station received letters and tapes. And there was also the apotheosis of their return.

"Look, the scotch, wow. You're so distracted."

"I'm looking at the touristy decor."

"They paid two hundred thousand for it."

"I could travel to Europe ten times with that money."

Too much ice and too little scotch. This way anyone can offer a party. Cheap.

"I wonder if they'll bring me a gift when they get back."

"Write your name on the envelope, place it in the box, as you're supposed to. Something will come out of it."

"Will you let me know when they get back?"

"They haven't even left yet."

"I don't want to miss their arrival."

A caravan of VW vans waits at the Viracopos airport, carrying painted banners. Gifts of all kinds appear, from water mattresses to mysterious little cans from which miles-long penises jump out, greeted by laughter.

"Don't they have orgies here?"

"They probably do. Otherwise, why such a large garden? For strolls?"

"You know everything about the town's history. Is it true he copied Florence's gardens? The Medicis' gardens?"

"I think so. Or the Finzi Contini's."

"The Fizi Contini didn't exist. It was a movie."

"That's right."

"I want to explore those labyrinths in the back."

"And me, I want to eat."

Maria Aparecida doesn't cook anymore. However, for more than ten years she was stuck in the kitchen while people gambled in her house all night long. Candinho had found out at the Club that there were complaints about the bar's awful food. He invited a group of people to play in his house. Maria Aparecida prepared a stew, the group grew larger, the house turned into a clandestine casino and then it too expanded. Maria Aparecida managing the kitchen, Candinho taking care of the cards and the drinks. It's said there's a sumptuous basement in the house full of roulette tables, but that sounds more like something from *The Untouchables* movie.

"Look at this!"

"Little gambling machines."

"Slot machines. Wow, I've never seen one before in my life."

"It must be to recover the money spent on the party."

"Refined, the utmost refinement! Slot machines just like the ones in Las Vegas."

"At least Candinho doesn't deny the source of his fortune."

"Deny what? It's common knowledge. This man is an asset for our town. He's fighting for the legalization of gambling and he'll get it. Then Araraquara will have a damn big casino, it'll be in the old Araraquaran Club. He's already bought the building."

"Is that why it hasn't been demolished?"

"Can you imagine? Araraquara and Monaco, the world's gambling centers."

"All it needs is a princess."

"We've already had Brazil's coffee queen."

"And if the gambling law doesn't pass? The military isn't so sure, the Church is against it. The pope has even been banning sex, have you heard?"

"If it doesn't pass, it'll become a restaurant."

"That big?"

"Or a small shopping center."

"Let's get some coins to play a little."

"Do you think I'm going to give my money to these millionaires?"

"I've never tried a slot machine in my life."

"I didn't come to the party to gamble. If I want, the town has all kinds of video-game arcades."

"It's all Candinho's."

"I know it. But I came to eat and get drunk."

"How rude."

"I'm following the general trend."

"You don't like the people here, do you?"

"They are the ones who don't like me!"

"You think you're something. That everybody is concerned about what you're doing."

"Stop being a pain. That's not something to talk about right now."

"I'm going to the lake."

"To catch some fish?"

"To catch something, but not fish."

"See if you get laid tonight."

"There's no use trying. I've dried up."

Black women standing next to wood stoves were serving stroganoff with fluffy rice. I'd give anything to have Nancy here. She would enjoy it. She was happy, danced like nobody else. The orchestra pours out boleros, stops, starts again softly with Glenn Miller. I'm walking around the Club's ballroom, waiting for someone to dance with me, I don't have the courage do ask anybody. Today nobody would pay attention to my face, but in the old times it was different, I scored points. And it hurt to spend the whole dance watching, tired from walking around.

"You here? In a bourgeois party? Has Leftie changed sides?"

Marcelo, called Corvino, I don't remember why, maybe one of

Danilo's jokes. Fat, with his wife and children. His grandfather, a lawyer; his father, a lawyer; his son doing Pre-Law. The family keeps all the diplomas on their office's facade: generations and generations, a judiciary genealogical tree.

"Would you like to sit down?"

"No, I want to go for a walk, see the gardens, the house."

"Go to the sauna. It's incredible. Will you have a scotch with us?"

"I'll come back later."

"Make sure you do."

I don't want to sit down, he doesn't want me to sit down. Courtesy. We have nothing to talk about, absolutely nothing. It doesn't even feel like Marcelo was one of our group. He was a nice guy, even wrote poetry. I can't reconcile the Marcelo who has his diploma under the family's diplomas with the one who got home drunk one night and threw up on his father's feet. Leftie! Shit! Is that what they think of me? And why? On the night of the rally I stood against the *Integralistas*, but that's because I didn't like those people. I didn't like them, personally. A bunch of snooty intellectuals, full of shit. It wasn't because of politics. At sixteen I didn't know anything about politics. Does Marcelo see me that way? We never see each other and when he greets me, I'm Leftie?

"I'll see you later."

"Do you want to get together for a sauna at five in the morning? Then we'll be recovered for the raffle."

"At six."

"At five there'll be fewer people."

"Do you remember when we screwed up the outdoor mass on Largo da Câmara? Tell your wife about that one."

"I don't want to know anything about the trouble you got into when you were single, Marcelo. I've told you a hundred times."

She doesn't even look at me.

"I'll stop by here at five."

"Do it, do stop by."

I hug Marcelo tight, out of spite for his wife. If I'm still standing at five, I'll come by. I want to see the famous sauna, where in the morning people recover from a night of gambling. I've heard incredible things about this sauna, the showers, the pools, massage, the marble they used. Men went straight from the sauna to their offices, arrived fresh and feeling good, better than if they had slept all night.

I walk through a tunnel of small cedar trees, and end up in a clearing decked with flags. There we go. The waiter saw what I did:

"Why did you throw your glass in the bushes?"

"I wasn't paying attention, I'm sorry."

"When you finish your drink, just wait a minute. We're covering the whole grounds."

"On foot?"

"How else could we do it? By plane?"

"Such a huge operation needs some form of transportation."

"It's all divided into sections. Twenty-three waiters for each section."

"So many?"

"And we don't stop moving for one second. It's the liveliest party I've seen."

"Did the waiters come from São Paulo?"

"The food did."

"The food?"

"It was brought in ice-packed containers, like those used in airplanes. Have you seen those? No?"

"Yes, I have. Just like in airplanes. I thought those black women were cooking on the stoves."

Is it in good taste to hold a conversation with a waiter? Or isn't it elegant? What an awful doubt, God!

"The stoves and the black women are for decoration. We hired them."

"Damn, that's a lot of money!"

"These folks in the interior are very rich. And they're not as stingy as the people in São Paulo."

"If Ziza heard this, he'd make fun."

"I'm sorry?"

"I was thinking out loud."

The waiter finds the glass, stands up with dignity, and takes his tray after leaving me another whiskey. I can't decide if it's domestic or foreign. I've been told Candinho was paid big money to serve domestic whiskey. Now I enter a labyrinth of fragrant bushes that seems never-ending. How incredible: it doesn't even feel like I'm in Araraquara. Who knows, maybe I'm not. People have no idea what a revelation this is. Waltzes explode, echo through the foliage. Being in a foreign place is like this: not being able to recognize anything, even the smells, to lose the comfort of familiarity, to enter the insecurity of the unknown.

"Are you lost?"

"Clarice?"

"Do you know me? How come?"

"Who in town doesn't know you?"

"That's right, I'm famous. Clarice Party-Girl, isn't it?"

"I didn't say that, only Clarice."

"But you thought it."

What a beautiful woman. Some people disagree. I like her long body very much, and the defiant attitude she shows. I always have the feeling she's sniffing the air, trying to find something out through her sense of smell. Clarice is rich, even though the rumor is that her father has disinherited her. I don't believe it. She's still living in their house.

Her hair is curly, hippie style, fashionable for a twenty-year-old girl, and it's becoming on Clarice, who must be thirty-six. She looks at me and caresses her neck with her left hand.

"I'm not lost. Just walking around, then I'll be leaving."

"So soon?"

"I've seen everything there is to see."

"But there'll be much more."

"Oh, yes? What?"

"Dinner, desert, dance, a samba school, magicians, maybe even a strip-tease."

"Strip-tease?"

"If one of these crazy women is brave enough to do what she's thinking."

"Never."

"Mariazinha Peixoto has guaranteed she'll take her clothes off at dawn, all she needs is to get high."

"To get drunk."

"To get high, really, dude."

The "dude" sounded strange. Do you know when a word doesn't fit someone? As if it were a foreigner talking. Clarice was forcing it, using young people's slang, and she didn't have to.

"If that's so, I'll wait. Because it's very boring."

"It's not boring. This is just the way parties are. What did you expect?"

"I don't know. I guess, nothing."

"So? What's up? It's really very funny."

"What?"

"People, turning up their noses. Making fun of Candinho's parties. Tell me, who has ever held a party like this? No one. Have you noticed there are all kinds of people here? Rich, poor, ugly, beautiful, whores and honest people? Everything's cool, right, everybody having fun. What do they want? Nothing ever happens around here, and when it does, people turn up their nose. Like you."

"It's just that I don't like parties."

"When I don't like something, I don't do it. There!"

"You're right. That's why I'm leaving."

"Stay. It'll get better."

"Think so?"

"Hell, it'll get better for the two of us!"

"For the two of us?"

Clarice threw her arms around my shoulders and glued her lips to mine. She smelled like alcohol and pot, and her face was slightly damp with sweat, clear sweat smelling like flesh, and that aroused me. How I had wanted this to happen twenty years earlier, when Clarice drove her car around, the only Cadillac in town, to pick up men on the streets, anyone, especially if he was from out of town. Was that true or not? I could ask her now. But what does it matter? If it's true it'll validate my frustration. If it isn't, what does it help? Will it serve as consolation? Consolation for what? Is it time to be thinking about these things? Not one man here wanted to marry Clarice, in spite of her money. Her brothers-in-law got rich. The only thing they had to do was give their sons, as their family name, the old man's name. Because he only had daughters, and wanted to see his name continue on. They all accepted it. The old man is paralytic. Politicians visit him, particularly those who need money. There was a book that told his story, but it's very rare, out of print, the police confiscated it as soon as it was published in 1946. The old man had people buying every single copy. He burned every one he could get his hands on.

Until recently they had a house in Rome, his daughters spent summers there. That's what I envied, and that was the distance between us: those five girls in the José Bonifacio Street mansion weren't normal, they weren't ordinary Araraquarans. They were out of reach, legendary.

She's pressing her whole body, glued to me, shaking. And I'm distant because I can't stop thinking. My damned head, wretched memories. Here's Clarice, she finally has picked me up, it doesn't matter that it's taken twenty years. When you live near someone, they don't seem to get old. For me it's the same Clarice in her Cadillac, the one who lost her virginity behind the stadium bleachers while everybody watched the game. Now I'm feeling it, I pull her, squeeze her arms, grab her breast, and my tongue twists around hers, and I bite her sweaty neck, sweat mixed with fresh perfume.

I try to open her dress, but she's faster: the dress is already on the ground. She doesn't wear a bra, never has, since she was a girl, even in her school uniform. Her small breasts protruding, we used to surround her in the patio and hated it when the bell rang for classes to start. Inaccessible and mythological Clarice, who leaves me with an uncomfortable feeling: I know nothing about you, except for what people say, have said for twenty years. What is true and what isn't? Doubt holds me back a little, but the excitement contained for so many years finally overcomes me. We roll on the lawn, under cedar trees that entwine, forming an arbor with a star sitting on top —an exact reproduction of the one at Largo da Matriz. A speaker nearby pours a cascade of sound: "Hernando's Hideaway." It was the opening song at the Club's Sunday dances, but she probably won't remember it. I'm the only one who cares about these things. Me: stuck in time, pensive, stagnant. People who really live don't keep so much inside, they always let go, add, renew themselves daily. I live off subtractions. Someone like me never adds, just takes away.

"Give me more, but don't take it out. How can you last so long?"

"Did I last long?"

"Wonderful. The kids here are like roosters."

I brag, "Experience, Clarice, simply experience. And because I enjoy it."

"No, don't take it out!"

"I'm tired. I'll lie down next to you."

"Stay where you are. Lie down on top of me. Go ahead, you're skinny."

I relax my body. I was tense, my arms and legs hurt. Relax. I hadn't let myself go like this for a long time. It's not only the weight of my body she's holding. This time it's all the weight of the anguish I had repressed. I need you, Clarice, I need you a lot. That book wasn't only about her father. It talked about all of President Getúlio's depravities. Only two or three pages were about the old man, including his name, documents and testimonies.

"What are you thinking about?"

Always the same question. Always. We're thinking, looking up, recalling how good it was, and the question comes up, "What are you thinking about," loaded with a tone of mistrust, as if the next minute we were going to leave and never come back.

"About you."

"Liar."

"I swear."

And it's true. In a sense, to think about the sacks of coffee her father sold in Italy below the legal market price is to think about her. The town found out and forgot it, or decided to forget. Or it was convenient to forget. Or else, people forget everything anyway, for their own reasons. It's been more than forty years ago, in 1936, the old man was Getúlio's friend. I don't know why. Maybe the fact he was from Rio Grande do Sul helped.

"What were you thinking about me?"

"I've wanted you. You have no idea for how long!"

"How long?"

"Twenty years."

"Liar."

"I swear."

"Twenty years? How cool. Twenty years, really?"

"Really. I've always been crazy about your legs. Do you remember when the kids hung around you during recess? Everybody kept staring at your little breasts."

"They did? I don't remember. I'll tell you something. I don't care if you tell people. At that time I was interested in Sylvinha. She always hung out with me, remember? A little brunette who lived in the Carmo district. She killed herself in a sanitarium."

"Sylvinha was a real knockout."

"I thought so too. She never wanted anything to do with me. I tried all my life, even after she got married."

"Is that why she killed herself?"

"Nobody knows. She was very complicated."

"She didn't look it. Her face was so peaceful."

"Sylvinha didn't want to live in Araraquara. She wanted to move to Rio, do something with her life, find a good man. She ended up with an itinerant salesman who owns a store now. She didn't want children, or a comfortable home, but the guy did."

The orchestra starts up a rock song. Clarice pulls me.

"Now. With this song."

We're sweating and sticky. It smells like grass, honeysuckle and sex, and this violently arouses both of us. She screams and the speakers muffle her screams. I've never heard anybody scream like this.

"Let's finish together with the song."

"I'm not there yet."

"Take your time, take your time, but finish with the song."

"You want more, you want more!"

"Yes. Music, keep going. Orchestra, keep going. Play, play nonstop. I love music, I love a party. I go crazy at parties. Give me more. Push harder, push harder!"

She screams, screams so much I get a little scared. The music is only halfway through and I'm almost coming. I think about the old man. He got thousands of sacks of coffee from Getúlio to hand out in Italy, as advertising. One of the Department of Coffee directors who didn't want to go along lost his job, which shows the old man's influence, his inexplicable power. Obviously the coffee wasn't handed out, but sold at a price that was much below normal. It was dumping. But what the old man wanted was money, and he made so much he even bought a house in Rome and in Viareggio. He didn't have to do it again. A single deal was enough. Later he invested his money and, for as long as Getúlio was in power, it multiplied, thanks to the information on the financial markets he kept receiving. People say there was a permanent direct phone line between the house on José Bonifácio and the Catete Palace, something that's never been confirmed or denied. If only he had the courage to open up, to write his memoirs! If he knew times have changed. But he can't now, he had a stroke and suffers from Parkinson's.

"Like that, dear, hold it. Hold it a bit. Wait for your Clarice to come. Let's come together. Together, when the song ends. No, no. Hold it. Wait for the song. Wait."

She stays still for a second, as if she had fainted. Then she violently pushes me off of her.

"I asked you to wait for the song to end."

"I couldn't hold it anymore."

"And I didn't come, okay?"

"I did what I could. I wanted you to come."

"You don't know how to do it. You still have a lot to learn. Few people here know."

"Is that why you pick up guys from out of town?"

"Maybe it is. You got it!"

"I can try to learn, if you teach me how you like it."

"Me? Teaching an old guy?"

"We're practically the same age, Clarice."

"But look at me and then look at yourself. I take care of myself, but you're screwed up."

"You get tough when you don't come, don't you?"

"Is there anything worse? I'll have to find another guy tonight, now. And it won't be easy here at the party because in a little while everybody will be drunk. I know: in the sauna. It's very nice inside, in the middle of the steam."

"Can you do that?"

"You haven't been to Candinho's sauna yet?"

"I've just heard of it."

"You've never been here to gamble?"

"I don't play."

"Not even once, out of curiosity?"

"Only canasta, but not for money."

"You can't fuck right, you don't gamble, and don't smoke."

"I drink."

"Everybody here does. That's nothing special. It's unbelievable how much they drink. What about pot?"

"Once in a while. I don't have the money to keep buying it."

"It's good for your health. And it helps if you live in this town, it helps a lot. Whenever you need some, get in touch with me. But don't call my house. I have some cool friends."

"Listen. I've heard this several times. Who knows, maybe you've heard it too: they're saying the police are out to get you."

"I know. But I'm discreet. It's ridiculous. So many people smoke. Why me?"

"Because arresting someone insignificant won't do any good. They want to arrest a big fish to teach everyone a lesson. You'd better watch out. By arresting someone big they'll show they're ready for anything."

"How much do you think my father will pay to set me free?"

There's one town I don't know, or don't know any longer. A new one inside the one I experienced. Transplanted. It might even have buried my old one. That's why I can't find Araraquara. It's as if it were Atlantis. Not that I want to know it. As time goes by we're naturally excluded from things. Or we let ourselves be excluded. I never expected to pick up Clarice Party-Girl. Or maybe I've expected it all this time. Everybody here in town does. It's like when someone wins the lottery: everybody gets happy waiting his turn. Except that the prize was less rewarding than it was promised to be, I can't explain why.

"If you want, you can go around telling everybody you've fucked me."

"I'm not going to tell."

"But you can. Just nobody will believe you."

"I won't, I swear!"

"I'm saying, you can. Do it"

"I don't understand. It's like you want me to tell."

"I do, of course I do. I'm saying it again!"

"Why?"

"God damn it, you men want an explanation for everything!"

"Okay, then I'll tell."

"But there's one thing: no one will believe a piece of shit like you has fucked me."

Did I really come? Or did I just resolve a long-standing doubt? I've been obsessed with Clarice for too many years. What if moving to São Paulo had been just another obsession? An obsession that would end up exploding like a balloon. From now on it won't be as fun to look at Clarice. I won't be dreaming of the glorious day when I'll pick her up.

"I was looking for you. You disappeared."

Marcelo, with one of his kids. A limping boy who'd had polio. If a doctor had seen him in time, he would have been cured. I don't know the story exactly, it had something to do with a doctor who had moved out of town. Or maybe it wasn't polio, it was an accident. Is this the time to think about it?

"What were you doing? Look at your face!"

"Fucking Clarice Party-Girl."

"Clarice?"

"Do you believe it?"

"Yes. And you'll get gonorrhea."

"Why?"

"She fucks everybody. She's got to have diseases. She isn't picky. With so many good-looking women at the party, you had to pick up that old rag?"

"Who's old? She's younger than us!"

"Are you out of your mind? She's been around a lot. She's almost fifty. Her father is going to send her to a clinic. She's really gone mad, can't keep it quiet anymore, picks up men anywhere. She's even taken them to her house."

Marcelo, the bastard, he had to spoil everything. Why? Why?

"I wanted to tell you I'm not going to the sauna."

"Why? I was coming to get you, so we could go sooner. The party's kind of boring."

"My wife wants to go home. She's got a headache."

"You know what you've got to do. I'm not going by myself either. I don't feel comfortable, I've never been to a sauna."

"Whenever I have an opportunity to have fun, my wife comes down with a headache. Right on schedule! She can't stand any of my old friends. I wanted to invite one or two of you, or everybody, to have dinner at my house. Or have one of our get-togethers, with lots of wine. Wouldn't it be nice to get everybody together again in Araraquara? But she doesn't want to. And if she finds out there'll be a party she won't let me go."

"Does she boss you around?"

"It's not a matter of bossing me. You know, you've been married. Marriages are complicated. Sometimes we have to make concessions."

"I ended mine for that reason."

"But I don't have the courage to end mine. And I like her."

"No, you don't. You've just gotten used to the situation."

"How do you know?"

"We all end up adapting, Marcelo. And you can't break up like that, suddenly. You're the great lawyer of families, of businessmen."

"There's some of that too, of course there is. And it's different with Marina. You know her father: the old man's family received a land title from the Portuguese king at the same time as the town's founder. But that's not the problem. I don't want to break up with anybody, I'm fine, I'm really fine."

"You think you are!"

"At least I'm better off than you."

"You think you are. I beat you in one thing: I'm my own boss."

"Boss? Do you know who you are? You're the town weirdo. You. Everybody calls you weird. Always depressed, annoyed, angry, mad. I'll tell you: My kids are afraid of you. My sixteen-year-old daughter gets scared when you stop by to talk, disheveled, unshaven, your curly hair a mess. You don't even take care of yourself anymore."

"Go home with your wife, go. Go, fatso."

"You've always had a bad temper, you don't like anything, you can't have fun with anything. You're unhappy."

"You're the unhappy one, tied to this town's skirt. Not me, I do what I want."

"I bet you hate the party."

"I do. I'm leaving."

"You never like any place. Nothing is ever good. You'd go from here to there, and say it's just as shitty over there. You haven't changed."

"I'm consistent."

"Or backward."

"I've changed. You're the ones who've stayed behind."

"You're a failure."

"And you're a piece of shit."

"An old rag fucker. It's the only thing you can get."

I jump at Marcelo, hit my head against his nose. He falls on his back, more from the surprise than from the impact. I'm skinny and he's fat. He rubs his bleeding nose. The limping boy is crying. Marcelo gets up and throws his arm with all his strength against my chest. I can't catch my breath. And now? There's no time to think, he hits me again, on my Adam's apple, I feel like I'm suffocating, it's horrible, I try to jump to one side, but he kicks me. The limping boy is crying, standing in front of me, I push him. How can I get out of here except by running? And I do. Marcelo won't be able to catch me with all his flab. And he doesn't even try. I look back: he's walking away holding his son's hand, the other hand on his face. I lose myself in the gardens, in the labyrinth of bushes. I need to find an exit. I still have part of the night ahead of me. I keep walking, always followed closely by "Siboney" on the speakers. And I exit onto a large clearing behind the orchestra. Everyone's dancing, lively. I get a whiskey, and drink it in one gulp. I sit down at a table. I don't know who's sitting there, the plates are still on the table. There's a bottle of pink champagne. I drink it. I move to another table, and another.

"This party is divine. Now the samba school will come out. Come dance the samba."

"What samba, Ziza? If I try to get up I'll fall."

"What's this blood? Is it the *foulard*?"

"I had a fight."

"With who?"

"I don't know, it was dark."

"There's all kinds of stuff happening at this party."

"Nothing is happening."

"Look, look. The Portela samba school. Portela in Araraquara, the whole school. Only that crazy Candinho would be able to do this."

It may not be the whole school, but there's a hell of a lot of people. They're coming up the main alameda lined with acacias, the wide avenue leading up to the mansion. An endless stream of people. Ziza climbs up on the table, pushes the plates and glasses aside with his feet, and dances the samba.

"Climb up, climb up. Come. Look, everybody is doing it."

I climb up.

"Let's break everything."

He starts to throw plates on the ground, glasses, silverware. Others accompany the beat with forks and bottles. Full and empty bottles, champagne glasses explode on the ground. Tons of tables gone mad. Okay, now. I pick up a chair and smash it against the table, and my gesture is being repeated everywhere. I push Ziza who's dancing the samba and continues to dance on the ground, as if in a trance. I turn the table over, grab a bottle of whiskey from the tray of a waiter who's watching everything, frightened. I'm taking the bottle home. Shove it, Candinho. Women run by on the lawn, kind of dancing, kind of running away.

MUSCLES

Memoirs

Things get worse at six-thirty in the evening. That's when you find yourself standing at the window completely alone. There's nothing to see, not one soul, the theater is closed. There's no one in the café either, except the cashier. It's dinnertime, people don't go out, the café comes back to life after eight, but not every night. I'm tired from trying to remember. It takes effort to reconstruct a memory.

Such reconstitution is valid when it's possible to re-establish all aspects of a situation: colors, smell, mood and dimension. When the recollection is interrupted, that's when we realize how useless our memories are. You may enjoy it, and find consolation in this retraction, but you find yourself in this same situation when you return. Nothing has changed, except inside yourself, as you become sour and disenchanted. So that, when sitting at the window, at six-thirty, you feel like those old women who lean out the window to look at who's passing by and then talk to the neighbors.

Except that old women don't sit at the window anymore. They stay in their living rooms, immersed in TV, their opaque eyes lit by the bluish metallic rays.

At this moment a feeling of power invades me: it's up to me to re-institute healthy customs and traditions in this town. I could put my chair on the sidewalk and wait for people to bring their chairs too, to talk. They wouldn't, and would think I'm even crazier. They might even forbid me to stay in my chair. This is a busy main street, they'd say I'm disturbing everybody. Maybe they'd allow me to stay behind the gate, locked up. Everybody would call me the "Third Street Madman," ridiculed by the people standing in line at the theater. Although it's been a long time since this theater saw any lines. I'm afraid the renovation will begin soon. Yesterday they were taking pictures of the building. I don't know why anyone would take pictures, maybe it's for the last news report they'll do about it. They should interview me, I've been attending the Paratodos for twenty-two years. I know everything: I saw the French movies on Mondays during the 1950s, the science fiction movies, the serials, almost screwed an old faggot in the balcony, Ziza Femmina's predecessor. I wonder if I can use the word "faggot." With all the censorship these days the newspaper would never publish it. But *Pasquim* uses that kind of language. I would have to say "homosexual." Or pederast. Or sexual deviant. It's better to forget that old man's story. He was a desperate loner, marginalized, condemned by all. He walked on the street close to the walls, practically against them, and never went downtown. He left the balcony and ran into the darkness of São Paulo Avenue.

Now it's time to read the newspapers I bought in the morning, and arranged on the table: four from São Paulo and two from Rio. I read them with suspicion. They want me to believe their information. I could very well believe it. I think: this is the information they want me to have. And why only this and not other news? I gradually stop knowing what's going on in many areas; I forget they exist. I forget about the people who say and declare just because they have something to say and declare. I've come to accept only channels of information that reach me directly, however greatly distorted. Every day, reading these newspapers, I have the impression I'm in a foreign country. They talk about a reality I don't see around me. When they report, I can't recognize what they're saying, I can't read their language, it's foreign. But I try, nevertheless. After trying I find out I'm getting used to the distortion, almost to the point of accepting it as truth. If I continue, I'll get to the point where I'll recognize in it my own truth.

88

Once every two weeks I go up Fifteenth Street and stand in front of our house. I don't know who lives there now. I see the house as it was before, when we bought it, Nancy and I. And who we were then. We didn't grow inside this house. We moved in and pretended we were living. We seeped away slowly, thinking we were enough for each other. For us, living was the reassuring day-to-day life: going to work, lunch, coming back home in the afternoon, the warm bath, the smell of Gessy soap invading the hallway, the lights off in the back of the house, the quiet living room, the radio (and later the TV), clean sheets, the dark bedroom, the street noises quieting down, waking up at dawn. Waiting for the noises to start over, the man from the bakery bringing the bread, the clinking of the milk bottles against the door, the neighbors' voices. To get up, boil water, shave, make coffee, the warm bath, the smell of Gessy soap invading the hallway. The table set, the red-checkered tablecloth through Thursday, the blue one from Thursday through Saturday, and, on Sunday, the flower-printed one. The coffee kept warm in a pan with hot water, the milk that sometimes got burned, the potato bread, canned (*Aviação*) butter, sweet crackers, hard-boiled eggs. You have a single white hair, either you dye it or pull it out, the neighbors, the barber closing his shop. The cicadas in the trees (where? invisible), Nancy watering the plants, the delivered newspaper never read, the warm bath, the pajamas, a slight smell of soap dying out in the hallway, hot soup (winter), potato salad (summer), potato bread, steak, tomatoes, rice, lights out, the TV, the covers, the white chamber pot, young men walking by at three in the morning making noise, back from a ball (at the time when balls existed).

Something was lacking. We felt a great void in every corner of the house. And we started to fill it with objects, until the house began to look like a strange warehouse, a small bazaar with a unique combination of items: dishes, towels, figurines, vases, pictures made of butterfly wings, framed prints, rosaries, images of saints, calendars.

Calendars: she didn't pull off the pages, nor did she let anyone else. There was one or two in every room that she chose from among the ones we received free at the end of the year from the baker, the grocer, the barber, the store clerk. Or that she bought at church, since she was a devout follower of the Sacred Heart. She chose it for the picture, and the calendar always showed the first of the year, a huge 1 in red, the Universal Day of Fraternization. As the months went by, the red began to fade and looked almost pink by the end of year, the paper yellowing.

"We don't need days, we don't need months. Time belongs completely to us. We don't have to mark the passage of time. What for, what good does it do, to know what day it is today, or what month? It's better to live a long, endless day, so that we end before it does." It didn't sound like her, a quiet woman, she never said anything. She accepted what happened, and just showed irritation or disagreement by scratching below her eye. The place she scratched became slightly wrinkled and her eye closed a little, which stretched its ends, like a Japanese person's eye.

THE WIRE VEGETABLE GARDEN

Every Sunday morning, while other men got together at the bar on the corner or went out to the field, he stayed in the yard, turning the soil. The yard was thirteen square feet, the most provided by the management of the apartment complex. There he grew lettuce, beets, and collard greens.

That morning, using the rake, he felt something grabbing onto the tool's tines. He pulled hard, but it resisted. He squatted and noticed silver threads coming out of the soil. They were wire, new wire. When he had turned the soil in order to fertilize it, he had dug deep without finding anything. Besides, old wire should be rusty. He tried to pull the wire. It was firmly secured. He found some pliers, but wasn't able to pull much. He dug. The wire went several feet deep in the soil. He dug some more. How could someone have done something like this overnight? Worrying about the garden, he stopped his investigation. He watered his seeds a little, wondering whether the wire would hurt the germination process.

The next day he got up very early to take a look. The wire had grown. There were four-inch-high sprouts in the three vegetable beds: little wires, tall, lively, strong. Could it have been the wrong pack of seeds? Wire seeds?

At night the wire seemed to have stopped. The same the next day. Weeks went by, and the vegetable seeds didn't sprout. Only the wire grew, and spread. It was sprouting all over the yard. His wife complained: she couldn't hang clothes on the line, the wires pricked her.

He requested help from the nursery. It took months. When the expert showed up, the wire was tall. The bushes twisted around one another. The expert had never seen anything like it. He advised the man to stick rods next to each plant, otherwise harvesting would be difficult. "But who wants to harvest wire?" the man asked. "I want to get rid of it." "We don't have any poison for that," the expert said. "We can exterminate ants, aphids, burr, all kinds of pests, but not wire," he said, taking notes in a small black notebook. "Not wire. You're going to have to harvest it. And I would like to know how it turns out."

The wire twisted around the rods, and within two months the man was able to harvest rolls and more rolls of a special kind of stainless steel wire. "You'll have a great market for this," his friends said.

He piled the harvest in a corner of the living room, his wife complaining. And complained more when he wasn't able to sell any at all, despite stopping by every household. A month later the wire was growing again in his yard.

Another harvest came: piled in the living room. His wife said, "I'll throw everything away." She didn't. The harvested wires kept piling up. The plants were fertile, producing wire monthly. The house filled up.

In the small house, 164 square feet, the maximum allowed, there was no room to keep the stock. The man began to distribute it around his neighborhood in the afternoon, after getting off work. He expanded the door-to-door distribution to the whole town. He advertised in the newspapers. Farmers had it sent to them. Hundreds of trucks jammed the street. The neighbors couldn't stand it. They drew up petitions.

Various city governments accepted the wire in order to fence in the counties. The state government did too. And the federal government used up the harvest of several months. Until the day when the whole country was fenced in.

Impenetrable fences made up of eighteen wires. The stores that sold wire complained, and started legal actions. Soon the city inspectors came with notices and court orders.

And taxes, on this and that. The Ministry of Finances talked about the market being saturated, about exports. Global prices took a dip. In the yard, the wire grew, twisting upon itself. The trash collectors refused to take the rolls, they didn't know where to put them.

The city prohibited its manufacture. He said he couldn't do anything, the wire grew by itself. The inspectors laughed, and didn't even want to look for themselves. "Nothing grows by itself." He began receiving fines and more fines.

Fines for illegal manufacturing, for failure to register, for sales without invoices. The (good) stores in that line of business won in the courts: it was dumping. He had to pay them compensation. The court ordered him to stop production. The market price for wire fell to zero. The man went out at night on his own, to throw the wire out into empty lots, in the farthest neighborhoods in town. His wife didn't want to bother. She just wanted the yard back.

The man stopped harvesting the wire. It grew, all twisted, fell onto the neighbor's yard. It grew everywhere, climbing up the fences and walls of other houses.

The neighbors complained: the wire damaged the walls. Police intervention became necessary. He cut the wire, brought healers in. Two weeks later the wire was growing strong.

It grew under the house, climbed like a vine, sprouted on the sidewalk, made the asphalt split. One morning, stepping out onto the yard, the man understood. Using a broom handle, he picked his way through the wire.

He walked through the threads of wire. They were still young, and gave way easily. The man let himself be enveloped by that wire forest. He kept walking, further and further toward the center, until it became impossible to go back.

He was lost—and happy. No one would find him there. The others would be afraid of penetrating that forest, where the afternoon heat was overwhelming, but the nights were cool and pleasant. And he wouldn't die from hunger either.

On the very first day he found some small silvery insects. He also discovered that the new wire sprouts were soft and thin. He found that in the center of the forest there was a kind of thick wire, and at the bottom of the plant there lay some water bulbs. During the day, the sun that penetrated through the dense foliage of stainless steel wires produced reflections and patterns. The wind shook the wires which, rubbing against each other, produced sounds.

Sounds and forms that distracted Danilo during the long trip he had begun.

OLD AGE

Memoirs and Facts

As the sun came up on the second Wednesday of the month, the participants waited at the station, ready to board. They were leaving for a party, but there was silence and emotion, and more than that, tension. I attended many departures for the Railroad Games and found the solemn mood curious. The party was for those who were staying: a noisy crowd tossing firecrackers, blowing whistles, carrying portable radios.

By that time the line had already been shut down, but the tracks were still there. Ten years later they were removed. People say it was because of the Railroad Games that it took so long for the tracks to be destroyed. The Games began on the second Wednesday of October and continued through the last Wednesday, under the burning sun. On the day of departure, before the sun comes up, all the families open their windows and bring out the most beautiful piece of fabric they have: a rug, tablecloth, sheet or tapestry. On top of it they place a vase with gladioli or roses. I've never seen any rose or gladiolus of the color and size found in the town gardens. The participants' families light a lamp.

If the person died or disappeared at the Games, the lamp was extinguished. People would come and light candles in the middle of the street, in front of the house, and cry together. The dead person's family would serve hot coffee, despite the heat, or soft drinks and cakes. They sing the dead person's favorite songs, tell stories about him, and all contribute toward the purchase of a coffin. Because the Games were the town's pride and glory, those who didn't participate contributed in some way, either toward the survivors' prizes or the burial of the dead. They believed the pain would be shared if all cried together. The family felt their sorrow minimized.

As children, we grew up with the myth of those Games, their beauty and violence. As difficult as chess, they demanded intelligence, reasoning, talent for the plays, and precision in every move—the precision of a computer. Taking part in the Games was the most important thing. Those who competed put up plaques on their doors. When they walked into the theater, the Club, the church, or when they passed by on the street, you could feel their pride. You could practically smell it, that's how strong a participant's presence was. The winners, then—with the white-tooth necklaces they wore at parties, dances at the university or at the Tennis Club, and on parade days—were the kings.

I remember standing in front of their houses for hours, waiting for them to come out so I could see the way they walked, moved their arms, lifted their heads, smiled and looked. They never saw me. The winners only looked up. So high up they never saw children or dogs. I grew up with two ambitions: to have a job and to participate in the Games, two things as difficult as becoming president, or as unlikely as poor people going to school, or as impossible as me leaving my exile.

Only a select few could compete for the tooth necklaces: members of the Tennis Club, the Nautical Club or the Golf Club; people with money, power, prestige, or all three. The others could get in as the audience, to applaud, as secondary elements to create the mood, the noise. There were so many requirements to participate in the Games, sometimes it took a young person years to cultivate the necessary qualities and accumulate all the proper accessories. If the parents had influence, he would be admitted into the circle in less than a year.

Clothes, weapons, flags, servants, cars, boots, and the gold wires to string the teeth. No, it wasn't easy. The rich kids had shooting instructors, got their weapons when they were still little, had trainers, strategists, employees, assistants, and advisors. Even so most returned dead, disappeared, or lost all their teeth. I know poor kids who moved up and were able to participate in the Games. They can't tell me anything: they didn't come back alive. And we were aware of that because all recourses are used in the Games, and there is no loyalty, no honesty, there are no rules, just total freedom of life and death over the other.

We were kids and pretended to play the Games. We made up our own Railroad Games, playing on the tracks, in the abandoned stations, in empty warehouses, in rotting railroad cars. We shaped rudimentary teeth out of plaster stolen from construction sites, strung them with twine and paraded around the neighborhood. My father (what a curious thing: I remember very little of my father; he was a resentful man, always wanted to move away) beat me every time I came back from playing—he knew I had been pretending to play the Games. "This is a disgrace. It's got to stop one of these days."

The Games were the opportunity the poor had to eat. I was among those who had enough to live on, maybe we were a little worse off than that. At home, sometimes there wasn't any food. I went out asking around the neighborhood, I could always get a bowl of soup. At six o'clock in that town every household had bean soup with small star-shaped macaroni noodles. While the Games were going on we went out around the streets, stopped in front of the windows of the player's houses waiting for news of some death, and were happy when the lights were turned off. Immediately we started to cry, sitting on the curb, waiting for the coffee and cake. If it was a rich house, a plaintive crowd stood outside. And the rich didn't serve just coffee, but also tea, milk, beer, wine, fine sandwiches, buttermilk cookies, crackers. And if it were one of the rich people from the most luminous districts, ham and cold cuts would be served in abundant quantities.During the months preceding the Games, the distributors' trucks constantly came into town bringing all kinds of things, some never seen before, some things we didn't even know what they were. And we would remain ignorant, for we weren't invited into those houses. The trucks stopped, the men got out carrying strange-looking crates. The kids were kept at a distance.

Food. We knew it was food because of the strong smell. In September the city was overwhelmed by the aroma of meats, baking bread, and ground coffee. So strong it overpowered even the fragrance of honeysuckle. It was horrible if we were hungry: our stomachs turned, our mouths watered. Everything that was brought into the houses would be used, whether the young men came back as winners or dead. We hoped they would die, that was the only way we'd eat better during those weeks. Many of my friends didn't eat anything at home. Their mothers didn't prepare anything. They dressed in their Sunday best and went out looking for the dead from the Games.

And there was plenty of food, we could even take some home.

It made up for the frustration of not competing. One of the rules was that nobody could be denied food. They had to feed everyone.

No matter how big the crowd, everyone should get something because they were all crying together. The bigger the crowd, the more the sorrow was shared. There were cases when the family didn't feel anything, after having shared their pain with two, three thousand people.

Days of sun, abundance, dances on the squares, smells, drunk people on the streets, cars racing by, full of young women in ethereal (were they ethereal?) white dresses. The Club had the orchestra playing on the street the day the winners returned, stumbling, their heads held high, looking up and stepping on dogs and children. The more they fell, the prouder the winners felt, the more they were applauded. Many looked directly at the sky, always, always, always—even when talking to the people.

A holiday was declared. Nobody bothered with anything. The mayor had the ice-cream parlors give out free ice-cream, the orange juice factory handed out small cans in the poor neighborhoods (the empty cans got made into mugs), the bells tolled all the time, the factories blew their sirens. The chamber of commerce held contests among the kids and hired the ones who screamed the loudest. It formed the Screaming Kids choir, gave them uniforms, held rehearsals in preparation for the return.

There was tension during those weeks. Who would come back alive, who would come back dead? The trains left. The day of silence came, everybody stayed home. They could only go out three days later, to make bets, comment, wait for some news.

The news arrived by the end of the first week. I don't know who brought it, but everybody talked, the news spread by word-of-mouth, the radio gave a report, the newspaper reprinted it, the loud-speaker system gave bulletins, with Pedro Schiavon's and Cesar Brasil's voices echoing over the *footing* along the Roses Esplanade.

The dead arrived the second week, sent from various stations. They came with their mouths sealed: a yellow ribbon around the mouth held by a lead seal, the kind used on the doors of railroad cars. Specialists from the Railroad were hired to do the seals. An uncle of mine, who had sealed car doors for many years, participated in many Games.

The only thing he ever told us was that the bodies arrived ready. He just had to place the ribbon around the mouth and put the seal on. Nothing else. In a small notebook he noted the dead man's name, delivery and departure times. Once he tried to look inside one of their mouths and lost his job. He had to go into exile. He thought he'd find the identity of the winner inside, the same person who had pulled the dead man's teeth to string them through the gold wire.

With time, as I grew up, I began to understand there was nothing bloodier and more savage than these primitive Games. I started to investigate why. It was necessary to have a very strong reason that would lead generation after generation to think only about themselves, in spite of all the risks, of one's own life.

The losers preferred to kill themselves. Either that or they fought to the very end to preserve their teeth, the teeth that would be raised and shown to the crowd in the sunny afternoon of the great parade. Teeth that sparkled on the gold necklaces, as a symbol of their great victory—a prize, medal, a crown of laurels. I have the feeling the Railroad Games changed my life. Because of them I fought against the town. From that point on, I began to be curious about humankind's essential nature. That's when I felt there was something wrong, one afternoon when I smelled the honeysuckle mixed with the bread and the meat, and I saw the white, polished teeth being raised. That day I felt a deep discomfort and apprehension. There was something wrong in our world. Suddenly, all that was familiar drove me crazy with its strangeness.

Blood and death. I understood clearly the town was cleansing itself from that night in 1897. It sacrificed itself. But not everyone; it was the elite, a distinguished group, not even all of them natives—there were many outsiders who had made a fortune in our town.

I saw the condition of those who, defeated, came back toothless, their mouths withered: the supreme courage of returning home. I witnessed the humiliations they endured, the kids running after them, screaming. I saw the shut doors, the jobs they were denied. Marginalized. But why did they come back? I think I know. Now that I'm exiled I can see we go back if we can, even if we suffer. Because that's where our roots are. The smell of the soil, of the fresh baked bread in the afternoon: a long, soft baguette, the toasty crust crumbling like a cookie. The fragrance of honeysuckle that I smelled the day I was born: it penetrated my skin, it's part of who I am.

That's what the toothless men searched for: themselves. Defeated, they attempted a re-encounter. Ridiculed, despised, spat on, nameless—for their ID cards had been taken away from them—they slept under bridges, in the squares, fell drunk on the curbs, without saying one word, so as to not reveal their empty gums, the symbols of their disgrace.

They risked everything on one stroke and lost. Tough people. The Games were their only chance of ascending, and they had tried. As winners, they would show off their teeth necklaces. Defeated, they faced their punishment. No, I didn't feel sorry for them. Had they won, their attitude would have been the same as today's winners. But they fell. On the wrong side.

The toothless men formed their own little caste. In spite of everything they were full of pride because they had participated in the Games, knew everything that happened there. I tried to interview some of the defeated. I talked to one of them—only once. It was in the red-light district in São Carlos. He was drunk, had no woman. However, the only thing I got from him was a belch and a few garbled words.

The Railroad Games came to an end twelve years ago: our last great tradition. All the stations were demolished. The tracks are now a tree-lined avenue that divides the town in half. The necklaces can still be seen in many houses, hanging on the wall. Necklaces of yellowed teeth, of past glories. They sit next to helmets from 1932, São Paulo flags, reproductions of the Sacred Heart, framed hand-painted photos. Many things have changed in the town, I know. People don't go out on the streets, there are no parties, the windows remain shut. Only the sun is the same, and the bean soup with small star-shaped macaroni noodles on Wednesdays after six o'clock.

THE MEMORY
Memoirs

The ground covered in confetti, the remains of streamers forming a paper paste. The drizzle fell all night long. It just stopped now, at dawn. The buses, full, leave for São Paulo, for Rio. People lean on benches dozing off. Crowded bars, groups of people walking toward the Largo da Câmara. They're going to eat empanadas at the Japanese's. That's what has remained: the empanada in the wee hours of the morning on Ash Wednesday. The milkman goes by. He has a VW van, has retired his horse and his carriage.

"What's that crowd doing over there? Has someone been killed?"

"No, it's Caldeira's sports car. He's in town."

"Is he still the same?"

"The same. Each time a different car."

"And always surrounded by women?"

"Of course. He parades around downtown and goes to his farm. The ritual hasn't changed."

"Only Caldeira changes. Once in a while I see him in São Paulo. He owns a car dealership. That's why he's always changing cars. Everything is for sale. Big Caldeira is looking sick, flabby."

"Now he's famous only among these punks who are into cars. Nobody else."

"And young women?"

"They think he's an old guy, out of it."

"And it's true, he's fifty."

"Full of whiskey and amphetamines."

"And a glass eye. Remember what the town was like that night? Everybody talking about Caldeira going to the hospital? All those women in the hallways of the Santa Casa Hospital, the nuns going crazy, Caldeira's mother coming from São Paulo, and his friends hiding the women."

"People talked about that bullfight endlessly! They envied Caldeira, his manners, always unshaved, sitting on the floor in the Club, walking around with his head smeared with cow shit."

"Nowadays everybody sits on the floor in the Club."

"And wears jeans."

"And smokes a fine joint."

"And young girls fool around more than ever."

"Screw these shitty playboys who bossed everyone around!"

"We all got screwed. At least Caldeira had fun."

"We behaved when we should have blown up everything, and kept quiet when we should have shouted."

"At least you left."

"To have left and not done anything is the same as staying and not doing anything."

"Sounds like something a drunk would say."

"And isn't a liter of gin enough to put anyone on the floor? I'm going to throw up a little. You left me drinking by myself, not fair."

"I've had enough to drink."

"You can't drink anything."

"I never could."

"How can you drink draft beer?"

"I like draft beer a lot."

"Mix it with something."

"Then I'll be on the floor."

"Beer is good only for making you pee."

The last members of a samba school stagger along banging on boxes, out of rhythm. A family—the father, the mother, two daughters, a son—slowly walk up the street, overtaken by Ash Wednesday, their hair full of confetti. The old man carries a wolf mask in his hand.

"Don't aggravate me, Danilo. In our day everybody only drank beer."

"Our day, our day. Do you know how long it's been since *our day*? Do you? How many years has it been? Tell me."

"Twenty-three."

"Shit. Twenty-three years and you're still drinking draft beer. Our day. Have you never considered that time belongs to others too?"

"Come on, Danilo, it's just a figure of speech. That period of time was nice, our friends united, thinking alike. We wanted to excel in life."

"Our friends were united in drinking, nothing else. A nice, carefree time! No. Hardship, exams, lack of perspective, anguish all the time, meaningless dates, parties, a hard time getting laid. Our day? A stupid time, that's what it was! Ask any of our friends if he wants to go back to *our* day. And even if he does, it's over, it's not coming back."

"I don't want to go back either. It's just an expression."

"Which you can't leave behind."

"You can't leave everything behind, something has to stay."

"Something stays when it exists. Look around. Do you recognize the town we live in? No. Everything has changed. It's another town, other people, other customs. The girls from our time are marrying away their daughters. The thirty-something women have already been buried. Their children are these damn beautiful women we see around. Nothing has anything to do with us."

"The spirit is the same."

Someone has opened the piano, is playing "Cumano." It has to be Paulinho, the pianist who has only one hand. No one can stand hearing "Cumano," and he plays and plays it non-stop. A cowboy fills a plastic bottle and sprays a thin, cold jet of beer in Paulinho's ear.

"What spirit? Nonsense, don't be foolish. What is that supposed to mean?"

"You're drunk, Danilo."

"I've always been. I've been drunk for thirty years and will continue to be."

"What you're saying doesn't make any sense. You've always hated the town, but it's not that bad."

"It doesn't exist. A small town, full of shit because it has five high-rises and a half-dozen more being built. Cement, lime dust, the wind always blowing this damn sand that gets in your eyes. Not one restaurant. The bars closing because there's no business. No place to go, not one bookstore or magazine stand. Not so bad—what is it then?"

"A calm, pleasant town where anyone can live well."

"Who? You?"

"Not me, because I bother them."

"Who do you bother?"

"Them."

"Them, who?"

"You know. You're the one who's always told me, 'Don't let them defeat you. Look out.' I learned from you to be careful, to defend myself."

"You never imagined I had the right to say foolish things? Or that I enjoyed saying them? Or that I wasn't the infallible voice of God, or anybody's mentor? Don't you remember how full of hot air I was? How pretentious I was? So willing to show off to these damn people? Why did I answer my math tests in alexandrine verses? Because I didn't know? No. So I would get everyone talking. I dreamed of being a poetic idol, a mix of Yevtushencko, Dylan Thomas, Allen Ginsberg, Castro Alves, and Mayakovsky. Today I don't even know a rhyme for 'heart.'"

"I can't imagine that. You were different from the rest of the group, you didn't participate like the others. You were always distant, a bit critical."

"Dart, start, fart, heart."

"Sometimes we felt you were watching us, and didn't do certain things because you didn't agree with them. And then we were left with the feeling that we had been childish."

"Heart, tart, smart, part. I wasn't different at all! I was just a shy guy who envied Luís Carlos's bright ideas. Nobody came up with pranks like he did: breaking open mailboxes, peeing in milk bottles, putting adhesive tape on doorbells, gathering the kids on the streets, feeding them yams and telling them to start farting inside the theater until nobody could stand it. That was creativity."

It stopped drizzling. People returning from carnival dances walk by people going to work. Groups of girls from the sock factory laugh at people in costumes sleeping on the hotel doorsteps.

"Disappointed?"

"I don't know, something strange."

"Did you think I was a cool guy?"

"I did."

"I'm not anymore?"

"Yes . . . and no . . ."

"Look, my friend, I'm a person, do you understand?"

"I do. But I'm thinking, thinking. I've got pieces loose in my head. I need to find their right place, and then tighten the screws."

"Thinking. Thinking about what?"

"You know, Danilo, many times I stop wondering where your genius has gone and where I've stuffed my ambitions, to try to understand the big return, in other words, "the overstep." I've developed the overstep theory. It's this: there are two steps, but only the second one exists, not the first. What happened to this first step? It's the base. You can't take a second step without having taken the first. And that's where the future is. The first doesn't exist, but the second does. In other words, the world has skipped over a void. And who's floating in this void, Danilo? Us, forty-year-old men who live like cartoon characters. They run fast, throw themselves into space, and suddenly realize there's no ground under them. And do you know what's worse? They don't fall and don't know why they don't fall, when all logic and the laws of physics are pushing them. I wonder what it is. Fear? No. Anguish, because they ask themselves, "Why didn't we fall if there's nothing holding us up?" Isn't that just fake? And how can we live in it all the time?"

Paulinho plays "Cumano" faster and faster, as if he were running a race against the song itself, and it were getting farther and farther ahead of him. Paulinho showed up and there was no other pianist like him in town. He played at the Club, was hired to play in houses. He said he had come from Rio's nightclubs, and I couldn't understand why someone who played like him would exchange this town for Rio. He never explained that. One day he left and came back without his left arm. He never brought up the subject. The Club didn't want him anymore. He plays in a beer and pizza bar, where he's the attraction on Sundays.

"Let's go to the station to watch the 6:10 train leave?"

"Nobody takes the 6:10 train anymore."

91

One night I stayed in the office alone doing extra work. I had stopped in front of the typewriter, fascinated, contemplating its cylinder, the levers, the keys, the ribbon, the space key, the tab, the capital and small letter keys devices. And suddenly I grabbed the typewriter and threw it through the window into the building's central courtyard. I could hear the noise it made as it crashed below. I threw the second, third. Twenty-two typewriters crashed, spreading keys, cylinders, pieces across the ground. Then I placed a pen and a bottle of ink on each desk, put on my jacket, washed my hands, put some gel on my hair and went home.

At home I wrote three letters in oval-shaped handwriting, embellishing the capital letters with some flowers. I went to bed. The next day I found the police at the office. I gave my deposition.

"I left at eleven at night, after finishing my work, which consisted of some bookkeeping that was overdue. Everything was calm, the other offices in the building closed, only the hallway light was on.

The elevator was on automatic. It went up. The doorman on the first floor saw me. Nothing had happened when I left. Actually, I think I noticed two lightbulbs were out, which left the right corner of the room a little in the shadows. The darkness was dense, strange, a little scary, but I distracted myself by working."

The doorman confirmed I had in fact left around eleven. He hadn't heard anything (how come he didn't? The typewriters had made a lot of noise); he was setting the time clock, adjusting it to the watchman's watch. The police interrogated us one by one, investigated, suspected, hovered around my desk for two weeks, the boss acting suspicious, my co-workers avoiding me. And new typewriters were brought in, and the typists began to type violently, faster, trying to make up the time they lost. They had stopped for five hours and in the end, when they retired, instead of seventy-two thousand hours they would have worked only 71,995, which wouldn't speak well of a professional who was used to typing 190 keystrokes per minute. On the first day after the crash, I went to talk to the doorman at quitting time.

"Why did you say you hadn't heard anything?"

"Because I didn't."

"But the typewriters made a loud noise."

"But I didn't hear it."

"They were coming down for more than 10 minutes. And you didn't hear it?"

"I didn't hear it."

"I threw the typewriters carefully, one by one. And you didn't hear it? You know I threw the typewriters, don't you?"

"Yes."

"So, why didn't you tell the police, tell my boss?"

"I know why I didn't tell."

"What do you know?"

"If I didn't tell the police you threw the typewriters, I'm not going to tell you I know why you did it either."

At work ten days later, I sensed a nervous commotion. The boss was talking loudly, the employees leaned against the wall, the police were there. The investigator—the same as before—approached.

"Did you work late last night?"

"No."

"Did you leave at the regular time with everybody else?"

"Yes."

"Can you prove it?"

"Yes. I stepped on that typist's foot at the door, that brunette over there. I stepped hard, apologized, she laughed, said it was all right, that I could step on her as many times as I wanted. I didn't understand, asked why, but she refused to explain, I insisted. We walked together all the way to the street corner."

The office was in turmoil. The nervous typists screamed, "AAAA, YYY, TTTTT, MMMMMM, GGGGGGGGGG, FFFFFFFF, RRRRR, EEEEEEEEE, IIIIIIIIII, UUUUUUU, VVVVVVVVV," and symbols, "&&&&, ----, §§§, (((((((, £, ;;;;, """"""""." A more desperate one had a nervous attack and cried without stopping, "ooooo." They had some rented typewriters brought in, gave the typists tranquilizers.

I went down, straight to the doorman.

"You went up there last night and threw the typewriters through the window. Why?"

"You did the same thing. Why?"

"I had to do it. I know why I had to. But what about you?"

"I had to do it too. Maybe for the same reasons as you."

The doorman turned away, walked to the information window to answer the questions from people who had questions. I went up. The investigator investigated, asked, shouted. I pulled out some files, papers, began to do the bookkeeping, hearing that noise, now unbearable, of the screeching letters coming from the typists who waited for the typewriters. I paused a little, watching the young girl from the night before, the one whose foot I had stepped on. She was looking at me too, without looking away even for one second. And we continued staring.

Following police orders, nobody left the office. We had lunch there, and I ate an empanada, sugarcane juice, two *sfihas* and caramel custard. The typists refused to eat. They wanted their typewriters. They kept tapping their fingers on their desks, typing invisible documents on invisible typewriters so their hands wouldn't lose the habit, nor their fingers their flexibility.

At the end of the workday I ran. I wanted to get to the door at the same time as the typist from the day before, step on her foot, accompany her to the bus. But she stayed to do overtime, because the typewriters had come late in the afternoon and they had a lot of extra work. So I stopped by the post office; I hadn't checked my mailbox for two days. I had rented a big one, and that's where I got my mail. The mailbox was completely full, and there was a notice for me to stop by the counter to pick up the rest: more than four hundred letters.

The clerk asked, "Are all these for you?"

"Yes . . ."

"Why? What do you do?"

"It's none of your business."

"And the stamps, can't you give me some of them?"

"No."

"Why not?"

"Because I don't feel like giving you the stamps."

At home I organized the letters according to their country of origin. I looked at the rubber stamp, and organized them by date. I organized the senders by first time, second, third time. This was something I was good at: the great archivist. First came the letters from people who were replying for the first time, then the rest, in order. I knew if it was an urgent matter or not by the name. In fact none were urgent. Many letters were written in their native language. They were written in Bantu, Swahili, Greek, Finnish, Chinese. They were placed in a box: "To be translated." There were 2,657 letters to be translated. At ten *cruzeiros* each, that would cost 26,574 *cruzeiros*. I would have to work for who knows how long and not spend anything, in order to pay for it. But I couldn't spend twenty months without writing letters, buying paper, envelopes, stamps. In any case, in twenty months the number of letters would have increased, and I would have to calculate it all over. There was no other solution but for me to learn Bantu, Swahili, Greek, Finnish, Chinese, and the other languages on my own.

I ordered catalogues at the bookstores. There are only three, and they were more stationary stores than bookstores. I was going to have to write to New York, Paris, Stockholm, Helsinki, Johannesburg, and Bergamo, and wait. It wouldn't matter: I had plenty of time on my hands, years and years to accomplish these things. I didn't have any other objective. I didn't go out, didn't talk to anyone, didn't have a family: a perfect Araraquaran.

But one day they came, perhaps following a tip from the clerk at the post office. I don't know, it doesn't help to blame anybody; the fact is they came. They opened my closets, boxes, packages, and took them. They set fire to them, destroyed everything.

"Why?"

"   "

"But why? What's the problem with writing and getting replies?"

"   "

A man can't watch his belongings being destroyed and stay quiet. That's his life. Everything torn, gone. I shouted, threw myself at them. So they tied me up. They didn't have to, but they tied me up. That's the worst humiliation for an Araraquaran. You can do anything to a man, except tie him up.

Has anyone been tied up before?

Having tied me up, they placed the typewriter in front of me. I got furious. The days went by, and I kept staring at the keys, the cylinder. Then I slowly realized what a curious thing a typewriter is. I started to try one key, another key. I noticed a long, black key, with no mark on it, on the bottom of the typewriter. It occupied a whole row. I typed and waited for the effect: none. That key's purpose was to produce an empty space. What for? I believed that bigger things didn't always produce voids.

And, worried, I continued to type page after page. I pressed the big key and an empty space appeared. It should have some use, otherwise the key wouldn't exist. Every space is useful in some way. I was fascinated by my new objective: what's the purpose of an object that produces nothing? For a whole year I considered the question, studying physics books. Finally I solved it: I've bought reams and reams of paper and spend my time filling them with empty spaces.

IT'S NOT ONLY MY NAILS
THAT ARE FALLING OFF

They all were happy in the bank. They worked inside on nine floors of concrete, with tinted windowpanes, air-conditioning, soft armchairs, anatomic desks, snacks served every hour on a cart that brought hot sandwiches and cold drinks: a day-long happiness. Typewriters typing, calculators calculating, cashiers counting money, clients depositing money, money multiplying interest. Computers, IBM cards, framed pictures on the walls, high salaries. The bank's engines were well oiled, the employees happy, their clothes clean.

On Monday, as he signed a document, the president noticed the nail on his little finger was practically falling off. He pulled it slightly: it fell. He thought about the manicurist, cursed her, had his secretary call a doctor. The president didn't know what to do. He had never had a nail fall off. When he hung up the phone, the nail on his forefinger fell off too, and he was astonished, because there was no blood. The nail simply fell on the table, a strange body, as if it had never belonged to him. He tapped his fingers on the glass table. And when he did he saw that all the nails, on all his fingers, were falling off. He got up alarmed, grabbed the phone (he didn't want to call his secretary), and waited for the tone.

When he dialed he realized his forefinger had become disconnected from his hand. He began to move his arm slowly toward his face. Before his hand reached the mouth all his fingers—from both hands—had fallen on the floor.

The president ran to lock the door but couldn't move the key—he had no fingers. In the effort his hands became loosened from his wrists and fell. Then his secretary opened the door, and the president saw the pandemonium and heard the screams coursing throughout the whole building. He saw his secretary had already lost her hands, arms, nose and ears. He felt like crying. The tears ran down his face and brought his eyeballs with them.

The president suddenly felt a deep silence overtake the glass and steel building, and he realized his hair was falling out, his teeth becoming loose, his nose coming apart, his ears drooping. And his skin was dissolving, his bones becoming disjointed, his cartilage springing like coils. His veins fell on the floor, his muscles seemed like high-voltage wires buzzing. The president's body (and the bodies of all the employees) fell apart on the floor. And livers, kidneys, lungs, pancreases, stomachs, hearts, intestines, and backbones rolled everywhere. And those pieces began to dissolve, turning into a paste that dried up quickly and split like parched soil. And then it turned into dust.

And when there was not one person left, and everything was dust, the building began to crack from top to bottom.

The shingles snapped, the bricks cracked, the windowpanes broke, the walls fractured, the wood frames splintered. Everything shattered into tiny pieces: toilet bowls, computers, desks, chairs, typewriters, adding machines, calculators, safes, lamps, electric switches, boilers, air-conditioners, fans, money, papers, inkwells, pens; disintegrating until it all became dust. And the dust that had been the people mixed with the dust that had been the building. And the wind blew that human-edifice dust away toward the river, to the trees on its banks, to the far-away town. And the dust was like fine, yellowish sand that settled on windows, on furniture, on the streets, on people's clothes.

THE ELEMENTS
AIR
Memoirs and Facts

"That black mourning band, which Colonel José Amaro had had painted on his house, a sign of protest and rebellion that many families imitated, shows that the town didn't commit the crime, but rather a powerful group did. You have to put a stop to your anachronistic naiveté and understand what the power struggle is. The old man who died represented power and everything relating to it, bc it corruption, abuse, paternalism, authoritarianism, or tyranny. Having complete power enslaves the individual, puts him outside the boundaries of reality. It's an acid trip, in which the person travels dazzled, without limits, his perception completely open, all barriers removed, aware of his control over himself and others."

I'm surprised, because every afternoon for the past five days, we've calmly walked through all the doors, and sat at the tables in the quiet Legal Archives, examining pages written in a hand we have to painstakingly decipher, like hieroglyphs. If they were actual hieroglyphs, I'd call Luís Carlos. He's been studying them for ten years, has grammar books, dictionaries, he can even speak the language. The funny thing is that Luís Carlos used to only be interested in things that related to the future. He never talked of the past, and now he's a specialist in a dead language. Which moment in his life, which instant, made him choose the opposite, made him change into what he already is, he, who incarnated the future? I'd like to determine the fatal moment in my life that made me become an is-not. I, who should have been.

On the first day Danilo grabbed me by the arm saying, "Let's go over there now. Let's look at all the records you want on this damn case that obsesses you."

"I don't go to the Court."

"And it's going to be right now."

I was almost paralyzed. We climbed the stairs, walked by two security guards. Neither one made the slightest movement. We went through four doors and nobody stopped us or even asked who we were or what we wanted. And being and having are both important in this town. I mentioned it to Danilo when, in front of the steel doors leading to the archive of cases dating from before the beginning of the century, the guard hesitated for a moment.

"I don't know anything about this key. I never heard of anyone who's consulted these books even once."

"We'll wait. It has to be somewhere. Look for it!"

Danilo knows how to speak assertively to these people. Either because he's a lawyer, or because nothing intimidates him, always aggressive, authoritarian, demanding, very self-confident, clear about what he wants. The fact is the guard returned with the key. I was sure we wouldn't find the records (or part of the cases). It's never been easy to access information about the case that shamed the whole town, caused a revolt, and left an indelible mark upon the whole population.

"What do you want to know?"

"Everything."

"Do you want to take the records home?"

"Is that allowed?"

"If it isn't we'll make photocopies."

"I can't believe it."

"There it is! Is the mystery over?"

"It wasn't a mystery. I simply was never able to consult them."

"For a while they were renovating and reclassifying the archive."

"I tried many different times."

"I'm sorry, but I don't believe you. Access was never prohibited. A judge would have given you authorization. You could have petitioned for a writ. It's illegal. Besides, it's been more than ninety years. What damage could it possibly do? The old man doesn't have any relatives left. At least not in Araraquara. Do you know what it is? You've always had delusions. You exaggerated everything, remember? That's why everybody thought you were going to be a writer. You were able to transform and elaborate any situation, adding dimension and details in a way that nobody else could."

"You manage to make things seem so simple, Danilo."

"I don't manage to. What is simple, is simple."

We read a good part of the case. Danilo translated the legal terminology when it got too complicated. We spent the day talking and reconstituting the facts.

"Who was the old man? What did he want to do?"

"A colonel, very rich. He owned two farms in town, a coffee farm and a cattle ranch. He was the Republican Party leader. When he died they inventoried his estate. It was the second largest in the 1890s."

"How do you know all this stuff?"

"I had an interest in it too. I'm familiar with the whole case."

296

"And you never told me?"

"I wanted to know what you found out—nothing."

"I had a lot of trouble."

"That's bullshit."

"What did you want to know all this for?"

"I wanted to know the town's social history."

"You hated the town."

"It wasn't the town itself that fascinated me. It was the power struggle, the various ways of doing things, the different people. You know, I wanted to do something big, compare the old man to Macbeth."

"And what was the result?"

"Nothing. When did I have time? I graduated, got married, put everything aside that wasn't necessary."

"Don't you regret it? Aren't you frustrated?"

"I dropped it because I wanted to. I chose to. I don't think about it anymore."

"Escapism."

"You're going to analyze me, are you?"

"Why don't you tell me what you know?"

"So you won't do anything with it?"

"Was the old man the mayor?"

"No. He liked to exercise his authority, but without the responsibility of an elected position. He governed, in fact, without making it official, without suffering any consequences. He's the kind of person that fascinates me. Power for him was a personal, intimate form of self-realization, not showy or vain. He stayed behind the scenes, but wanted to keep the reins of power."

"The world is full of them."

"It's hard to talk to you, isn't it? I'm serious, and you're full of nonsense."

"It was just a comment."

"Well, don't make any more comments. The Northeasterner was a well-known and well-liked person. He worked as a nurse during the yellow fever epidemic. Later he almost died from the disease. He had a sense of justice, and so he defended a man who had been tortured in the local police station, and ended up provoking the old man's rage."

"And he killed the old man?"

"Two shots. One in the heart."

"But people talk about two prisoners who were lynched."

"The little *Caboclo* and his brother."

"Did they both get killed on that same night?"

"No, a week later at the memorial mass. Everything had been planned, deliberate. The farm's employees were invited to attend the mass, and they arrived armed. There were supposedly one thousand people on the square the night of the crime. The old man's sons were the first to go in, disguised in shabby clothes with kerchiefs covering their faces. Others painted their faces black. Look, this is all from the records. They dragged the prisoners to the sidewalk and shot them, beat and stabbed them, hit them with their fists and bats."

"What a movie this could turn into."

"You just need a script."

"Yes, and now it's possible to write one."

"It's always been possible. I don't understand you."

"Will you believe it if I give my word? I was never let in here. Everything I know is from hearsay. For example, the priest's curse."

"The jail was next to the church. When the priest opened the door before the first mass, he saw the shattered bodies. He knew about everything, the rumors, the promise made. So he cursed the town. That's part of the folklore: nannies tell babies the story. I don't know if it's true, but it's a good opening."

"Just think: the deserted town. It's dawn. The church doors open; the slumbering priest."

"Slumbering? Isn't there another word?"

"Sleepy, yawning. The priest's terrified face. A close-up of the bloodied bodies. The opening credits. The movie starts. Good, isn't it?"

Danilo looks at me, an ironic half-smile on his face. As if he thought, "He's not going to write the script." Suddenly I understood everything clearly. For five days Danilo has tested and provoked me. I think he's been provoking me for years, and now I understand why. Desperate, he's tried everything, even shown me the legal records, aware of the risk he's running. That's why it was so easy. I knew it was strange. Something didn't seem right, didn't click, like two positive poles together. Danilo hanging around me, wanting to find out about my research, my book, my stories, the material I have in my hands. I kept resisting, until this last desperate tactic! He showed me the records, told me the facts to get me to trust him. Are these actually the real facts? How can I believe the man who is the Guardian of the Records?

The Facts

THE OLD COUPLE AND THE WIND

It was Saturday and the woman had just finished washing the verandah and the sidewalk. She went back inside carrying the bucket, the broom and the mop. She saw her husband staring rigidly at the lamp. It hung from a long wire that was covered with dead mosquitoes. He was sitting still in his rocking chair. The wire and the lamp swung rhythmically, and at first the woman thought it was the wind. But all the doors and windows were closed. Her husband hated air currents, and the house was never open. It even smelled muggy and moldy, like some abandoned houses do. She remembered that it was a beautiful summer day, and that the air was still, dry, and hot. The woman thought it was a joke her husband was playing on her. Maybe he had tied a string and was pulling it without her seeing it. The kids on the street often played pranks: they tied money on a piece of string, left it on the sidewalk, and hid behind the wall. When someone bent over to pick up the money, the kids pulled the string and laughed. But her husband was motionless, quiet, looking at the lamp, and hadn't realized she had come in.

They watched the lamp's rhythm slowly increase, and noticed that other things in the room had begun to move: the flowers she placed on the table every two days, some papers that had been sitting on the china cabinet. And the husband felt a cold draft under his feet. "You must've left a door open," he grumbled. She said she hadn't. Nothing had been left open, not one crack, because she was so used to the airless house that even a crack in the door bothered her too. It was as if the house had been caulked. Nevertheless, the air current could be felt in all the rooms, very low, on their legs and feet. Probably the wind was coming from a gap in the roof. He lay down under the covers, asked for some very hot tea. He could hear the wind whistling as it passed under the bed. He'd better put on some wool socks too. The two of them closed the doors one by one, and covered the keyholes with newspapers and scotch tape. Then they sat down to watch TV and wait for bedtime. The lamp wire swung violently, hitting the ceiling. He thought it would be better to take the lamp down before it broke. Lit by the TV's bluish gray light, they could feel the wind gradually getting stronger. It was knocking over everything that was on the furniture. The woman hurried to put away vases, crystal and plastic figurines, took pictures off the walls, removed the calendars. They were frightened, wondering if they should go to their son's house, but he was having dinner out, eating pizza, dancing, and drinking beer with his wife.

The TV's picture trembled. Husband and wife sat together on the couch, while the wind shook everything, the windows, the furniture, and pushed the doors in. The newspapers that covered the doors blew away. The wind surrounded them and pushed them. They fell on the couch, tried to get up but weren't able to. The whole living room had been overtaken by the wind. The china cabinet broke to pieces, the table slid toward one wall, and then to the other. The two dragged themselves along the hallway, trying to reach the kitchen. Chairs flew and stuck in the ceiling, doors slammed. The door locks were ripped off and whistled by like projectiles. The curtains floated in the air. The windowpanes shattered. They could hear pans hitting against pans, the stove tumbling, dishes, glasses, silverware shaking and hitting the walls. Everything fell and was lifted, flying over husband and wife. Knives cut their arms and legs, glasses broke against their heads. The wife's face was covered in blood. Now they were both still, hugging each other in the middle of the hallway, not shaking, and not frightened. They weren't crying. They just watched the wind twist like a hurricane, furious, at an incredible speed. It blew over them, shredding their clothes, pulling the rags off their bodies. And in its fury, the wind splintered the furniture and peeled the walls. Pieces of the bed, chairs, cabinets, bedside tables, china cabinet, refrigerator, cups, dishes, figurines, pictures—everything mixed together, banging against each other in the air, grinding, crushing, turning floorboards, glass and china into a thick dust. The dust took over the house. Husband and wife, hugging, naked, couldn't see anything, and coughed, suffocating.

They tried to move, were pushed, screamed, but were unable to hear their own screams. They just hoped the neighbors would hear that horrible noise, and would break the doors open. The front doors remained shut, and the rough dust, rubbing against the husband's and wife's bodies, began to scrape their skin off, at the speed of 1,000 kilometers per hour. And once all the skin had come off, the dust quickly ate away the rest of their flesh, until it reached the bones. The cyclone went on, peeling off the wall plaster, slowly eating away the bricks, while more dust accumulated and twisted rapidly in the air. And the dust from their bones joined dust from wood, glass, fabric, lime, plaster and bricks. Soon there was so much accumulated dust that the wind wasn't strong enough to move it. With all the rooms filled from ceiling to floor, the house exploded, a kilometers-high geyser—gushing up.

THE ELEMENTS
FIRE
Memoirs

Bernardo came to cover the inauguration of another bus line to São Paulo and Rio. He's furious. He says a journalist of his stature shouldn't be doing paid advertising. But the opportunities to do reporting are dwindling, the newspapers are in crisis. He's assured me he wants to move to TV. The company's office is located where Pedro's Bar used to be. We sit in the bar across from it, owned by a Turkish woman who still can't speak Portuguese, but who already knows how to charge practically double for her strange empanadas.

"And what do you plan to do with these stories?"

"Publish them, of course. What did you think of them?"

"Publish them how? You have to organize them, define them, give them unity."

"And what if they don't have unity or definition?"

"It'll be a mess."

"Does that mean I can't write a bunch of stories, put them together and send them to an editor?"

"Of course you can. But they'll reject it."

"What a small, narrow-minded world! Full of rules and regulations. What do you think of the stories?"

"You say they're all true. It's incredible. I've lived in this town for twenty-one years and never knew a fraction of all this stuff. What an imagination."

"Maybe they didn't happen during your time. You left eighteen years ago. What do you think of them?"

"I'd like to follow your process, see where you get your material. Good stuff for a book. I don't like the title. 'The facts behind the walls' doesn't tell me anything. I don't know, it sounds like something to do with jail."

"I get it from out there, what's in front of me. All kinds of things happen at every moment. You just have to be paying attention. I go out for walks and watch. Sometimes there is so much going on that I don't even have enough time to take notes. The other day I took two short stories to the newspaper. Now it has a literary supplement. It's the only cultural activity in town, did you know? It's not like in our day, when there was a film club, a visual arts movement, theater groups, debates at the library."

"What about the university?"

"The university keeps to itself. Exclusive stuff. Elitist, you know? The others don't participate. The town hasn't changed one bit because of the university. And we expected so much—that it would intervene, make things better, provoke, motivate. Do you remember a conversation we had the day Sartre gave a talk at the Municipal Theater? 'Now it's going to happen, too bad we're leaving,' that's what we said. Maybe it hasn't been long enough to evaluuatue—less than twenty years. But many classes have graduated, and the university continues to be a stranger among us."

"And did the supplement publish them?"

"No. The guy said I was crazy. What do you think? Everything's real, I just gave it a literary treatment. Maybe it killed the authenticity. It's like a shoe that's polished too much, too shiny. It looks ugly, out of date. I think that's what bothers you about the stories. Too elaborate."

"It's funny, sometimes when I see you on the street I have the feeling you're a deeply anguished man. Now I see it differently. I believe you're happier inside this world you see and from which you get so many stories. I confess I don't understand them, or what they're getting at. It's my problem. I've been contaminated, I'm too caught up in normalcy. They'd never accept your book at the press where I work. And if they asked me for my input, I'd have to reject it. It's going to be years before you can get this book published. And when it happens, maybe it won't be worthwhile anymore. Do you know what I'm saying? There's something very important in this book that I can't grasp. That's what happened to me: I've stopped grasping things. And I've stopped writing. Now I just live off the news about the next book that I'm supposedly writing, the news you read and that makes you envious. It's nothing more than news about something that doesn't exist. I've stopped at those three miserable novels—there's nothing else. All these years I was stretching myself thin: working at the newspaper, and doing freelance work for advertising agencies. I write well, was called to do TV ads, pseudo avant-garde TV plays, movie reviews in newspapers where I had already worked, decadent newspapers, like all newspapers are. I was commissioned to write books, which I wrote to make more money and be able to travel. I wrote press releases for pharmaceutical products. On Saturdays and Sundays I edited companies' newsletters. I imagined it'd be only for a while, but I kept at it, and kept doing it. And I couldn't travel because I didn't have time. And the TV ads gave me experience to do other ads, and the avant-garde theater was nothing but a cheap soap opera shot with better equipment, as compromised as any other product. I stopped writing and have no desire to resume it. I feel lazy just thinking about sitting at the typewriter and spending hours on a story that I don't know if I'm going to sell. I got used to adapting, to getting ideas from other people, instead of producing, creating. Sometimes I feel the need to, but it happens less the more settled I get. To say 'React!' doesn't help. I can't, it's awful, I don't know how to get out of this situation. And to think it's only been five years, sixty months working day and night non-stop. If I leave everything, come back to town and lock myself in the house, maybe things will change. I can't stand São Paulo and its violence anymore. After twenty years I found that it's not where I want to live. Not that I don't want to. I can't, I can't stand it. I have no interest in it. I envy you. You stayed, chose to stay. I thought you were frustrated, but you aren't. Someone who writes stories like these can't be. I feel that behind these stories there's a satisfied man. True?"

The Turkish lady brings two more empanadas and two beers. Bernardo is talking to himself. He's let loose. He's crazy, irremediably crazy. Completely crazy, and I can't do anything, except feel sorry for him. How can someone so accomplished, successful, a guy so much in demand, talked about in the newspapers, to whom the town has paid homage, be saying stuff like this? He wants to please me, cheer me up. He thinks I'm a fool, that I deserve pity. That's enough for me. Really, I don't want to hear anymore. I bet he hasn't even read my stories.

94

I'm sucking on an orange I stole from Cândida's backyard. A strong fruit that tastes like the earth, not like the grafted fruit the Japanese produce, huge and colorful, but without taste. I throw the peels on Drunk Rio, who is sleeping on a bench in the garden. It's three in the afternoon, he's crashed early. Usually he's bothering everyone until late at night. Maybe he's losing his resistance. I don't remember him. People say he's from here, left to study law in Rio and never showed up again. Only now, like that: drunk, practically unconscious. When he's lucid he addresses some people by their names, asks about people from his time, from twenty-five years ago. He must be only forty-five years old, but looks older, like sixty. Right after he returned he told stories about Rio, so they started to call him Drunk Rio. He wants to open a law office and is looking for a room and a partner. He's been looking for a year and a half without much determination, maybe he's a little afraid he might find them.

Suddenly, a person at the other side of the garden makes me shiver: Ceres Fhade. He approaches at his staggering pace and greets me, taking off his hat. He keeps walking, but I step in front of him, like a mid-fielder blocking a forward.

"What are you doing on the streets during the day?"

"I was doing some shopping for my wife."

"Aren't you exposing yourself too much?"

"Exposing?"

"You know. It's better not to provoke *them*."

"Them who?"

"Well, you know."

"I just went out to buy two pounds of potatoes. What's wrong with that?"

"Potatoes may be the excuse *they* have been waiting for."

"They who?"

"I don't have to tell you. Nor should I. I don't even know who they are. I know they act and do incredible things. *They*. I don't know anything else."

"What's wrong with buying potatoes? You're scaring me."

"I don't want to scare you. But you can be sure that sometimes potatoes may be just the reason they need to get you again."

"Who's going to get me again? And why? What are you talking about? You come up with these stories! Explain what you're talking about!"

"I don't want to say anything else, Ceres. Go. Go home. We'll see each other tonight at the movie theater, okay?"

"I'm going. I'll take my potatoes and go. My wife's waiting for me. So long."

"No, Ceres. I can't let you. I think it's ridiculous, a full professor buying potatoes at three in the afternoon. Even more ridiculous is your wife, with a degree in Social Sciences, making gnocchi on a Tuesday."

"My wife doesn't have a degree. She didn't even finish high school."

"Ceres, I know everything."

"Look, I don't understand the things you tell me very well. But you're good company. The nights at the theater were boring until you showed up. Besides, my father taught me to be patient and tolerant, and I think I've been both. Now, my dear friend, I need to go.

My wife is waiting for me, I have to have dinner at a certain time, at six-thirty I start at the theater."

"I repeat: I don't know, but potatoes may be a good excuse for them."

"Who's going to get me again? They never did. What is this? A joke, a game? Get me for what? What are you talking about? I think you must know something. Maybe you're friends with the theater owner. Or a spy for the distributors watching to see if I'm doing everything right. There are many theaters out there that are laundering the money from the ticket sales, especially for Brazilian movies. That's it, isn't it? You're doing a report on me. Yes, they want to fire me and not pay me. Twenty-nine years on the job, since they showed *Yolanda and the Thief.* I missed work only twice in my life: when they showed *The Wizard of Oz*, and the day they showed *The Wild Ones*; only these two times. Why are they doing this? And why are you doing this to yourself? Now everything is clear: they want to interfere in my life outside the theater too. Tell me: what's wrong with buying potatoes?"

"That's not it. You don't understand me. I have nothing to do with the theater owner. My business is different."

"This sounds very strange, my friend, very strange. You mention *them*, mention the potatoes. What do you want? Why are you after me?"

"I'm a friend, Ceres. I like you. I know of your fight against doors. You beat the town, Ceres."

"You like me. So what? I want peace. I want you to leave me alone. I don't understand your friendship. I lived much better before you showed up. Really. I didn't have friends and didn't miss them.

I just cared about my work, about doing exactly what they told me to do. Then you showed up, sitting there, distracting me, trying to drag me into the room, wanting me to watch the movies. Me, a guy who has never stepped into the theater during a movie. Leave me in peace. Leave me alone. Don't come near me again."

"Come on, Ceres. I'm your friend. Really. I'd do anything to defend you. The two of us are alike; the city doesn't like us. I know your secret, your two great secrets: your identity and the Manual. I haven't told anybody. Never, do you understand? I never told anyone what I found out about you. It's between us. It's our revenge against the town."

"What revenge? What secret? I don't have any secret. What is this Manual that you're always talking about? Well, enough. Leave me alone, get off my back. Leave me in peace. I have things to do."

"Yeah, you really do. Get your bag and go buy potatoes and beans. Go please your wife, you big coward. Hurry, or she won't make that delicious gnocchi for dinner. What a shitty bourgeois you've turned into."

"What does that mean? If you're calling me names, I need to know. I don't take insults home."

"No, it's not an insult. It's praise. Praise you can take home along with your potatoes. The best thing a man can be is a bourgeois."

"Really?"

"Really."

"And you really think I am? Aren't you just being nice?"

"No. You're a wonderful bourgeois."

"Aren't you one too? It'd be good if you were. I just wish good things for good people. I think you're a good person, despite your weirdness."

"Don't worry, I'm one too. I'm nothing more than that."

"Now I have to go."

"Hurry, go get your potatoes."

"Ciao, bourgeois."

He winked at me in complicity. I'm going to go back to Fifth Street to see if they're done with the trees.

95

What my marriage was—I don't know. The only real, concrete decision I made, my own decision, was our separation. It didn't require an act of courage. Leaving was something very simple, like opening a door, stepping down from the sidewalk. Practically no words were being said, it was silent like our relationship: tacit understandings. If I think now about us, I see we had sensitivity and intuition and were able to connect. We were constantly communicating. Any couple can achieve the same, it's just a matter of knowing how to do it in order to know what the other thinks, how they're going to react, if they're telling the truth or lying. No, knowledge doesn't mean routine, and it must be made use of. Nevertheless, we spent too much time within a circle formed by her family, our few friends, even the neighbors, who decided to stick their noses in our life. We didn't even know how to face each other, much less the outside world putting pressure on us. We gave in, and the cracks got bigger until the dam crumbled, and it wasn't possible to contain the waters. The worst part is that these waters never did us any good. We never used them. They were simply destructive.

96

It doesn't rain, it's not cold, there are no movies showing in the theaters, no party anywhere, no game. It's a Friday like any other, and
I don't see a single soul downtown. I've been leaning against this
tree for the past hour and nobody has walked up or down the street.
Drunk Rio doesn't count, all soaked, passed out at the Club door.
The café is empty, the employees look at the TV set. I know, Fridays
have always been dead, but not like now. There's something in the
air, a conspiracy against me. *They* want to know how long I can bear
to stand next to this tree. They'll get tired if they're watching me.
They'll see I'm tough. I can spend the whole night here just to deny
them the pleasure of winning. At least I'm in the open, exposed,
and they're not. They're hiding, fearful, behind inviolable doors and
windows. Invulnerable.

THE MAN WHO STUCK HIS HAND OUTSIDE

He stuck his hand outside the door. The sun burned his palm. It was two o'clock in the afternoon, and in one hour the temperature would reach the highest point for the month of October. The village twenty miles from Araraquara had 272 houses on a plain hit hard by the sun. The houses were painted white, in order to reflect the light, and scientists had been there to study why it was the hottest region in the country. And in addition to the scientists, sociologists had come to find out why the people didn't move away, since the field was rocky and didn't produce anything, and the hillsides were dry and bare. There were 1,500 inhabitants who lived off of small animals in the extremely hot environment. Organisms had adapted to living without water, and the scientists had discovered that the people of the white sunny village descended, in part, from camels and dromedaries. Their eyeballs had adapted also, because they had never seen any green. That color didn't exist for them. There was nobody outside at two o'clock in the afternoon. The population spent the afternoon sleeping, and left in the evening to hunt brats, a mix of bats and rats, and toaduses (a type of toad from dry regions whose thin skin was tanned) for the manufacture of clothing that was resistant to the sandy wind. A half-hour later the man stuck his hand out. Three seconds, and the hand turned red. A little longer and the skin would have come off. In the house across the street, the neighbor heard the door and the squeaking from the stretchers holding brats' skins, which they tanned for four days in the sun and two nights in the light night dew. The neighbor peered through a crack, finding it strange that the man would stick his hand out twice. What was he trying to do? Two days earlier his wife had mentioned that the neighbor didn't look well. He spent the afternoon sticking his hand outside; he was probably losing his mind. Soon he'd be up on the roof offering himself to the sun, which will come out to lick his flesh and bleach his bones (they didn't bury their dead; they let them sit in the sun, which acted like soda ash, eating away the flesh and corroding the bones until everything became a fine powder that mixed with the dust from the ground). The apprehensive neighbor watched, waiting for the 12th, the day the sun would be the strongest. And he sat there peeking, worried because the man had two kids, and if he lost his mind nobody would take care of the children. He waited. The 12th went by. All day long he watched, and on the 12th the man didn't as much as stick his hand outside, which probably meant he had calmed down. As the neighbor was watching the front of the house on the 12th, he didn't see the man go out through the back door with his two kids inside an aluminum washbasin. The man placed the washbasin on top of the flint in the middle of the yard and went back to the kitchen, into the shade. And he waited until evening to check on the two boys, who had blackened, turned into charcoal. Then he left to hunt for brats and toaduses. For one person only.

THE PERCEPTION

Memoirs

Nobody can believe it. They're saying Miss Maria do Carmo has been arrested and is incommunicado. Her husband's lawyers are coming from São Paulo. The family doesn't trust the local lawyers. That must be it: they're afraid their secret will be revealed. People are surrounding the police station. The doors are closed: nobody can go in, not even the press, and nobody can come out. Silence. I can see Bueno with a camera, Magno with a microphone, and Terto, a guy from Bahia who used to work as a miner, and now is a reporter. Something must be going on, if the police station is locked up like that. The corporal has assured us they locked the doors only after people started acting crazy. Such a commotion has only happened once before—when the government closed down the Vales Bank. Everyone was desperate, hurried to withdraw their money. For two days the people have filled the street. There are whispers that the shock troops and a water truck are coming to disperse the crowd.

98

Sweaty, filthy, covered in dusty, dry mud.

"You haven't finished your part. You have to go all the way to that mark, the straw over there."

"I want a snack, Dad."

"Already? It hasn't been half hour since we started."

"Just a sandwich, or I can't do it."

"If we continue this way, this vegetable garden is going to be very expensive, considering the price of a sandwich."

"One for each of us."

In each bag, four sandwiches. That's something I can do very well: sandwich bread with margarine and cheese. A damp napkin wrapping it all, to keep the bread fresh.

"Give me a ham and cheese."

"We only have cheese."

"Why?"

"Ham is expensive these days. And cheese is healthier. I don't trust the ham we find in supermarkets. It has an ugly color."

"Come on, Dad. You are too picky. One of these days you're not going to eat anything."

"Finish it off. We have to turn all the soil by twelve. I'll have to come back by myself to finish fertilizing it."

"Tell me and I'll come too."

"You have school."

"I can miss it, can't I?"

"No, you can't."

"Do you mean the garden isn't important?"

"Of course it is."

"If it is, missing a few classes won't hurt."

"If you miss school and your mom finds out you've missed because of me, she'll get mad at me. We may not be able to go out together anymore."

"It's not because of you, it's because of the garden."

"It's fine with me. But keep it secret!"

"Look."

He crossed his fingers over his mouth and promised. He winked at me.

"We have a date: Tuesday. I'll go by the Santa Cruz stop at seven."

"Do it. Don't mess up."

"Have I ever?"

"Yes."

"Let's work some more?"

"Let's."

Eduardo drank some water from the tap. The water is brought from the source by a plastic hose, less than a quarter mile away. The owner gave me permission, as long as nothing gets built there. And it's going to take a while, this is not a commercial zone. The mayor and his cohorts have a development on the other side, a place where asphalt, water, electricity have pushed up the property value—all a sleazy deal.

"We should dig a well here and put in a pump. The water can't be very deep here."

"We'll have lots of money after we sell our vegetables, won't we, Dad?"

"If it works out, it won't be much. Enough to make some things better."

Digging, turning the soil, cleaning out rocks, stumps, grass roots. Eduardo pulls weeds, useless plants. He pulls them up by the roots, so they won't grow again.

"Water break."

"Dad, can't we come here really early, before school?"

"Will your mother let you?"

"Maybe, if we tell her everything. She's not a monster, Dad. She just doesn't like it when you take me to a bar after the matinee so you can have a beer. I bet she'll think the garden is cool. She may laugh, but she'll agree. I'll talk to her, okay?"

"It would be nice to come here every day. I don't even know if I'm doing this right, but I think I am. According to what I've read, we have to fertilize it. And we'll use cow manure because I don't have a penny to buy fertilizer."

"Do you know what we can do? We'll grab two sacks and look around the streets. There must be donkey dung somewhere."

"The baker and the milkman used to use donkeys to pull their carts. The milkman's horses and donkeys stopped close to our house. You weren't even born yet. The manure smell was strong in the morning. It smelled like the damp earth, like grass on a farm, right on the corner near the house. One day the health department showed up, and made him take the animals away. The neighbors had complained. Soon the milkman bought a van and sold the horses. Now I don't even know where to find manure. I rarely see a horse anymore. Unless we go to the racetracks or look in one of these small ranches around town."

"Dad, what's this garden for? Why so much work?"

"Isn't it fun? Digging in the earth? Doesn't if feel good?"

"It's funny."

"Just funny? Don't you enjoy it?"

"Yes, I'm starting to like it. But why don't we buy vegetables in the supermarket like everybody else?"

"We do for now. The day will come when we won't have the soil anymore."

"Why, Dad?"

"The time will come when the soil will be exhausted, the population will be enormous and everyone will be living in town. The fields will be deserts, nobody will live or grow anything there. Artificial fertilizers will exhaust the land. Synthetic food will have been invented, because otherwise the world will starve. So, whoever has a small piece of land and is able to plant will be saved."

"But won't my piece of land be exhausted too?"

"No, because we'll have a schedule, to plant and to let it rest."

"You're funny, Dad. Why did you buy a lot?"

"This is all I could afford with the money I made at the Railroad, at the very beginning. I don't need much more."

"Let's eat another sandwich?"

"Let's eat it all, that's it."

The *guaraná* bottles were inside the water tank to keep them cool.

"Do you like working, Dad?"

"Working, working, no, I don't like it. Or rather, I like to work on what I like."

"And what do you like?"

"Not much."

We lay down under the sparse shade of a big bush and fell asleep for a while. Or maybe for a long time: when we woke up the sun was going down, and the smell of earth around us was strong. We picked up our stuff and hit the road. A small *Caboclo* man walked by us, his big shoes hitting the ground firmly. He greeted us with a movement of his head and kept walking ahead quickly. The road was narrow, full of turns: a private shortcut, not even a municipal road. A small truck went by raising a cloud of dust. I saw the driver's scared face.

We walked a little more, and after a bend we saw something hopping in the middle of the road. As we approached, it hopped less and less, like a chicken with a broken neck. It was the little *Caboclo*, all covered in blood. He had lost an arm. His head was practically turned backwards, his big shoes had come off. He was dying, uttering a strange howl. Eduardo didn't want to look.

"Let's go, Dad."

"No, Eduardo. Sit down."

"I don't want to look, Dad, poor guy."

"You have to see, son."

"It's awful. It scares me."

"Fear and sorrow. This is death, Eduardo."

"I don't like it. I don't want to look."

"Look. You have to."

The man was still. He just howled, a little more weakly each time.

"He's dying, Eduardo. A man's life is coming to an end in front of us. Everything comes to an end. Open your eyes."

"I don't want to see, there's too much blood."

"Look, look. You must look. That's how you're going to live life, always. It's full of people dying every day. You have to get used to it."

We kept watching for a long time. The night had fallen. We walked to town and I called the police from a public phone.

99

They closed the house for two years and never came back. They disappeared without ever saying anything. Maybe someone knows something. It doesn't matter. The couple wasn't significant. The grandfather had been the last person in the family to hold power. The father, in turn, had preferred to distance himself from politics. He had his shop of household electronics (which his son ruined), was the first one to offer a payment plan system, using coupons. It was the grandfather's grandfather who, in 1897, left town in a golden coffin covered by the town's flag, a freemason flag, and another flag nobody recognized. It was a yellow flag with a blue oval in the center. According to the town's history, this was the flag of some secret society. It reproduced the gound plan of the Independence Gardens exactly, in the center of which—before the oval flowerbed was put down—a black man was hanged. The afternoon of the funeral, many people closed their houses, others had a sign of mourning painted on the facades, while the old man's followers filled streets and squares, muttering quietly and promising revenge. This was his house, the family's home since it was built in 1885. In spite of everything, the old man was a historical figure, a despotic colonel, wealthy landowner, political boss, and the mansion should have been preserved as a historical site or something like that. They haven't been able to rent it out. Everybody is afraid, nobody knows of what. It was the first three-story house, and later an elevator powered by a steam engine, a conveyor belt for the food, heating system, gas lamps, an alarm system, and hot water showers were installed.

My hands were numb from the cold, but I managed to dismantle the keypad and remove the deadbolt. Nobody could see me kneeling down. Weeds had taken over the garden, the bushes are overgrown. This house never had a good view of the street because of the tall wall surrounding it. I took the deadbolt with me. The house is abandoned: soon the looting will begin.

I've never seen anything like this lock: it has double plates and the bronze parts seem to be handmade, judging by their rough construction. The system is extremely complicated, with bolts that lift and come down as the key is turned. And it's necessary to turn it the exact number of times, because one turn too many stops the whole system and locks the bolt; like a code. I've never seen anything more complex, or skillful, in all the locks I've examined, and there were three thousand of them. You'd need to take a class to learn how to use it. People say that not only was the old man the only one to handle the keys, but also that he (personally) killed the men who made and installed the locks. In the same way that pirates killed the sailors after burying their treasures on desert islands, so that their secret would never be revealed.

100

I walk through the greasy brown velvet curtain, and look at the last two seats in the row on the right. I sat in that place with Nancy on Sunday nights. We sat with our faces together, waiting for a dark scene so we could hug each other tight. I walked in, and saw the empty seat. I waited for the bell to ring, for them to turn off the lights, and sat down. My mouth, dry, my tongue, sticky, chewing mint gum or Torino candy. The whole movie theater smelled like Chita candy, mint gum, cheap perfume, sweat, foot odor. The air was stuffy. The matinee had ended just a little while before. The Sunday shows were all those odors combined and an indefinite murmur that lasted the whole movie. People talking in whispers, children screaming, bathroom doors slamming—what was the bathroom like? God, I don't remember—young guys walking up and down the aisle all the time, looking for the sluts who never went to the Sunday shows. Women fanned themselves with magazines, pieces of cardboard and sandalwood fans. The men folded their jackets over the back of the seats, took their shoes off, shouted for the candy man. They went outside to have a soft drink at the bar next to the stairs, and looked at the huge, hand-painted photo of Jeanette MacDonald. The kids couldn't wait or didn't want to miss the movie, so they peed right there, the urine streamed down the floor, got shoes and naked feet wet, people cursed, stood up, slammed seats, others shouted "sit down, sit down, sit down." From the balcony people threw crumbled papers, pieces of seats, popcorn bags, wet paper. A big uproar. Everybody screamed when the actors kissed, and counted the score: one – zero, two – zero, three – zero. They whistled, clapped, stomped their feet, when the hero chased the villain they shouted, "There he is, look, watch out," laughed and cried, got mad at the villain, hid to smoke by lowering their heads and hiding the cigarettes in their hands. The movie theater turned into a universe of emotions and reactions, of communication among those people who knew each other, between the townspeople and the outsiders on the screen who never replied to the provocation. There was tension: electric shocks between people who touched each other in the dark, hands squeezing each other, hands sneaking down under dresses, noses blowing, teeth being sucked on, chairs squeaking, moms screaming at their kids, babies feeding on bottles and on breasts. For two hours we were bound to one another, bound to the screen and to the projector's bright light, fascinated with the cities shown in the movies, the cars, the adventures. It was a real jolt. That's why we spent the day feeling tense, waiting for the moment to cross the threshold of golden metal and penetrate the magical circle. We forgot everything outside, tomorrow was no more, we became, not isolated individuals, but a whole that lifted from the ground and rose, completely dizzy, as if we had been continuously drinking to the point of exhaustion, which coincided with the climax of the serialized show: "To be continued next week." When the lights came back on, people recovered their everyday unhappy demeanor and left dejected, to cross again the golden brass rails—the end of illusion, the frontier of a fantastic world—plunging into the melancholic ending of a Sunday, gateway to Monday.

THE DOOR
101

Technical innovations began to emerge in the second half of the nineteenth century, such as doors that opened and closed automatically—using a hydraulic, pneumatic, or electric system—as well as innovations in free-standing doors: double doors, sliding doors, rolling doors, revolving doors and canopy doors. The most common type of hinged door opens in both directions. The revolving door was created around 1900 in the United States. It consists of four glass panels set up in a ninety-degree angle that revolve around a central axis. The double doors became popular during the nineteenth century. They have a series of panels that can be folded in one direction or the other. The type used in the twentieth century is similar to a curtain: it runs over a rail attached on the top using a system similar to the pantograph, and is made of light and foldable material, such as pressed-wood panels, rubber, leather, or plastic. The sliding door (with wood panels) emerged in the nineteenth century: it sits on small casters that run over a rail embedded in the wall.

The sliding door (with glass panels) was perfected around 1900, and is based on the sliding room dividers in Japanese homes. Large sliding doors are very common in warehouses and factories. The type made of iron is often used for large areas such as airplane hangars, and may be up to seventy-two feet wide and forty-two-and-a-half feet high. The rolling door (made in the nineteenth century) built with (galvanized or stainless) aluminum or steel astragals at regular spaces, and set on a rail, became very common in industrial facilities. Some reached forty-six feet in width and thirty-six feet in height. This type of door is also used as a rolling window. Other types include the canopy door, which may be up to fifty-nine feet wide and twenty feet high, or the folding doors that collapse when raised. (*E. B.*)

MYTHS
Memoirs and Facts

"Is Miss Maria do Carmo inside?"

"She, her husband, and a maid."

"The big black maid?"

"That's the only one I know."

"She's Miss Maria do Carmo's confidant. They're always together."

"What happened?"

"Nobody knows. The police chief arrived with the couple in a van, with a São Paulo license plate."

"A crime?"

"Nobody's saying anything. They've even closed the police station."

"Makes it easier to assail the old man."

"I'm not sure. There are some Federal agents too."

"What about these nosy people?"

"Soon enough they'll use violence to disperse the crowd."

"What if we go to Miss Maria do Carmo's house?"

"To do what?"

"Everybody's here. Who knows, maybe we'll find something there. It'll be good for your newspaper. We're not going to find out anything here for now."

"We won't be able to go into the house either."

"We'll try."

We went by bus to the final stop, walked the rest of the way, about a mile and a half. We didn't want to take a taxi in order to avoid a gossipy driver who could cause complications later. I don't know exactly what it was, but something had hit me, a need to see Miss Maria do Carmo's house. It wasn't for the lock or the door. It was for the house itself, the inside of the house. The imposing brick wall looked very different from up close: poorly built, poorly finished, as if done in a hurry. Made of exposed bricks not for the sake of style, but rather for lack of time or money to finish it. Here and there a shriveled ivy plant climbed up, but didn't spread out. It sat on an elevated point, like a fortress with no battlements, with a good view of the town. The rear was well protected. It had a gate, a dirt road, and marks of big tires.

"How are we getting in?" asked Bueno. He was the photographer at the new newspaper, anxious for a good lead, so that he could get in the spotlight.

"I don't know. That's what I'm trying to figure out."

"You said you knew."

"Just so you'd come along. I don't think anybody knows the house."

"Doesn't the house face the street?"

"That's what people say."

"Where's the verandah where Miss Maria sits?"

"You can't see it from here."

"But when the guy knocked on the door he could see her."

"Who knows, maybe they raised the wall later. It was low, had a railing."

"You're full of it. It's all bullshit about her."

"Look at the small gate, right at the corner."

"Open it. You said you could open any lock."

"I can."

It wasn't necessary. It wasn't locked. We entered the patio: dirty; heaps of rocks, shards of brick and shingles, empty bottles, medicine containers, liquor bottles piled up. Iron furniture that once had been white, now peeling, rusting, stacked up in a hole that was lined with bricks—the unfinished pool. There was no garden, no flowerbeds; just wild rose bushes on pallets. The house was big and old; the eaves had eagles, alligators, small birds, gargoyles—all made of grayish plaster. The walls were black, as if water had run down them from the roof, the gutters being broken.

"I don't get it. Where's the mansion?"

"This is it. I think I was right."

"Where are all the servants? There's not even a watchman."

"I think the big black woman is the only one."

"Did you get smart all of a sudden?"

"Everything is so obvious you don't need to be a genius to piece together the story. What do you say?"

"I don't say anything. I'm going to take some pictures."

In the rear, roofless sheds full of firewood, the servants' quarters and the garage, neither ever finished. Forty- or fifty-years old, I'm not sure, I don't recognize the style. And this house followed some kind of style, maybe the coffee planters', who moved here at the beginning of the century. I'll have to research it. This was probably the site of some old farm.

"These guys don't even have a watchdog."

"She hated dogs."

"Why?"

"Their son was bitten by a German Shepherd and died."

"Where did you hear that?"

"I didn't. I made it up. You can pass it on: one more story about them won't make any difference."

"Let's go. They may come back soon."

"They won't be getting out of the police station so quickly. Will you be brave enough to publish your report tomorrow?"

"I will. I don't know if the editor will let me. He's friends with Miss Maria do Carmo's husband."

"Candinho's going to love it. Show the photos to him first. He'll pay to have them published."

"Do you think so?"

"Do you know what? He'll buy all the material on the spot. The two families hate each other. The doctor is always saying Candinho makes money off prostitution."

"And that's true."

"Sure, but who wants to hear that? And it's not quite like that."

"No? What about the people who have rendezvous in the sauna?"

"Candinho doesn't get anything from that."

"That's what we don't know."

"The sauna serves as a meeting place for married folks."

"The photos are his if he pays good money. I'll take some more."

"Document everything."

The windows missing their glass panes, boarded up; the plaster peeling off the walls; putrid stagnant water near the kitchen door.

"Look at that stain on the door. It looks like dried blood."

"It may or may not be. Do you have color film?"

"Yes, in the Rollei."

"Take a picture while I scrape it a little."

I pulled the plastic cover off my Voter Certificate; I've been using it since I lost my ID card. I scraped the dry stain. We'll give everything to Candinho. Something will come out of it, and we'll leave the fight for the big fish.

"What if Candinho isn't interested?"

"I'm not worried about that, a lot of people in town don't like this couple."

"Miss Maria do Carmo's husband might also pay. He may pay more than Candinho, especially if we imply that the other is interested. That's good: a power game between these hypocrites. We'll make them pay."

"Let's find a way in."

"You just have to kick in the door."

Bueno's taking pictures. Brush growing around the house, a small granite flight of steps with no handrail, an easy-to-open lock of the most common type. I should be a burglar. It never occurred to me before, but it's not a bad idea. To steal from people I don't like. And I don't like anyone, so I can steal from everybody. No big robberies, only enough for me to live for a week, a month, some money and objects of sentimental value. I could steal portraits, jewelry, stuff hidden in drawers, books with dedications. Objects people are attached to: that's what hurts. Attachment is an easy feeling to abuse. I'll think about it. I can lift documents, ID cards, titles, paycheck stubs, deeds, and it'll make people run to the Notary, despair about their taxes, rot in the police station waiting for affidavits. Everything is very monotonous, old, and poor like this illustrious woman's house. Ah, Miss Maria do Carmo, how I feel like kissing your feet for the good you do me!

"There's just one thing I don't understand: the parties they held. Guests from out of town came, it filled with cars."

"That's what people said. Nobody in town was ever invited. Why not? They talked about the parties the next day, when the doctor went downtown and had coffee with the bank managers. Then the managers spread the news, each telling the story in his own way, exaggerating it. Don't you think?"

"I don't know, I guess I heard what was probably the third or fourth version. It was even published in the newspaper. But what about money—do they have any?"

"What if we check it out?"

"Check it?"

"Check with the banks. All those managers kissed the doctor's ass because they wanted to have his account. Who knows, maybe each one thought the others had it. And nobody said anything so as to not give in. Do you think?"

"I'm not sure. Banks don't give out information to third parties. You're acting like you read *Mystery Magazine*."

"I do. I have the whole collection."

"Then that's it. Keep on digging."

"But that's a good version, isn't it? Now we'll begin to spread the other side of the story, to really screw up everything."

The front door, or what should have been the front door, opened to a tiled portico with a glass roof. Vases and pots hung from chains hooked onto beams. But there were no plants, the roof glass was filthy, and barely any light got in through it. It felt like this entrance had never been used. Ahead, a large room, the floor made of wide wood boards, a lightbulb hanging from a socket, three pieces of furniture covered by soiled sheets. The broken windows let the rain in, and the floor next to them was musty.

"Is there enough light to take pictures?"

"Yes."

"Keep taking them, don't miss anything. We may have to leave in a hurry."

"This is all very strange, sinister."

A hallway led from the room to the bedrooms on the left, and to the bathrooms and a first, intermediary kitchen on the right. I didn't get it, because the main kitchen was in the back, where a big electric stove with rusty burners sat, and a gas stove with four burners for daily use. There was hardened boiled milk in an aluminum pot, cold coffee, pieces of bread, sausage, margarine. An attached room was likely the pantry, but it was empty, except for a bag of rice that was full of cockroaches.

"Look at this," shouted Bueno who was investigating the other side of the house.

The bedroom (it must have been the couple's) had a box spring on the floor, clothes thrown on top of crates, vodka bottles. There were two doors, one of them nailed closed with boards. The other one was loose on its hinges. We went through it: a central patio, isolated, accessible only through the bedroom. There was no other exit. Three peeling walls formed a *sanctum sanctorum*, like the internal patio of a prison, a solitary square open toward the sky, with no apparent purpose. It felt oppressive, claustrophobic. It was practically in ruins. At the top the walls ended in volutes and capitals, most of them broken or cracked. A fret in a faded color that had once been red went around the whole patio. The marble floor, covered by a layer of hardened dust, was full of pieces of wall plaster, bricks, pieces of lime that had fallen from the walls, rocks, cement, shards of blackened mirrors, broken glass, cigarettes stubs, trash. The door paint had dried, burst, the wood split. And we could almost feel time standing still in the middle of the patio: not today, not yesterday, a thousand years ago. The same feeling I have sometimes at the movies: splitting in two, both belonging to a place where I had never belonged, and floating in a space I don't recognize and that fills me with anguish, as if the world had been reduced to that and nothing else. I realize suddenly that this house represents the town's truth, its synthesis. Dream and reality, seen from out there and from inside—synonym, hope, ideal. What's the right word to define it? Maybe all three. Miss Maria do Carmo is the only person in town whose feet are firmly grounded, who is authentic in her defiant arrogance and disaffection.

"Let's go."

"We're not in any danger."

"It's going to rain, look, the dark sky, the black clouds."

"I'm going to hide here until they come back."

"I'm out of here."

"If you want, go ahead. But first, look at what I've found."

A room filled up with cardboard boxes and wood crates, sealed by steel bands. The stamps in English referred to I don't know what kind of business companies. The boxes were new and seemed to have arrived recently. There wasn't one speck of dust on them.

"Are you thinking what I'm thinking?"

"Of course."

"Photograph it, this is precious. This will make us lots of money."

THE VOICE AT DAWN

103

"This is getting dangerous. The couple couldn't have gotten into this alone. Let's go."

"Don't be a fool, Bueno. For the first time in your shitty life you sense adventure, it's at your fingertips. And you want to leave. Let's look some more."

And there were other rooms, some dark, but all were filled with boxes of varying sizes. Other rooms were lit up and full of equipment. We climbed a staircase and ended up over the garage, where we found a kind of laboratory. There were test tubes, pipettes, Bunsen burners—a whole arsenal arranged on impeccable white tile tables.

"I don't understand any of this."

"It doesn't matter if you understand or not. Photograph it."

"There's something big going on here. They'll kill us."

"I think I'm beginning to understand the disappearances."

"What disappearances?"

"Do you remember a guy who people said had planted wire? The one who disappeared in the wire?"

"You told me it was your friend Danilo."

"I'm sure he disappeared in this house. There must be a cellar where they bury people."

"Cut it out! I'm getting out of here!"

"Stop being a coward."

"Coward, but alive. Ciao! I won't stay one minute longer."

"I'm going to look for the cellar."

"Let me know if you find it."

"You have the story of your life in your hands. You can sell it to any magazine in Rio or São Paulo."

"Me? No! I'm not a reporter. I just take photos. Ciao!"

THE DOUBT

"Hello, 567-8967?"

"Yes" (sleepy voice).

"This is Ron Lopes."

"Who?"

"Ron Lopes, from Araraquara's Culture Radio Station, PRD-4, *This Is Your Call* show."

"Ah."

"Ma'am, can you answer a question?"

"Now that I'm awake I can."

"The question is worth ten music CD's."

"Go ahead."

"Who discovered Brazil?"

"I don't know."

"What do you mean, you don't know?"

"I don't know."

"That's impossible.

"It's not impossible."

"Yes, it is."

"No, it's not."

"Well, I don't know. I didn't even know Brazil had been discovered."

"Well, it was."

"Are you sure?"

"Sure, no. But Brazil is out there."

"What if it's not Brazil?"

"Of course it is."

"That's what you're saying. But you're not sure. And I say it is not."

"It is."

"It isn't."

"Why do you say that?"

"Because I know."

"If it isn't Brazil, what country is it?"

"There's no country."

"No country?"

"No, there's nothing here."

"You're crazy."

"Yeah? Then look out the window."

"Hello, you're right, there's nothing around us. What's going on?"

"There's nothing going on."

"How come?"

She didn't answer. She hung up. She knew everything that was going on.

THE SENSES

Looking at the hospital ceiling (hospital?) I think about hallucinations. Like the ones I've been experiencing: people I meet who don't exist, cups spilling hot coffee on me. It can't be *delirium tremens*, the most I ever drink is a few beers with gin. And I've been reducing the doses, nobody wants to sell me anything on credit. I can't imagine those shots were meant to kill me. He was probably pretending, so as to not compromise me. It was naive of me to step in front of him, but he didn't realize the cashier had a gun and was going to kill him. And when I moved, making it seem unintentional, I stepped in front of the cashier's line of fire, and he preferred not to hit me. Derly probably thought I was going to recognize him, and he felt threatened. I could see the fear in his face. It was so concrete, so dense, you could touch it, pick it up and cut it with a scissors. You could feel the heavy air, like fog, in the bank.

It was the second robbery in Araraquara. We couldn't believe it could have been robbed even once, and when it happened we thought the town had had its share. That was 1968, a very violent year, and Bernardo's long letters, which read like novels, talked only about murders, bombs, assaults, tortures, arrests. The impression they gave was that he had nobody to vent to. He said they didn't let anything get published in the newspaper. They censored everything. And it was a big load for a man to carry alone, keeping everything in his head. So he wrote me, non-stop. I was, and still am, afraid he was involved in something, and could put me in some embarrassing—or worse—dangerous situation. I was going to say "fatal," but thought it would be too strong, dramatic. I tried to answer him many times, but my letters seemed empty compared to Bernardo's. I kept putting it off, leaving them for later, writing drafts, but never finishing a single letter. Nevertheless he kept writing to me, indifferent, it seemed to me, to what I could have to say. I began to feel like a bottomless pit where he dumped his anger, impotence, and frustration, because his letters were a mix of all these things. I imagined that his confessions signalled the renewal of our friendship, the strengthening of a relationship. Bernardo had treated me strangely for many years, accusing me of not leaving town, as if I had committed a crime. He couldn't understand that I felt good here and didn't want to leave, that I was afraid of leaving. What's wrong with being afraid? He always accused me of succumbing to fear, of not overcoming it, not facing it, but only someone who never experienced fear can say something like that, because it is one thing to diagnose the disease, and another to be the sick person. The prescribed medications don't always work as planned, the organism must be predisposed to them, and so must we.

The first time the bank was robbed it was practically a holiday. Everybody worked only a half-day. An unprecedented crowd gathered in front of the bank, and the police had to seal it off to be able to work. It was very hot that evening. Everybody stayed on the street, talking, trying to find out how much had been stolen. The bank employees were told not to say anything. For some reason—not even the employees who were harshly interrogated knew why—all of them were taken to São Carlos, placed in a hotel, and returned the next day.

Some complained that it was humiliating. They were discrediting innocent people, they could ruin their careers. Nothing was ever established. Still, they moved the manager and fired some employees, suspecting that someone inside the bank had helped.

Then, no one expected the robbers—or other robbers—would come back. Of course it wasn't the same bank. I had gone in to cash my pension check, get that humiliating money I had to give to Nancy every month. Hand it to her so she could curse me at her door, or have the maid get the check and tell me she wasn't home, or was taking a shower. When she's in the shower I imagine her olive skin, her pointy breasts. The maid closes the door and I don't even notice. I stay there, waiting for I don't know what. Waiting. I do nothing but wait, I have all the time in the world. When someone asks me what I'm waiting for, what should I answer? If anybody asks me at all. All I get asked for is my ID number. They also ask what I'm going to have, depending on the bar—otherwise they just bring the draft beer and an order of Gorgonzola. Derly didn't need to shoot me.

105

Excerpts from the book that divided the town's history, *The Safe Guide to Leaving Home*. With technical and philosophical knowledge and no bias, it shows how it is possible to safely abandon one's home and reach the sidewalk. The author didn't finish his work. Subsequent volumes would have had directions on how to reach the next corner and downtown. His objective was a series of manuals that could be juxtaposed. I excerpted from the book (completely out of print) the basic paragraphs about the final move, that decisive step that puts the individual on the street. There were huge problems, legal suits for the sake of the town's security. The author was cornered by leagues, organizations, the police, religious groups. Having proposed an entirely new, revolutionary idea, the most violent reactions were expected. Local police stations banned all experiments with the Manual—they wouldn't be held responsible for any consequences. The Church wanted the author to recant in a public square (to whom? to an empty square?). A small segment of the population accepted the new principles, in the same way they had accepted the sexual revolution. There was an uprising, and another segment of the population demanded the author be exiled. Accused of subverting order, destroying the family, endangering public safety, obstructing peace, corrupting customs, wiping out tradition, the author had no alternative but to withdraw whatever books he could and admit he was wrong. But I know he was right, because I did the experiment and took it to incredible lengths, like crossing all the streets and going anywhere I wanted. I began by observing the author's investigations, positioning myself in front of his house, hiding like I hid when I was fifteen to look into the windows of Nilcéia's house—I liked her very much. It was surprisingly simple, and maybe that was what caused the shock, the feeling of absurdity and impossibility. I laughed when I read the Manual for the first time. It was so incredible that someone could have had such an idea and developed it over nine-hundred pages, that I kept reading it to the end. Astonished, I concluded that he was right, *it was possible*. On that same day I went out on the street; straight out, encountering no obstacles, a little scared. It all happened very fast. I didn't need any preparation, concentration, meditation, consultation, or to verify the wind, sun, humidity or temperature. The Manual was a hit. The reactions began. I thought I could have helped the author to keep up his fight by demonstrating the truth. But he recanted (did he really?). I hesitated. Who knows if maybe the town's truth was the real one?

"4 – Between the house and the street there is a door (see appendix), a traditional device consisting of one or two panels of wood, glass, corrugated zinc, iron, or aluminum.

5 – On one side the door is attached to the wall by hinges; on the other by the latch and lock.

6 – The door normally opens from left to right, and the individual should be positioned at a reasonable distance, so as to be able to:

a) Extend the arm and turn the key or latch.

b) Pull the door without the panel being obstructed by the individual's body.

§ In case this happens, it is advisable to step back once, and step to the left, extend your hand and push the panel.

. . .

12 – Some doors lead straight onto the street. They are dangerous, because they leave the individual completely exposed. Others lead onto porches, and are safer (see 'SAFETY RULES').

. . .

17 – Once the door is open, the individual is faced with two noteworthy institutions in the history of humanity: the sidewalk and the street (on their specific influence on the town's history and development, see the works of Alberto Ramos).

. . .

21 – Some doors are located at the sidewalk level; others are two or three steps above it. The town's baroque houses are located on a much higher level, for obvious reasons that don't need to be mentioned here.

. . .

29 – Once the door has been opened, look straight ahead. Having finished the spiritual preparation (see 'SPIRITUAL AND MENTAL CONCENTRATION'), carefully place your head out, looking attentively to the left and to the right.

30 – Move your body, without any hurry, climbing down the steps until you reach the sidewalk. Don't let panic overcome you. It is advisable to do this slowly, in order to get used to it. Practice twice in the morning, twice in the afternoon, once at night, but not after eight o'clock.

31 – This sequence should be repeated until you are able to remain relatively calm, standing on the sidewalk for five full minutes.

. . .

36 – Remain still, then turn your head.

§ In order to determine the length of immobility, consult the tables at the end of this volume.

. . .

44 – No step should be taken before the individual feels that it is absolutely safe to do so.

45 – Complete safety does not exist. Safety is just synonymous with complete insecurity. To accept insecurity means to float calmly, without struggling, in a sea of insecurity.

46 – How to take the first step: Instructions in the chapter 'STEPS AND THEIR CONSEQUENCES.'"

106

I'm not sure I'm going to the movies. If I don't, this will be another evening spent leaning against the tree. The trunk already has a callus: the place where I lean my shoulder is smooth. I'll stay here, keep watch, read Bernardo's letter. Why does Andrade walk so slowly, staring at his own feet? Is that how they walk in prison? He spent eight years there, was just released, came back to town. Andrade was dangerous. That's what the newspapers said. The town is not proud of him, after all he was involved in a big opposition movement, he led the high-school students. One of his arms hangs motionless at his side. We walk up together, side by side. I'm going to the other theater.

"Going for a walk?"

"Doing some exercise."

"I never see you during the day."

"I don't go out during the day. I'm not used to the sun. I lost a lot of my eyesight, and my eyes always irritate me. I'm getting used to normal life little by little. What amazes me is being able to walk around without limitations. I spent six years in a six-by-ten-foot cubicle. I walked all day, back and forth, so I wouldn't get stiff. Now, all of sudden, I can walk, walk. I can't believe it. Sometimes I catch myself walking three steps and stopping.

"Is everything okay now?"

"More or less."

"Are you living at your father's?"

"No, he moved right after my conviction."

"That's why I hadn't seen your old man for a long time."

"What have you been doing?"

"Some odd job in a shitty office."

I let him go on. I'm going to the movies. The room is practically empty. I open Bernardo's red envelope, typical of him, he bought stationery in Italy or something like that:

"I simply don't remember; it happened twenty-three years ago. I don't know if I was in town or traveling. Do you remember how our indoor soccer team traveled so much? But why is it important to know where I was that night?"

Well, Bernardo, do you think it's all so simple? I can't be satisfied with this, it's very different. What are you trying to do? Fool me? Always cheating me? I've had it with you, this doorman, the theater, the empty street, the closed doors, Nancy. I've been thinking and have come to the conclusion that nothing is going to be resolved: nothing about these facts, and nothing about the events that night in 1897. What's the point in connecting isolated dots? The night of the curse, questions without answers, the rally on the Largo, disappearances in the swimming pool, the man in the telephone lines. Will everything, if put together, solve the puzzle, or do these pieces belong to separate games? I'm exhausted, tired of watching in vain, of thinking continuously, and realizing I'm still thinking.

I hate the wind on my back. It's this son-of-a-bitch doorman who doesn't take care of things. He should have closed the curtains. This damn movie theater. This is going to be good, ah, today it's going to be good. The wind on my back, leaks dripping on my head, half of the lightbulbs out, the projector jamming all the time. And the smell of urine and excrement coming from the bathrooms. There's only one couple on a date. Right in the front. They're waiting for the lights to go off so they can start making out. The floor is covered in sand. The wind is going to bring much more, and if it keeps up, the whole room will fill up. I think they fixed the film—the lights are off. The wind. Ceres Fhade, no way, that fucking guy. Cowards. I go out into the lobby, don't find him. In a little while he shows up, eating a hot dog. He's got ketchup on the collar of his jacket.

"Would you like some?"

He smiles, inviting. Is he a faggot? I slap his mouth. The ketchup spreads on his face, the hot dog rolls on the floor. A black hot dog from the Turk next door. He only sells junk to people like Ceres Fhade, life's excrement. And his look of surprise? As if he had never been slapped before. I push him inside the theater, to the damn room he hates, where he refused to go. Inside the dark room I see his face contorting so he won't see the movie. I keep pushing him, this man who has fooled me for years and years. The years I wasted sitting on that rotting couch, trying to make conversation. Trying to find answers to the Manual, trying to find out about new and non-existent chapters, or whatever could save me. Ceres, or whoever this impostor is, tries to take my hands off his jacket, his greasy and frayed clothes. There's nobody to help him. The woman at the ticket counter has left, the candy counter is closed, Nelson from the newsstand went to get something to eat.

"What's wrong? Are you upset today?"

"Upset? Here's what's upsetting."

I hit Ceres with my body, throwing him over the seats. He moans. He's hit his ribs against the back of a seat. I knee him in the stomach: another moan.

348

"Coward, son of a bitch, fight with me. Come on, Ceres, fight."

"You're crazy. I'm not Ceres. I've always told you my name isn't Ceres."

"Liar. You're scared. Tell me you're scared. Tell me or I'll smash you."

"I'm shitting my pants out of fear."

"Really?"

"Yes. Stop this."

I slam my two hands on his ears. He's bigger than me, much bigger, but doesn't react. And somebody who doesn't react needs to take a beating. I pound him, and pound, and pound. He falls, crawls along the aisle between rows. I kick him, he cries.

"Shout, you son of a bitch. Call the police. Ask for help. Today I'll kill whoever comes in here. Shout like you've never shouted in your life. They did everything they wanted to you, and you never reacted."

He goes down a row of seats. I follow. He falls under a seat and I hit him hard on the head with the cushion: I hit, and hit, and hit him.

"You piece of shit, what have you done with your life? What? Buried in this town. Most of your life buried in this filthy theater. A tomb, this is a tomb for you, for the old movies, for these dead actors."

"No, no."

Not enough strength to scream. I stomp on his face with my shoes. He collapses.

"Liar, always a liar, saying you were someone you weren't. Escaping, escaping."

Ceres (or whoever he is) is lying still. The couple continues making out, maybe they hadn't even looked back. Ceres moans softly. I step on his hands, on his fingers, crushing them: the crushed man.

"Wake up, shout, run away. Run. Get out of this town. Go fight for your rights. There's still time. Get up, you've been lying down all your life."

I step on his legs, drag him to the flooded bathroom. The water runs from a clogged toilet; the valve is broken, pieces of excrement float in the water. And that smell of rotten urine, the urine of many generations of Araraquarans, stuck to the walls, infiltrating, juxtaposed urines forming a layer of un-breathable gas—fatal.

"Shit, that's what you are. Why did you let yourself be destroyed like that, Ceres?"

From where I was I could see part of the movie. From that angle Laurence Harvey looked disfigured. The images were distorted, the faces contorted. I'd seen that movie many times before: *Room at the Top*, the portrait of a son of a bitch. Except that, he got there. As for Ceres, he can't see anything, his face is submerged in the drain's stinky water. In any case, he doesn't like movies. I don't know what he likes, this useless piece of shit. To die or to keep on living at the door of the theater doesn't make any difference. He doesn't even know it, but this theater is dead, they're already talking about the hotel they're going to build here. What would they do with Ceres? They'll fire him or give him a job as a janitor, someone to clean up. An ex-university professor picking up trash. He isn't going to like it. It'll be a big change. Humiliated, trampled on, besides the trauma of seeing the theater demolished. People said he'd been working here since it opened.

It's better for Ceres. He's not going to be persecuted anymore. He lived in fear of being arrested, tried to hide, denied his own identity. He never invited me to his home to meet his wife and kids. His head is out of the toilet, I push it back in with my foot. Too bad he's swallowing filthy water. He didn't deserve it, he was a nice guy.

I take apart the other toilets as best I can. I open faucets all the way. My feet, my shirt, my pants are soaked. I clean the faucets with my handkerchief (fingerprints). Why am I carrying a hankie today? I wait, until I see the clogged drains unable to draw off the water. I sit down next to the door and watch. Ceres' body floats. If he had left he wouldn't have met me. He'd be in another town, in a better situation than he is now. It must be horrible to drown. Water in my nose has always bothered me. When I leave I need to stop by the supermarket and buy a fountain pen. Writing with a ball pen doesn't work. Just brushing the paper with my sweaty hands smudges everything. The water flows out of the bathroom, runs along the wall. It's a flood, and I can hear the water flowing violently out of the pipes. Ceres' body moves with the water but gets stuck at the door. It hits the door a few times and floats back. His face is looking up. That's better: he'll swallow less water this way. It doesn't even look like Ceres. He'll have to wash and iron all his clothes. His wife will be furious. The water forms a puddle by the screen. It's growing quickly, soon it'll catch the couple's attention. They must be screwing, those wretches. I'd better go, before they set off the alarm, and before the supermarket closes. I'm not even sure it'll be open on a cold night like tonight—the desert nights are freezing. I drag myself over the sand that covers the seats. I hit my head on them. I need water, my forehead is boiling. Just a cup would be enough. If I see the ticket counter woman, or Nelson from the stand, they may be able to help me. No, Nelson is eating a sandwich at Pedro's bar, the bar that was demolished last Sunday. I make it to the lobby, walking with difficulty. The right side of the stairs is gone. The *Once upon a Time in Hollywood* poster has disappeared under a dune of yellow sand. That's too bad, I really wanted to see that movie. The dune slopes down gently toward the street, extends for miles, disappears in the darkness. I never imagined the desert could be so dark at night. But I've never been in a desert. I've only seen deserts in movies. Poor me, I'm ashamed to admit, but I've never seen an airplane in my life. It's unbelievable, in 1976, a forty-year-old man who's never seen an airplane. And astronauts now go to the moon, satellites connect me to Paris instantaneously, computers are becoming more human. Two or three times some politicians came to Araraquara by plane. The last time I was watching Eduardo. He was six months old, and Nancy had to go out. She sewed and had to make the prom dress for some girls at the Tennis Club. She was upset. I think the girls humiliated her. Nancy was complicated, too sensitive, distrustful like only poor people can be. She dreamed of being a member of the Club. So she could dance on Saturday nights, have fun at Carnival, spend New Year's Eve there. They come back during Carnival and the New Year Eve's festivities.

On Airplane Day I thought of picking up Eduardo and going to the airport. But it was a Wednesday and it was windy. Nancy was afraid of wind, because of the stupid way her grandparents died. One night the old folks were at home. A horrible wind began to blow and nobody knew where it was coming from. Nancy's grandfather had certain neuroses. He always kept doors and windows closed, had all the holes and cracks in the house caulked, as if it were winter in Versailles. That wind almost blew up the house. Only the walls remained standing. Everything inside, walls, furniture, blew away.

I feel like disconnecting, being like the man who one day didn't ride his car, didn't walk, simply stopped and stood there. Be just like him. I can stand. But I don't stop. My mind keeps going. And I see the street giving birth to men, children roasted in washbasins, men living in telephones. What does all this mean? I know it makes sense within the context of my life, because even the worst chaos has order.

So I sat on the floor with Eduardo, surrounded by sheets of paper. He was full of curiosity, showed an interest in everything. At that time I worked in the Railroad accounting department. I hadn't yet been punished with banishment to that lonely station. I brought home what was left from the used notepads. I sat with Eduardo to draw hats with ants on their brims: an ant on each hat. It's easy to draw an ant:

1 – Draw an oval, with one of the sides pointing slightly upward.

2 – Another oval, much smaller, positioned above the first one.

3 – A thin line connecting the two ovals.

4 – On the bigger oval, four thin, slanted lines, on the bottom part, to represent the legs.

5 – On the smaller oval, two thin vertical, upward lines, to represent the antennas.

The ant is ready.

I've kept the sheets with the hats and ants. If I'm able to cross this desert and make it home, I'll look at the drawings again and will burn all of them. They no longer have any interest for me. I thought the desert sand was white, like on the beach. It's my fault. I never bent over to pick up the grains that fell, or gathered them from the windowsill. I could have examined them, seen their color, and learned a lot.

I couldn't imagine the desert would have come so soon. It didn't catch me by surprise. I have the necessary equipment: the tall boots that keep the sand from getting on my feet. I should have worn the boots, my shoes are full of sand. They're heavy, and hurt. I'm taking my socks off. Ceres Fhade is better off than me, more comfortable. We can float in the water. All we have to do is to flap our arms, and there we go, wherever we want to. If he doesn't have enough strength to keep up, the current will take him to the wide pool under the screen. There's a whirlpool there; he may go under. And no one knows what lies under old theaters. Everybody must have heard: not only the basement, but also the underground floor—and the earth underneath. I can't explain. It's something to do with the preservation of dialogue, sounds, noises, and the actions that took place on the screen and in the rooms during the shows. All that was said and done in the seats, preserved like the memory in a computer. It just needs to be activated. It plays back faithfully. That's why people are so afraid that the theater will be demolished. Everything is kept there, recorded I don't know how, and preserved in the layers of soil and rock. The other day Bernardo told me, "You're so good in math and physics, why don't you take a course on computers? Everybody needs technicians, they're well paid." But I don't want to work with electronic brains. I want better things, living things. I was thinking about that while they tore down the theater and I saw the stacked bricks. Pieces of columns, plaster friezes, rotten curtains, glass from the light fixtures being piled up. My cathedral: altars, friezes, columns, niches. The screen-sacrarium, the balcony-choir, the actor-saints, the show-ritual, all continuously renewed. Everything taken apart, brick by brick. Witnesses of my life. And they meant nothing, to no one—not even (surprisingly) to me. Coldly, I let them pile together the remains of the cathedral-theater. I didn't feel resentment or loss. Now I understand why certain places emit sounds and images. They're nothing more than a leakage in the underground memory. I'm tricking you all with these stories, while I try to orient myself in the desert. I try to seem at ease, as if I were an expert. Until recently I thought: if I go to a restaurant or nightclub with an elegant woman, I should take a lighter, to light her cigarette with a firm gesture, at the right time. Such gestures have always impressed me. To extend my hand, holding the lit match or lighter, showing indifference and, at the same time, assertiveness and casualness; to do something as if I had done it all my life. The accumulation of gestures I'd considered making before, but didn't. That's my life. How can I orient myself if I had never walked in the desert? I don't even know how to walk. I'm crawling. If the wind stopped, my mouth would be clean, it wouldn't be dry. Sand hits against my teeth, an unpleasant feeling. It's harming my dentures. I'd better take them off, bury them. These teeth were good for three years. They helped me eat, helped me bite. Now in the desert, I say good-bye to them. I decided to take care of my teeth long after Nancy. When we were together, they began to hurt, to rot. I didn't go to the dentist. I walked by the office, but didn't go in. I wanted to pull my mouth off, remove it from my face, nullify it. I'll leave my dentures in the cold, in the dark night. Poor things. I'm afraid I'll dig and bump into Araraquara down in the hole. I finally freed myself from it, it's disappeared. Poor dentures, I didn't take good care of you. Yellowed, they practically disappear in the sand. I dig carefully, open a sufficiently comfortable hole. Dentists recommend Corega and a huge hole. I don't have Corega. I'm not prepared. Nobody carries Corega around in their pockets, for emergencies. I have the feeling, I'm not sure, that the School of Odontology has passed a decree making all Araraquarans carry Corega with them. If I followed the rules, I'd now be able to pay my last and respectful tribute to my dentures. If Bernardo were here he'd laugh at me. I'm serious when I talk about a respectful tribute. The desert is the only dignified tomb for a dental prosthesis. I'll be famous for this sentence. All I have to do is wrap myself in the College of Pharmacy flag and dive in the sand. The students attended the dances with their girlfriends, and in the middle of the night left for the desert, taking the girls from out of town and the fiancées they had in town to try to explain things to them. With the girlfriends and fiancées from their hometowns. And there was a stream of tears, a downpour that washed passions and hearts, and drowned the feelings and dreams of the poor girls who had been deceived during the whole term, having served only to entertain the young men, as a protection against loneliness. Instead of remembering the happy moments, they just cried for the moments in the future when they would no longer be happy. They lived the future and the future didn't exist. They plunged into a vacuum and stayed that way: unable to see reality. I cover the dentures with sand; can't find a flower anywhere to throw in the tomb. I've just learned something new: deserts don't have flowers. Judging by the position of the clock at the sock factory, the old Araraquaran

Club must be right underneath here. And I'm happy that my teeth are resting above the Club they attended so many times. The next task the desert demands from me is finding in this jumble, in this maze, in the insignificant pebble that was my life, one action that makes sense, that justifies my having lived. It must exist, or I wouldn't be here. The question is: how can I find such a microscopic point in a period of forty years? The glowing clock face is now at ground level. The neon light looks ghostly, it produces a terrible sensation of loneliness in the desert night. I walk by it. The clock face used to be twenty feet high. But now I can reach it, I can touch the hands, move time forward or back. I won't do that. The buried town doesn't need the time. The desert travelers may. The clock is much bigger than me and projects my shadow on the sand. It'd be nice to take my pants off and show the clock my ass. Psychiatrists would interpret that as homosexual; the hands would be phallic symbols. Psychiatrists tie our lives down; they're stifling. Everything I do has a meaning I don't want it to have. According to them it'd be better to stay home, sitting still, my eyes closed, my ideas interrupted. I lose my sense of direction thinking about psychiatrists. If the factory clock is behind me, that means I have to walk three hundred feet and turn right, toward the village. I realize I'm walking around the glowing clock, fascinated by the white light. To think that I guided myself by this clock for years, going to class and to work. One could check it day and night. It was the only clock in town after the old church was demolished. I'd like coffee, hot and very weak: *Caboclo*'s coffee, the way Nancy knew how to make it. We made love on the sandy beach. She liked it a lot. She was a nice girl, I just shouldn't have married her. It wasn't her fault she wanted the things she did, she was only following the general trend. There were few girls in town who didn't want all the things she expected in a husband. I didn't want to be a husband-provider, nor did I have the means to be one. How can I explain? It's very hard for me to talk, to reason. What Nancy didn't know was that those things irritated me too, because I always ended up losing, and I know all the things I've lost. Now, I'm sure Bernardo didn't play indoor soccer. There wasn't any team. That means he was somewhere on the Largo. I wasn't happy. I can't orient myself. The four faces of the clock look the same. I've walked around them a lot. I've walked too much around everything. It's better for me to sit down and wait for the sun to come up; someone will walk by here. This is the way the caravans of Ferroviária's fans take. I'll have to wait till Saturday, and I'll have only the shade from the clock to protect me.

I'm an idiot. All I have to do is break one of the glass faces and go into the tower. There must be food and water, whatever I need. I can live in the tower. It'll be better for me. I'll always be able to find my way around, and to know the time. The glass is thick. I hit it with my shoe heel and learn another lesson: hammers are necessary in the desert. The glass yields and falls to the ground six feet below. I don't see any openings on the tiles. There must be one, otherwise, how would they fix the clock when it stops working? That's not my problem, it's up to the repairman to reach an agreement with the factory owners. For years and years they've watched over Araraquarans' feet and time. They sold socks and lit up the big clock, which could be seen from anywhere in town. Later came the high-rises, and there were places where you couldn't see the clock.

I jump inside, twist my foot, roll when I fall and hit my head on the wall. And I thought I had some agility, just because I'm tall and thin. I haven't exercised since school, and suddenly I realize it's been eighteen years. I didn't imagine it'd been so long. I'm going to take a nap, and then go down to inform Ceres' family of the accident. They must be worried. If they don't find the body soon, it'll bloat. He's lucky there aren't any carnivorous fish in the lagoon under the screen. Actually, I don't know if there are any fish at all there. Araraquara doesn't have fish like Bauru and Vera Cruz, where they have sharks and smoked salmon. Looking up, I see the clock face from behind and can barely make out the numbers because of the strong lights. The hours are reversed. If I stay here, I'll go back in time and reach the moment I want. So I'll be able to decide then. I know: no, it wasn't a rally. It was the voter meeting—my conviction. They took twenty years to inform me of my sentence. They all were there to write my name on the ballots. And the revolt was my group reacting against that foolish act. This town commits only foolish acts. To be afraid of just one man reveals weakness. They were afraid of the old man too, but that was different: he had power. That's why I need to know where Bernardo was that night, to know if he voted along with the fools, of if he was with the ones who overturned the truck. But all I can see is a slice of the Largo, the crowd scattering because of the water jets. I'll go back in time, reconstruct my life. By the time they arrive I'll have gone several days backwards. This is a difference they can't take away from me anymore: that of time. Only the clock repairman comes up here from time to time. It must be Bazoli, my childhood friend; I'll ask him not to tell anyone. He'll be surprised, especially when he finds out he's getting older and I'm not, because my life goes in the opposite direction from his. Again

I face some crucial problems. Tonight is the decisive night. After the desert, I need to adapt to the new world awaiting me, create an inverted calendar, so that I don't get lost in time and don't go too far backwards. Maybe I can use a pencil to take note of the days, weeks, months and years on the wall, making small lines. I need some material for the anti-calendar. There must be different habits and customs down there. If I had traveled a lot, as I had intended, I would have experience facing the unknown. The language—how would it be? I liked to study languages. To not have fear. Facing the unknown is exciting. I go down, slightly apprehensive, as if I were leaving the uterus. Why be born? I walk like a robot, and don't want to leave anymore. We think about something all our lives, and the instant we're about to accomplish it, we step back. The walls around me are black, "silver-plated according to Dr. Rob Hottinger's famous process. In two hours it turns the person inside hygienically sterile, safe from harmful microbes. Its continuous use ensures good health."

Now I need to find the man who used to sit in the square every day, so I can learn the new language. At that time I didn't have the clarity of mind to understand the times he lived in, to see that malaria is spelled with an x, or that 76 take away 18 equals 986. He's the one who knows. But where is he?

Perspective on what's going to happen, even if hasn't happened, is worthwhile. It's the same as if it had happened. Realization itself is no longer necessary. We've reached a meeting point—that's what matters. On the streets, women wear short dresses that expose their shoulders. The air in the line to the movies smells like soap. The faces getting out of the cars are fresh and happy, and I know them all. I feel confident. We're very young, and our future hasn't crashed against the currents, it's still kept safe inside ourselves. Our skins are clean and tanned. It was very sunny today, and people spent the day at the pool in the Club, or on farms. Nancy. I liked to watch her in the afternoon at the pool. Watching, waiting for her to get out of the water. That moment produced a happy feeling in me. Five hundred times I see her getting out of the water. That's all I see: her body emerging from the chlorinated waters, as if propelled by a coil. And there was no coil, only her splendid, taut muscles pushed her. I saw her shining torso, the reflection of the sun between her breasts. Her leaving the water lasted one hundred years, and I could think about everything. I had time, and nevertheless I found myself incapable. I just shouted inside myself, "I love that girl, I love that girl!" And every day was a party: her flight toward the sun.

"tekcit s'tneduts a em eviG."

I take my ticket. Soon we'll be ready, and available, for whatever happens. I go in for the eight o'clock show. I lost part of myself when they demolished this theater. The people who count, and matter, are here.

The lights are out.

The aroma of honeysuckle, Sunday nights, and perfume in the movies have remained. Things that are so close to me, standing here next to my face, and so distant and incomprehensible for you all. Sitting in the red leather seat, I watch the young women coming in for the eight o'clock show: Suely, Gilda, Elide, Norma, Vera, Cleide, Marina, Maria Ernestina, Alda, Marilu, Lurdinha, Maria Ignez, Marisa, Laurinha, Marília, Vanda, Maria, Corina, Maria das Rosas, Magda, Alair, Margarida, Costinha.

They walk in. Tchaikovsky, the *baião* song "Delicado," gongs, Elvis Presley, the movie begins.

This show will never end. It's been fixed, like a movie. With time the images may fade, but they've been imprinted, the people will remain even if the town is destroyed—as it has been, by the desert.

The only thing left from the town is this clearing, which comes from somewhere underneath the earth, or over it. I don't know. I'm not allowed to investigate, which is what I like to do.

If I ask a question, they don't answer. If I speak, they become silent. If I laugh, they break my teeth. If I ask for something, they don't give it to me. If I steal, they punish me. If I escape, they lasso me. If I move my hands, they tie me down. If I paint, they take away the canvas. If I write, they steal my papers. I don't hear the roosters at dawn, only a delicate voice, the nurse's, with his hands on my shoulders.

THE NEW WORLD
Memoirs and Facts

Nancy never visited me. I kept wondering, when I left the hospital: why did I stay there for eight months, if the bullet just scraped me? I spent a lot of time today looking at the whale. It was in an eighteen-wheeler, under a canvas awning. On the outside there were banners ("the biggest whale in the world"), photos of whale hunting, scenes from *Moby Dick* with Gregory Peck, drawings. It was hot inside, and there was Cidinha Dick-on-Thighs. The hoarse sound of a stereo playing boleros and *marchas*. After a few minutes I got used to an odor I had never smelled before. It didn't smell like anything rotten or old, or like mold, or old, rancid lard. It was all these things together. The whale wasn't so big. Its skin was flaccid and had creases, and there was a wood framework sustaining it. I looked at it and wanted to smell the sea, hear men shouting, the noise of whalers, see Moby Dick and Captain Ahab, or something like that. And feel the emotion of the men who risked their lives in storms, fights, islands, inns in the harbors. I couldn't think with all the heat, the smell, and Cidinha staring at me, me thinking of her nickname and looking at her legs, at the whale, and hearing boleros. She walked by me, toward the door. I'd have to run if I wanted to talk to her.

She walked up to Santa Cruz Square, stopped at the ice-cream truck, had a green soda. I walked by her and sat on a bench under the tree, looking at her legs, feeling the heat from the granite under me, and hearing a woman singing in a backyard somewhere. Cidinha bought some ice-cream and came toward me. My heart beat fast. I thought, it's got to be now. I was going to stand up, the electrical bus went by, I cooled off. If anyone I knew saw me with that little slut, it'd be a shame. The bus was gone. Cidinha climbed on the edge of the fountain (and that fountain was built in the same place as the old lamppost where we met before going out on serenades). There she was, a foot and a half above the ground, sitting on the narrow wall and dipping her feet in the water. She had pulled her dress up—I could see her dark thighs—and kicked her feet in the water. She didn't smile, was expressionless. Something was running inside me. I hadn't picked up a hooker very often, this was my chance. Cidinha stopped, looked at me, was practically calling me. Then she ran to the corner, holding her shoes in her hands. The square filled with students.

With no money for the bus, I walked to Nancy's house, wanting to see Eduardo. They didn't come to visit me even once. He wasn't allowed or didn't he want to? I wonder if he took good care of our vegetable garden. The door was shut. Nancy is just like everybody else in town. I knocked, and knocked: nothing. I knocked again.

"Nancy, open the door."

"What do you want?"

"Open the door, Nancy."

"What do you want?"

Stupidity irritates me. If I'm asking her to open, it must mean I want to go in. Nancy's idiocy has always angered me.

"I want to come in, that's all."

"Not here, you don't."

"I want to see my son, Nancy, or I'll break this door down."

"You think you're that strong?"

"Open it."

"I'll call the police right now."

"Eduardo is my son too, Nancy. You can't do this."

"Go away, go. Stop disrupting my life."

"Open it."

"You know I'm not going to open it. I don't want to see your face."

"You don't have to come out, Nancy. Just let Eduardo come to the door. Or to the window, behind the glass. I just want to see his face. I don't want him to forget his father."

"Father? Is that a father?"

"Just one minute, Nancy. Ask him if he wants to go out with me. There's a carnival in town, with a Ferris wheel, a merry-go-round, a haunted house—everything. Eduardo, Eduardo, let's spend all day at the carnival. I can hear his voice, Nancy. Let him come out. Please, I'll bring him back before dinner."

"Go drink some *pinga*, you bum. Go. It's the only thing you can do."

I've never been much of a drinker, except with my friends in the old times. Beer, all I drink is beer. I can't stand *pinga*.

"I'll bring Eduardo back this afternoon, Nancy. Otherwise he'll end up forgetting who his father is. I think he doesn't even remember anymore. Eduardo, do you remember that I drew ants so you'd learn? He must be so big, Nancy. Let's finish our vegetable garden."

"He's very big. Ah, go away, go! Stop acting so crazy. Go away and don't bother me. Go. I have to go to work."

"Today is Saturday, Nancy."

"I'm on duty today. Come on, let me go."

"Go ahead."

"No, not while you're out there."

"I'm not going to do anything to you. I just want to come in."

"Go away, go. I need to work."

"You can come, Nancy."

"I'm not crazy, I was fooled once. Only once, and that's it. Don't you remember? I just give one chance. Go away."

"Wait. Two minutes. Let me see Eduardo for only two minutes."

"You have two minutes before I call the police."

"Wait a second."

"Go on, I want to open the door. Go away."

"Wait, Nancy."

"I want to go. Let me go, for God's sake!"

I head straight to Pedro's. The bar doesn't exist. Not knowing what to do, I lie down in the garden, on the granite bench, a gift from Racy's Store. I greet everybody who walks by and not one person fails to respond. The Tennis Club president, surprised, looks at me with curiosity, but waves. I kiss the priest's hand. I run after him and kiss it, holding the fingers of Christ's son on Earth. He pushes me, "Today is Saturday, I don't have time." I think he's going to clean the church. Saturday is cleaning day. Women wash and wax their homes. The horrible new church. Good for them: nobody contributes to finish the construction anymore. Around five o'clock, when the aroma of roasted coffee invades town, mixed with the stink from the juice factory (or wasn't it five o'clock?), I go to the School of Medicine.

At the window:

"I want to donate my body."

"What for?"

"So the students can study it, after I die."

"Okay. But there are some formalities. Sit down. Someone will come talk to you. Are you sure you want to do it?"

"Look, kid. If I didn't want to, what would I be doing here?"

This body is no longer mine. I'm sitting next to me, looking at myself, saying goodbye. For forty years this body helped me, carried me around. No, there's no sadness. The students will lean over me. They will see me wide open, will look at my stomach, my heart, my liver. A few beers won't have affected my liver. It still works well. Other students will come, and others still. Forever. All I'll ask for is that they put a little sign with my name. Nothing else.

On summer nights after dinner, people went out to the sidewalks carrying chairs. The elders, or the hosts, sat near the door. The others sat around. First, those most intimate, whether they were relatives or not. Next, friends, acquaintances, and occasional visitors, in a hierarchy that excluded the children. When visitors arrived, the hosts would be waiting at the door. It wasn't required, simply a habit. But if the hosts weren't there, the conversations began in the living room with the coffee and moved to the sidewalk as more people arrived. The topics of interest were family affairs, the kids' education, politics, the school, the widows' weddings, the genealogical trees, who did and didn't do, the Tyrone Power movie, the church condemning the Gypsies who were camping in town, the troops returning from the war. The groups on the sidewalk sometimes stretched along the street. There was no danger. In the whole town there were two buses, thirty trucks to transport milk, lumbermen and coffee sacks, eight rental cars, and fifty private vehicles. Children ran, sang in circles, crossed the street on one foot, played tag. The men smoked, the women drank sodas, *jaboticaba* or fig liqueur. Coffee was served when the guests arrived and again at the end of the night, when the factory blew its whistle at ten-thirty. The guests started to get up. They stood around a little finishing their conversations, while fathers gathered their children and mothers picked up their sleeping babies, covering them with blankets because of the cold air. In fifteen minutes the street was empty.

SELECTED DALKEY ARCHIVE PAPERBACKS

SELECTED DALKEY ARCHIVE PAPERBACKS

LADISLAV MATEJKA AND KRYSTYNA POMORSKA, EDS., *Readings in Russian Poetics: Formalist and Structuralist Views.*
HARRY MATHEWS, *The Case of the Persevering Maltese: Collected Essays.*
Cigarettes.
The Conversions.
The Human Country: New and Collected Stories.
The Journalist.
My Life in CIA.
Singular Pleasures.
The Sinking of the Odradek Stadium.
Tlooth.
20 Lines a Day.
ROBERT L. MCLAUGHLIN, ED., *Innovations: An Anthology of Modern & Contemporary Fiction.*
HERMAN MELVILLE, *The Confidence-Man.*
STEVEN MILLHAUSER, *The Barnum Museum.*
In the Penny Arcade.
RALPH J. MILLS, JR., *Essays on Poetry.*
OLIVE MOORE, *Spleen.*
NICHOLAS MOSLEY, *Accident.*
Assassins.
Catastrophe Practice.
Children of Darkness and Light.
Experience and Religion.
The Hesperides Tree.
Hopeful Monsters.
Imago Bird.
Impossible Object.
Inventing God.
Judith.
Look at the Dark.
Natalie Natalia.
Serpent.
Time at War.
The Uses of Slime Mould: Essays of Four Decades.
WARREN F. MOTTE, JR., *Fables of the Novel: French Fiction since 1990.*
Oulipo: A Primer of Potential Literature.
YVES NAVARRE, *Our Share of Time.*
Sweet Tooth.
DOROTHY NELSON, *In Night's City.*
Tar and Feathers.
WILFRIDO D. NOLLEDO, *But for the Lovers.*
FLANN O'BRIEN, *At Swim-Two-Birds.*
At War.
The Best of Myles.
The Dalkey Archive.
Further Cuttings.
The Hard Life.
The Poor Mouth.
The Third Policeman.
CLAUDE OLLIER, *The Mise-en-Scène.*
PATRIK OUŘEDNÍK, *Europeana.*
FERNANDO DEL PASO, *Palinuro of Mexico.*
ROBERT PINGET, *The Inquisitory.*
Mahu or The Material.
Trio.
RAYMOND QUENEAU, *The Last Days.*
Odile.
Pierrot Mon Ami.
Saint Glinglin.
ANN QUIN, *Berg.*
Passages.
Three.
Tripticks.
ISHMAEL REED, *The Free-Lance Pallbearers.*
The Last Days of Louisiana Red.
Reckless Eyeballing.
The Terrible Threes.
The Terrible Twos.
Yellow Back Radio Broke-Down.
JULIÁN RÍOS, *Larva: A Midsummer Night's Babel.*
Poundemonium.
AUGUSTO ROA BASTOS, *I the Supreme.*
JACQUES ROUBAUD, *The Great Fire of London.*
Hortense in Exile.
Hortense Is Abducted.
The Plurality of Worlds of Lewis.

The Princess Hoppy.
The Form of a City Changes Faster, Alas, Than the Human Heart.
Some Thing Black.
LEON S. ROUDIEZ, *French Fiction Revisited.*
VEDRANA RUDAN, *Night.*
LYDIE SALVAYRE, *The Company of Ghosts.*
Everyday Life.
The Lecture.
LUIS RAFAEL SÁNCHEZ, *Macho Camacho's Beat.*
SEVERO SARDUY, *Cobra & Maitreya.*
NATHALIE SARRAUTE, *Do You Hear Them?*
Martereau.
The Planetarium.
ARNO SCHMIDT, *Collected Stories.*
Nobodaddy's Children.
CHRISTINE SCHUTT, *Nightwork.*
GAIL SCOTT, *My Paris.*
JUNE AKERS SEESE, *Is This What Other Women Feel Too?*
What Waiting Really Means.
AURELIE SHEEHAN, *Jack Kerouac Is Pregnant.*
VIKTOR SHKLOVSKY, *Knight's Move.*
A Sentimental Journey: Memoirs 1917-1922.
Theory of Prose.
Third Factory.
Zoo, or Letters Not about Love.
JOSEF ŠKVORECKÝ, *The Engineer of Human Souls.*
CLAUDE SIMON, *The Invitation.*
GILBERT SORRENTINO, *Aberration of Starlight.*
Blue Pastoral.
Crystal Vision.
Imaginative Qualities of Actual Things.
Mulligan Stew.
Pack of Lies.
Red the Fiend.
The Sky Changes.
Something Said.
Splendide-Hôtel.
Steelwork.
Under the Shadow.
W. M. SPACKMAN, *The Complete Fiction.*
GERTRUDE STEIN, *Lucy Church Amiably.*
The Making of Americans.
A Novel of Thank You.
PIOTR SZEWC, *Annihilation.*
STEFAN THEMERSON, *Hobson's Island.*
The Mystery of the Sardine.
Tom Harris.
JEAN-PHILIPPE TOUSSAINT, *Television.*
DUMITRU TSEPENEAG, *Vain Art of the Fugue.*
ESTHER TUSQUETS, *Stranded.*
DUBRAVKA UGRESIC, *Lend Me Your Character.*
Thank You for Not Reading.
MATI UNT, *Things in the Night.*
ELOY URROZ, *The Obstacles.*
LUISA VALENZUELA, *He Who Searches.*
BORIS VIAN, *Heartsnatcher.*
PAUL WEST, *Words for a Deaf Daughter & Gala.*
CURTIS WHITE, *America's Magic Mountain.*
The Idea of Home.
Memories of My Father Watching TV.
Monstrous Possibility: An Invitation to Literary Politics.
Requiem.
DIANE WILLIAMS, *Excitability: Selected Stories.*
Romancer Erector.
DOUGLAS WOOLF, *Wall to Wall.*
Ya! & John-Juan.
PHILIP WYLIE, *Generation of Vipers.*
MARGUERITE YOUNG, *Angel in the Forest.*
Miss MacIntosh, My Darling.
REYOUNG, *Unbabbling.*
ZORAN ŽIVKOVIĆ, *Hidden Camera.*
LOUIS ZUKOFSKY, *Collected Fiction.*
SCOTT ZWIREN, *God Head.*

FOR A FULL LIST OF PUBLICATIONS, VISIT:
www.dalkeyarchive.com